About the

Award-winning author **Jennifer Faye** pens contemporary romances. With more than a million books sold, she's internationally published with books translated into more than a dozen languages and her work has been optioned for film. Now living her dream, she resides with her very patient husband and Writer Kitty. When she's not plotting out her next romance, you can find her with a mug of tea and a book. Learn more at jenniferfaye.com

Donna Alward lives on Canada's east coast. When she's not writing she enjoys knitting, gardening, cooking, and is a *Masterpiece Theatre* addict. While her heart-warming stories have been translated into several languages, hit bestseller lists, and won awards, her favourite thing is to hear from readers! Visit her on the web at donnaalward.com and join her mailing list at DonnaAlward.com/newsletter

USA Today bestselling, *RITA*®-nominated, and critically acclaimed author **Caitlin Crews** has written more than 130 books and counting. She has a Master's and PhD in English Literature, thinks everyone should read more category romance, and is always available to discuss her beloved alpha heroes. Just ask. She lives in the Pacific Northwest with her comic book artist husband, is always planning her next trip, and will never, ever, read all the books in her to-be-read pile. Thank goodness.

Once Upon a Time

Once Upon a Time:
The Beast

JENNIFER FAYE

DONNA ALWARD

CAITLIN CREWS

MILLS & BOON

First Published in Great Britain 2023
by Mills & Boon, an imprint of HarperCollins*Publishers* Ltd,
1 London Bridge Street, London, SE1 9GF

www.harpercollins.co.uk

HarperCollins*Publishers*
Macken House, 39/40 Mayor Street Upper,
Dublin 1, D01 C9W8, Ireland

Once Upon a Time: The Beast © 2023 Harlequin Enterprises ULC.

Beauty and Her Boss © 2018 Jennifer F. Stroka
Beauty and the Brooding Billionaire © 2020 Donna Alward
Claimed in the Italian's Castle © 2020 Caitlin Crews

ISBN: 978-0-263-31950-7

BEAUTY AND HER BOSS

JENNIFER FAYE

PROLOGUE

"THIS CAN'T BE HAPPENING."

Gabrielle Dupré frowned as she perched on the edge of a hard, black plastic chair. The room was small with gray walls. Outside the little room, there was the buzz of voices and phones ringing. But inside the room, a tense silence hung in the air like a dense fog. This was a place she'd never been in her life—a police station. How had things spiraled so far out of control? Her head pounded and her stomach churned.

After being here for more than two hours, the situation wasn't looking good. Not good at all. She'd just played her final card and she'd been praying ever since that it would pay off.

"Don't worry, daughter." Her father stared at her from across a black nondescript table. "Everything will be all right."

"All right?" She struggled not to shout in frustration. "Things are so far from all right." With each word, her voice crept up in volume. Realizing that losing her cool right now would not help their cause, she paused and swallowed hard. "Father, do you know how much trouble you're in?"

"Gaby, don't you understand? If I got word out about that monster, then it was worth it." His voice was filled with conviction. "Sometimes a man has to do what he has to do."

"And sometimes he needs to think before he acts," she said in a heated whisper. Anger pulsed through her veins, but it wasn't her father that she was upset with—it was herself.

Her father reached out and patted her hand. "You'll see. This will all work out."

She blamed herself for not being there to reason with her father. And to stop him from acting rashly. For the past six months, she'd been working two jobs to pay their outstanding bills but she was still losing financial ground. Things were so bad she was considering taking on a third job. With her father's health declining and him now in a wheelchair, it was up to her to make ends meet.

And through it all, she'd made sure to be there for her father every single day. He had been grieving ever since her aunt's deadly car accident almost four months ago. And it didn't help that the police had failed to release the truth about the accident. Although, that didn't stop the gossip sites from pointing fingers, including the magazine she'd recently started doing an admin job for, *QTR*. By way of some unnamed source, they were accusing an award-winning movie star, Deacon Santoro, of being at fault.

Gaby was still trying to figure out the how and why of her father's actions. "So you've been sneaking off to Deacon Santoro's estate all week?"

His gaze narrowed. "I wasn't sneaking. I didn't want to bother you so I took the bus."

She shook her head in disbelief. "I thought you had a girlfriend that you weren't ready to tell me about. If I'd have known what you were up to, I would have stopped you."

With her father's elbows resting on the table, he leaned toward her. His bloodshot eyes pleaded with her. "Don't you want the truth?"

"Of course I do. How could you question that? I loved her, too. She was like a second mother to me. But there are better ways to get to the truth. You shouldn't have staged a loud, disruptive protest in front of the man's house and accosted his staff."

Her father expelled a heavy sigh as he leaned back in his wheelchair. "Nothing else has worked. I've made phone call after phone call to the authorities. All I get is the runaround. They keep saying the accident report will be released as soon as the investigation has been completed."

Gaby couldn't believe what she was about to say, but someone had to reason with her father. With her mother and now her aunt gone, the responsibility landed squarely on Gabrielle's straining shoulders.

"Do you even realize how much power Mr. Santoro wields?"

Her father's bushy, gray eyebrows drew together. "Why do you think I went there? The police aren't helping us get the truth because he bought them off."

Gaby shushed her father. "Don't say those things."

"So I thought the media might help. After all, they'd do anything for a big headline."

"You certainly got their attention." Sadly, she didn't think this tactic was going to work, but she sure hoped she was wrong because the not knowing was eating at her, too. "There were so many reporters standing outside the police station that I had to be escorted through the back entrance."

Her father's tired face, with its two days' worth of

stubble, lifted into a satisfied smile. "It's working. You'll see."

Her father had a bad habit of acting first and thinking later. And she was left with the task of cleaning up his messes. But this was his first and, if she had any say in it, his last arrest. "And is it worth you going to jail or paying a stiff fine that will financially wipe us out?"

Before her father could answer, the door swung open. A tall police officer with salt-and-pepper hair stepped just inside the room. "We've contacted the complainant."

"And…" Gaby knew this was the time for restraint but there was so much on the line.

The officer shook his head. "He refused to meet with you."

That was not what she'd wanted to hear. She was hoping to plead with the man and hopefully get him to drop the charges. Her father was not physically well and punishing him would not help anyone, least of all Deacon Santoro. "Surely there has to be some way I can speak with him."

The officer cleared his throat. "I was about to tell you that he's on the phone. You may speak with him at my desk."

That was all the invitation she needed. In a heartbeat, she was on her feet and rushing out the door. She didn't so much as pause to assure her father that she'd straighten out this mess—because in all honesty, she wasn't sure she could fix things this time. But she was willing to do anything to protect her father—even from his own misguided sense of justice.

The police officer led her to his desk, where he handed over the receiver. Before she got a word out, the officer was called away to help with an unruly arrestee, who appeared intoxicated and quite belligerent.

Turning her back to the scene, Gaby said, "Hello."

"I am not dropping the charges." Deacon Santoro didn't even so much as utter a greeting, friendly or otherwise.

And yet his voice caught her attention. It was deep and rich, like a fine bourbon. She didn't need to verify who she was speaking to. After watching each and every one of his movies countless times, she would recognize Deacon's voice anywhere.

"I would really appreciate if we could talk this out."

"I've done all of the talking that I intend to do." His sexy voice was short and clipped. "Now, I've spoken to you. That is all I agreed to. I must go—"

"Wait!"

"This is a waste of time. Your father is guilty. He will have to take it up with the judge."

With each syllable the man spoke, her body betrayed her by being drawn in by the deep timbre of his voice. Logic dictated that he was the absolute last person she should be fantasizing about, but there was another more primal part of her that wanted to hear his voice again.

Gaby gave herself a swift mental jerk. She had to stay on point. Her father's future was depending on her getting this right.

"But he didn't do anything serious—"

"I'd call stalking a serious charge."

"Stalking?" This was the first she'd heard of this allegation. She couldn't help but wonder what else her father had failed to tell her.

"Yes. He's been making harassing phone calls, skulking outside my residence with binoculars and hounding my entire staff."

"I'm sorry. He hasn't been himself lately. He wouldn't hurt a soul. If you knew him—"

"I don't. And I don't plan to. None of this is my problem."

Mr. Santoro was right on that point, but would it hurt him to be a little generous? Perhaps she needed to explain the situation better. "My father, he isn't young. And his health is failing."

"Again, not my problem."

This man wasn't going to give an inch. His stirring voice ceased to affect her as she went into protective mode. "Listen, Mr. Santoro, I am sorry for the trouble my father has caused you, but pressing charges against him won't fix anything. Surely there has to be another way to work this out."

"Your father should have thought of all of this before he decided to cause trouble for me."

Why did this man have to act as though he was the innocent party here? If it weren't for his actions on that fateful night, her father wouldn't have bothered him. Angry accusations bubbled up within her and hovered at the back of her throat. It would be so easy to lose her cool—to tell this man exactly what she thought of him, which wasn't much.

What good would that do her? Yes, it'd temporarily make her feel better.

But in the long term, would it do anything to help her father? Definitely not.

Gaby's jaw muscles clenched. Her back teeth ground together.

"If that's all, I must go."

"It's not all." He wasn't getting off that easy. "My father was doing what he thought was best for my aunt."

"What does your aunt have to do with this? Or was she one of those misguided people that he coerced into shouting lies and throwing garbage onto my property?"

Gaby wasn't going to let this man go on about her father and aunt. Did he really not know who her father was? "My aunt wasn't outside your house. She—she died in the car accident."

There was a swift intake of breath as though at last he understood the gravity of the situation. A long silence ensued. Was it possible she'd finally gotten through to him?

Still, she didn't breathe easy—not yet. In just the short period of time that she'd spoken with this man, she'd learned that he didn't change his mind easily. And yet, she couldn't give up.

Every muscle in his body tensed.

Deacon Santoro didn't utter a word as he processed this new piece of information. How was this the first he'd heard of the woman in the accident having a family?

He searched his impaired memory for an answer. And then he latched on to the vital information. The police had said the woman had no family—no living parents, no ex-spouses and no children. Just a surviving brother. Deacon had never thought to ask about nieces and nephews.

Deacon swallowed hard. "You're her niece?"

"Yes. My name's Gaby."

"As in Gabrielle?"

"Yes. My aunt was the only one who called me Gabrielle."

Take care of Gabrielle.

Those words haunted him each night in his short and troubled sleep. Until now, he'd never understood what they meant. He didn't know anyone named Gabrielle. But suddenly a jagged piece of a memory from the accident came back to him. It wasn't an image but rather a voice. The woman from the accident had told him to take care of her niece.

And it was his chance to make sure the woman's final words were fulfilled. The need to help Gabrielle was overwhelming. But how? He needed time to absorb this revelation—to form a viable plan.

Deacon cleared his throat. "I didn't know she was your aunt. No one told me."

"Now you can understand my father's actions. He's grieving for his younger sister. He isn't thinking clearly."

"But that still doesn't make up for what he's cost me." Thanks to her father, another in a string of employees had quit. And thanks to the negative publicity, associates were shying away from doing business with him.

"I will do whatever I can to make this right."

He applauded her for trying to clean up a mess that wasn't hers. "How much are you talking about?"

"You want money?" Her voice took on a note of distress.

No. He had enough of his own, but he didn't want this conversation to end—not until he knew a bit more about this woman. "You did offer to make things right and I lost a lot of money when two promising business ventures fell through thanks to your father's actions."

"I—I don't have any money. Please believe me. I work two jobs to keep us afloat."

"Us?" The word rolled off his tongue before he could stop it. Suddenly he pictured this woman with a husband and children—her own support system.

"Yes. Me and my father."

At this point, Deacon should just hang up, but he couldn't do it. The father may have stepped over the line, but the daughter hadn't. And those words kept haunting him—*take care of Gabrielle*.

"What do you have in mind?" he asked.

"I could go outside and talk to the media. I could explain my father's actions—"

"Don't. The less said the better." All the while, he was considering how best to help this woman, who obviously had too much on her plate.

"So if my father and I agree not to say another word, you will see that the charges are dropped?"

"No. Not only has my name been slandered in the news, but my assistant was coming back from lunch when your father's protest was at its height. She was verbally assaulted and had things thrown at her. She has quit. And the temp agency doesn't want to send anyone else."

"Oh." Gabrielle paused. "I don't know what you want me to do to make this right."

"You don't need to do anything. You did not cause this mess." Something told him this wasn't Gabrielle's first time cleaning up after her father. Perhaps taking care of Gabrielle meant freeing her from being constantly at her father's beck and call. "Your father must face up to what he's done."

"But he's in no physical condition to go through the legal process—"

"This isn't your first time fixing things for your father, is it?"

"No." She quickly added, "But he needs me."

"Your father, can he cook for himself?"

"Yes, but—"

"Do his own laundry and shopping?"

"Yes, but—"

"You do most everything for him, don't you?"

"Of course I do. I'm his daughter. Now tell me what I can do to remedy things."

In that moment, Deacon knew what needed to be done.

Without giving himself a chance to back out, he said, "There is one thing and it's nonnegotiable."

"Name it."

"Come work for me."

CHAPTER ONE

Two days later...

WHAT EXACTLY HAD she agreed to?

Gabrielle Dupré's heart beat faster as she turned into the gated drive of the Santoro estate. Her gaze shifted to the clock on the dash. The drive from Bakersfield had taken more than four hours. She definitely wouldn't want to deal with that long commute each day. Thankfully Newton, an old friend from the neighborhood, had recently moved back to town and was renting a room from her father and had agreed to keep an eye on him while she worked here at the estate. Newton had changed since she'd last seen him, but he was happy to be there for her father, and they seemed to get on.

Deacon had offered her more money to work here than both of her jobs combined. It also included free room and board. Under different circumstances, she'd be excited about the opportunity. But with her father convinced that Mr. Santoro was the reason her aunt had died, being here felt uncomfortable to say the least.

She swallowed hard and reached out the driver's side window, pressing a finger to a button on the intercom. She waited for someone to speak to her. However, without a word the gate swept open. She had to admit she was curious to see what awaited her on the other side of the wall. She'd done an internet search, but it hadn't turned up any pictures of the estate.

Gabrielle eased her father's vintage red convertible onto the overgrown grounds. It certainly wasn't the grand estate that she'd been anticipating. Perhaps at one time this place might have been beautiful, but now it was woefully neglected. The grass appeared not to have been cut in ages. The bushes were overgrown and gangly. The flower gardens were overrun with weeds that were strangling out the few remaining flowers.

The internet sites said that Deacon Santoro had become a recluse since he'd been involved in the deadly accident. Apparently for once, the paparazzi hadn't been totally wrong. There was definitely something amiss on this estate.

The Malibu beach house was a stunning piece of mid-century architecture. Gabrielle slowed the car to a stop to have a better look around. Feeling as though someone was staring at her, she glanced up at the massive white mansion. There was no one standing in any of the windows. But there was a window on the top floor where the sheers moved. Cold fingertips inched down her spine.

Stop it. You're just being melodramatic. It's not like this is a haunted mansion.

No matter what she told herself, she couldn't shake her uneasiness. If it wasn't for her father, she'd turn around and leave. But a deal was a deal.

When she'd handed in her immediate resignation at the library, they'd refused to accept it. The staff was small and they were all close, like a family. So, she was on sabbatical leave until her deal with Deacon was concluded. She was so grateful to have a job to return to. It was one less thing she had to worry about.

However, when she'd resigned at the tabloid, she'd made the mistake of letting Deacon Santoro's name cross her lips. That spiked everyone's interest. She'd been passed up the chain of management until she'd been sitting across from the managing editor. And when the whole sordid truth came tumbling out, the editor had assured her that she didn't need to quit. In fact, they'd increased her pay.

The editor was putting Gaby on an assignment. The money was most welcome as her father's mounting medical expense were beyond her means. She had been shocked until it became clear that they wanted her to feed them every bit of dirt she could dig up on Deacon Santoro. She'd initially refused. Finding out the truth about her aunt's death was one thing. Digging up information about his private life just for sensational headlines was something else.

In the end, they'd all agreed that she would remain on the payroll and submit a daily report with information regarding the deadly accident. After all, if the legal system wouldn't do anything about it, someone had to seek justice in whatever way possible. And so Gaby had come here not only to protect her father, but also to uncover the truth about the accident and to expose Deacon's actions to the world.

At the time, the plan had seemed so easy. She'd play along as his assistant and befriend the man, which from the looks of the desolate place wouldn't be hard. Then she'd get him to open up about the accident. She would prove that he was responsible for her aunt's death. At last the world would know the truth, just like her father had wanted for so long. And then she could return to her life—a life that was temporarily on pause.

Gabrielle wheeled the car into a parking spot next to

a late model gray sedan. She'd arrived early this morning as she'd wanted to make a good impression on Mr. Santoro. She didn't want to give him any reason to go back on his agreement to drop the charges against her father, and that included keeping her connection with *QTR* magazine hush-hush.

She climbed out of the car and lifted her head to the blue sky. There was a gusty breeze. The forecasters said there was a storm brewing over the Pacific, although it hadn't reached them yet. But there was an ominous tension in the air.

She turned to head inside, but she wasn't sure where to go. There was yet another fence surrounding the building. There were numerous gates but no signs indicating where each led.

A movement in the corner of her eye caught her attention. Her gaze strayed across the outline of a figure in the distance.

"Excuse me," Gabrielle called out as she rushed forward.

The man's back was to her.

She called out again.

The man straightened from where he was bent over a rosebush. He was wearing jeans, a black long-sleeved shirt and a ball cap. He didn't turn around. Did he hear her?

"Hey, could you tell me where to go?" Not about to continue screaming across the grounds, she started down to a set of stained concrete steps leading to the garden.

By the time she reached the bottom step, the man was gone. Perhaps he hadn't heard her. He could still be around here somewhere. She started walking around in hopes of spotting him again. However, he was nowhere to be found. How was that possible? He was just here a second ago. She turned around in a circle. Where had he gone so quickly?

She sighed and was about to walk away when she paused to take in her surroundings. She stood on the edge of an expansive rose garden with a winding footpath. Unlike the rest of the overgrown yard, this section was neat and tidy. She found this shocking. What made this garden so special? It was just one more question that she had for Mr. Santoro.

Gaby headed back up the steps to the parking area. If worse came to worse, she would try all the gates and open all of the doors she encountered until she found where she belonged. You really would think Mr. Santoro would greet her or at the very least call her.

Time was getting away from her. If she didn't hurry, she was going to start off this arrangement by being late. Talk about making a bad situation worse. She picked up her pace.

At the top of the steps, she glanced around. On both sides of the parking area were doors. There was the large main house and there were six garage doors with what appeared to be a guesthouse atop them. Would he have put the office in the guesthouse?

Her gaze moved back and forth between the two structures as she tried to make up her mind. Just as she decided to try the main house, a gate swung open. At last, Mr. Santoro had come to greet her.

She rushed toward the door, but she came to a halt when an older woman with white hair and a round, rosy face came hurrying out. The woman was muttering something under her breath and shaking her head, but Gaby wasn't able to make out what she was saying.

When the woman's gaze met hers, a smile softened the woman's face. She had kind eyes and a warm smile.

"Ah...hello, dearie. You must be Mr. Santoro's new assistant."

Gaby smiled back at the woman. "I am. My name's Gaby Dupré."

"Welcome Ms. Dupré. And you can call me Mrs. Kupps. Mr. Santoro, he likes formality."

"I'm pleased to meet you, Mrs. Kupps." Gaby held out her hand to the woman. "But please feel free to call me Gaby."

The woman giggled and placed her hand in Gaby's for a brief shake. "I'm pleased to meet you, too," she whispered, "Gaby."

"Will you be showing me what I need to do?"

The woman shook her head. "Not me, dearie. I wouldn't have a clue. I'm the housekeeper and cook."

Gaby was disappointed. Working with Mrs. Kupps would have certainly made her workday interesting. "Do you know who will be showing me what I need to do?"

"I assume that would be Mr. Santoro."

"Oh, will he be out soon?"

The woman clucked her tongue. "Mr. Santoro does not get out much these days."

"Not even on his own estate?"

The woman shook her head as a serious look came over her face. "He prefers to stay in his suite of rooms."

This arrangement was getting stranger by the minute.

"But how will I be able to work with him?"

"He will phone you."

And then Mrs. Kupps pointed out the way to the office. Gaby made it there with ease. Once inside, she glanced around the office, taking in the white walls and two desks that faced each other from across the room. They were both sparsely set up, but the one to her left looked a bit haphazard, as though the person had been in a rush to get out the door.

The room was adorned with beach decorations and a couple of prints of the ocean. It was pretty, but there was nothing of the man that owned this spacious estate. There were no movie posters, no snapshots of Mr. Santoro with costars and no awards. It was though he'd purposely removed himself from the room. But why?

Gaby moved to one of the desks and placed her purse as well as her pink-and-white tote on the desk chair. Her gaze scanned the desk as she searched for any instructions of what was expected of her or a number that she was supposed to call upon arrival.

Then the phone rang.

He should have never agreed to bring Gabrielle here.

The decision had been made in haste.

And it was a mistake.

Deacon paced back and forth in his private study. This woman with the honeyed voice was dangerous, as she was poised to be a distraction from the stark reality of his situation. She would make him think about all of the damage that had been done. If only he could remember the accident—remember if he was at fault.

He would need to be on constant guard around her. With her being the niece of the woman who had died in his arms, she would be out to finish what her father started—destroying him.

And then he'd almost been caught by Gabrielle while he was in the rose garden.

It was his oasis. His chance to feel like a normal person, not a man hunted and hounded for the truth—something he didn't possess. How exactly had she missed the sign that explicitly said Do Not Enter?

Luckily he'd had enough time to make a clean escape. But as her sweet voice called out to him, he'd hesitated. An overwhelming urge came over him to capture a glimpse of the face that went with such a melodious voice.

In the shadows, he paused and turned back. He'd been awestruck. He didn't know how long he'd stood there in the shadows watching her move about the garden searching for him. Her long hair had bounced around her slim shoulders. Her face—it was captivating. It wasn't the type of beauty that was created with powder and makeup. No. Hers was a natural, undeniable beauty.

Her creamy complexion was flawless. He was too far away to catch the color of her eyes. He imagined they would be blue. His gaze strayed down past her pert nose and paused on her lush, rosy lips. Oh, she was definitely going to be a big distraction.

He jerked his meandering thoughts to an immediate halt. What was done, was done, as his mother would say. Now he had to deal with the consequences.

Deacon Santoro gripped the phone in his good hand and pressed the number for the office. He lifted the receiver to his ear. Two rings later, Gabrielle answered. The tone of her voice was a sweet blend of vanilla and caramel with a touch of honey.

He did not have time to get caught up in such nonsense.

Focus.

Deacon resumed pacing. "I see you decided to abide by our agreement."

"I don't see how I had any choice?"

"Everybody has choices—"

"Not in this case."

"And you were able to find someone to check in on

your father?" He didn't know why he'd asked except that when he'd first made this proposal, Gabrielle had been quite hesitant to leave her father.

"I have a friend staying with him. Newton just moved back to the area and my father had a spare room. It seemed like a good idea at the time."

"I take it you've since changed your mind about this Newton."

Gabrielle hesitated. "Let's just say I've gotten to know him better and he's not the same as I remembered."

"I see." Deacon's curiosity spiked, but he forced himself to drop the Newton subject. "At least you won't have to worry about your father."

Deacon was impressed by her allegiance to her father, but that wouldn't be enough to sway him to concede. Her father had cost him more than just bad press, a mess in his yard and upset employees—her father had stirred up the paparazzi. Once again, there were news reports on television and the internet. His phone—with its private number—was now receiving calls from journalists wanting "the truth."

The little sleep he did get was once again riddled with nightmares—fiery, jagged dreams. But when he woke up, the images blurred and the memories receded to the back of his mind. With each dream, he hoped he'd be able to latch on to the elusive truth of what happened on that deadly night. But try as he might, his memory had holes the size of craters and images blurred as if in a dense fog.

The doctors had warned him that the memories might never come back to him. That was not the answer he'd wanted to hear. He needed the truth—even if it meant he was responsible for taking another person's life. Trying to live with the unknown was a torture that had him knotted up inside.

"If you would just tell me where to meet you, we can sit down and go over what is expected of me." Gabrielle's voice cut through his thoughts.

"That won't be necessary."

"Of course it is."

He could hear the confusion in her voice. She wasn't the first assistant that had been uncomfortable with his distant style of management, but it was the way it had to be. He didn't need anyone eyeing him with pity. He didn't deserve anyone feeling sorry for him. It was best for him to keep to the shadows. The accident had left permanent scars on him both inside and out. His career as an actor was over. And he was now struggling to find a new position for himself in the background of Hollywood.

He cleared his throat. "All of your instructions are on your computer. The password is capital B-e-a-c-h."

"Will you be stopping by the office later?"

"No."

"I don't understand—"

"We will conduct our business via the phone or preferably by email."

"But what if I have papers for you to sign? Or mail. I'm assuming that I'll be receiving your business correspondence."

"You will. And if you check next to the interior door, there is a mail slot. Drop whatever correspondence needs my attention in there and I'll get to it."

"But that doesn't seem very efficient. I don't mind bringing it to you—"

"No!" His voice vibrated with emotion. He clenched his jaw and swallowed hard. He didn't want to have to explain himself. After all, he was the boss. In a calmer voice, he said, "This is the arrangement. If you don't like it, you are free to leave. Our deal will be null and void."

"And my father?"

"He will face the judge and pay for the trouble he caused."

"No. I can do this." Her words were right, but her voice lacked conviction.

In all honesty, if she quit, he didn't know what he'd do for help. The temp agencies had blacklisted him after he'd gone through a dozen temps in the past couple of months. But he'd make do, one way or the other. He always had in the past. "You're sure?"

"I am."

"Then I will let you review the document that I've emailed you. It should explain everything including the fact that I work late into the night, but I don't expect you to. However, I will have work waiting for you each morning." When sleep evaded him, he found it best to keep his mind busy. It kept the frustration and worries of the unknown at bay.

"Does anyone else work in the office?" she asked.

"No."

She didn't immediately respond.

He hadn't considered that she wouldn't like working alone. It had been one of his requirements through the temp agencies, but Gabrielle hadn't given him time to get in to specifics when they'd spoken on the phone. Maybe this was his way out—even if the voice inside his head kept saying that he needed to watch out for her.

He cleared his throat. "If working alone is going to be a problem, we could end this now."

The silence on her end continued. He really wished he could look into her eyes. For the first time, he found communicating via the phone frustrating.

"No. It won't be a problem." Her voice sounded confident. "But I have a stipulation of my own."

"And that would be?"

"I need to speak with my father at least once a day—"

"That's fine."

"Would you reconsider letting me visit him? He will miss me."

This separation was to punish her father—not her. He'd cost Deacon and now the man had to pay a price—even if it wasn't dictated by a judge. Her father would learn not to take Gabrielle for granted.

"He should have thought of that before he allowed you to pay the price for his actions. Our arrangement will hold. You will stay here and work for three months."

Deacon knew what it was like to be alone. Both of his parents had passed on and he had no siblings. Other than Mrs. Kupps, the housekeeper, he was alone in this big rambling estate—except now Gabrielle was here. And somehow her mere presence seemed to make this place a little more appealing and less like a prison.

"My father didn't make me do anything. I volunteered." Her indignation came through loud and clear.

"Now that everything is settled, I'll let you get to work." Deacon disconnected the call.

Something told him this was going to be a very, very long three months. But it definitely wouldn't be boring.

CHAPTER TWO

THIS DEFINITELY WASN'T her best first day on the job.

In fact, it ranked right up there as one of the worst.

And the day wasn't over yet.

A loud crack of thunder shook the windows at the same time as lightning lit up the sky around the guesthouse. Gabrielle rushed to close the French doors. Somehow the weather seemed rather fitting.

She had one more piece of business before she curled up with a book and escaped from reality. She had to file her first report with *QTR*.

Gaby sat down at the granite kitchen bar and opened her laptop. She stared at a blank screen with the cursor blinking at her...mocking her. What would she say? She didn't even know what format to use. Did they expect her to tell a story or stick to bullet points?

Sure, she'd earned a bachelor's degree in journalism, but with a downturn in the economy, she hadn't been able to land a position in publishing, so she'd returned to school. She'd gone on to get a second degree in library science. Books had always been her first love.

And as much as she loved words, right now they wouldn't come to her. She typed a couple of words, but they didn't sound right. She deleted them.

This is ridiculous. It's not an article for the public to

read. It doesn't have to be perfect. It just needs to be the facts. So start writing.

The man has closed himself completely off from others. Is it the result of guilt? Or something else?

As she pressed Enter to begin the next point, the landline rang. That was odd. She hadn't given anyone that phone number. Her father had her cell phone number.

She picked up the phone. "Hello."

"Did you find everything you need?" Not a greeting. Just straight to the point.

"Yes, I did."

"I wasn't sure what you like to eat, so I had Mrs. Kupps prepare you a plate of pasta, a tossed salad and some fresh baked bread. You will find it in your kitchen."

Outside the storm raged on with thunder and howling wind. Gaby did her best to ignore it. "Thank you." Had he called purely out of courtesy? Or was this his way of checking up on her? Perhaps this was her opportunity to flush him out of the shadows. "Will you be joining me?"

"No." His voice was firm and without hesitation. He was certainly a stubborn man. "In the future, you can let Mrs. Kupps know what you eat and don't eat, so that she can plan the menu appropriately."

"I—I can do that." She hesitated. "The guesthouse is nice." There was some sort of grunt on his end of the phone. She wasn't sure what it was supposed to mean, so she ignored it. "What time would you like to get started in the morning?"

"I start before the sun is up. You can start by eight. Will that be a problem?"

"No. Not at all." She was used to opening the library

at eight each morning. "I have a few things that I'd like to go over with you. Shall we meet in my office?"

"I thought you understood that this arrangement is to be by phone or email. I don't do one-on-one meetings—"

"But—"

"There are no exceptions. Good night."

And with that terse conclusion, he'd hung up on her. She stared at the phone. She could not believe that this man was so stubborn. Working for him was going to be difficult, but trying to get information about the accident from him was going to be downright impossible—unless she could get past this wall between them. And she hadn't come this far to give up.

Gaby hung up the phone and turned her attention back to the report for *QTR*. She'd lost her concentration after speaking with Deacon. She was back to staring at the blinking cursor and wondering what she should write.

QTR had assured her that before anything was published, they would get her approval. She wouldn't have agreed to the arrangement otherwise. After all, she didn't want them getting the facts wrong.

Although at this point, there wouldn't be much to write about the elusive Mr. Santoro. Giving herself the freedom to write about anything she'd learned so far, she resumed typing.

His estate in in disarray with overgrown vegetation. Was it always this way?

He's run off multiple assistants. What has happened? Has he fired them? If so, for what?

Locked door between the office and the rest of the house. What is he hiding?

The man lacks social niceties. Has he always been this way? Or is this a new thing?

It certainly wasn't a stellar first report. Would they be upset that it contained more questions than answers? Or would they appreciate her train of thought and look forward to the answers?

Accepting that it was the best she could do now, she proofread the email. Gabrielle pressed Send and closed her personal laptop.

She moved to the French doors and stared at the sky—the storm had now moved away. She opened the doors, enjoying the fresh scent of rain in the air. In the distance, the lightning provided a beautiful show. Was Mr. Santoro staring at the sky, too? She instinctively glanced in the direction of the main house, but she couldn't see it as it sat farther back than the guesthouse.

Still, she couldn't stop thinking about her mysterious boss. There had to be a way to break through the man's wall. She would find it, one way or the other.

CHAPTER THREE

Two days…

Forty-eight hours…

Two thousand, eight hundred and eighty minutes…

One hundred seventy-two thousand and eight hundred seconds…

No matter how Gaby stated it, that was how long she'd been at the Santoro estate and how long she'd gone without laying eyes on her new boss. It was weird. Beyond weird. What would that be? Bizarre?

Gaby sighed. Whatever you called it, she wasn't comfortable with this arrangement. Not that her accommodations weren't comfortable. In fact, they were quite luxurious. And unlike the estate's grounds, the guest suite was immaculate, thanks to Mr. Santoro's housekeeper, Mrs. Kupps. The woman had even written her a note, welcoming her.

Gaby glanced at her bedside table and realized that she'd slept in. She only had five minutes until she was due at the office. She had to get a move on. She slipped on a plain black skirt to go with a gray cap-sleeve blouse. There was a jacket that went with the outfit, but she rejected it. It was a warm day and she was more comfortable without the jacket. After all, it wasn't as if she had any business meetings. When Mr. Santoro said that he would limit their interactions to strictly email with the rare phone call, he hadn't been exaggerating.

She stepped in front of the full-length mirror and slipped on her black stilettos. With her height of only five foot two, the extra inches added to her confidence.

A knock sounded at the door, startling Gaby. She knew who it was without even opening the door. It would be Mrs. Kupps trying to lure her into eating breakfast. Gaby already explained that she didn't eat much in the mornings. In all honesty, she loved breakfast but never had time for it. She'd grown used to her liquid diet of coffee, with sugar and milk. It was easy to grab when she was on the run. Upon learning this, Mrs. Kupps had clucked her tongue and told her that she would end up with an ulcer if she didn't take better care of herself.

Gaby rushed to the door. "Good morning."

Mrs. Kupps stood there with a bright smile, a tray full of food and a carafe of coffee. "Good morning to you, too. I just brought you a little something to eat." Mrs. Kupps rushed past her and entered the small kitchen, placing the tray on the bar area. "I know you're in a hurry, but I'm determined to find something you can eat quickly."

"Mrs. Kupps, you don't have to do that." And then, because she really didn't want to hurt the woman's feelings, she added, "But it is really sweet of you. And the food looks amazing."

Mrs. Kupps beamed. "Oh, it's nothing, dearie. I enjoy having someone around here to spoil. Lord knows Mr. Santoro doesn't let anyone fuss over him since the accident. He's like a big old bear with a thorn in his paw."

"So he wasn't always so standoffish?"

Mrs. Kupps began setting out the food. "Goodness, no. He was always gracious and friendly. Perhaps he was a bit wrapped up in his acting career, but that's to be expected with his huge success. But now, he lurks about all alone in that big mansion. He doesn't see guests and rarely takes phone calls. I cook all his favorites, but his appetite isn't what it used to be. I'm really worried about him."

"Do you know what's wrong with him?" Gaby couldn't help but wonder if the guilt over the accident was gnawing at him.

Mrs. Kupps shrugged. "I don't know. And I really shouldn't have said anything. I just don't want you to leave. We need someone young and spirited around here. Lord knows, we've gone through assistant after assistant. He's even tried to run me off but it's not going to happen." The woman smiled at her. "You're a breath of fresh air. I have a good feeling about you."

Mrs. Kupps checked that everything was as it should be and then made a quick exit. It wasn't until the door shut that Gaby thought of a question for the very kind woman. Why did she stay here? Mr. Santoro was not the easiest person to work for. In fact, he was demanding and expected nothing but perfection with everything that Gaby did. And when she messed up, there was a terse note telling her to fix said error. And he didn't spare the exclamation points.

Still, she had agreed to this arrangement to save her father—a father who was now more eager to know what dirt she had dug up on her boss than worrying about how she was making out in such strained circumstances. It was all he'd wanted to talk about on the phone. His full attention was on making Mr. Santoro pay for the accident.

Gaby's gaze scanned over the croissant and steaming coffee. There was also a dish of strawberries. Okay. So maybe she had enough time to enjoy a few bites. Her stomach rumbled its approval. Perhaps some nourishment would help her deal with the stress of the day.

She couldn't help but wonder if this would be the day that Mr. Santoro revealed himself to her. He couldn't hide from her forever.

Deacon awoke with a jerk. His gaze sought out the clock above the door. He'd slept for more than two hours without waking. That was a new record for him, but it had come at a cost. He'd had another nightmare and, even worse, he was late.

It'd been another night spent in his office. He preferred it to staring into the dark waiting for sleep to claim him. Because with the sleep came the nightmares.

A couple of months after the accident, his nightmares had started to subside. But then Gabrielle's father had staged his protest with a megaphone, and he'd shouted horrible accusations. It was then that the nightmares had resumed. Sometimes Deacon remembered bits and pieces. There were brutal images of fire, blood and carnage. He had to wonder how much was real and how much had been a figment of his imagination.

Other times, he was left with a blank memory but a deep, dark feeling that dogged him throughout the day. It'd gotten so bad that he dreaded falling asleep. That's when his insomnia had set in with a vengeance. After spending one sleepless night after the next, he'd given up sleeping in his bed. In fact, he'd given up on sleep and only dozed when utter exhaustion claimed him.

It'd helped to keep his mind busy. And so he'd become a workaholic. Knowing the movie industry inside and out, he was working on starting his own production business. But being the man behind the curtain meant he had to find people he could rely on to do the legwork for him. That was proving to be a challenging task.

He'd just sat down to read over the lengthy letter that

Gabrielle had typed up for him. It had been late in the night or early in the morning, depending on how you looked at it. He'd made it to the last page when his eyes just wouldn't focus anymore. Blinking hadn't helped. Rubbing them hadn't made a difference. And so he'd closed them just for a moment.

He jumped to his feet and gathered up the papers that he'd reviewed. If he didn't get these on Gabrielle's desk before she arrived, it would have to wait until lunchtime. Because the mail drop in the wall only went one way. There was no way for him to deliver any documents anonymously for his assistant. He would have to see about rectifying that, but for now, he had to beat Gabrielle to the office.

He strode toward the door. When he reached out his hand for the doorknob, he couldn't help but notice the webbed scars on the back of his hand. They were a constant reminder of the horror he might have caused that impacted so many lives—especially Gabrielle's.

It was no secret that he'd liked his cars fast and he'd driven them like he was on a racetrack. He couldn't remember the details of that fateful night, but it wouldn't surprise him if he'd been speeding. If only the police would just release their findings. Gabrielle's father wasn't the only one anxious for that report.

His attorney had told him there were a number of complications. There had been an intense fire that destroyed evidence followed by a torrential downpour. Deacon didn't care about any of it. He just needed to know—was he responsible for taking a life?

Deacon moved through the darkened hallway, past the dust-covered statues and the cobwebs lurking in the corners. He didn't care. It wasn't like there was anyone in the house but him. Not even Mrs. Kupps was allowed in this part of the house. She kept to the kitchen and the office suite.

He descended the stairs in rushed steps. When he reached the locked door that led to the office area, he paused. There was no light visible from under the door and no sounds coming from within. He hated sneaking around his own home, but he didn't have any other choice. He didn't want to startle her with his appearance.

He recalled what had happened when his friends, or rather the people he'd considered friends, had visited him in the hospital right after his accident. They were unable to hide their repulsion at seeing the scars on his face, neck and arms. And then he'd held up a mirror to see for himself. The damage was horrific. After numerous rounds of plastic surgery, his plastic surgeon insisted the swelling and red angry scars would fade. Deacon didn't believe him. He'd already witnessed the devastating damage that had been done. It was so bad that he'd removed all the mirrors in the house as well as any reminders of how he used to look.

Deacon banished the troublesome thoughts. What was done, was done. He moved into the office and placed the stack of papers on Gabrielle's desk. That would definitely keep her busy today and probably some of tomorrow.

He noticed that her desk was tidy. However, there were no pictures or anything to tell him a little about her. It was though she wasn't planning to be here one minute longer than necessary to repay her father's debt. Not that Deacon could blame her—no one wanted to be here, including him. But he couldn't go out in the world—not until the accident was resolved and answers were provided.

Without tarrying too long, he turned to leave. He was almost to the door when he heard a key scrape in the lock. For a moment, he wondered what it would be like to linger in the office and have a face-to-face conversation with Gabrielle. In that moment, he realized how much he missed human contact. Maybe if he were to stay—maybe it would be different this time. Maybe she wouldn't look at him like he was a monster—a monster that killed her aunt.

He gave himself a mental shake. It was just a bunch of wishful thinking. He moved with lightning speed to the other door. He grasped the doorknob and, without slowing down, he gave it a yank, slipped into the outer hallway and kept moving. He needed distance from the woman who made him think about how one night—one moment—had ruined things for so many people.

CHAPTER FOUR

Didn't this man sleep?

It was almost lunchtime and Gaby hadn't even scratched the surface of all the tasks her boss had left for her. It didn't help that the phone rang constantly. Most calls were from reporters wanting to speak with Deacon. She had been left strict instructions to tell them "no comment" and hang up. With business associates, she was left with explaining that Deacon didn't take phone calls. When she explained that they would have to deal with her, it didn't go over well. Still, Gaby persisted. She had a job to do.

With a sigh, Gaby pressed Send on an email requesting the script for a film that Deacon was considering backing. But from what she could gather from prior correspondence and the files in the office, he had requested a lot of screenplays, but had yet to back one. She wanted to ask him how he decided which would be worth his money and which wouldn't.

Gaby got up to place the mail in the allotted slot for Mr. Santoro. When she approached the mail slot, she noticed the connecting door was slightly ajar. She slipped the papers into the slot and then turned back to the door. It beckoned to her.

What would it hurt to go see what was on the other side?

She knew if Mr. Santoro caught her, he would not be happy. In fact, it could very well blow up their whole deal. But if she didn't take a chance now, would she ever find out what he was hiding?

And to be fair, she was never told that she couldn't enter the house—only that mail was to go in the slot and communication would be phone or email. She had a hard time believing that he was as bad off as Mrs. Kupps had let on. This place wasn't exactly a dungeon by any means. He probably was just avoiding all the unanswered questions about the accident. And it was high time he stopped hiding from the truth and faced up to what had happened.

With a renewed determination, Gaby placed her hand on the doorknob and pulled the door open. It moved easily and soundlessly. There were no lights on in the hallway, but a window toward the back of the house let in some sunshine, lighting her way.

She didn't know what she expected when she crossed the threshold—an enraged Deacon Santoro, or a dark, dank house?—but she found neither. The house was done up in mainly white walls and marble floors. What she did notice was all of the empty spaces on the walls. There were mounted lights as though to illuminate a work of art or a framed photo, but there was nothing below any of the lights, as though even the hangings had been removed. *How odd.* The oddity was beginning to become a theme where Mr. Santoro was concerned.

The first set of doors she came to had frosted-glass inserts. One door stood ajar. She peered inside, wondering if at last she'd come face-to-face with Deacon Santoro, the larger-than-life legend. But the room appeared to be empty—except for all of the books lining the bookshelves.

Her eyes widened as she took in what must be thousands of titles. She stepped farther into the room, finding the bookcases rose up at least two stories. Like a bee to honey, she was drawn to the remarkable library. There was a ladder that glided along a set of rails to reach the top shelves. And a spiral staircase for the second floor of shelves with yet another ladder. It was truly remarkable.

She didn't know whether she had walked onto the set of *My Fair Lady* or the library of *Beauty and the Beast*. She'd never seen anything so magnificent. She moved to the closest bookshelf and found an entire row of leather-bound classics. It was then that she noticed the thick layer of dust and the sunshine illuminating a spiderweb in the corner. Who would neglect such a marvelous place?

Gaby ignored the dust and lifted a volume from the shelf. She opened the cover to find that it was a first edition—a *signed* first edition. It was probably priceless or at least worth more than she could ever pay.

And then she realized that if it was so valuable, she shouldn't be holding it in her bare hands. When she reached out to return it to the shelf, she heard footsteps behind her. She paused, not sure what to do. She moved the book behind her back. The time had come to face Mr. Santoro and suddenly she was assailed with nerves. It probably wouldn't help her case to be found hiding a collector's item. Her hand trembled and she almost dropped the book, but with determination, she gently placed it back on the shelf.

She leveled her shoulders, preparing for a hostile confrontation, and turned. The man had just entered the library and caught sight of her at the same time she had spotted him. He wore jeans and a long-sleeved shirt, which struck her as odd considering it was warm outside. And then she realized he was the man she spotted the first day that she'd arrived. He was the mysterious man from the rose garden.

"Who—who are you?" She didn't take her eyes off him.

His dark eyes narrowed. "I'm the one who should be asking questions here."

The voice, it was familiar. Was it possible that this was Deacon Santoro? She peered closely at him, trying to make up her mind. She supposed that it could be him. But it was his hair that surprised her. It was a longer style, if you could call it a style. The dark strands brushed down over his collar and hung down in his face.

She'd never seen him wear his hair that long in any of the movies he'd played in and yes, she'd seen them all. At one point, she'd have been proud of that fact, but after the accident, she'd wondered what she'd ever seen in the man.

When her gaze returned to his face, she had to tilt her chin upward. He was tall, well north of six feet.

And by the downturn of his mouth, he was not happy to find her in here. Her heart picked up its pace. She should turn away, but she couldn't. She needed to size up the man—all of him. She swallowed hard and jerked her gaze from his mouth. She really had to get a grip on herself. After all, he was the enemy, not some sexy movie star… Okay maybe he was that, too.

Ugh! This is getting complicated.

Her gaze took in the full, thick beard. It covered a large portion of his face. Between the beard and his longer hair, his face was hidden from view, for the most part. Except for his eyes. Those dark mysterious eyes stared directly at her, but they didn't give away a thing.

"What are you doing here?" His voice was deep and vibrated with agitation.

"I was looking for you." She refused to let on that his presence unnerved her. She clasped her hands together

to keep from fidgeting. "I thought it was time we met."
She stepped forward and held out her hand. "Hello, Mr.
Santoro."

His eyebrows drew together and he frowned as he
gazed at her hand, but he made no move to shake it. "I
told you I don't do face-to-face meetings. And you may
call me Deacon."

Gaby recalled what Mrs. Kupps had said about him
preferring formality and was surprised he'd suggest she
call him by his given name. Perhaps he wasn't as stuck
in his ways as she'd originally thought.

"And I don't like to be kept isolated." Ignoring the
quiver of her stomach, Gaby withdrew her hand. "If I
am going to work with a person, they need to have the
decency to meet with me—to talk one-on-one with me."

"You've seen me. Now go!"

She crossed her arms, refusing to budge. It was time
someone called him out on his ridiculous behavior. "Does
everyone jump when you growl?"

"I don't growl."

She arched a disbelieving eyebrow at him.

"I don't." He averted his gaze.

"You might want to be a little nicer to the people who
work for you." And then she decided that pushing him too
far would not help her cause, and said, "I have a request
that just came in today for you to make an appearance
at the upcoming awards show to present an award—"

"No."

"No? As in you don't want to attend? Or no, as in you
won't be a presenter?"

"No, as in I'm not leaving this house. And no, I'm not
presenting any awards. Have you looked at me? No one
would want me in front of a camera."

The fact that he'd dismissed the idea so quickly surprised her. For some reason, she thought he would enjoy being in the spotlight. Isn't that what all movie stars craved?

Deciding it might be best to change the subject, she said, "You have an amazing library."

At first, he didn't say a word. She could feel his gaze following her as she made her way around the room, impressed that the books were placed in the Library of Congress classification system. Was it possible Mr. Santoro... erm, Deacon loved books as much as her?

"I see you have your books cataloged." She turned back to him. "Do you also have a digital catalog?"

He nodded. "The computer that houses the database is over there."

She followed the line of his finger to a small wooden desk next to the door she'd entered. "This place is amazing. I've never known anyone with such an elaborate private library."

His dark eyebrows rose behind his shaggy hair. "You like books?"

"I love them. I'm a librarian and..." Realizing that she was about to reveal that she was an aspiring journalist would only make him more wary of her.

"And what?"

"I was going to say that I read every chance I get." She turned back to him. "I take it you read, too."

He shrugged. "I used to. These days my reading is all work-related."

"That's a shame, because books are the key to the imagination. You can travel the world between the pages of a book. Or visit another time period. Anything is possible in a book."

"What is your favorite genre?"

"I have two—suspense and romance. And cozy mysteries. And some biographies." She couldn't help but laugh at herself. "I have a lot of favorites. It depends on my mood." Perhaps this conversation was her chance to get past his gruff exterior. "How about you?"

"Mysteries and thrillers." He turned toward the door but paused. Over his shoulder, he said, "You—you may make use of the library while you are here." Then his voice dropped to the gravelly tone. "But do not wander anywhere else. The rest of the house is off-limits."

He certainly growled a lot, but she was beginning to think that his growl was much worse than his bite. So far, so good. Now if she could just get him to open up to her, perhaps she could find the answers to the questions that were torturing her father.

But before she could say another word, Deacon strode out the door.

Why had he gone and done that?

Later that afternoon, Deacon strode back and forth in his office. He never gave anyone access to the house. Even Mrs. Kupps, who had been with him for years, had restricted access. Now, his house was being overrun by women and he didn't like it.

He'd rather be left alone with his thoughts. His repeated attempts to uncover the truth had been unproductive. He kept coming back to one question: had he been responsible for Gabrielle's aunt's death?

As long as Gabrielle stayed in the library and the office, he could deal with her unwelcome presence. If he wanted a book to distract him from reality, he would make his visits late at night, when he was certain that Gabrielle would be asleep.

The thought of having that beauty staying on the estate gave him a funny sensation in his chest. It wasn't a bad feeling. Instead, it was warm and comforting. Dare he admit it? The sensation was akin to happiness.

It was wrong for him to be excited about Gabrielle's presence. He didn't deserve to be happy. But there was something special about her and it went beyond her beauty. She was daring and fun. He admired the way she stood up to him. He could only imagine that she was just as fiery in bed.

In that moment, his imagination took over. The most alluring images of his assistant came to mind. He envisioned Gabrielle with her long coppery hair splayed over the pillow while a mischievous grin played on her lips. With a crooked finger, she beckoned him to join her.

Eagerness pulsed through his veins as he shifted his stance. He'd been alone so long and she was an absolute knockout. He imagined that she could see past his scars and—

Knock. Knock.

Immediately his lips pulled down into a distinct frown. Who was disturbing his most delicious daydream? Wait. Who was in his private area?

Deacon spun around. Heated words hovered at the back of his mouth. And then his gaze landed on Gabrielle. A smile lifted her glossy red lips. Her eyes were lit up like they had been in his fantasy. He blinked and then peered into her eyes once more. Instead of desire, there was uncertainty.

"What are you doing here?" His words came out much gruffer than he'd planned.

"I—I have some correspondence for you to approve, and I have an idea I want to run by you."

"And for that you marched up here to my private office? You couldn't have emailed me?"

Her lips lowered into a firm line just as her fine eyebrows drew together. "I didn't think you were serious about resuming that ridiculous nonsense of emailing each other. I thought now that you've granted me access to your home, we could start working together like two professionals instead of being pen pals."

His prior assistants never would have been so bold. His respect for Gabrielle grew. And that observation caught him off guard. If he wasn't careful, her tenacity would lead them into trouble. However, she certainly did liven up his otherwise boring existence. Maybe he could risk having his life jostled just a bit.

"Well, you're here now, so out with it. What's your idea?" He had to admit that he was curious.

"I've been thinking over your concern about your public image. And I know that my father didn't help with that. But I've thought of something that might help—"

"Help?" He was utterly confused. "You want to help me?" When she nodded, he asked, "Why?" He was certain there had to be some sort of catch. There was no way she would want to help the person that was involved in an accident that killed her aunt. No one had that good of a heart.

Gabrielle lifted her chin. "During our first phone conversation, you appeared to be upset with the negative publicity, and I've thought of a way to negate some of it."

Some people may call him a pessimist, but the possibility of countering the bad publicity was definitely too good to be true. There was a catch and he intended to find it. "And what's in it for you?"

Her eyes widened. "Why does there have to be more?"

"Because you aren't here out of choice. There is absolutely no reason for you to help me. So out with it. What do you stand to gain?"

She sighed. "Fine. There is something—"

"I knew it." He felt vindicated in knowing that behind that beautiful face was someone with an agenda. "Well, by all means, don't keep me in suspense. What do you want in exchange?"

She frowned at him. "Why do you have to make it sound so nefarious?"

"And why are you avoiding the answer?"

"If my idea works, I was hoping you'd see fit to shorten my time here."

He smiled. "I was right. There is a catch."

"I just think we can help each other is all. Would you consider sponsoring a fundraiser?"

A fundraiser? He had to admit he hadn't seen that coming. "I am the last person who should be asking people for money."

Gabrielle shrugged. "I don't agree. People know who you are. You're up for a couple of awards for your latest movie release. And you have another movie about to be released. I think you'd be surprised by the public's support."

Deacon shook his head. "It's not going to happen."

"Consider it your way to put some good back in the world."

"You mean my penance."

She shrugged and glanced away. "I suppose you could put it that way."

There was no penance big enough, generous enough or selfless enough to undo his actions. "No."

"Because you don't want to do something good?"

Why did she have to keep pushing the subject? He had to say something—anything—to get her to let go of this idea. And then he thought of something that might strike a chord with her. "Have you looked at me?"

"Yes, I have." Her gaze was unwavering.

"Then you know that I have no business being seen in public."

Her gaze narrowed. "I think you're trying to take the easy way out."

"Easy?" His hands clenched. "There is nothing easy about any of this. You of all people should know that."

"You're right. I'm sorry. That didn't come out the way I meant."

He wanted to know what she had meant but he decided the subject was best left alone. "I need to get back to work."

"I think with a haircut and a shave that you'd look..." She stepped closer to him. At last, she uttered softly, "Handsome."

Too bad he didn't believe her. There wasn't a stylish enough haircut to distract people from his scars. And a shave would just make those imperfections obvious. He shook his head. "It isn't going to happen."

"What isn't? The haircut or the shave? Or the fundraiser?"

"All of them." Why couldn't she just leave him alone? It would be better that way.

She crossed her arms and jutted out her chin. "I can do this. And you can participate as much or as little as you want."

"What do you know about fundraisers?"

"Enough. I've organized one for my library each of the past five years."

"A library fundraiser?"

She nodded. "Funds are being withheld from libraries across the country. Lots of them are closing. In order to keep doors open, libraries have become creative in raising money. So many people need and use the resources made available by the library, but the government is of less and less help at keeping the lights on. It's a real struggle."

"I didn't know." It'd been a very long time since he was in a public library. "My mother used to take me to the library when I was very young. I remember they had reading time where all the kids sat around in a circle and they read a story to us. I think that's when I got the acting bug. I'd listen to the librarian use different voices for the various characters and it struck a chord in me."

Gabrielle's smile returned and lit up the room. "As a librarian, that's the best thing I could hear. I love when we are able to make a difference in someone's life, big or small."

"So, what you're saying is that you'd like me to do a fundraiser for your library."

She shook her head. "Not at all. The library is what is close to my heart. You need to find what's closest to yours."

He took a second to think of what charity he'd most like to help and the answer immediately came to him.

"You've thought of something. What is it?" She stared at him expectantly.

"Breast-cancer research. *If* I were going to have a fundraiser, that's what I would want it to be for."

"Why?" she asked, curiosity ringing from her gaze.

He shook his head. He wasn't going to get in to this. Not with her. Not with anyone. It was too painful and still too fresh in his mind.

After a few moments, Gabrielle asked, "Will you at least consider the idea?"

It would be more efficient and less hassle to just write a hefty check, which he did every year in memory of his mother. But Gabrielle seemed to have her heart set on this. Perhaps if he didn't readily dismiss the idea, with time she'd forget about it.

"I'll think about it." When a smile reappeared on her face, he said, "But don't get your hopes up."

She attempted to subdue her smile, but there was still a remnant of it lighting up her eyes as she placed some papers on his desk. Those eyes were captivating. They were gray, or was it green? Honestly, they seemed to change color. And they had gold specks in them. They were simply stunning, just like Gabrielle.

And then as he realized he was staring, Deacon turned away. "I'll get these back to you by morning."

He gazed out the window at the cloudless sky until he heard the clicking of her heels as she walked away. It was then he realized he'd forgotten to tell her something.

He turned around but she was out of sight. He was going to tell her not to enter this part of the house again—that it was out of bounds. But something told him she would have just ignored him anyway.

CHAPTER FIVE

THE NEXT MORNING Deacon couldn't concentrate.

He should be working, if he was ever to get his fledgling company firmly ensconced in the movie business. He'd made a lot of inroads so far. The legal documents were all signed and filed with the appropriate agencies. Financial business accounts were opened. Sunsprite Productions was at last ready to do business.

In front of him sat a stack of proposed movie scripts to read. However, every time he sat down, his mind would venture back to Gabrielle. Why had he agreed to keep the door unlocked? To give her access to his space?

He'd avoided the library like the plague and, so far, she hadn't returned to his office. The way she'd looked at him—well, it was different than others. She hadn't shuddered. And she hadn't turned away. If anything, she'd been curious. In fact, she'd even stepped closer to him. What was he to make of that?

No one who'd come to see him in the hospital, people who were supposed to be his friends, had been able to look him in the eye. Most had hovered at the doorway, unwilling to come any closer. But not Gabrielle. She was different. And his curiosity about her kept mounting.

He had to wonder why her aunt had found it necessary to use her last breath to tell him to take care of her niece. He had to be missing something. Gabrielle Dupré was quite capable of taking care of herself.

She hit things straight on and treaded where others feared to go. And she was smart, as she'd demonstrated by coming up with that idea to improve his public image—though he doubted it would work. He needed to tell Gabrielle that he wasn't going to take her up on the offer; he just hadn't gotten around to telling her yet. It wasn't like he had to worry about letting her down. Gabrielle was no damsel in distress. She was sharp and would always land on her feet. Deacon wondered if her father knew how lucky he was to have her by his side.

He halted his train of thought. Listing all of her positive qualities was doing him no favors. No matter how much she intrigued him, nothing could ever come of it.

Because there was a look in her eyes, one that was undeniable. She looked at him with anger. She blamed him for her aunt's death. And for all he knew, she might be right.

Feeling the walls closing in around him, Deacon made his way down to the rose garden. It was the one place where he found some solace. With the gentle scent of the roses that reminded him of his mother and the sea breeze that conjured up memories of sailing, his muscles relaxed. It was here that the pulsing pain in his temples eased.

He moved about the garden. His doctor and physical therapist had told him to make sure to get plenty of movement as that would help heal the injury to his leg caused by the crash. He wasn't about to venture outside the estate gates. He knew the press would soon catch up to him. And then the probing questions would begin.

And so he spent time here in the spacious rose garden. He hadn't spared any expense creating this retreat. The garden ran almost to the edge of the cliff overlooking the ocean. Wanting a wide-open feel, he'd declined building a wall around the garden. He used to think that this garden was a little piece of heaven on earth.

Deacon took a deep breath, enjoying the fresh air. Out here he could momentarily forget the guilt that dogged him. Out here, he could pretend there wasn't the most amazing yet unobtainable woman working for him. For just a few precious moments, his problems didn't feel so overwhelming.

He followed the meandering brick path to the far edge of the garden. He paused to prune a dying purple rose from a newly planted bush. He'd surprised himself by finding that he didn't mind gardening. In fact, he found the whole process relaxing. Who'd have ever guessed that?

A glint of bright light caught his eye. He glanced around, finding an idle speedboat bobbing in the swells not far off the shoreline. The light must have been a reflection. It wasn't unusual for the water to be filled with boats on these beautiful sunny days. And today, with the brilliant sunrise, it wasn't surprising that people were out enjoying the warm air and the colorful sky.

He didn't give the boat any further attention as he turned back to his task. He continued to trim the dead blooms from the bush when a movement out of the corner of his eye caught his attention. Was it animal? Or human?

Deacon swung around. He didn't see anything. Perhaps it was just his exhaustion catching up to him. With a shake of his head, he returned to his task.

"Good morning."

The sound of Gabrielle's voice startled him. He turned with a jerk. "You shouldn't be here." Did she have to invade every part of his life? Frustration churned within him. "Go!"

Her eyes widened. "I... I'm sorry."

She stepped back. Her foot must have struck the edge of a brick because the next thing he knew, her arms were flailing about and then she was falling. He started toward her, but he was too far away to catch her. And down she went. Straight into a rosebush.

Deacon immediately regretted his harsh words. He didn't mean to scare her. He inwardly groaned as he rushed over to her.

The first thing he spotted was blood. Little droplets of blood dotting her arms and legs from the thorny vines. And it was all his fault. Since when had he become such a growling old bear—so much like the father that he swore he would never turn into. And yet it had happened...

Take care of Gabrielle. There it was again. Her aunt's last dying wish. He was certainly doing a dismal job of it.

As he drew near her, he watched as Gabrielle struggled to sit up. Her movements only succeeded in making the situation worse and a pained moan crossed her lips.

"Don't move," he said, coming to a stop next to her.

This was one of the rosebushes he hadn't gotten to. The limbs were long and unruly. He pulled the shears from his back pocket and hastily cut the bush. He worked diligently to free her.

And then he had her in his arms. Her eyes glistened with unshed tears. She sniffled but she refused to give in to the pain. Her strength impressed Deacon. He was used to women who lashed out or gave in to the tears. Gabrielle was stoic—or perhaps stubborn fit her better.

He started toward the house with her in his arms.

"I can walk," she insisted.

"I've got you."

"Put me down." There was steely strength in her voice and the unshed tears were now gone.

He hesitated, not wanting to put her down. To his detriment, he liked holding her close. She was light and curvy.

And she smelled like strawberries. His gaze lowered to her lips. They were berry-pink and just right for the picking. He forgot about their awkward circumstances and the fact that he hadn't shaved or had a haircut in months.

In that moment, all he wanted to do was pull her closer and press his mouth to hers. Her lips were full and shimmered with lip gloss. It had been so very long since he'd been with a woman—

"Now." Her voice cut through his wayward thoughts.

When his gaze rose up to meet her eyes, she stared up at him with determination. Did she know where his thoughts had drifted? He hoped not. Having her know that he was attracted to her would just make this uncomfortable arrangement unbearable. He lowered her feet to the ground.

"Come with me." This time he was the one issuing orders and he wasn't going to take no for an answer.

He led the way into the darkened house. He knew that in its day the house was impressive, but now the blinds were lowered and dust covered most everything. But it didn't matter to him. He never spent time on the first floor. He stuck to his suite of rooms. And that's where he led Gabrielle.

Into the expansive foyer with its white marble floor and large crystal chandelier. He turned toward the sweeping staircase that curved as it led to the second floor.

"Where are we going?" she asked.

"To get you cleaned and bandaged."

"I'll be fine."

She didn't trust him. That was fine. She had no reason to trust him. He wasn't even sure he trusted himself now that he had a faulty memory and tormenting dreams. But this wasn't about her trusting him. This was about her welfare and making sure she didn't have any serious injuries.

"You need someone to help you." He turned to her at the bottom of the stairs. "You can't reach the cuts on your back. And as fate would have it, today is Mrs. Kupps's day off."

He started up the steps, hoping she would see reason and follow him. The very last thing he needed on his conscience was her being injured because of him and then getting an infection. He may have royally messed up the night of the accident and no matter how much he wanted to go back in time, it was impossible. However, right now he could help Gabrielle. If only she would allow him.

At the top of the steps there were three hallways—one to the left, which was where his mother had had her suite of rooms, another hallway to the right, where the people he'd considered friends used to stay, and then the hallway straight back, which led to his suite of rooms and his office that overlooked the ocean.

He stopped outside the last door. He hadn't made his bed. He hadn't straightened up in forever. And it hadn't mattered to him for months. But now, it mattered. Now he was embarrassed for Gabrielle to see his inner sanctuary. Later tonight he would do some cleaning.

"Is something wrong?" she asked. "If you changed your mind, I can go."

"No. Nothing's wrong." And with that he swung open the door. It wasn't like he was trying to impress her. That ship had sailed a long time ago. In fact, he'd lost any chance to impress her before they'd even met.

The room was dark as the heavy drapes were drawn as they always were, but he knew his way around without bothering with a light. However, he realized that Gabrielle would have a problem, and he reluctantly switched on the overhead light.

"Why is it so dark in here?" she asked. "You should open the curtains and let in the sun."

"I like it this way."

"Maybe the sun would give you a cheerier disposition."

Why did she want to go and change him? He didn't want to be changed. This was now his life and he would live it however he chose. "My disposition is fine."

"Really? And you think it's normal to go around scowling at people and barking out warnings for them to go away?"

"I do not bark and I do not growl." He turned on the bathroom light.

"Apparently you don't listen to yourself very often."

"You are—" he paused, thinking of the right word to describe her "—you are pushy and…"

"And right about you."

He sighed. "You don't know everything."

"But I do know that you're going to turn down my offer to help you."

He arched an eyebrow and stared at her, finding that she was beautiful even with her hair all mussed up from the rosebush and cuts crisscrossing her arms. It was then that he recognized just how much trouble he was in. There was something about Gabrielle that got under his skin, that made him feel alive again. And made him want to be worthy of her affection.

And if he wasn't careful, he was going to fall for her—head over heels. And that couldn't happen. She would be crazy to fall for him after the car accident. And he didn't deserve to have love in his life—not that he was falling in love with her. He wouldn't let that happen.

But knowing that it was even a possibility had him worried. The best thing he could do for both of their sakes was to keep her around here for as little time as possible. Maybe he should accept Gabrielle's offer to plan the fundraiser. Not that he relished having more attention cast upon him, but he could shorten her time on the estate without arousing her suspicions. She would never know how she got to him.

"What are you smiling about?" Gabrielle was eyeing him suspiciously.

"Who, me? I don't smile. Remember, I growl."

"Oh, I remember. But I saw a distinct smile on your face, so out with it."

What did he have by holding back? He'd strike the deal, set the timetable and soon his life would return to the way it used to be. Why did the thought of his quiet, lonely life no longer sound appealing?

"I accept your offer," he blurted out before he had an opportunity to change his mind.

Her eyes widened. Today, they looked more blue than green. "You do?"

He nodded. "How long do you need?"

"A few months would be ideal."

Months? He was thinking in terms of weeks. "You'll need to do it faster than that."

She thought about it. "How grand do you want to make it?"

"That's up to you."

"Instead of say a grand ball, we could do a garden party."

"That might not be enough of a draw."

"Okay. Give me a little time and I'll come up with some other ideas."

"Just don't take too long. I'd like to do this in the next few weeks."

Her eyes widened. "You don't give a person much room to work, do you?"

"If you're not up to the challenge—"

"I'll do it."

"Good. Now let's get you cleaned up." He led her into the bathroom and set to work cleaning and medicating her injuries.

He felt terrible that she'd been injured because of him. He would work harder in the future not to be so abrasive. He'd obviously been spending too much time alone.

He stood in front of her as she sat on the black granite countertop. He'd just used a cloth to wash the wounds on her arms with soap and water. Now that they were rinsed off, he was gently patting them dry.

As he stood there, he could sense her staring at him. He glanced up to say something, but when his gaze caught hers, he hesitated. And then her gaze lowered. Was she staring at his lips?

CHAPTER SIX

WAS THAT DESIRE reflected in her eyes?

Deacon swallowed hard. Suddenly the walls seemed to close in around them and the temperature was rising... quickly. He should turn away because if she kept staring at him, he was going to start to think that she wanted him—almost as much as he wanted her.

"You shouldn't do that," he said.

"Do what?" Her voice carried a note of innocence.

He inwardly groaned. "You know what."

"If I did, I wouldn't ask."

Surely she couldn't be that naive. Could she? "Look at me like—like you want me to kiss you."

She didn't blush, nor did she look away. "Is that what you think I want? Or is that what you want?"

Why did she have to insist on confusing matters? He was already confused enough for both of them. "Forget I said anything."

"How am I supposed to do that now that I know you're thinking about kissing me?"

"That's not what I said." He huffed in exasperation. "Turn around."

"Why?"

"Do you have to question everything?"

She shrugged. "If I didn't, I wouldn't know that you want to kiss me."

"Would you quit saying that?" Heat rushed up his neck and settled in his face, making him quite uncomfortable. "Turn around so I can tend to the wounds on your back."

For once, she did as he said without any questions. Thank goodness. He wasn't sure how much longer he could have put up with the endless questions. It would have been so much easier to smother her lips with his own. And then he'd know if her berry-red lips were as sweet as they appeared.

But this was better. With her back to him, he could get a hold on his rising desire. They were oh, so wrong for each other. She was pushy and demanding. She was definitely not the type of woman he normally dated. If he hadn't been alone all these months, he wouldn't even be tempted by her. He assured himself that was the truth.

And then she lifted her shirt, stained with thin traces of blood, to reveal the smooth skin of her back. His assurances instantly melted away. All he wanted to do was run his hands over her body and soothe away her discomfort with his lips, fingers and body.

"Is something the matter?" she asked.

His mouth suddenly grew dry. He swallowed and hoped when he spoke that his voice didn't give away his wayward thoughts. "I—I'm just figuring out where to start."

"Is it that bad?"

He wondered if she was referring to his level of distraction or the cuts and punctures on her back. He decided that she'd given up flirting with him and was at last being serious. "It could be worse."

"That's not very positive."

He was beginning to wonder if along with his memory

loss he'd lost his ability to talk to women. He used to be able to flirt with the best of them without even breaking a sweat, but talking to Gabrielle had him on edge, always worrying that he'd say something wrong, which he seemed to do often.

"I didn't mean to worry you." He grabbed a fresh washcloth from the cabinet and soaked it with warm water. He added some soap and worked it into a lather. "Let me know if this hurts."

"It'll be fine."

He wanted to say that the skin on her back was more tender than that on her arms or hands, but he didn't want to argue with her. It was then that he noticed how her skirt rode up her legs, giving a generous view of her thighs. His hand instinctively tightened around the washcloth as his body tensed.

With great reluctance, he glanced away. It took all of his effort to concentrate on the task at hand. And it didn't help that the task involved running his fingers over her bare flesh. Talk about sweet torture.

He pressed the cloth gently to the first wound. When he heard the swift intake of her breath, he pulled away the cloth. "I'm sorry."

"It's okay. Just keep going."

"Are you sure?"

"Keep going. I obviously can't do it myself."

And so he kept working as quickly as he could. When her wounds were cleaned, rinsed and dried, he grabbed the antibiotic cream, which, thankfully, had something for pain relief. A few of the cuts had required bandages. The others had already started the healing process.

He lowered her top. "There. All done."

She turned to him. "Thank you."

"Don't." He waved off her gratitude. "I don't deserve your thanks."

"Yes, you do. You fixed me all up."

"I'm the one who caused your injuries." He just couldn't seem to do anything right these days.

"No, you didn't. I stumbled and fell. End of story."

"You stumbled because I startled you."

Her green-gray eyes studied him for a moment. "You do have a way of growling—"

His voice lowered. "I don't growl."

She laughed. "You just growled at me."

Had he growled? No, of course not. He wasn't some sort of animal. He was human—a damaged human, but human nonetheless. Still, his tone might have been a bit gruff.

She stepped toward him. "I see the doubt in your eyes."

He narrowed his gaze on her. "If I growl so much, why are you still here?"

"Good question. I guess I'm just holding up my side of our agreement."

For a moment there, he'd forgotten that she was there at his insistence. He knew that if she had a chance, she'd be anywhere else. And he couldn't blame her. He definitely wasn't the most hospitable host.

But when he was this close to Gabrielle, he wanted to be someone else. His old self? No. He'd been too selfish—too self-absorbed. Right now, he wanted to be someone better.

"I'm sorry that I startled you earlier." He made sure when he spoke that his voice was soft and gentle. He would not growl at her. "I never meant for you to get hurt."

She stared into his eyes. "You really mean that, don't you?"

"Of course." His voice took on a rough edge again. He swallowed hard. And when he spoke, he made sure to return to a gentle tone. "I'm not used to having anyone out in the gardens."

"The rose garden is beautiful. That's why I was out there. I could see them from my bedroom window and I wanted to get a better look. Unlike the rest of the grounds, they are well-maintained. They must be special to you?"

"They are. I had them planted for my mother." He missed his mother. She had been kind and gentle. She had been the exact opposite of his brutal father. "Roses were her favorite. She used to spend hours out there. It's where she spent her last days."

Gabrielle's eyes filled with sympathy. She reached out to him. Her fingers wrapped around his hand. She gave him a squeeze. "I know that saying I'm sorry isn't enough, but it's all I have."

He continued to stare into her eyes, and he saw something more than sympathy. There was…understanding. He searched his memory and he recalled her mentioning that she'd also lost her mother. "You understand?"

She nodded. "My mother died giving birth to me, so I never knew her."

Instead of offering her the same empty words, he nodded and squeezed her hand back. It was then he realized her hand was still in his. The physical contact sent a bolt of awareness through his body.

He should let her go. He should step away. But he could do neither of those things. It was as though she were a life-sustaining force and without her, he would cease to exist.

His gaze lowered to her lips. Today they were done

up in a striking purple shade. Against her light skin, her lips stood out. They begged for attention and he couldn't turn away.

This wasn't good—not for his common sense. Because right now, all he could think about was her mouth—her very inviting mouth. He wanted to kiss her. He needed to kiss her. He longed to feel those lush purple lips move beneath his. A groan swelled in the back of his throat, but he choked it back down. He didn't need Gabrielle realizing how much power she had over him.

Because there was no way her kiss could be as amazing as he was imagining. Nothing could be that good. Not a chance.

He needed a heavy dose of reality to get her out of his system. And then he'd be able to think clearly. Yes, that would fix things.

Without giving his actions further thought, he dipped his head. He captured her lips with his own. At first, he heard the swift intake of her breath. She pulled back slightly and he thought she was going to turn away.

Then her hand lifted and smoothed over his beard. It must have caught her off guard. He should shave it, but it never seemed like the right time, until now.

And then her lips were touching his again. Tentatively at first. She didn't seem to know what to make of this unlikely situation. That made two of them, because kissing her was the absolute last thing he thought he'd be doing this morning.

As if he were acting in a trance, he drew Gabrielle closer and closer. He expected her to pull away. To slap him. Or at the very least stomp away.

Instead her hands came to rest on his chest. Her lips began moving beneath his. Her hands slid up over his shoulders and wrapped around his neck as her soft curves leaned against him. Mmm…she felt so good. And she tasted sugar-sweet, like the icing on a donut. And he couldn't get enough of her.

Their kiss escalated with wild abandon. It was as if she were the first woman to ever kiss him. No one had stirred him quite the way she did. He never wanted to let her go.

In the background, there was a noise. He couldn't make it out. And then it stopped. Their kiss continued as his body throbbed with need.

And then the sound started again. He wanted it to stop—for them to be left alone to enjoy this very special moment. The next thing he knew, Gabrielle braced her hands against his chest and pulled back.

It was too soon. He wasn't ready to let her go. And yet she moved out of his embrace. She reached for her cell phone, which was resting on the countertop.

"Hello, Dad. Is something wrong?" She turned her back to Deacon.

He ran the back of his hand over his lips. Instead of getting Gabrielle out of his system, he only wanted her more. He was in so much trouble.

Gabrielle turned back to him. She didn't have to tell him how much she loved her father. It was there in her voice when she spoke of him. It was in her eyes. It was in her actions by coming here and working for Deacon. She was a devoted daughter. Deacon just hoped her father deserved such devotion.

When she ended the call, Deacon asked, "Is everything all right with your father?"

She nodded her head. "He's fine."

Deacon noticed how her gaze failed to meet his. "But he's not happy about you being here."

"No. He isn't." She sighed. "My father used to

be such an easygoing guy. But the accident, well, it changed everything—for both of us."

Right then the wall went back up between them. Deacon could feel the warmth slip away. The chill was as distinct and real as the kiss they'd shared—the kiss that would not be followed by another. He would be left with nothing more than the memory.

"I know how death can change people." His mother changed after his father's death. Even though the man didn't deserve her undying love, she'd given it to him anyway. When his father passed away, his mother was cloaked in sadness. She moved on with her life, but it was never the same. She was never the same again.

Gabrielle's gaze briefly met his. "About what happened between us—"

"It was nothing." He was a liar. A bold-faced liar. "We lost our heads for a moment. It won't happen again." At least that part was the truth.

Gabrielle glanced away. "You're right. It was a mistake."

Her sharp words stabbed at him. He didn't know how much more of this he could take. It was best that they parted ways until he got his emotions under control.

He wasn't mad at her. He was angry with himself for losing control—for complicating an already messy situation.

"I should go." She just turned and walked away.

This situation was such a mess. An awful mess. How in such a short time had Gabrielle taken his dark hopeless life and filled it with light? He didn't know how he'd go back to the dark again.

CHAPTER SEVEN

THE SUN WAS sinking into the sky when Gaby called it quits for the day. Deacon had made himself scarce the rest of the day and perhaps that was for the best—for both of them.

Things were confusing enough. That kiss only intensified the conflicting emotions within her. She had no business flirting with him—coaxing him into kissing her. She should keep a respectable distance from this man. He was trouble.

Wait. Was that the answer? Could she be drawn to Deacon because he was so different from the other professional men she'd dated? Did Deacon's dark side act like a magnet?

Whatever it was, she had to get a grip on it. Because her reason for being here had absolutely nothing to do with becoming romantically involved with Deacon Santoro. And she'd do well to remember the circumstances that had led her here.

Gaby sighed as she let herself inside the guesthouse. There was still enough light filtering in from outside that she didn't turn on the lights. Instead she kicked off her heels and moved to the couch.

Her cell phone rang. She didn't recognize the number.

She was about to ignore it when she thought of her father. Something might have happened to him.

Needing to be certain her father was all right, she answered the call. "Hello."

"Gabrielle Dupré?" The male voice was unfamiliar to her.

Concern pumped through her veins. "Yes."

"My name's Paul. I'm with *Gotcha* magazine. Do you have a comment on the photo?"

"Photo?" She had no idea what this man was talking about. Thinking it was probably a scam, her finger hovered over the end button.

"The one of you in Deacon Santoro's arms. Would you like to comment on why you're in the arms of the man that *allegedly* killed your aunt?"

"There is no photo."

"If you don't believe me, go to our website. It's on the home page, front and center. I'll wait," he said smugly.

Gaby pressed the end button. It didn't matter what they had posted on their website, she wasn't giving a comment. But she wanted to see what had prompted the reporter to call her.

Her fingers moved rapidly over the touch screen and then the website popped up. She gasped. It was true. They did have a photo of her and Deacon.

Her face felt as though it was on fire. That man had made the situation sound so scandalous. Deacon had only been helping her after she'd been an utter klutz.

She studied the photo more intently. She didn't recall Deacon looking at her like—like he desired her. Surely they'd done something to alter the photo. She'd heard they do that all the time to make people thinner or prettier.

Thankfully there hadn't been any cameras in Deacon's house. Her face burned with embarrassment when she

recalled how she'd flirted with him and then that kiss—
oh, that heated kiss had been so good.

And yet, the kiss could not be repeated.

No matter how good it was, it was a one-time thing—
a spur-of-the-moment thing. It didn't matter if his touch
had been so gentle and so arousing. There could be no
future for them. It was impossible. She was the niece
of the woman who'd died because of Deacon's actions.
There was no way they could get around that.

And she wouldn't do that to her father. She owed everything to her father—a man who'd always stood by her
and who'd encouraged her to follow her love of books
and sacrificed so that she could go to college.

She needed to talk to Deacon. She needed to tell him
about the photo. She headed out the door. She also needed
to make sure he'd heard her when she said that she regretted that soul-stirring, toe-curling kiss—because she
did, didn't she?

Now that she had full access to the house, she knew
her way around. She knew where Deacon would be,
where he spent most of his time—in his office. It was
like a one-room apartment. From what she could tell, it
was where he took his meals, where he slept—when he
slept—and where he worked.

Her footsteps were silent over the carpeting. When she
reached his office, the door was open and the soft glow
of the desk lamp spilled out into the hallway. But there
were no sounds inside.

She stepped just inside the door. Her gaze scanned
the room, with its long shadows. The desk chair was
empty and so was the leather couch. Her gaze continued
around the room until she spotted him standing in the
open French doors that overlooked the ocean.

He didn't move. He must be lost in thought. She wondered if she was too late. Had he seen the photo?

She softly called out, "Deacon."

He didn't turn to her as she'd expected. Instead he said, "You shouldn't be here."

"We need to talk."

"If it's business, it can wait."

She crossed her arms and leveled her shoulders. "If you're going to talk to me, you could at least have the decency to face me."

He turned to her. His face was devoid of expression. She didn't know how he managed that when she was certain he was anything but calm—not after that spine-tingling kiss. She supposed that was what made him such an accomplished actor. She, on the other hand, wore her emotions on her sleeve. She didn't like it, but she didn't know how to hide her emotions.

"I'm facing you," he said matter-of-factly. "Now, why are you here?"

"I just had a phone call from a reporter. There's a photo of us on the internet."

A muscle in Deacon's jaw twitched. "Let me see it."

Recalling how the photo made it seem like there was something going on between them, she didn't think Deacon would take it well. "I don't think you want to see it."

He approached her and held out his hand.

She pulled up the picture on her phone. The headline read: Evading the Police in the Arms of a New Lover. Maybe bringing it to Deacon's attention wasn't a good idea after all.

She handed him the phone and waited for his reaction.

For a moment, he didn't speak. He scrolled through the article. With a scowl on his handsome face, he returned her phone.

"I don't even know how they got the photo," she said.

"I do. There was a boat not far off the shoreline. I hadn't thought much of it at the time, but there must have been a photographer on board."

"How can they publish this stuff? The headline is a lie."

"Welcome to my world. The tabloids will do anything for headlines. They are vultures."

"But they know it's not true."

"They don't care about the truth. It's whatever makes them money. I'm sorry you got caught up in it." He raked his fingers through his hair. "Until the police report is released, I'll be in the headlines."

They'd both been dancing around the subject of the car accident for far too long now. She needed some answers and she didn't know how to get them other than being direct. "Deacon, tell me about the accident."

"No." He moved to his desk and started moving papers as though he were looking for something.

"Don't dismiss me. I need to know—I need to know if what my father is saying about you is true."

Deacon straightened and his dark gaze met hers. "Why would you doubt him?"

"Because I feel like I'm missing something. And yet I keep thinking if you were innocent, you would have given your statement to the police. You would have cleared up this mess. Instead you remain tight-lipped about the facts, which says you're guilty. Is that it? Are you guilty?"

His jaw tightened. "I know in part you agreed to this arrangement to get information, but I'm not talking about the accident. Not now. Not ever. So if that's what you're after, you can go back to Bakersfield."

"So you can say I broke the arrangement and have

you press charges against my father? No thank you. I'm staying until my time has been served."

"This isn't a prison." His voice rumbled. "You're free to go."

"When our deal is fulfilled and not a minute sooner."

She paused and studied his face. "You might feel better if you talked about it."

"That subject is off-limits," he said with finality.

She sighed. "Okay then. I'll go work on the plans for the fundraiser. I'll let you know how it goes."

"At this hour?"

"It's not like I have much else to do around here. This place is so big and yet so empty."

His eyes grew dark. "It's the way I like it."

She didn't believe him. He didn't live alone in this big house because he wanted to. There was so much more to him closing himself off from the outside world. How would she get him to open up to her?

Gaby moved to the door. She paused in the doorway. She still hadn't told him the other reason she'd sought him out. She worried her lip. With him standing there looking so cold, it wasn't easy to talk to him. He reminded her of the man she'd met that not-so-long-ago day in the library, but tonight he hadn't told her to get out. Nor had he growled at her. Maybe he was changing.

"What?" he prompted.

"I just wanted to make sure that things were straight between us. You know, about the kiss."

He brushed off her concern. "It's already forgotten. I won't be kissing you again if that's what you're worried about."

"Oh." She wasn't sure what she'd wanted him to say, but that wasn't it.

Without a word, he turned his back to her and stared out at the moon-drenched ocean.

She had been dismissed, quickly and without hesitation. And so had their kiss. Was it just her that had been moved when his lips touched hers?

As she walked away, she felt as though she had lost her footing with Deacon. Her fingers traced her lips, recalling the way his mouth had moved passionately over hers, bringing every nerve ending to life. Her lips tingled at the memory.

He may deny it, but he'd felt something, too. And for the life of her, she didn't know what to do about this attraction that was growing between them.

CHAPTER EIGHT

HE COULDN'T STOP thinking about that picture.

The next morning, Deacon set aside his pen and leaned back in his desk chair. Although he didn't like the invasion of privacy, that wasn't what was eating at him. Nor was it the inflammatory headline. It wasn't any of that stuff.

He pulled up the photo on his computer with the larger monitor. The part that he couldn't get past was that she looked good in his arms. In fact, if he didn't know better, he'd swear they were lovers. And he was certain that's what anyone who caught a glimpse of the photo would think.

He scrolled down, finding there were hundreds of comments. He knew he shouldn't read them, but he couldn't help himself. There were, of course, mean, nasty comments, but to his surprise, there were others in support of them. They commented that sometimes love comes at the most unexpected times. Those people were all wrong—very wrong. Others said he was taking advantage of Gabrielle. That, too, was untrue. He was trying to help her, both financially, with an inflated salary, and so that she could gain her independence from her father. And it certainly had nothing whatsoever to do with love.

Deacon shut down the site. He'd read enough. He

checked the time. It was almost time for him to leave for his appointment.

He moved to his bedroom to change clothes. Still, he couldn't stop thinking about Gabrielle.

He knew she wanted answers, but he didn't think she'd buy his amnesia story any more than the police had bought it. There had been the skeptical looks followed by the prodding questions that went on and on with the same answers. It was as if they believed that if they asked the same questions a hundred and one times, his answers would change from "I don't remember" to something they could use against him.

In the short amount of time he'd spent with Gabrielle, he'd come to respect her. And having her upset with him for not opening up about the deadly accident was better than the look she would give him upon hearing that he couldn't remember it. In her shoes, he probably wouldn't believe him, either. He couldn't bear to have her look at him as if he were a liar. He was a lot of things in life, and some of them were not so good, but he wasn't a liar.

Maybe today he would get those elusive answers. His attorney had said he had news, but he wouldn't say on the phone whether it was good or bad. Something told Deacon that it wasn't good news. But he didn't want to say anything to Gabrielle until after his meeting, when he'd hopefully have more information.

Once he left the attorney's office, he had a doctor's appointment, where they'd run some tests to make sure he was healing properly. The accident had done significant damage to his body. If he were to pass through the metal detectors at the airport, he'd surely set them off with his newly acquired hardware.

In the end, he'd spend most of the day in Los Angeles. He didn't like these outings. They were fraught with the stress of being hounded by the press and wondering if the attorney and doctors would have more bad news for him.

Refusing to dwell on the unknowns awaiting him, he gathered the screenplay he'd finished reading. He was on the fence about this one. It was a mystery and he recalled Gabrielle mentioning that she enjoyed reading mysteries. He'd like to get her take on this one before he went any further. He did have a few changes he'd like to see incorporated when the screenplay was rewritten, but he'd run those past Gabrielle after he got her initial reaction.

However, when he opened the door to the office, Gabrielle wasn't at her desk. He walked farther into the room and found the outer door slightly ajar. He dropped the stack of papers on her desk and headed out the door. Once outside, he spotted Gabrielle at the end of the walk.

Deacon called out to her, but she must not have heard him as she kept moving. She turned the corner away from the beach and the guest cottage. Where was she going?

As he followed her, the sidewalk soon became surrounded by overgrown bushes, tall grass and weeds. He frowned. To be honest, he never walked toward the front of the house. It was too close to the road for his comfort with the paparazzi lurking about.

Surely she couldn't be enjoying a leisurely stroll through this thick vegetation, could she? He kept walking. His steps were long and quick as he hustled to catch up with her.

He turned a corner and there she was on the opposite side of the house. She stood in the shadows with a legal pad in one hand and a pen in the other. She was so intent on writing something that she didn't appear to notice his presence.

Once he was within a few yards of her, he called out to her.

Her head jerked up.

"Oh. It's you." And then she flashed him a smile that filled his insides with warmth. "Good morning."

"I stopped down to speak with you and didn't find you at your desk."

She turned back to the legal pad and continued writing. "I had an idea and I needed to check it out. Now, I'm not sure how to make it work."

An idea? Suddenly he grew uncomfortable. If he knew anything about Gabrielle, it was that she wasn't afraid to shake things up. And the fact that she was standing in his overgrown yard making notes didn't sit well with him.

She sent him a mischievous grin that lit up her eyes and intensified that fuzzy warm feeling in his chest. He swallowed hard. "Gabrielle, dare I ask what you have in mind?"

She glanced around. "This used to be a golf course, didn't it?"

He glanced over the neglected grounds and a fresh wave of guilt washed over him. "At one point, it was a private course."

"Wow." Her gaze was glued to the lush green grounds. "How many holes?"

"Nine." He used to spend a lot of time out here entertaining friends and associates. They said he had the best private course in the country. "But it doesn't matter anymore."

"Of course it matters. Why don't you golf anymore?"

"After the accident, my injuries made it impossible."

"And now, can you play?"

"I don't know. I haven't tried." He rotated his left shoulder. There was a dull pain, but thanks to lots of therapy, his range of motion was almost one-hundred-percent. "Not that anyone could golf out here."

"It looks like at one point it was beautiful."

"It was." His mind conjured up an image of the golf course in its prime. It had come with the house and it had been gorgeous, with water hazards and sand bunkers. It might have been a short course, but it had been a fun way to while away a lazy summer afternoon with friends. Those carefree days seemed like a lifetime ago now.

"It's a shame to let it go to ruin. Have you ever considered restoring it?"

He shook his head. He just couldn't imagine golfing when he had so much uncertainty and guilt weighing him down. "I stopped by to let you know that I need to go out for a while."

Her eyes widened and her mouth gaped open, but she quickly recovered her composure. "I didn't know you ever left here."

"I don't unless it's necessary."

Unasked questions filled her eyes, but she was smart enough to leave them unspoken. "Is there anything you need from me while you're gone?"

"Yes. I put a screenplay on your desk. I know you enjoy mysteries and I was interested in your thoughts. The sooner, the better."

"Thoughts? As in a pro-con list?"

He hadn't thought of that, but it wasn't a bad idea. "Sure. That works for me." And then he added, "I'd really appreciate it."

"Well, when you put it so nicely, I'd be happy to do it."

So nicely? He didn't think he'd said it in any special manner. Perhaps she meant since he didn't growl at her. Was Gabrielle having that much of an effect on him?

"I'll be gone most of the day." He turned to walk away.

"Do you mind if I ask where you're going?" When he turned back to her, she added, "You know, in case something comes up while you're gone."

"I'll have my cell phone. The number is listed on your computer."

"Oh, okay." She tried to hide it, but he caught the hint of a frown. "But there's something I want to discuss with you."

He checked the time on his phone. "It'll have to wait."

When he turned to walk away, Gabrielle said, "But it won't take long—"

"I can't be late. I'll talk to you when I get back."

Without another word from either of them, he strode away. He could have told her about his meeting with his attorney, but he didn't want to get her hopes up. He felt the pressure every time she looked at him. She wanted the truth as much as he did. If only he could remember.

This was pointless.

Gaby sat behind her desk later that afternoon. Deacon still hadn't returned. The fact that he'd been gone for hours worried her. Perhaps she should have pushed harder to learn his destination, but she doubted there was anything she could say to get him to open up.

She was quickly coming to the conclusion that no matter what she tried, Deacon wasn't going to let his guard down with her. He was a very determined man. But at least he didn't growl at her any longer. That had to mean something, right?

And now that she had him considering the fundraiser, she had to make it extra special. It was her ticket out of here without jeopardizing the deal for her father.

The fundraiser needed to be something different. Something that would attract big names with big money and also attract the press. She told herself that concluding their deal early was the only reason she was so invested in these plans that kept her up at night. Because there was no way she was trying to improve Deacon's image.

Her gaze scanned across the manuscript that Deacon wanted her to read. It could wait until later. Right now, she was wound up about the fundraiser. It could help so many people, not just Deacon.

After making some notes, Gaby looked up the name and number of the printing company she'd used for the library fundraiser. Lucky for her, she could use a lot of the same contacts for this event. It would cut down on her workload because getting this estate ready for the event was going to take a lot of time.

Gaby recalled seeing a list of estate employees on her first day here when she'd been checking out everything. Now where had she seen it? Her gaze scanned her desktop. Nothing there. Then she turned to the bulletin board behind her desk. No names and numbers.

She logged on to her computer. Maybe they were in here. A lot of pertinent information was stored on the network. She clicked on directory after directory. And then she stumbled across a file titled Personnel Listing. Under Grounds Crew, there were six names listed. Was it possible they were still employees? She knew it was a long shot, but hope swelled within her.

She reached for the phone and then hesitated. Should she do this without checking with Deacon?

She worried her bottom lip. He did give her the lead on this fundraiser. And it wasn't like he had much interest in the plans. But if she could show him what she had in mind, she was certain he would agree. She hoped.

Without letting any more doubts creep into her mind, she picked up the phone and dialed the first number on the list.

CHAPTER NINE

IT HAD NOT been a good day.

Not at all.

Deacon stepped out of the dark SUV and sent the door flying shut with a resounding thud. He pulled the baseball cap from his head, scrunched it with his hand and stuffed it in his back pocket. He removed his dark sunglasses and hung them from the collar of his shirt. He was done with disguises for today.

For all of the good it had done him, he might as well have stayed home. His attorney didn't have any good news for him. In fact, it was quite the opposite. The television network he'd been negotiating with had pulled out of the deal. They felt he brought too much bad publicity to the table and it would ruin their chances of having a hit. Apparently they didn't subscribe to the notion that there is no such thing as bad publicity.

Perhaps Gabrielle was right. Maybe he needed an image makeover. But would that work before the police report was released?

People might think that he'd refused to answer the officer's questions, but it was quite the opposite. In fact, at his meeting with his attorney, he told him in no uncertain terms to light a match under the powers that be. If he was innocent, he needed to be cleared ASAP. And if he had caused the tragedy, then he'd deal with the consequences.

When he'd moved on to his doctor's appointment, he grilled his physician about the gaping holes in his memory and the nightmares that plagued him. The doctor said the memories might all come back to him at once, or they might come back in pieces. His dreams were indicative of them coming back to him bit by bit. The doctor did warn him that the dreams might be real memories or they could be figments of his imagination. Or a combination of both.

When Deacon stepped out of the garage, he ran straight in to Gabrielle. He was not in the mood to be social right now. "What are you doing here? Shouldn't you be working?"

Her eyes widened. "I am going up to my rooms. And no, I shouldn't be working as the workday is over."

He pulled out his phone. It was much later than he'd been expecting. His appointments had taken up his entire day and he still didn't know any more than he had when he'd left that morning.

"I—I didn't realize the time." Not wanting to chitchat, he said, "I'll just be going."

"Wait. I wanted to talk to you."

"About?"

"The fundraiser. I've come up with some really good ideas. I was hoping for your input."

Deacon shook his head. He was in no frame of mind to deal with Gabrielle or the fundraiser. "I don't think this evening is a good idea."

"Are you feeling all right?"

"As good as can be expected. I just..." He paused as he grasped for any excuse to make a quick exit. "I'm just hungry."

"Then I have the perfect solution. It's Mrs. Kupps's night off, so I'll cook us up some dinner."

"I don't want you to go to any bother."

"It's no bother. We both have to eat, don't we?"

Her insistence surprised him. Of course, he realized that her interest was purely for business reasons. And she was right, they did have to eat. So what would it hurt to combine food and work?

"Okay. Count me in." He arched an eyebrow at her. "I take it this means you know how to cook."

She nodded. "Does that surprise you?"

"It's just that I don't know much about you."

"What would you like to know?"

A bunch of questions sprang to mind, like was she seeing anyone? If circumstances were different, would she go out with him? He immediately squelched those inquiries. They were none of his business—no matter how much he longed to know the answers.

He swallowed hard. "How well do you cook?"

A smile lifted her pink lips. "Don't you think you should have asked before agreeing to this meal? Now you'll just have to find out for yourself. Come on."

She didn't even wait for his reply before she started up the steps to the guesthouse. He watched the gentle sway of her hips as she mounted each step. No one had a right to look that good. And oh, boy, did she look good.

He hesitated. Right now, he was truly regretting agreeing to this meal. And it had absolutely nothing to do with his bad day or his uncertainty about her cooking skills and everything to do with how appealing he found the cook.

She glanced over her shoulder. "Well, come on."

Not wanting her to notice his discomfort, he did as she said. He started up the steps right behind her. A meal for two. This was a mistake. And yet he kept putting one foot in front of the other.

He'd spent so much time alone that he wasn't even sure he remembered how to make small talk. Just stick to business. It wasn't like she wanted to have this dinner for them to get closer. She was just anxious to get on with this fundraiser—a fundraiser that he was certain would fail if it had his name attached to it.

What had she done?

Gabrielle entered the galley kitchen. It was small and cozy. If Deacon were to be in here with her, they'd be all over each other—as in bumping in to each other. But now that the seed had been planted, she started to think of other things they could cook up together that had absolutely nothing to do with food.

Her imagination conjured up a shirtless Deacon in her kitchen. Oh, yes, things would definitely heat up. And then she'd be there in him arms. Her hands would run over his muscled chest. And there was a can of whipped cream—

Heat rushed to Gaby's face. This was a mistake.

But as she heard Deacon's footsteps behind her, she knew that it was too late to change her mind. She just had to keep her attention focused on the main course and not the dessert.

She moved to the fridge and pulled the door open. There on the top shelf sat the whipped cream. She ignored it. "What are you hungry for?" She was hungry for... The image of licking cream off Deacon came to mind. She gave herself a mental jerk. "Maybe I, ah, should tell you what I have ingredients for and, um, then we can go from there."

"Are you okay?"

"Um, sure." If only she could get the image of having him for dessert out of her mind. "Why?"

"You're acting nervous. If it's dinner, don't worry. We can order in."

"No." Her pride refused to give up. "I've got this."

Deacon took a seat at the kitchen counter. "I'm not a picky eater. So anything is good."

"Let me see what's in here." Mrs. Kupps had kindly offered to fill her fridge for the times when she was off and for the evenings when Gabrielle might get hungry.

"I've found a steak." Gaby opened the produce drawer. "There are some fingerling potatoes. And some tomatoes, onions, Gorgonzola cheese and arugula."

Her gaze skimmed back over that tempting whipped cream, but she absolutely refused to mention dessert. When he didn't respond, she glanced over her shoulder. "What do you think?"

"Sounds good. I'll just look over this information about the fundraiser while you cook the food."

She closed the fridge and turned to him. "I don't think so."

His dark eyebrows drew together as his puzzled gaze met hers. "What?"

"I'm not cooking us dinner. We're both doing it."

He shook his head and waved off her idea. "That is not a good idea. I don't know my way around a kitchen. That's what takeout menus are for."

"It's about time you learned your way around it." She wasn't about to wait on him. She didn't care how much money he had or how famous he was. "Come on. You can wash the potatoes and get them ready to go in the oven while I get out the ingredients for the salad."

And so with a heavy sigh, he got off the bar stool and made his way into the kitchen. She gave him detailed instructions and they set to work. This wasn't as bad as she'd been imagining.

Gabrielle finished rinsing the lettuce and turned to grab a bowl from one of the cabinets over the counter when she ran in to Deacon. To steady herself, she reached out with both hands. They landed on his chest—his very firm chest. The breath caught in her throat.

He reached out, catching her by the waist. His hands seemed to fit perfectly around her. It was though they fit together. But how could that be?

Deacon was the man who was responsible for her aunt's death. At least that's what her father and the papers were saying. But there was a voice deep inside her that said there was so much more to this man. Was she only seeing what she wanted to see?

Neither of them moved as her gaze rose from his chest to his full beard to his straight nose. And then she noticed his hair. It looked like it hadn't been cut in months. It fell just above his eyes. When their gazes at last connected, her heart pounded. Each heartbeat echoed in her ears.

Was it wrong that she wanted him to kiss her again? That kiss they'd shared was stuck in her mind. No man had ever made her feel so alive with just a kiss. And she hadn't gotten enough. Maybe it was the knowledge that it was wrong that made this thing—whatever you wanted to call it—between them that much more enticing. Deacon was the bad boy and she was the good girl.

Her gaze slipped back down to his mouth. It was surrounded by his mustache and beard. Though they were both well kept, she wasn't sure she was a fan of so much facial hair. Still, she wouldn't pass up the chance to kiss him, beard or no beard.

At that moment, Deacon stepped back. He released her. When she glanced at him, he turned away. Did he

know what she was thinking? Did he know that she'd almost kissed him again?

"I just need the olive oil," he said, as though nothing
had happened between them.

"I think I saw some in the cabinet to the right of the
stove."

"Thanks."

And that was it. They were both going to act as though
sparks of attraction hadn't just arched between them like
some out-of-control science experiment. Well, if he could
pretend nothing happened, so could she. After all, it was
for the best.

Refusing to let her mind meander down that dangerous
road, she focused on preparing a delicious dinner. In no
time, Gaby filled their plates with seared steak, roasted
potatoes and a fresh salad tossed with a wine-and-cheese
dressing. They took a seat at the kitchen bar and ate in
silence. In fact, Deacon was so quiet, she couldn't tell if
he was enjoying the meal.

"Do you like it?" she asked.

"Yes." His gaze met hers but then he glanced away
as though he wanted to say more but wasn't sure if he
should. He stabbed a potato with his fork. "It's the best
meal I've had in a long time."

"I doubt it. Mrs. Kupps is a marvel in the kitchen.
But thank you for the compliment." It'd been a long time
since anyone had taken notice of her cooking, including
her father.

She was truly happy he was enjoying the meal. This is
the point where she should once again probe him about
the accident, but she just couldn't bring herself to ruin the
moment. The questions had waited this long, surely they
could wait a little longer.

They continued to eat in a comfortable silence. Deacon

emptied his plate first. He politely waited for her to finish before he carried both of their plates to the sink. Together they cleaned up the mess they'd made in the kitchen.

After the dishes were placed in the dishwasher, Deacon said, "I should look over those notes for the fundraiser."

Gabrielle spied a beautiful sunset splashing the sky with brilliant pinks and purples. "Or you could go for a walk with me."

He shook his head. "I don't think so."

"Oh, please? It's such a beautiful evening."

He shook his head.

"Do you ever get out of this estate?"

He frowned at her. "Of course I do. I was just in the city today."

"I don't mean for business or whatever drew you away. I mean get out of here and do something relaxing."

"Not since the accident."

"Because of the paparazzi?"

He nodded. "It stirs up interest in me. And it's not my reputation so much as the people closest to me being harassed. When the reporters start their feeding frenzy, Mrs. Kupps can't even go to the grocery store without being harassed in the parking lot. I thought staying out of public sight would help and it did for a while."

"And then my father stirred things up."

Deacon lowered his gaze and nodded.

"I'm sorry." So he wasn't hiding out here for purely selfish reasons. "Is that why you gave your grounds crew time off?"

"Yes. It just got to be too hard on everyone. Although Mrs. Kupps refused to take paid leave. She said she wasn't going to let the reporters bully her."

Gaby glanced away. Guilt settled over her like a wet,

soggy blanket. Here he was telling her how hard the media had made the life of those around him and she was writing daily reports for *QTR*. She was starting to wonder if her idea to publicly out him was the best approach.

"What's the matter?"

Her gaze lifted and she found him studying her. Apparently the guilt was written all over her face. "It's nothing."

"You're upset because I don't want to go for a walk."

It was best to let him think that was the source of her distress. "Oh, come on. There's no one out on the beach. Let's go."

"I thought the fundraiser stuff needed to be dealt with."

"It does. But there's plenty of time for it. Right now, I'd like to see more of this area. I must admit I'm not used to hanging out in Malibu. And the beach here is so nice. Come on." She reached out and grabbed his hand. "Show me around." She started toward the door, hoping that he'd give in to her tug of his arm.

"But there isn't much to show. It's a beach."

"A beautiful beach with a gorgeous sunset."

He followed her to the door and then stopped. "But I have work to do."

"Don't you ever just want to play hooky?"

There was a twinkle in his eyes. "So that's what you do? Play hooky instead of working."

The smile slipped from her face. She couldn't decide if he was being serious or if he was just giving her a hard time. She removed her hand from his. "I promise you that I work all day. I do a lot—more than what you've asked—"

"Slow down. I was just teasing you." He sent her a small smile.

She studied him for a moment, determining if he were serious or not. "Don't do that."

"Do what? Harass you a little?"

"Yes. Because I don't know you well enough to know if you're being serious or not."

"Perhaps I am too serious these days."

"You think so?" The words slipped across her lips before she could stop them.

His eyes widened. "I didn't know I was that bad."

"Let's just say that a bear with a thorn in its paw is more congenial than you."

"Ouch." He clasped his chest. "You really know how to wound a guy."

"Well, if you want to make it up to me, let's go for that walk."

He hesitated. She waited for him to say no, but instead, he said, "Fine. Lead the way."

She didn't say a word, not wanting to give him a chance to change his mind. Instead, she headed down the steps as quickly as her legs would carry her.

CHAPTER TEN

WHY EXACTLY HAD he agreed to this walk?

Deacon pulled the navy blue ball cap from his back pocket and settled it on his head. And even though evening was descending upon them, he put on the sunglasses that had been dangling from the neck of his shirt. These days, he always took precautions.

He shouldn't be out here, in the open for anyone to approach him—especially the press. The thought of being hounded with question after question about one of the most horrific events in his life almost had him turning around. Instead he pulled the brim down a little farther on his forehead. But the lure of stepping outside of his self-imposed confines was almost too tempting for him.

How could he resist walking along the sandy shore with the most beautiful woman he'd ever known by his side? The truth was, she'd cast a spell over him and he'd follow her most anywhere. And so he kept moving—kept in step with Gabrielle—as they made their way down to the beach.

He scanned the beach, looking for any signs of trouble. There was a man jogging along the water's edge. And coming from the other direction was an older woman walking her dog. Other than that, the beach was quiet.

Before his life had crashed in on him, he would jog on

the beach each morning. And sometimes in the evening, if he had time. He'd come out here to clear his head. It was funny to think that he'd ever taken those simple liberties for granted—

"Don't you think?" Gabrielle's voice cut through his thoughts.

He had no idea what she'd been saying. "What was that?"

"I said the sunset is exceptional tonight. I wish I'd have grabbed my phone from the kitchen counter so I could take a picture of it."

Deacon stopped. This was one small thing that he could do for her. "I've got mine."

He pulled out his phone and snapped a picture. And then he handed it over so Gabrielle could forward it to her phone. When she was done, she returned the phone and that's when their fingers touched. How could such a small gesture get to him? And yet, a zing of nervous energy rushed up his arm and settled in his chest, making his heart beat faster.

"Thank you." When she smiled at him, it was like having the sun's ray on his face.

"You...you're welcome." It'd been a long time since he'd used his manners, but it made him feel more human—she made him feel like a man again. He didn't want this evening to end. "What are you waiting for? Surely you don't want to turn around already."

Her eyes lit up with surprise. "Certainly not."

They set off again at a leisurely pace. Every now and then they passed someone else with the same intention of enjoying such a perfect evening. Deacon couldn't recall the last time he was able to let go of the guilt, the remnants of the nightmares and the worry of what tomorrow would bring long enough to enjoy the here and now.

"I can see why you live here," Gabrielle said. "If I had the opportunity, I'd get a little place along here and wild horses couldn't drag me away."

"Actually I've been considering moving. It's time for a change. Maybe I could move someplace where they don't recognize me."

"I don't think that place exists."

He shrugged. "Perhaps."

"You aren't returning to the movies?"

Was she just being polite? Or had she not really looked at him? He stopped walking and held out his hand in front of them. "With scars like these, no one would want to hire me."

"These are from the accident?"

"Yes."

She reached out and ran her fingertip ever so gently over his skin. "It's not so bad. Maybe some makeup could hide what's there from the camera if you're self-conscious about it."

But makeup could not hide the scars in his mind. They were there—they kept him up at night, walking the halls in the dark. "It's not going to happen."

"Why not try?"

"Because…" Because he didn't deserve to be in front of those cameras any longer. She of all people should understand that. "Why are you being so nice to me?"

She shrugged and then started to walk again. "How am I supposed to act around you?"

"Like you hate me."

"Should I hate you?"

He inwardly groaned. Why did she have to keep turning things around on him? "It's not for me to say how you should feel. It's just that if circumstances were reversed, I'd probably act more like your father."

"And what has that accomplished? He has broken the law and has his daughter bailing him out."

Deacon really wanted to understand her. "So you think by taking the high road that you'll accomplish more?"

"Such as you telling me what happened the night my aunt died?"

"There it is." He stopped next to an outcropping of rocks. "I knew that's why you dragged me out here. You wanted to get me someplace where you could interrogate me."

"That's not true. I didn't drag you out here—"

"But you can't deny that you didn't think about questioning me. You were hoping to wear me down into a confession."

Her gaze searched his. "Do you have something you need to confess?"

He should turn and leave. That's what he'd do if he were thinking clearly. That's what his attorney would advise him to do.

But his feet wouldn't cooperate. He stood there staring into Gabrielle's eyes and could only imagine the pain that she'd been through. And the not knowing, well, he knew all about that. Much too well.

He swallowed hard. "If I told you, you wouldn't believe me."

"Try me."

He wanted to trust her. He wanted to believe that whatever he said would stay between the two of them. But he hardly knew her. And right now, he could count on one hand how many people he trusted.

Instead he turned and climbed up on the rocks. He made his way to a large boulder on the water's edge. He sat down, letting the sea breeze fan his face, and hoped the lulling sound of the ocean would ease the storm raging inside him.

He sat there for the longest time, trying to get his thoughts in order. By then the sun had sunk below the horizon. It was an overcast night with the moon peeking out here and there. Deacon found comfort in the long, dark shadows. He glanced around and found that Gabrielle hadn't left. Instead, she was sitting just a few feet away. She was too far away in the dark to make out her face. As she sat there with her knees drawn up to her chest, he couldn't help but wonder what she was thinking. He hated the thought that he continued to cause her pain. But nothing he could say would fix things.

"If you're waiting for a confession, you're wasting your time." He turned back to the ocean.

Gabrielle moved to settle on the rock next to him. "Is that because you didn't cause the accident?"

Why was he holding back? So what if she didn't believe him. Once he said it, it would be out there. Perhaps she'd believe him. Perhaps she wouldn't. But it was time he told the truth.

"I don't remember." Somehow it was easier having this conversation under the shelter of darkness.

"What don't you remember?"

"The accident." He could feel her intense stare.

"What part don't you remember?"

"All of it. They called it retrograde amnesia or some such thing."

"That's pretty convenient." She said it as a fact.

He turned to her and now that she was closer, he could make out the disbelief written on her face. "Actually, it isn't. I want to remember the accident as bad as you need me to remember. I need to know what I've done." His voice cracked. "I—I need to know if I'm responsible."

For a moment, Gabrielle didn't say anything. "So you're not holding out and trying to bury the events?"

His jaw tightened. He knew that she wouldn't believe him. But then again, why should she?

"No. I'm not lying." He shook his head. "I knew you wouldn't believe me."

"And the delay with the police report?"

"I've had my attorney pressing for its release, but without camera footage or an eyewitness account, it complicates matters. Once the police have finalized the report, it must go up the chain of command, ending with the DA's office. When my attorney checked yesterday, he was told the report should be released soon." When Gabrielle didn't say anything, he glanced over at her. "I'm sorry. I know that's not what you want to hear."

Her gaze met his and she placed a slight smile on her lips. "It's the truth and that's what matters."

"You believe me?" If she did, she'd be the first person to do so.

"Are you saying I shouldn't?"

"I'm just surprised is all."

Gaby paused. "So tell me more about yourself."

"You don't really want to hear about me?"

She nodded. "I do."

"Where do I start?"

"How about at the beginning."

"Well, I was born on Valentine's Day. My father died when I was thirteen. My mother finished raising me on her own. I split my time between the fishing boat and watching movies."

"Fishing and movies. Those are two diverse interests."

"The fishing wasn't a hobby. It was my job. I started when I was thirteen, getting paid under the table, in order to help my mother pay the bills." It hadn't been an easy

life and his schooling had paid the price, but he'd graduated by the sheer willpower of his mother. "The movies
were my passion. I drove my mother crazy telling her
that one day I would be a movie star. And do you know
what she told me?"

Gabrielle shook her head.

"She used to say, 'Deacon, you're a smart boy. You
can be anything you want to be as long as you work hard
and don't give up.'"

"She sounded like a smart lady."

"I thought so, too. And then she met my stepfather. In
the beginning, he wasn't so bad. And then they got married. That was when I decided to move to California. I
just couldn't stick around and watch those two argue. I
tried to talk my mother in to coming with me, but she
insisted that her place was with her husband."

"I'm sorry. That must have been tough on you."

"And what's even worse is that when she first found
a lump in her breast, that—that man told her it was her
imagination. By the time I talked her in to going to the
doctor, the cancer was advanced. I brought her here to
California. Oh, they tried to help her, but by then the
cancer had spread."

Gabrielle reached out, taking his hand in hers. She
gave a firm squeeze. It shouldn't, but it meant a lot to
him. And it even meant more because she wasn't supposed to be here giving him support. She was supposed
to hate him—hate his very existence. The fact that she
didn't confused him, yet also intrigued him. There was
definitely something different about Gabrielle.

CHAPTER ELEVEN

SHE DIDN'T MOVE.

Gabrielle left her hand securely within Deacon's hold. His hands were large and his fingers long. And his hand fit perfectly around hers. It was as though they were made for one another. Not that she was letting her heart get ahead of her mind. She knew that nothing could ever come of their relationship, whether he'd caused the accident or not.

Because in her father's mind, Deacon would always be responsible for her aunt's death. And she highly doubted that anything would change her father's mind. He was a very stubborn man. She'd inherited his stubborn streak. Or at least that's what her aunt had told her.

However, Deacon was far from the spoiled movie star that her father and Newton had accused Deacon of being. There was a lot more to this man than anyone would guess. He was like an onion, with layer upon layer, and she had an overwhelming desire to keep peeling back the layers until she reached his heart.

"Maybe we should head back." Deacon released her hand and got to his feet.

"So soon?"

He laughed. "We've been out here a long time. It's getting late."

"But we have the whole beach to ourselves." And then she dropped her voice. "We can do whatever we want and there's no one around to see."

"Be careful. Or I just might take you up on the invitation."

A shiver of excitement raced through her. She knew she shouldn't be flirting with him, but she couldn't stop herself. There was something about Deacon that she couldn't resist.

"Maybe I *want* you to take me up on the invitation."

Deacon stood there in the shadows. She wished she could make out his eyes. He was so quiet. Was he considering taking advantage of her suggestion? Her heart thudded against her ribs.

"Gabrielle, don't make offers you aren't ready to fulfill. Let's head back before something happens that we'll both come to regret. I don't want to hurt you."

He held out his hand to her and helped her to her feet. For a moment, they stood there face-to-face. Her pulse raced and her heart pounded. With darkness all around them, a few moonbeams silhouetted Deacon's face. She wanted to tell him that she wasn't fragile. But her tongue refused to cooperate.

Instead of turning and heading back to the estate, Deacon continued staring at her. Was he considering kissing her again? Was it wrong that she wanted him to pull her against his chest and lower his head to hers?

And then he turned away and started climbing down off the rocks. When he was standing on the sand, he turned back to her and held out his hands in order to catch her. Even though she could make it down on her own, she didn't resist his offer of assistance.

He placed his hands on her waist and lowered her ever so slowly. Her body slid down over his. It was tantalizing and oh, so arousing. She was so caught up in the crazy sensation zinging through her body that she never noticed when her feet touched the ground.

Beard or no beard. Scars or no scars. Long hair or short. There was something magnetic about this man. She knew that it wasn't rational. And right now, she didn't care.

Her heart pounded so loud that it drowned out rational thought. She was going to live in the moment and damn the consequences. She tilted up her chin and lifted up on her tiptoes. Her mouth pressed to his.

His lips were warm and smooth. And the kiss, it was full of emotion, of need, of desire. Her hands slid up over his broad shoulders and slipped around his neck. She could get used to this.

Except for the beard. It tickled her. And when he moved to trail kisses down her neck, it tickled so much that she pulled away. A smile lifted her lips as she struggled not to laugh. He sent her a concerned look as though wondering if he had done something wrong.

"It's not you." But when he went to press his lips to her neck again, she placed her hands on his shoulders and held him back.

"What?"

She wasn't sure if he would take offense or not. And so she stood there not saying a word.

He frowned. "Just tell me."

"It…it's your beard. It tickles."

His eyes twinkled with mischief. "It does?" He leaned toward her. "How much?"

Before he could tickle her again, she yanked away from him. "Catch me if you can."

And with that taunt, she ran up the beach. A big smile was plastered across her face. For once, she wasn't the dutiful daughter working two jobs to keep the bills paid and she wasn't answering her father's numerous phone calls to check up on her. She was just Gabrielle Dupré, a woman with a dangerously handsome man chasing her. She could hear Deacon calling out to her, but she didn't stop until she was out of breath.

When she turned around, she fully expected Deacon to be standing there, but he wasn't. She squinted into the shadows. He was quite a way down the beach. What in the world? Hadn't he wanted to catch her?

Disappointment socked her in the gut. They'd been having so much fun. Where had it gone wrong?

Her wounded pride urged her to keep going. But another part of her wanted to wait and find out what was up. The curiosity in her won out. She started to walk back to him.

When she was within a few feet of Deacon, he said. "Sorry. I couldn't keep up. My leg is getting better, but it's not that good yet."

And suddenly she felt foolish. She was worried about him being upset with her when in fact he had an injury. It never even dawned on her that the injuries he'd sustained to his face, arms and hands had extended further.

"I'm sorry. I didn't think."

"It's not your problem. And how would you know?"

They started to walk side by side. She felt awful. She'd just assumed that he was fine. "Are you okay to walk back?"

"Yes. I'm just not up for running. Maybe one day, if I keep going to therapy and doing the exercises."

"You go to physical therapy?" She hadn't noticed him leaving on a regular basis, but then again, she hadn't been here that long.

"Not anymore."

"Why not?" She knew from her father's accident how important physical therapy could be to making a full recovery. "It's really important."

"I'm fine." His dismissive manner bothered her.

"If you were fine, you would have kept up with me or surpassed me. You are not fine. Your therapy is important. You can't just dismiss it because you don't want to do the work."

He arched an eyebrow. "And since when does my welfare matter to you?"

"It—it doesn't." Did it? She glanced away from him, not wanting him to read anything in her eyes. "But that doesn't mean it shouldn't be important to you."

"I don't think it's going to matter. All I do is haunt that place." He gestured toward the mansion in the distance.

"If you refuse to leave home, I can help you with the exercises."

"I don't need help." His voice rumbled with agitation, letting her know that she'd pushed as far as he was going to let her go.

And so they walked in silence. She wasn't sure what to say now. He'd made it clear he didn't want her help and he refused to go anywhere to get help. She couldn't believe this, but she'd met someone who was as stubborn or perhaps more stubborn than her father. They at least had that in common.

The thought of who could be more stubborn made her smile and the more she thought about it, a giggle started to form. And before she knew it, she was laughing. Maybe it was her nervousness or maybe it was the stress, but it felt good to laugh. Talk about a cathartic moment.

Beneath one of the estate security lights, Deacon stepped in front of her. "What's so funny?"

The frown on his face just made her laugh some more. It was almost like an out-of-body experience. She couldn't help herself. And it just felt so darn good.

"Stop it. Right now." His eyebrows were drawn into a firm line.

"I—I can't." She laughed some more.

She could see that the more she laughed the angrier he was getting. She really had to pull herself together. She had no idea what had come over her, but she needed to get a grip.

With a frustrated groan, Deacon turned and started to walk away. That was definitely not a good sign, at all. The elation in her started to ebb.

"Wait." She rushed to catch up with him, all the while trying to catch her breath.

"I don't care to be laughed at."

"I wasn't laughing at you. Not really." And then she thought about it a little more. "Well, maybe some. But it really wasn't that bad."

"I don't want to be laughed at."

Totally sober now, she said, "I just started thinking about you and my father and what you two have in common."

Deacon came to a stop and she almost ran in to him. "You were comparing me to your father?"

"Yes, in a way."

"What way?"

"You are both so stubborn. I was trying to figure out which one of you is the worst, but I couldn't decide."

"And that made you laugh."

"Yes, I guess it did."

He shook his head. "I don't understand you."

"That's okay. I don't really understand myself, either." It was the truth. She understood the parts of her that were like her father, but the other parts, the silly parts, sometimes surprised her. "I honestly don't know why I laughed. But once I did, it felt good. It's been a very long time since I laughed like that. You should try it some time."

He looked at her like she'd just grown an extra head. "You want me to laugh for no reason at all."

She shrugged. "Don't put it down until you've tried it."

He shook his head again. "It must be a woman thing."

Before they went their separate ways, Deacon asked for the fundraising plans. She ran upstairs and retrieved the papers. She was kind of hoping he'd follow her upstairs. His kisses were more addictive than the squares of chocolate with caramel centers that she enjoyed each night while reading.

She hurried back down the steps. "This is everything I have so far."

When she handed over the papers, their fingers touched. To her surprise, he didn't rush to pull away. Neither did she. Their gazes met and her heart careened into her throat.

Her gaze lowered to his mouth. She'd never been so tempted by anything in her life. What was it about this man that muddled her thoughts? It was as though he had some sort of magnetic force and anytime she was near him, she was drawn in.

And then he stepped back. "Thanks for these. I'll look them over tonight."

She choked down her disappointment. "Good. The sooner I jump on these plans, the better."

"Then how about a breakfast meeting?" When she didn't immediately respond, he asked, "You do eat breakfast, don't you?"

At last, she found her voice. "Yes, I do."

"Good. We'll discuss this in the morning." He gestured toward the papers. "Good night."

She stood there for a moment watching him retreat to the main house. What was wrong with her? She knew better than to fall for him. It was the ocean breeze and his deep voice that caused her to lose focus for just a few moments. She was fine now. Realizing that she shouldn't be standing around staring at Deacon like some besotted schoolgirl, she turned and headed up the steps.

Before it got much later, she needed to file her daily report with *QTR*. She carried her personal laptop to a chair on her private balcony and sat in one of the comfy chairs.

She opened the laptop and typed in her password. Once she had her email open, the words came pouring out of her.

Tonight we walked on the beach. It was like a scene right out of a movie, with the lull of the water in the background and the gentle breeze. It was amazing.

Beneath the moonlight, we kissed. I don't think my feet were touching the ground. His touch—it was amazing. I know that I shouldn't feel anything for him because of the accident, but the harder I fight it, the more attracted to him I become.

His kiss awakened a part of me that I'd forgotten about. There was a rush of emotions unlike anything I've ever experienced before. It's all so confusing. Maybe I'm just lonely. It has been over a year since I dated anyone. Work and caring for my father has consumed my life. When I leave here perhaps I need to revisit the dating scene and update my online profile. Because there's no way what I'm starting to feel for Deacon is real. It can't be!

She read back over what she'd written. What was she thinking? She could never tell anyone her most intimate thoughts—most especially a tell-all magazine. Talk about creating sensational headlines.

With a shake of her head, she highlighted it all. Then she pressed the delete key. But she still had to find something to write in her report.

And after what she'd learned today, she was beginning to suspect there was no story here. But she had promised that she would document the details relating to the accident. And she liked to keep her word. So she started to write out in as much detail as she could what little Deacon had told her about the night of the accident.

But with every word she typed, guilt weighed on her. How could she betray Deacon's trust? Even if now it was to help *clear* his name?

Her emotions warred within her. She knew how Deacon felt about the paparazzi and tabloids. He would consider what she was doing as an utter betrayal. Could she blame him?

She hadn't taken any of this into consideration when she'd agreed to this plan. Getting close to Deacon, gaining his trust, was changing everything. And now she was utterly confused. More than anything, she wanted to leave. Each day that passed, her confusion over where she stood with Deacon grew.

Gaby saved her report to the drafts folder. She wanted more time to consider her actions. In the meantime, she jotted a brief email stating that there was nothing new to report.

She closed her laptop and leaned back in her chair. Her presence on the estate had nothing to do with the accident and everything to do with protecting her father from prosecution. And so she would keep her word to

Deacon and stay until the fundraiser. And once it was a huge success, she could return to her life. A life without a brooding movie star with the ability to make her laugh and feel lighter than she had in years. Suddenly, returning to her prior life didn't sound so appealing. But life here on this Malibu estate wasn't reality. It was some sort of dream and soon she'd wake up—probably about the time the police report was released. And she worried about the steep fall back to earth.

CHAPTER TWELVE

MAYBE THIS HAD been a mistake.

Deacon sat across the table from Gabrielle. The table was done up with a light blue linen tablecloth. Fine china was laid out. The yellow napkins were folded into the shape of bow ties. A vase of yellow roses had been placed in the center. This was Mrs. Kupps's doing. The last time the table had been so fancy had been before the accident. These days, he ate at his desk with a tray of food. No flowers. No company.

What had he been thinking to invite Gabrielle to breakfast? Perhaps it was the fact that when she smiled, the whole world was that much brighter. And when they talked, she didn't hold back. She was filled with optimism. He gave himself a mental jerk. That line of thought could get him into trouble—big trouble. It was best to focus on the business at hand.

But that would be easier said than done with the table all decked out to impress Gabrielle. When he'd mentioned all the needless fuss to Mrs. Kupps, she'd clucked her tongue at him. She told him he needed to do everything he could not to run off Gabrielle, as she was the sunshine in his otherwise gloomy world. It was as if she was worried that he'd grow old alone. He was not some beggar, desperate for anyone's attention.

Is that what Gabrielle thought of him, too? Did she think that he was pathetic and deserving of her sympathy? He would show her. He did not need anyone's pity. He was not some charity case.

"You know this isn't going to work." His words came out terser than he'd intended.

Gabrielle glanced up from where she unfolded the yellow napkin and placed it on her lap. "Which part doesn't work?"

"All of it. Every single last piece of it." That wasn't exactly true, but he was in no mood to be generous. If they were adversaries, then perhaps she wouldn't feel obligated to be nice to him—to let him kiss her.

He watched her closely. He was waiting for her to leave. However, the only visible sign of her discomfort was in her eyes. They widened, but she didn't move. He knew a lot of people would have turned tail and fled by now. But not Gabrielle. She was made of sterner stuff. But he should have figured that when she'd volunteered to take her father's punishment.

She adjusted her napkin and at the same time avoided his gaze. When she glanced back up at him, she said, "I'm assuming you are referring to the fundraiser plans and not the meal."

"Of course."

She nodded. Then she set about removing the lid from the dish of scrambled eggs. She was going to eat? He was setting up for an argument and she was acting as though everything was perfectly fine. Everything wasn't fine.

He couldn't take her lack of reaction any longer. "Are you just going to sit there and ignore me?"

"I'm not ignoring you, but Mrs. Kupps went to a lot of work to prepare this meal and I think it'd be a shame to let it go to waste."

"You're hungry?"

She smiled at him. "Of course I am. I'm sure you'll feel better after you eat."

He wanted to disagree, but his gaze moved to her plate. The food did look good. "But what about the problems with the fundraiser?"

"They aren't going anywhere. We can deal with those later." She scooped up some bacon and added it to her plate. When he didn't move, she said, "Do you want some bacon?" When he didn't respond fast enough, she added, "If you don't hurry, there might not be any left. I love bacon."

He did, too. He held out his hand for her to pass the serving plate. She hesitated as though she weren't so sure she wanted to share, but in the end, she passed it to him.

It was really hard staying upset with her. She was either a very good actress, good enough to be in the movies with him, or she tried not to let things ruffle her. Either way, he was going to have to figure out a different way to deal with her. Because all his huffing and puffing didn't appear to deter her.

Gabrielle continued to fill her plate. "I can't believe Mrs. Kupps made us all of this food."

"She was more than happy to do it. For so long now, she's been begging me for things to do and I've been putting her off."

"I take it you don't have breakfast like this very often."

"No. Not at all. Not since, well, you know." He didn't want to bring up the accident. Not this morning. But since Gabrielle had entered his life, his appetite was back.

Gabrielle buttered her toast. "Well, I will make sure to tell Mrs. Kupps just how good this is."

"I'm sure she would love to hear it. I must admit that I've been lacking on the compliments lately."

"I'm sure she understands that you've been going through a lot."

When they'd finished their meal, which took much longer than he was accustomed to taking to eat, he found himself in a better frame of mind. He assured himself that it had nothing to do with what Gabrielle had said about him needing to eat, and more to do with the fact that he was right about this fundraiser and he would prove it to her.

Mrs. Kupps brought more coffee and then cleared the empty dishes. Both of them complimented Mrs. Kupps on the delicious food. The woman's cheeks grew rosy as she thanked them.

After Mrs. Kupps departed, Gabrielle turned to him. "Now, what were you saying about the fundraiser?"

"I don't think people are going to attend."

"Why would you think that? Are my plans that bad?"

He shook his head. "It isn't anything you've done." Surely he didn't have to spell this out for her. "I'm the problem."

"Oh." Her good mood seemed to have diminished a bit. She sat there and stared off at the shimmering ocean for a moment. When she turned to him again, she had a glint in her eye. "Actually, I think all of your notoriety will work to our advantage."

He had a feeling he wouldn't like where she was going with this line of thought. But it was too late, he'd already been drawn down the rabbit hole. "How's that?"

"You forget that in addition to the car accident, you also have a movie being released next month."

"What about it?"

"I couldn't sleep last night, so I turned on the television. And guess what I saw?"

He sighed. "I don't know, but I'm sure you're going to tell me."

"I saw the promo for your movie. Your name and face were all over the ad. Your movie sponsors aren't backing down from using your brand and you shouldn't, either."

If only people still thought he was that man. Now they all questioned him and his actions—including himself. "I'm not that man anymore."

"Which makes people all the more curious about you—"

"I'm not going to be some sort of freak show for them to come here and stare at."

"Relax." She reached across the table and placed her hand on his. "I promise you, it won't be like that. I believe that people will come out for the event. They will want to get behind a great cause because so many lives have been touched in one way or another by breast cancer."

When she put it that way, he felt guilty for making such a big deal about his circumstances. Some people had it much worse. "So you'll make sure to keep the emphasis of the event on the reason for it and not on the sponsor?"

"Um, yes." Worry clouded her eyes. "Does that mean you don't want to be mentioned at all?"

"That is what I'd hoped."

She worried her bottom lip but didn't respond.

"Go ahead and say it."

"It's just that without your name, I don't know how to make the event stand out."

He reminded himself that raising funds would help save other families from having to go through the pain, the uncertainty and, for some, the loss of a loved one, like he'd experienced. And when it came down to it, if using his name would help raise awareness of the event, didn't he owe that to his mother's memory?

"Okay. You can use my name, if you think it will help."

"I do." Gabrielle pulled out a legal pad from a colorful bag she had on the ground next to her chair. There were handwritten notes on the top sheet. It was a long list. It appeared they were going to be here a while. She sent him a sideways glance. "You aren't going to change your mind after we get this all started, are you?"

He knew once news of the fundraiser was out there that his world would get a lot smaller, with paparazzi hanging from trees and sneaking onto the property. It would be chaos and he'd want to back out. "No. I'll manage."

"Good." A smile eased the worry lines bracketing her beautiful face. "And I think they are really going to have a great time."

He filled his coffee cup, then added a dash of sugar. He'd forgotten how much he enjoyed sitting outside in the morning with the bright sunshine and the cool breeze. He could feel Gabrielle's gaze on him. She was anxious to hear his thoughts, but he didn't think that she'd like what he was about to say.

As he stirred the coffee, his gaze skimmed down over the printout that Gabrielle had given him the night before. She had certainly paid attention to details and made certain that there was plenty of entertainment.

He took a drink of the dark brew and then returned the cup to the saucer. "You do realize that you have so many events listed that it dilutes the entire event."

Gabrielle's eyebrows drew together. "But people need something to do."

"True. But not this many things. This is more like an amusement park than a fundraiser." Before she could argue with him, he intended to prove his point. "You have golfing, amusement rides, clowns, artists, dancing and games. That's a lot. A whole lot."

"But with each of those things, we can raise money."

"How much money are we talking? Really?"

She sighed and gazed down over the list of events. "What are you proposing?"

"That you narrow the list down to two or three things."

She frowned at him. Then she shook her head and looked away.

"What?"

Her gaze met his as she worried her bottom lip.

"Gabrielle, just spit it out." He wasn't good at guessing, especially where women were concerned.

"I was just wondering if it is the money. You know, if sponsoring the event is too much for you."

Oh, that was all. This was something he could deal with.

"It isn't the money." Though this fundraiser would cost a small fortune to pull together, he could handle it. He'd had a number of blockbuster movies and he'd carefully invested the money. When her gaze told him that she still wasn't reassured, he said, "I promise. I'm good financially."

His main concern was for Gabrielle. She had invested herself completely in making this fundraiser a huge success. She had her hopes so high that when it all fell apart, she would have a long way to tumble.

In the short time he'd gotten to know her, he'd learned that she had a big heart—big enough to even care about his welfare, which was more than he'd ever expected. He didn't want her to get hurt because of him and his now tarnished reputation.

"That's good to hear." There was a catch in her voice

as though there were something more she wanted to say, but she decided to refrain.

"You know it's not too late to pull out—"

"No. I really want to do this."

He knew what she meant. She was anxious to get away from him. And he couldn't blame her. She blamed him for what had happened to her aunt. And as much as he wanted to deny it, he couldn't. He didn't know. And his nightmares only confused him even more.

He thought about just calling off the deal. But he knew Gabrielle would take it personally. She had a lot of pride and would think he didn't believe in her ability to pull it all together. He didn't want to do anything else to hurt her. So he would do what he could to help Gabrielle— even at the expense of his privacy.

Deacon cleared his throat. "The events should either be big draws in order to up the ticket price or garner large donations once the guests are in attendance." And he had another observation. "Perhaps keep this an adults-only event. Without children around, people will relax and perhaps they'll be willing to spend more freely."

"That's the exact opposite of how I ran my fundraisers for the library. I did a lot of activities to draw in the kids and by extension their parents." She frowned. "I suppose you're going to want to remove all of the fun events."

He really did hate to disappoint her, but he'd been around these affairs many times in the past. And he knew a lot of the big fish she was hoping to hook would appreciate something more low-key.

"Trust me." He knew that was a poor choice of words where she was concerned, but they were already out there and he couldn't undo them. So he kept going with the point he wanted to make. "I do know what I'm talking about."

"But it'll be boring."

He had to admit some of the charity events he'd attended were boring, but he didn't want to tell her that. He knew Gabrielle would use any excuse to keep her current lengthy list of events.

"Ah… I see. I'm right." Her face lit up.

"What are you talking about?"

"The look you just made when I said that it would be boring. You couldn't deny it."

"I was thinking is all."

"Uh-huh. What if we compromise?"

Oh, no. He had a bad feeling about this. His experience of compromising with a female in his private life consisted of him giving up on what he wanted, so the woman wouldn't be mad at him any longer.

With great trepidation, he asked, "What sort of compromise?"

And so they started with the first activity on the list—dart toss. They discussed it and the type of atmosphere they'd like to present to the people. In the end, it was cut in an effort to make the fundraiser more sophisticated.

After they made it through a quarter of the list and had nixed all but one item, Gabrielle said, "Okay. So we should stick to just a handful of entertainments."

"Or even less. For the most part, the affluent people you'll be inviting will want to be seen." He explained a little more of his understanding of the elite of Hollywood.

Gabrielle nodded. "Okay. I can work with this."

"Now, what were you considering for the main focus of the event?"

She took a moment, as though considering everything he'd told her. "I think we should make it a golfing event. Lots of people golf, both men and women. And you do have an amazing golf course."

"How would you know? It's a mess."

"Mrs. Kupps showed me some pictures. The course needs some TLC, but I talked to your head groundskeeper. He said that with the help of the entire grounds crew, they could pull it together. They might have to bring in some turf, but it is possible to have it together in time."

He arched an eyebrow at her. "You really have worked hard on this."

"I saw an opportunity and I took it. This fundraiser will be great—if you'll agree to it."

His gut told him not to do it. But he saw the gleam of hope in Gabrielle's eyes. He just didn't have it in him to turn her down. What would it hurt to get this place cleaned up? He wasn't even sure if he wanted to live here any longer. It would have to be restored if he were to put it up for sale. So he would let Gabrielle move ahead with her plans and when no one bought the tickets, he would still abide by their agreement. Once the planning was over, he would let her go back to her life.

He told her to take what they'd discussed and refine her list. Include a few more details and they'd go over it tomorrow. And then he would give her his decision about whether they should move forward with it or not.

He had a gut feeling that he'd dug himself a hole. Gabrielle had a determined look in her eye that said she would never give up on the fundraiser. And he was going to have to find a way to be okay with all those people being here on his estate.

Unless…no one bought a ticket or showed up. But then Gabrielle would be crushed and he would be to blame. Either way he would be in trouble.

CHAPTER THIRTEEN

THE PLANS WERE coming together.

Later that afternoon, Gaby straightened her desk. It had been a very productive day. She recalled her breakfast with Deacon. He hadn't been very congenial at first, but once he realized she wasn't going to give up, he became helpful.

And though she hated to admit it, he was right. This event needed a different vibe than the events she'd planned at the library. This was his world and he knew these people, so she'd follow his lead.

It may not be the type of event she was used to planning, but she would work to make it perfect. People would come. They would enjoy themselves, and they would donate to a worthy cause.

By five o'clock she'd also finished reading the screenplay Deacon had given her. She'd made a list of pros and cons and sent it to him in an email. With her tasks done for the day, she shut down the computer and then made her way to the guesthouse.

She brought the fundraising plans with her. She was too excited to stop now. The plans were coming together really well and instead of this event being her get-out-of-jail-free card, it was turning into an event she believed in and wanted to see succeed.

Mrs. Kupps had placed some dinner in the fridge with a note for reheating it. Gaby smiled. The woman was the absolute sweetest. She wondered if Deacon knew how lucky he was to have someone so kind and thoughtful in his life.

Gaby settled at the table with her laptop, a legal pad and all the notes she'd taken during her talk with Deacon. She didn't know how much time had passed when there was a knock at the door.

She couldn't imagine who it might be. Mrs. Kupps had left long ago. And no one could get access to the private estate.

Gaby ran a hand over her hair and a finger around her mouth, making sure there weren't any crumbs from the chocolate chip cookies that Mrs. Kupps had left her. And she rushed to the door. Gaby peered through the peephole and was shocked to find Deacon.

What was he doing here?

Her heart started beating faster. She glanced down at her white shorts and old Support Your Library tank top. Not exactly the most attractive outfit, but it'd have to do.

She swung the door open. "Hi."

Deacon looked uncomfortable as he shifted his weight from one foot to the other. "Never mind. I shouldn't have bothered you."

"It's fine. Do you want to come in?"

He shook his head. "I saw your light on and figured you couldn't sleep, either."

Either? As in he didn't sleep at night? Interesting. "I was going over more plans for the fundraiser."

"At this hour?"

"You gave me until tomorrow to come up with a revised plan."

"I did, didn't I?" When she nodded, he frowned. "If you need more time, it's not a problem."

"Actually, I'm just about finished. Tomorrow works fine to go over the agenda." She was certain that wasn't why he stopped over. "What did you need?"

He glanced down. There was a book in his hand. When his gaze rose and met hers, there was uncertainty in his eyes. "It was nothing."

"Obviously it was something or you wouldn't be here. Are you sure you don't want to come inside?"

He shook his head. "I—I just finished reading this new book and thought you might enjoy it."

The fact he'd thought of her and wanted to share something personal filled her chest with a warm sensation. A smile lifted her lips.

She held out her hand. "What type of book is it?"

He handed it over. "It's a suspense book. But I'm sure you have other books you're already reading."

"Actually, I just finished one last night. So you have perfect timing."

"I do?"

She couldn't help but smile at his awkwardness. When it came to business, he was very sure of himself. But here, with it just being the two of them, he was nervous. And that bit of knowledge chipped away at the wall she'd erected to keep him out of her heart.

He shifted his weight from one foot to the other. "Usually I can figure out what's going to happen in the end, but this book kept me guessing until the last page."

She turned over the book and quickly read the blurb. "It sounds intriguing. I can't wait to read it. Thank you."

"I, uh, should be going." And with that he walked away.

As Gaby closed the door, she was struck by the gesture. It was so small and yet, it said so much about the man. The fact that he liked to read checked off a big box for Gaby—not that she was looking at him as a prospective boyfriend. But the fact that he used his mind for more than just work meant a lot.

And what meant even more was that he was thoughtful. The more she got to know him, the less he seemed like the monster that others had made him out to be after the accident. It was getting harder and harder to view him as the enemy.

"Okay. You have yourself a fundraiser," Deacon said the next day after going over her revised plans for the event in his office.

"I do?" Gabrielle smiled.

He tried to ignore the way her smile warmed his insides. *Focus on the fundraiser.* He cleared his throat. "Do you have a name for it?"

"Actually, I've given this a lot of thought. And you can change it, but how about the Diana Pink-Rose Tournament?"

The title that Gabrielle had chosen couldn't have been more perfect. His mother's name. She would have loved it. He was touched that Gabrielle had included her name in it. A lump of emotion swelled in his throat and for a moment he didn't trust himself to speak.

Misinterpreting his silence, Gabrielle said, "If you don't like it, I could work on some other titles."

He shook his head and swallowed hard. He wasn't the type to let himself get emotional, but Gabrielle was the first person to do something so kind and thoughtful in honor of his mother. She probably didn't even know how much it meant to him and perhaps it was better that way.

It's too bad the fundraiser would never become a reality. He thought it would definitely have been a great event.

His gaze met hers. "It's perfect. Thank you. What made you choose the pink rose for the title?"

She shrugged. "I guess because pink is the color of breast-cancer campaigns."

"Do you know what else pink rose means?"

She shook her head.

"Then come with me." He led her down to the rose garden, where he'd purposely planted a rosebush in every color that he could track down. As they made their way down the steps in the back of the house, he said, "My mother loved roses. And so I made a point of buying as many colors as I could find. I loved watching her face light up with every color that was added to the garden."

"That was very sweet of you. She was lucky to have you."

"No. I was the lucky one." And he meant every word of it. His mother had loved him even when he hadn't made the wisest choices. And she cheered him on when he reached for the stars. "I couldn't have asked for a better mother."

When they stood in the rose garden, Gabrielle's eyes searched his. "What are we doing here?"

"Did you know that each rose has a meaning?"

"I know that red roses mean love. But that's all."

"Ah, but not any love—true love. I'm sure you must get them all of the time."

"I must admit that I've never received any."

The fact that no man had given her roses really surprised him. Gabrielle was so beautiful. Her beauty started on the inside and radiated outward. He'd like to be the first to present her with one. "You should have roses and daily."

Color filled her cheeks. How was it possible that she grew more beautiful each time he saw her? His heart picked up its pace. He couldn't help but stare. He never got enough of looking at her. Was it possible for her to look even more radiant?

It was with great effort that he turned away. He walked down the brick path and stopped next to a white rose. "This one is the traditional rose of weddings. And it represents purity and virtue."

"How do you know all of this?"

"Each time I ordered a new rose, I would do my research. Roses are quite intertwined in history. I would distract my mother from her discomforts with stories that included the various roses."

Gabrielle gazed at him but didn't say anything. Yet there was a look on her face and he couldn't read it.

"What?"

"It's just that you continually surprise me."

"You mean you thought I was nothing but a conceited partygoer."

"Um, no. I don't know why you think that. It's just that I don't know any men who know so much about flowers."

His body tensed. It was even worse than he'd thought. "You think I'm a wimp—"

"No. Not at all. I think what you do here is wonderful." There was sincerity in her voice. She continued down the walk and stopped in front of a pink rosebush. "And how about these? What do they mean?"

"The dark pink petals mean gratitude and appreciation." He moved to a neighboring light pink rose. "And this one means sympathy."

He continued walking through the garden. When he came across his gardening supplies, he grabbed a pair of shears. He moved to some long-stemmed yellow roses. He searched for a perfect bloom and then cut it. He turned and presented it to Gabrielle.

A bright smile lit up her face. "Thank you." She lifted it to her nose and inhaled. "What does it mean?"

"Friendship."

She sniffed the petals again. "Is that what we have here?"

He hadn't tried to define what was going on between them until now. It was more complicated than friendship, but that title was safe and easy, so he went with it. "That's what I'd like to think."

Her eyes reflected her approval. "Me, too."

She'd slept in!

The next morning, Gabrielle awoke with a start. It was Deacon's fault that she'd been awake until the wee hours of the morning. He'd loaned her that book and it was good—no, it was great. She raced through her bedroom, trying to get ready for work as fast as she could. It wasn't that Deacon would be standing there by the office door waiting for her to arrive. It was more a matter of how much she wanted to accomplish that day.

She opened the door of the guesthouse and found a bud vase with a single yellow rose. She glanced around for Deacon, but he was nowhere to be seen. What had happened to the man who used to growl at her? She knew where she stood with his former self, but with this new version of Deacon, she was constantly losing her footing.

Deacon wasn't all good or all bad—he was both, but she was quickly learning that there was a lot more good in him than bad. She picked up the rose and lifted it to her nose. Its perfume was gentle but delightful. She'd never smell another rose without thinking of him.

She loved that each color of rose had a meaning. What

impressed her more was that Deacon had learned the meanings in order to delight his mother.

As she carried the flower into the guesthouse to find just the perfect spot for it, her aunt's words came back to her: *if you find a man that is good to his mother, he will also be good to you.* Gaby had only been a know-it-all teenager when her aunt had given her these sage pieces of advice, but somehow they'd stuck. Someday, some woman was going to be very lucky to have Deacon by her side.

But it wasn't going to be her.

Even if she were drawn to him, the cards were stacked against them. There was just too much baggage between them. Relationships were hard enough under normal circumstances, but theirs was outside the bounds of normal.

As she tried to dismiss the profound meaning of Deacon making this gesture, she recalled what he'd said about yellow roses: *they meant friendship.*

Did that mean he considered her a true friend? The acknowledgment stirred a rush of emotions. She tried to tamp down her reaction, but her heart refused to slow. She once again breathed in the flower's gentle perfume.

The fact that it wasn't her birthday and it wasn't a holiday made this gesture all that much more special. He'd done it just because he could. This was the most thoughtful thing a man had ever done for her.

She knew then and there that she was in trouble. Deacon was working his way through all the barriers she'd built around her heart. Why did it have to be him that got to her? He was the absolute last person she should be interested in and yet, he was the one that kept her awake at night. And when she did fall asleep, he was the one that filled her dreams.

She was still puzzling over what to do about her feelings for Deacon when he materialized in the doorway of the office. He looked quite handsome. The dark circles under his eyes were fading and when he smiled, it eased the worry lines bracketing his eyes.

"I hope you had a good night," he said.

Gaby yawned. She didn't know if there was enough coffee in the world to keep her awake today. "Morning."

His eyebrows gathered. "Don't tell me you were working all night."

"No. I was reading." She recalled the book, so she grabbed it from her purse and handed it to him. "Thank you. It was just as good as you said it would be. It had me guessing right up until the last chapter."

He accepted the book. "I'm glad. But you didn't have to read it so quickly."

"Yes, I did. Once I started reading, I had to keep going. It's the way I am when I get into a book."

When he nodded in understanding, their gazes met and held longer than necessary, and her heart began racing. Her stomach shivered with nerves. She'd never had a problem speaking with anyone until now. When she glanced away from him, her gaze skimmed over the yellow rose. "Thank you for the rose. It's beautiful."

"I'm glad you like it." He stepped back and leaned against the desk opposite hers. "I've been thinking that you have everything pretty much planned out for the event except for the menu."

"I guess I need to do that sooner rather than later so I can give the caterer the menu." She pulled out a pad of paper. "Do you have a preference for the format? Sit-down? Buffet? Finger foods?"

He paused as though giving each option due consideration. "This is going to be more of a garden party than anything else, correct?"

Gaby wouldn't exactly classify the event that way, but for the lack of a better term, she went with it. "Sure." Following his line of thought, she said, "So the finger foods might be best." When Deacon nodded, she added, "And we could have the wait staff mingle with trays."

"Sure, sounds good."

There was one more thing that she'd thought of. She didn't know how Deacon would feel about it since he was in favor of streamlining the event. But she thought that it would add a bit of fun to the event and it could be a big revenue raiser during the afternoon.

"I've been going over the plans and I think there's one more thing we should do."

Deacon's face grew serious. "What would that be?"

"A Chinese auction."

"No."

She frowned at him. "How can you just readily dismiss the idea?"

"Because the basis of the Chinese auction is to ask others to donate items or services. I don't want to ask anyone for anything."

She dropped the pen to the desk and lifted her chin. "Maybe that's your problem."

"What's that supposed to mean?"

"It means that you're trying to get through this difficult part of your life by yourself—by putting a wall up between you and everyone else."

He arched a dark eyebrow. "I let you in."

"No, you didn't. I made my own way past your walls in spite of you."

"This is my life, my choices—not yours."

She glared at him. "And this is my fundraiser and I'm telling you that there will be a Chinese auction."

His voice lowered and rumbled with agitation. "Are you always so stubborn?"

"My father says so, but I don't believe everything he says." She no longer believed what he said about Deacon.

"And you're going ahead with this auction no matter what I say?"

"Yes."

"Then I won't waste any more time trying to talk you out of it." He muttered under his breath as he strode out the door.

Something told Gaby that he regretted giving her that flower. But she wasn't backing down. That was Deacon's problem. When he growled, everyone backed away. He needed to learn that life was about give and take.

CHAPTER FOURTEEN

THERE WAS SOMETHING different about Gabrielle.

Something not quite right.

Deacon had kept his distance from her since their disagreement last week. He didn't know exactly why he'd taken such a strong opposition to her idea of the Chinese auction. It wasn't a terrible idea. He could think of much worse.

He was left with no choice but to admit the truth to himself. He'd created the disagreement on purpose to put some distance between them. And it was all because of that rose and the other ones he continued to leave at her door each morning.

He had mixed emotions about leaving her yellow roses. Part of him said that it was just a friendly gesture, but another part of him wanted them to mean more. And that made him uncomfortable.

Logic said that there was a fifty-fifty chance he was responsible for the car accident. If he were responsible, Gabrielle wouldn't want anything to do with him. But even if he were found innocent, would that really do much to change their circumstances? He was still the other party in a two-party accident.

But when he was outside in the rose garden, he would catch glimpses of Gabrielle. And when she didn't think he was watching, the smile vanished from her face. A glint of worry reflected in her eyes. Was it his fault? Had he upset her that much?

This time he didn't need to hear her aunt's voice in his head to know he needed to somehow fix things. Mrs. Kupps was right about Gabrielle being a ray of sunshine in his otherwise gloomy life. And when her light was dimmed, the darkness and shadows were too much for him.

He approached Gabrielle where she was sitting on the patio. She had pen and paper in hand, but she wasn't looking at either. Instead she was staring out over the ocean with a faraway look in her eyes.

"Mind if I join you?" He stopped next to the table.

She blinked and turned to him. "I don't mind, if you don't."

It wasn't exactly the invitation he'd been hoping for, but he sat down anyway. "Something is bothering you. I'd like you to tell me what it is."

She shook her head. "I'm fine."

"No. You're not. You haven't been happy in a while."

She sighed. "I didn't know that it was that obvious."

"Maybe not to others, but I've gotten to know you pretty well and I know when you have something on your mind. Is it the fundraiser? Are you worried—"

"No. It's not that. Things are going well. In fact, I'm already getting RSVPs to the digital invitations."

Frankly, that was quite a surprise to him. He'd assumed the event would be a failure. Actually, he'd been counting on it. The thought of opening his home to all those people was not something he relished, but it was a problem he'd deal with later. Right now, he was concerned about Gabrielle.

"If it's not the fundraiser, what it is? Maybe I can help."

Her tentative gaze met his. "It's my father."

"Your father? I don't understand. Did something happen?"

"No. At least not that I know of."

He should probably leave it there. It wasn't like he was friends with her father. But the sadness on her face had him searching for the truth. "Then what is it?"

"We've just never been apart for this long. It's always been just the two of us against the world."

Deacon hadn't expected this. "But isn't it nice not to be responsible for caring for him on a daily basis?"

She shrugged. "It never really bothered me. Maybe it should have. I guess I like being needed."

She did? "You mean you don't mind taking care of your father even to the extent of you not having a life of your own?"

"Is that what you think?"

"Well, when was the last time you had a date?"

She glanced away. "It's been a while."

"And when was the last time you did anything with your friends?"

"Lindsay and I went to the movies the other month."

"Other month? That sure doesn't sound like a busy social calendar."

"Why do I need a busy social calendar? So what if I don't have time to hang out. I have two jobs to hold down. And the cleaning and shopping to do." She paused as though she realized that she'd said too much. And then she frowned at him as though he was now the one in trouble.

He drove home his point with one final comment. "Maybe you take on too much."

"I do what I need to do."

There was no talking to her. She obviously couldn't see that she did so much for others that there wasn't any time left for her. He felt bad for her, but his persistence on this subject was only upsetting her more. "I didn't mean to upset you."

She sighed. "It's not you. I'm just frustrated. I'm not sure my father is taking proper care of himself."

This was Deacon's chance to pay her back for all the generous things she'd done for him. And he knew exactly what he must do.

When he looked at Gabrielle, he knew he didn't have any other choice. "Go to your father."

Her head jerked around until her puzzled gaze met his. "But our agreement—"

"I know about our agreement and I don't care. I won't stop you. Go to your father. Make sure he's okay."

"Really?" Immediately her face lit up. "You don't mind?"

"No." He was lying.

He knew that once she passed beyond the estate gates that she would not return. Why should she? She had a life that had nothing to do with him. She had a father that loved her. Friends to do things with. She had a full life.

And what did he have to offer her? He struggled to come up with any reason for her to return. The memory of their kisses passed through his mind. But he knew that had been a fleeting thing—a moment of pity on her part for a man who looked and sounded like some sort of beast.

"Do you mind if I go now?" She looked radiant, like Dorothy about to click her red heels.

He, however, didn't feel like the Wizard. "No. Go."

She ran over to him and hugged him. The moment passed much too quickly and then she pulled back.

He refused to let her see how much her departure bothered him.

Without another word, Gabrielle rushed away. He wasn't even sure that her feet touched the ground, she was so happy to get away from there. How could he take that happiness away from her? He sighed in resignation.

He was happy for her, but he was sad for himself. He just couldn't believe in the short amount of time that they'd been together that she'd come to mean so much to him.

And now he was on his own again.

CHAPTER FIFTEEN

IT HAD BEEN a lovely visit.

The weekend had flown by. It had been so good to see her father. The time with him had been exactly what she'd needed. And best of all, Newton had been out of the house. Everything had gone smoothly so long as she stayed away from the subject of Deacon.

She'd tried a couple of times to let her father know that Deacon was treating her really well, but her father hadn't wanted to hear any of it. All he'd wanted to hear regarding Deacon was if she'd gained any information to help move along the legal process. He was still convinced that Deacon had paid off people to bury the accident report. In the end, Gaby had given up because she didn't want to spend the short amount of time she had with her father arguing. Though she didn't believe Deacon was a monster, she couldn't confidently claim his innocence, either. They still didn't know exactly what had happened in the accident. To say she was confused was putting it mildly.

While she was home, she'd cooked for her father. She'd spent quite a bit of time in the kitchen preparing healthy meals. By the time she left, the fridge was full. The freezer was stuffed with meals that just needed re-heating. And her father's prescriptions were refilled.

Her father begged her not to return to Deacon's estate, saying that he could take whatever punishment the judge was likely to throw at him. But Gaby told him this was about more than just him. She was doing important work with the fundraiser and she needed to see it through until the end. And that soon she would be back home. With a hug and a kiss, she'd left for the long drive back to Malibu, knowing her father was doing quite well on his own. Perhaps she did fuss over him more than necessary.

Thanks to Deacon, both she and her father were finding that they didn't need each other quite so much. When her time was over at the estate perhaps she could stick her foot back in the dating pool. But as soon as she thought of dating, Deacon's image came to mind.

She tried to imagine him with his hair cut and his face shaved. He'd look like a whole new man and perhaps he'd feel like one, too. Maybe it was time to see how he felt about a makeover.

Monday morning, she opened the door to the guesthouse of Deacon's estate and paused to look around. After waking up for the past week to find a yellow rose at her door, today there was none. It saddened her, but she knew eventually they had to stop. Still, she'd come to look forward to them. And now she tried not to read in too much to their absence.

It wasn't until later that morning, with a check in hand for his signature, that she went in search of him. At that hour of the morning, Deacon was usually tending to the roses. But when she went to the garden, there was no sign of him and it didn't look as though he'd been there that morning. That was odd.

She went to his office, thinking he was working on an important project, but the office was empty and the lights were off. Concern started pumping through her veins.

In the kitchen, she tracked down Mrs. Kupps. "Do you

know where Deacon is?" The woman nodded, but her face said that something was definitely amiss. "You're worrying me. Where is he?"

"He's closed in his rooms."

"His rooms. But why?"

"I don't know. He hasn't said a word to me." Mrs. Kupps shrugged. "He went in there after you left and he hasn't come out. I'm worried about him."

Gaby recalled their last conversation. She thought things had been fine between them, but then she recalled how Deacon had been eager for her to go visit her father. She'd missed her father so much at the time that she hadn't paid much attention to Deacon's reaction, but looking back on things, she should have realized something was off with him.

"Leave it to me. I'm used to dealing with stubborn males."

A weak smile lifted the worry lines on the woman's face. "I knew as soon as I laid eyes on you that you would be the ray of sunshine this house needed. I was just preparing him a late breakfast. You could take it to him, if you like."

"Thank you. I would."

Mrs. Kupps put together a tray of eggs, bacon, toast, fruit and juice. When she handed it over, she said, "Good luck."

"Thank you. I'll need it."

Remembering the day that Deacon had taken her to his room to clean her wounds from falling in the rose garden, Gaby made her way upstairs. The tall double doors were closed, but that wasn't going to stop her.

She leveled her shoulders and then gave a quick knock. Without waiting, she opened the door. She was surprised to find the room so dark. She squinted into the shadows, looking for him.

"Go away!" His deep voice rumbled through the room.

It seemed that he'd regressed. "Your growl isn't going to scare me."

Suddenly he was standing in front of her. Frown lines were deeply etched upon his face. "You're back?" He seemed surprised.

"Of course."

His face quickly returned to its frown. "Well, since you aren't going to leave until you've had your say, get it over with. Quickly."

"I hear that you've been in your room since I left. What's the matter? Are you sick?"

"No."

"Something must be the matter." Now that her eyes had adjusted to the low lighting, she moved to a table and placed the tray. "You have things to do. There's no time for slacking."

"I'm not slacking." Again his voice rumbled. "Now go away. Shouldn't you be with your father?"

So *that's* what was bothering him? She worked to subdue a smile. He had missed her. Who'd have guessed that? In truth, she'd missed him, too. But she wasn't ready to admit it.

She moved past him with sure, steady steps. At the window, she stopped and threw open the heavy drapes, letting the bright morning sun into the room. She turned to find Deacon squinting and trying to block the sun's rays with his hand.

"Close that."

"And let you sit in here in the dark? I don't think so."

He grunted his displeasure. "I'm your boss. You're supposed to do what I say."

"I'm your friend, remember? And I'm doing what's best for you."

"No, you came back because your father probably kicked you out for working here. I bet you don't listen to him any better than you do me."

"When both of you make poor choices, I don't mind calling either of you out on them."

Deacon frowned at her. "I didn't make a poor choice."

"You mean sitting around in the dark is your way of being productive?"

He opened his mouth and just as quickly closed it again. He sighed and glanced away. "If you're going to stay here, shouldn't you be in your office doing some work instead of harassing me?"

"I will just as soon as you start eating that delicious meal Mrs. Kupps prepared for you." He looked at her but he didn't move. She crossed her arms and tapped her foot. "I have all day."

With a look of resignation, he moved to the small table and sat down. "You are certainly something."

"I'll take that as a compliment."

He took a bite of egg. It was followed by a half a slice of toast. Partway through his meal, he stopped and looked at her. "Why do you care?"

"Because you apparently need someone to care about you. You don't seem to do a very good job of it on your own."

"How am I supposed to, when I know what I've done?" The worry and stress lines etched his handsome face.

"I thought you said you didn't remember the accident?"

He let out a heavy breath, causing her heart to lodge in her throat. Did he know more than he'd told her? Had the police report been released? Her mind rapidly searched for the reason for his despair.

"Talk to me," she prompted, needing him to tell her that the worst hadn't happened.

"The nightmares are getting worse. It's hard to tell the truth from the products of my imagination."

"And…" She waved her hands as though trying to pull the information from him.

"And I remember bits and pieces, like the fire burning my skin. I remember your aunt. I remember her saying 'Take care of Gabrielle.'"

"What? She did?" When he nodded, she asked, "Is that why you gave me this job?"

His gaze met hers. "Yes."

Gaby had been right about him. Deacon was a good man—buried beneath a mountain of unnecessary guilt. Her aunt's words were the proof of his innocence that she needed.

"Why are you smiling?" His dark eyes searched hers.

"Don't you understand? You're innocent."

His eyebrows drew together and his forehead wrinkled. "Why would you say that?"

"Because if you were guilty, my aunt never would have asked you to reach out to me and take care of me—not that I need you to." Gaby smiled at him, feeling as though a huge weight had been lifted. When he didn't look convinced, she asked, "What's wrong?"

Deacon rubbed the back of his neck. "Your theory is not proof—not legally."

"It's enough for me. It'll all work out. You'll see." There was one more thing bothering her. "But if you really wanted to fulfill her wishes, instead of having me work here, you could have just offered me money or something, but you didn't. Why?"

Deacon hesitated. "When you went on and on about how you cared for your father after telling me that he could take care of himself, I wanted you to know that you could have a life of your own and you didn't have to sacrifice everything for him."

"It was more than that and you know it."

"Perhaps."

"Perhaps nothing. You wanted to separate me from my father in order to punish him for the pain he caused you."

Deacon's gaze lowered and he nodded. "Yes, I did. I suppose that makes me a bad person."

"No. It just makes you human." She eyed him as he returned to eating. "Speaking of making you more human. What would you say to a haircut and shave?"

"I don't think that's a good idea."

She wasn't going to let him wiggle out of this. He'd been hiding behind all of that hair long enough. "Really? You like having your hair hang in your eyes?"

"No, but it's better than seeing what's beneath it."

So he was worried about the scars. He couldn't hide from them forever. Maybe facing up to them would be his first step back to the life he'd left behind after the accident.

She stepped closer to him. "I'd like to see you. The real you beneath all of that hair."

He looked at her as though gauging her interest. "And what if I'm a scary mess?"

"I'll still think you're handsome." Now where had that come from? She couldn't believe she'd uttered those words, even if it was the truth.

His eyes widened with surprise. "Really? You're not just saying that because you pity me? Which is ridiculous considering I lived and your aunt didn't. Listen to me. I just keep rambling..."

She kneeled down next to him. With her hands, she smoothed his hair back from his face. "There you are. Yes, you're definitely the most handsome man I know."

There she went again, saying the first thing that popped into her mind. But this time, when Deacon reached up and wrapped his hand around her wrist, she didn't regret speaking the truth.

"Okay. I'll do it," he said, "as long as *you* do the haircut and shave."

That wasn't exactly what she'd imagined when she'd proposed the idea. Still, if he was willing to take this big step with her, who was she to deny him?

CHAPTER SIXTEEN

HER HEART POUNDED in her chest.

After gathering the supplies she needed, Gabrielle stood there in Deacon's bathroom holding a razor.

What if she messed up? She wasn't a barber or a hairdresser. Sure she could trim her own bangs when her hairstyle dictated. But there was a big difference between trimming bangs and trimming a man's entire head, on top of giving him a shave.

But with his dominant hand still not working well enough for him to manage a razor, what choice did she have?

Call a professional? The idea was so appealing and yet, she knew that it was an impossibility. Deacon was so certain that beneath all of that hair that he was a monster. And this was her one chance to prove him wrong.

The truth was she didn't know what she'd find beneath his beard. She prayed that in his mind, he'd made the scars much worse than they were in reality. No matter what he looked like, she had to let him know that he wasn't some sort of beast.

The fact that he trusted her enough to allow her to shave and trim him wasn't lost on her. They had come a very long way since she'd started working at the estate. She remembered how awkward it felt working in that office, knowing that he was on the other side of a locked door.

But at the time, she hadn't understood that he had such significant injuries from the accident. That certainly wasn't how the accident was portrayed in the news. In fact, she was beginning to think that nothing in the media was as it seemed.

"Did you change your mind about revealing the real me?"

Deacon's voice jarred her out of her thoughts. "No. Of course not. I'm just trying to decide if I should start with your hair or your beard."

"The hair. That way after you're done shaving me, I can jump in the shower."

"You're sure about this?" She had to hear his answer one more time.

"I am." He studied her for a moment. "If you are."

"I am." She sucked in a calming breath. It didn't work, but she focused on the task at hand instead of her lack of experience.

Trading the razor for a pair of scissors, she set to work. She drew on her memories from her own haircuts and her experience trimming her dad's hair when he was in rehab. Gaby took her time, not wanting to mess up. She knew there was a lot riding on this particular haircut.

Her stomach was a nervous, jittery ball of nerves. Lucky for her, her hands remained steady. A cut here. A cut there. The trimmed locks of hair piled up on the floor. And all the while, Deacon remained quiet.

She walked around his chair, checking for any uneven spots. There was one by his left ear. With great care, she trimmed it.

And in the end, he retained both ears, and no blood

was shed. It wasn't the most stylish haircut, but considering his hair before, it was a large improvement.

Deacon lifted a hand and ran it over the short strands. "Do you want to look in the mirror?"

"I don't have any mirrors. I got rid of them."

"But I have one." She held up a hand mirror.

He turned away and shook his head. "I'll see it when you're all done."

After the trimmings were swept aside, she grabbed a comb and the scissors. Then she set to work trimming his beard as short as she could. She'd never trimmed a man's beard before. Sure, she'd shaved her father when he'd been in the hospital but his stubble was nothing compared to Deacon's full-on beard.

But what got to her more was being this close to him. There was something special about him. It was more than him being a famous movie star. It was an air of strength and power that exuded from him. And she was feeling herself being drawn closer and closer to him.

She'd never experienced such an intense attraction and it scared her. Not the part about her father or the accident. No—it was the fact that she didn't know how she was going to return to a world without Deacon's reluctant grin, or seeing the way his eyes twinkled when he was happy.

As the fundraiser grew closer, her time with Deacon was running out. She wanted this time to count. If all she had left when this was over were the memories, then she wanted them to be earth-shattering, pulse-quickening memories.

Deacon didn't know how much time had passed.

His eyes were closed as he focused on Gabrielle's gentle touch. He didn't know that a haircut and shave could be so tantalizing. Thank goodness she didn't attempt to make small talk because he wasn't sure he'd be able to follow along.

Each time her fingertips brushed over his skin, it short-circuited his thoughts. And each time her body brushed up against him, he longed to reach out and pull her onto his lap. He ached to press his mouth to hers. He smothered a groan.

"Are you okay?" Gabrielle paused.

He opened his eyes to find her staring directly at him. "Um, yes."

"You're sure?"

She'd heard him moan? He smothered a curse. He thought that he'd caught himself. Deciding it was best that he change the subject, he asked, "How's it going?"

"Before I go any further, I need to soften your beard." She turned on the water.

He couldn't see, but he could imagine Gabrielle letting the water get hot and steamy. And the next thing he knew, she was draping a hot towel over his jaw. The heat gave him a bit of a start, but he soon adjusted to it.

All the while, he was tempted to ask for her mirror just to make sure his hair wasn't an utter mess, but then he decided at this point, it didn't matter. If worse came to worse, he'd shave his entire head. At one point in his life, his hair had only been touched by the finest stylist in the movie business, but that felt like a lifetime ago. These days his hair didn't matter to anyone.

Gabrielle moved in front of him. "I have to admit I've only ever shaved my father when he was in the hospital."

"Don't worry. I trust you." It wasn't until the words crossed his lips that he realized what he'd uttered. He would retract the words if he could. But now they were out there. They filled the room with silence as the heavy impact settled in.

Gabrielle immediately turned away so he was unable to read the emotions filtering through her expressive eyes. When she turned back, she removed the hot towel from his jaw.

He didn't know why he'd said such a thing. That wasn't exactly the truth. He knew. He just didn't want to admit it to himself or to anyone else.

He was a man who prided himself on relying on no one. He told himself during all these months of solitude that he was fine on his own because he couldn't trust anyone else in his life. And then Gabrielle burst into his world and little by little she'd chipped away at the crusty shell that he'd armed himself with. And now he was starting to care about her. He didn't know what to do with these feelings.

But it was getting difficult to ignore his body's strong reaction to her with her fussing all about him. And when she stood in front of him to shave him, he had to close his eyes to keep from staring at the most tantalizing view of her firm breasts. But it was too late. The image of her curves straining against the thin cotton top when she leaned toward him was permanently tattooed upon his mind.

Think of something else—anything else.

He didn't want to let Gabrielle know just how much this session of playing barbershop was getting to him. The truth was he was letting himself get too close to Gabrielle. And no matter how he tried to hold her at arm's length, she ended up getting so much closer. But that would all end as soon as Gabrielle revealed his scars.

He told himself that he was ready for her to be repulsed, but he wasn't. One look at him and she wouldn't be able to pack fast enough. The truth was that before Gabrielle, he'd forgotten how to smile—how to laugh. He'd forgotten what it was to sleep at night for more than two hours. She had totally turned his life upside down and made him think of all the things that he could still do.

"Relax." Gabrielle's voice drew him back to the present.

"I am relaxed."

"No, you're not. Your jaw is rigid and so are the muscles in your neck. If you don't trust me—"

"I do trust you. Keep going. I have things to do." The truth was he didn't have any other place that he wanted to be other than right here with her hands moving gently over his skin.

"Look at me when you say those words."

He opened his eyes and found her staring straight at him. "I trust you."

With that admission hanging between them, she continued shaving him. Her motions were slow and deliberate. He banished the worries and drew in a deep, calming breath. The more she worked on him, the more relaxed he became under her skilled hands. He sat there with his eyes closed, enjoying the way her fingers felt on his skin. Her touch was gentle, but it ignited a fire within him.

She ran a towel over his face. "You can open your eyes. I'm done."

When his eyes opened, she was smiling at him. "You're already done?"

"Already? That took close to an hour."

"It did?"

She nodded. "And it was worth every minute. Because just as I predicted, you're amazingly handsome. You'll have all of the women swooning at your feet," she added softly.

"I doubt it." He ran a hand over his smooth jaw. It felt so good to have all that hair removed. The beard had been itchy and too warm.

However, he refused to let himself buy in to Gabrielle's compliment. He'd seen the damage to his face at the hospital. He'd been a mess of angry scrapes and nasty gashes. She was just being nice.

"If you don't believe me, have a look for yourself." She handed him a hand mirror.

He really didn't want to look. He knew that he'd find an angry red map of scars. Still, it couldn't be avoided forever. He might have removed all the mirrors from his home, but he was quickly learning just how many surfaces were reflective.

Not allowing himself an easy out, he lifted the mirror. He blinked. Surely he wasn't seeing clearly. He turned his head to one side and then to the other. Where were all the ugly scars?

"See, I told you." Gabrielle continued to smile at him. "You're as handsome as ever."

"I can't believe it." He ran his fingers over his face. "I know that when they transferred me to another hospital, they mentioned something about bringing in a world-class plastic surgeon, but I didn't think there was any hope of salvaging my face."

"I'd say that surgeon is quite gifted."

The angry red lines had faded. The surgeon had hidden most of the scars. Others were fine white lines, but they didn't make him look like Frankenstein. He'd never be the way he used to be, but at least now he wouldn't scare children.

He turned to Gabrielle to thank her for helping him through this difficult step. But when he faced her, the words caught in the back of his throat. She looked at him differently. Not in a bad way. More like a woman who desired a man. Was that possible? Or was he reading what he wanted in her eyes?

As though in answer to his unspoken question, she bent over and pressed her lips to his. At first, he didn't move. He didn't want to do anything to ruin this moment. And yet she pulled back, ever so slightly.

Need and desire pumped through his veins in equal portions. When she looked at him, he felt like a whole man. Not like a man haunted by his past and worried about his bleak future. She looked at him as if she couldn't imagine him doing anything bad. And he so wanted to believe it, too.

Giving in to the urgent need consuming his body, he slipped his arms around her waist and gently pulled her back to him. Her warm, soft curves pressed against his hard muscles and a moan formed in the back of his throat.

He didn't know why fate had brought them together, and in this moment, it didn't matter. The only thing he cared about was Gabrielle's happiness. He wanted to give her a good memory—something to overshadow some of the pain he'd caused.

In all honesty, the memory they were creating would be something he'd cherish, too. He'd never known anyone as generous of heart, as understanding and as bossy as Gabrielle. And he knew no matter how long he lived, he'd never find anyone else like her.

As their kiss deepened, he longed to have all of her. But he had to be sure she wanted the same thing. He wouldn't rush her.

With every bit of willpower, he pulled back and waited until her gaze met his. "Are you sure about this?"

She nodded.

That wasn't good enough, he had to be absolutely sure

she wanted him as much as he wanted her before he carried her into his bedroom and laid her down on his king-size bed. "Gabrielle, do you want to make love?"

"I thought I made my desires clear just a moment ago."

"I need to be sure. I... I don't want to do anything to upset you."

Her eyes reflected the desire warming his veins. "Then let me make this perfectly clear. I, Gabrielle Dupré, want to make love to you, Deacon Santoro."

That was all he needed to hear. He scooped her up in his arms and carried her to the bedroom. He laid her gently on the bed. Nothing had ever looked so good—so right.

He knew after tonight that nothing would ever be the same for them, but he would deal with the aftermath later. Much, much later...

CHAPTER SEVENTEEN

THE NEXT MORNING Gaby awoke alone.

She reached out, running her hand over Deacon's pillow. It was cold to the touch. Her gaze searched the bedroom. There was no sign of him.

The convergence of disappointment, embarrassment and sadness left her grappling to keep a lid on her emotions. He regretted their night together. A sob caught in the back of her throat.

No. Don't lose it now. You're stronger than this.

As she looked to see the time, her gaze stumbled across a yellow rose on her bedside table. It hadn't been there last night. She was certain of it.

She withdrew the rose from the vase. As she stared at its velvet petals, she wondered what Deacon was trying to tell her. Did he want to go back to being friends? Or was she reading too much in to it? Maybe, in this case, a rose was just a rose.

She glanced at the clock. She realized if she didn't hurry, she'd be late to work. Finding out where her relationship now stood with Deacon would have to wait until later. She was expecting phone calls that morning about the fundraiser. And no matter what happened between her and Deacon, she intended to do her best job.

She scrambled out of bed and rushed to get dressed.

There was something else she needed to do that morning—conclude her arrangement with *QTR*. She may not know the exact circumstances of the accident, but she knew Deacon hadn't been at fault and didn't deserve any further bad press.

When she returned to the guesthouse, she knew she'd made a big mistake. Not the night she'd spent with Deacon. One minute, he'd been so tender and loving. Then in the next moment, he'd been hot and passionate. It was a night of surprises and delights. No, her problem was agreeing to do an exposé about him. Now that she knew about her aunt's request, she was certain he was innocent. Her aunt would never have asked a killer to look after her. And now Gaby had to try to undo some of the damage.

So far *QTR* hadn't printed anything that she'd given them, not that there was anything noteworthy. Hopefully it wasn't too late to call off the arrangement.

Gaby retrieved the number of the editor at *QTR*. The phone rang and rang. She began to worry that no one would answer.

Suddenly there was a male voice. "Hello."

Gaby was startled. This certainly wasn't the perky young female editor that she'd been assigned to. "I'm sorry. I must have rung the wrong number."

"This is Elle McTavish's desk."

Gaby swallowed down her nervousness. "I was hoping to speak with her."

"And who is this?"

"Gaby, um, I mean Gabrielle Dupré. And who is this?"

"Thomas Rousseau."

As in Quentin Thomas Rousseau II. Gaby's stomach clenched. Oh, boy. She'd heard stories about the man. None of it was any good. He was legendary. She wasn't sure what was going on, but she had the feeling that it wasn't going to be good.

She gripped the phone tighter. "Could I leave a message for Ms. McTavish?"

"I've taken over for her."

But he was the owner, not an editor. Gaby clenched the phone tighter. "I see. Then perhaps you are the person I should speak to."

"I'm listening."

"I've changed my mind about doing the story about Deacon Santoro."

"I see." His voice was smooth and patient. "But my understanding was that's what you wanted—for the world to know about Santoro—and how he's evading the law."

At the beginning, that was exactly what she had wanted. But now she knew that her aunt hadn't blamed Deacon and, therefore, neither should she. He was not the beast she'd originally thought. He was just a man—a man who had punished himself needlessly.

"That was before—"

She stopped herself from saying too much. The less she told this man, the better. She had learned firsthand how words and images could be twisted into something they're not.

"Before what?"

"It was an accident. That's all."

"Have the police said this?"

"No, but they will."

"Miss Dupré, what changed your mind about gaining the truth and forcing the police's hand in delivering their findings about the incident?"

She worried her bottom lip. What was she supposed to say now? She didn't want to break Deacon's confidence. She didn't want to share her aunt's last words with the world.

"Miss Dupré?"

"I want to end our arrangement."

"Is that because you're now romantically linked with Mr. Santoro?" The man's voice took on a hard edge. "Yes, I saw that photo of you in his arms. I was not happy to be scooped by another magazine."

"It wasn't the way it looked." At least at *that* moment, everything had been innocent. Now everything was exponentially more complicated.

"Tell me about it." His tone was more congenial. He wanted her to give him a story but she refused to do it.

"You and I don't have a signed agreement. Remember, your magazine wanted to wait until you could ascertain what information I would provide."

"There was a verbal agreement, was there not?"

"Sounds like a case of 'he said, she said.'"

Regretting the deal she'd struck with the magazine, and now this man that she didn't trust in the least, she said, "I am calling off the arrangement. Besides, I never gave you anything you could use."

The line went dead.

She had to admit that had gone a little better than she'd expected. And as she set aside her cell phone, she felt a bit lighter. She didn't care how hard up she was for money, she was never working for a gossip rag again.

Now she had to deal with Deacon. She had no idea what to make of his disappearance that morning. He did say that he didn't sleep much. Maybe he'd just gotten up early.

And to complicate matters, she needed to come clean about her liaison with *QTR*. She felt now that her relationship with Deacon had shifted, she needed to be completely open and honest—even if he didn't like what she was about to say.

How was he supposed to face her after last night?

Deacon moved to the window in his office. She was going to look at him differently. She was going to expect things of him—things he couldn't give her.

And yet he didn't want to lose her. He told himself that it was the fact she was the best assistant he'd ever had. And this fundraiser, if it worked out, might help fund a breakthrough in the fight against breast cancer. There was too much riding on them continuing to work together.

Was it possible to wind back the hands of time? If they didn't talk about it, could they pretend that amazing night of lovemaking had never happened?

"Deacon, we need to talk."

He didn't move as he stared out the window of his office. She'd just said the five words he'd been dreading. It was time he put his plan in action.

Deacon turned to her. "I wanted to talk to you, too. I have another screenplay and I'd like to get your thoughts on it."

"It can wait—"

"No, it can't. If I don't get the rights to it, someone else will. I know it."

"But what I have to say—"

"Can wait." He saw the frustration reflected in her eyes. He owed her more than a quick brush-off. He swallowed hard. "I wasn't expecting last night. It wasn't something I planned."

"Me neither."

That was good to hear. It meant she had to be as confused as him. "Then you'll understand when I say I need time to process this. My life—it's not the best time to start anything serious."

Disappointment dimmed her eyes. "I understand. But I feel I owe you the truth about something."

Revealing secrets and truths were things people did when they were establishing a relationship. When they were building a foundation. He didn't intend to do any of those things with Gabrielle. Because when that police report was released—when he was sure his whole world would come crashing down—he didn't want Gabrielle hurt any more than she already would be.

Whatever she'd done or thought she'd done, it wouldn't compare to his transgressions.

"Now isn't the time for sharing." He averted his gaze. "We can talk another time."

"But—"

"Please." She didn't know how hard she was making this for him.

Because in a different place, at a different time, under different circumstances, he would have welcomed her into his life with both arms. Turning her away was the hardest thing he'd ever done.

As he watched her walk away, he felt the distance grow between them. It was like the sun had been eclipsed from his life. And as much as he wanted to go after her— to pull her into his arms—his feet remained rooted to the floor.

He clung to the fact that she was better off without him.

CHAPTER EIGHTEEN

IT WAS ALL coming together.

Beneath the blue skies, Gaby stood to the side of the golf course and gazed out over the estate grounds. Deacon's grounds crew were miracle workers. Of course, it helped that they'd enjoyed months of paid leave and were now anxious to get back to work. Gaby couldn't imagine what it would be like to have all that free time. Right now, she didn't have enough hours in the day to do everything that needed done.

And ever since they'd made love, Deacon had held her at arm's length. She didn't understand it. Had she done something wrong? Had he not enjoyed it? Whatever it was, he wasn't talking and she was left with nothing but doubts and worries. Thankfully the fundraiser was only a couple of days away and there were so many last-minute details to attend to that she didn't have time to get lost in her thoughts.

Every last ticket for the event had been sold. Now if only they'd all show up. The food had been ordered. The catering service had been reserved. The rose garden was already in order. Deacon had seen to that. But there was something she was forgetting. She just couldn't put her finger on it.

"You wanted to see me?" Deacon's voice came from behind her.

"I did." She tried to hide her surprise at him actually seeking her out instead of calling her on the phone. "What do you think?"

"About what?"

She subdued a sigh. What was wrong with him? "Look around. The grounds are done. The men have been working on it every day from dawn until dusk."

Deacon remained quiet as he took in his surroundings. His expression was masked behind a look of indifference. How could that be? Didn't he notice what a mess the estate had been? Even she had been out here every day going over the details to make this place spectacular.

"It looks good." He still didn't smile.

"Good? That's it. This place is amazing. Anyone would be amazed by the transformation." There was something more to this. Something that he wasn't telling her. "Deacon, we need to talk about the other night—"

"There's nothing to talk about."

She was tired of being patient—of thinking he just needed time to adjust to the change in their relationship. "I don't believe you."

"What?" He gave her an innocent look.

"Don't go acting like you don't know what I'm talking about. You've been avoiding me at all costs ever since we made love."

"I've been busy." His phone chimed. He withdrew it and held it up as proof of his business. Then he silenced it and slipped it back in his pocket.

"Fine. We'll play it your way."

"I'm not playing. What happened was a mistake. One we shouldn't repeat."

She managed a shrug as she wasn't so sure she trusted

her voice. It took her a second to swallow the lump in the back of her throat. With a blink of her eyes, she mustered up what she hoped was a blank expression. He wasn't the only actor here.

Willing her voice not to waver, she said, "And the golf course? What do you think of that?"

"It's good."

She planted her hands on her hips. "After all this work, *good* is all you have to say?"

His gaze didn't meet hers. "I don't know what you want me to tell you."

"More than that. My lunch was good. Your haircut is good. But the transformation of this estate from an unruly jungle to a work of art is spectacular."

He sighed and then proceeded to rub the back of his neck. "I just can't shake the feeling that something is going to go terribly wrong." He turned to her and apparently her thoughts were reflected on her face because he said, "What happens if the report on the accident comes out between now and then?"

"We deal with it."

"What if it says I'm to blame?"

In all honesty, she wasn't sure how she'd cope if the report really did say that Deacon was responsible for the accident that stole away her aunt, no matter how sure she was that he was innocent. But now Gaby understood why he'd pulled away from her. The accident was like a deep chasm between them, and try as they might, it was hard to cross.

She wanted to believe she would be able to move past the accident—to not hate him if the truth turned out to be different than what she imagined. But she knew that emotions could be tricky. Her father was a prime example—who'd have thought he would be arrested for stalking and harassment? Her father had never been in trouble with the law before in his life.

Not wanting to get caught up in the what-ifs and may-bes, she said, "Would you like to give it a go?" She gestured toward the golf clubs that were all spiffed up and standing next to the house in a special shed. "The clubs are just waiting to be used."

He hesitated and she was certain he was going to turn her down. And then he said, "I'll do it, if you do."

She shook her head. "Not me."

"Why not?"

"I—I prefer to watch." She really didn't want to admit that she didn't know a putter from an iron. Those were terms she'd heard the groundskeepers throwing around.

Deacon arched an eyebrow as he stepped closer to her. "Are you afraid I'll beat you?"

He was challenging her? Oh, boy. Maybe it was time for her to fess up. "No. I'm not worried." There was a glint of excitement in his dark eyes. He definitely had the wrong idea and so she said, "I don't know how to golf."

His eyes widened. "But you're the one who suggested making this a golfing event."

"I know I did. You did happen to notice that most of your yard is taken up by a nine-hole golf course?"

"But usually when you host an event, you know how to do the said event."

Now she understood his confusion. "But see, I'm not the host, you are. The fundraiser is in your mother's name. This is your home. And the people are coming here because of you—"

"No. They are coming because they are curious to see the recluse and find out if I'm an ugly, scarred mess like the tabloids have portrayed."

"Whoa! Whoa!" She waved away all his worries.

"That isn't why they're coming here. They're attending the event to support a worthy cause."

"And I think you see only the good in people."

"What's that supposed to mean?"

"Look at you. You're always so positive. Wanting to believe people are truly good. But they aren't."

She didn't know where all of this was coming from. "I'm not some Pollyanna."

"Yes, you are. You're all smiles and sunshine."

She hadn't meant to mislead him. "I'm human just like you. I have my share of doubts and worries. I just try not to dwell on them."

He rolled his eyes.

"Don't do that. Don't make me out to be like someone up on a pedestal."

"Then tell me that you aren't doing everything you can to convince yourself that I'm innocent. Go ahead. Deny it."

"But my aunt—"

"She was probably in shock. She probably hadn't even understood what had happened. The only thing she could think about was her love for you."

She shook her head, refusing to believe his version of events. "Now that I've gotten to know you, I just can't believe you would be reckless with your life and that of others."

"But see, that's the point. I have been in the past. I've bought super cars and I've taken them out on the road to see how fast they could go—to push the envelope. Doesn't that make me reckless?" When she couldn't argue with him, she remained quiet. His gaze implored her to affirm his actions. "Go ahead, say it."

"No." She wasn't going to help convict him when there wasn't any evidence. Because if he were guilty—if he did act recklessly—she would have lost not one but two people that she cared deeply about in that accident.

"Gabrielle, you can't bury your head in the sand and pretend the accident didn't happen. The reality is my nightmares grow stronger every night. You have to accept that—that I'm responsible for what happened. No amount of positivity will be able to overcome the fact that I—I killed your aunt."

Each word he threw at her was a blow at her heart. Tears pricked the back of her eyes. "Why are you doing this?"

Deacon hated hurting her.

But he didn't have a choice. More of his memories were starting to come back to him. He remembered being in the car. He recalled the blinding headlights headed straight for him. The rest was bits and pieces, but he couldn't shake the guilt mounting within him.

And now he was making a mess of things with Gabrielle. He'd only wanted to help her. He should have done it from a distance. Bringing her here to his estate was his first mistake. The second mistake was getting caught up in her greenish-gray eyes and letting himself be drawn in by her pouty lips. Now he had to untangle the ties that bound them together. It was best for Gabrielle.

He cleared his throat. "I never should have let things get this far. You and I need to part now, before either of us gets hurt."

"Are you saying you never cared? That this thing between us is all in my imagination?"

Why did she have to make this harder on herself? He couldn't tell her what she wanted to hear—not if he wanted her to leave, if he wanted to save her from more pain.

"It was fun and nice." He glanced away, unable to

stand the hurt reflected in her eyes. "But it wasn't real. It would never last."

His phone vibrated again. What in the world was going on? His email was busier than ever. Using his phone as an excuse not to face the pain he'd caused Gabrielle, he pretended to check it. In truth, he couldn't care less about business right now—right when he was sending away the woman that he'd come to care about deeply—

The breath caught in his throat as his gaze strayed across a bit of news. There was a distorted picture of him with ugly scars, next to a photo of Gabrielle. The headline read, The Beast Wins Beauty?

"What is it?" Gabrielle asked. When he didn't respond, she asked again, "What's the matter?"

He ignored her as his gaze skimmed down over the slanderous piece of trashy journalism. The fact that Gabrielle was *quoted* in the article stabbed him in the chest. Each breath was painful.

All this time, he'd thought she was so amazing with her ability to see the good in him. At first, he hadn't wanted to believe in her generous heart, but she'd worn him down and snuck past the wall around his own heart. And it'd been a lie. All of it.

"Deacon, I'm getting worried. What's wrong?"

His gaze narrowed in on her. "Why? Are you hoping I'll give you another headline?"

"What?" She reached for his phone. The color drained from her face as she read the article. When she looked up at him, worry lines bracketed her eyes. "I can explain."

"Don't bother." His angry words died in his throat when he realized she'd done what most anyone would have done in her situation. "I probably would have done the same thing in your place."

"But you don't understand. I—I backed out of the deal.

Once I knew you better and you told me what my aunt said to you, I backed out."

He wanted to believe her but he couldn't allow himself. "It looks like you gave them plenty to work with."

"This isn't my stuff. They did a hatchet job on the information I supplied them. Please. You have to believe me."

Anger pulsed through his veins. He was angry at the tabloid for printing outright lies. And he was furious with himself for not listening to his gut. Instead, he'd let down his guard with Gabrielle. He'd let himself fall for her and it'd all been a lie.

"Just go." His voice rumbled.

"But the fundraiser—"

"Is taken care of. You said so yourself. All the arrangements have been made. Now that your end of our deal has been fulfilled, it's time for you to leave."

When she didn't move but rather stood there with tears glistening in her eyes, he said with a low guttural growl that he knew she hated, "Go now. And don't come back."

He turned his back to her because it was killing him to send her away. He would try to forget the happiness that Gabrielle had brought to his life. He would banish the image of her warm smile—a smile that she would get when he walked in the room.

Because none of it had been true. While he'd been falling in love with her, she had been figuring out how best to twist the knife. And she'd succeeded. Worst of all, he deserved it and more after causing the accident.

His last little bit of hope that his name would be cleared was also gone. The future looked bleak. He just hoped the article brought Gabrielle and her father some sort of satisfaction.

CHAPTER NINETEEN

THIS WAS THE absolute last place he wanted to be.

Deacon stood off to the side of his newly manicured lawn. Despite what he'd said to Gabrielle, the estate did look spectacular. She hadn't overlooked a single detail. And his staff had gone above and beyond to make everything perfect for this occasion.

After Gabrielle left, it had been too late to cancel the fundraiser. He knew it was up to him to see it through to the end. Only things weren't turning out quite as he'd imagined.

With not one, not two, but three scandalous headline articles in as many days that featured him in the worst light, he didn't think anyone would attend. Instead, everyone was in attendance. He didn't know if they'd come in spite of the article or to find out if any of the lies were true.

The only person not there was the one person he longed to see—Gabrielle. He knew he should be angry with her, yet when she said that she'd backed out of the arrangement with the magazine, he'd believed her. But it didn't mean they belonged together.

He drew his thoughts up short. Today he had to be a gracious host.

He really couldn't believe all of these people had

shown up. There were fellow actors, directors, pillars of the music industry and people he didn't recognize, but what they all had in common was that they were happy to be here. All were smiling, talking and greeting each other. Food and drink flowed freely. The golf course looked better than it ever had, thanks to Gabrielle's insistence.

He'd already had compliments and slaps on the back that his scars had healed so well. After that doctored photo in *QTR*, where they'd made him to look like some sort of monster, people were pleasantly surprised by his normal appearance. It felt surprisingly good to greet friends and acquaintances. And he had Gabrielle to thank.

A mariachi band played in the background as well-dressed people mingled. Deacon worked his way past the crowd. He was headed for the rose garden, hoping to gain a moment alone. Though people had been accepting of him, it was all a bit overwhelming.

And then Gabrielle appeared in the distance.

Deacon came to a halt. It couldn't be her, could it? Not after the way they'd ended things. He blinked and looked again.

She was gone.

He expelled a disappointed sigh. It must have been someone that resembled Gabrielle. He assured himself it was for the best. She would soon forget him and move on with her life.

And then Gabrielle came back into view. She had on a yellow crocheted dress. The spaghetti straps showed off her slim shoulders. The plunging neckline hinted at her voluptuous breasts. He swallowed hard. A slit ended high up on her thighs, letting the crocheted high-low skirt show off glimpses of her long legs. She really was a looker.

It was then that he noticed a man next to her. The guy was chatting her up. Deacon stood too far away to overhear what was being said, but Gabrielle was smiling. However, it wasn't an easy smile. It looked forced. Yet, the guy acted as though he didn't have a clue she was only putting on a show of being nice to him.

Deacon's body stiffened as this man had the audacity to reach out and put his hand on Gabrielle's upper arm as though they knew each other intimately. If Gabrielle's body gestures were anything to go by, the attention was unwanted. Deacon started forward. Before he reached the two, the guy leaned over and whispered something in Gabrielle's ear. She pulled away. What did the man think he was up to? Couldn't he tell Gabrielle wasn't interested?

Deacon's steps quickened. He would step in. Or should he? He slowed down. Was it his place to step in? After all, he had told Gabrielle to go away. What would he be telling her if he were to step in now?

Yet, this was his estate. He had a right to see that none of his guests were unduly harassed. Determined that he had a right to make sure things were all right, he continued in Gabrielle's direction. He could see that she was no longer smiling and her gaze was darting around as though to find an excuse to slip away from the guy.

Deacon was almost at her side, when someone stepped in his way, blocking his view of Gabrielle. "Excuse me."

"Deacon, old boy. It's so good to see you."

Deacon focused on the man speaking to him. It was his agent. A man he used to speak to at least once a day, but since the accident, his agent hadn't bothered to call. The man had obviously given up on Deacon, figuring his pretty face was gone forever. Now that his face had healed, Deacon wondered if his agent realized he'd given up too soon.

"Harry, it's good to see you." Deacon did his best to smile, even though he didn't feel like it—not for a man who, for all intents and purposes, had told him in the hospital that his future in Hollywood had gone up in flames along with his good looks. Of course, Harry had been smart enough to put it in friendlier terms, but that's what it amounted to.

"You know I've been trying to reach you—"

"I've been busy." Deacon knew whatever Harry wanted would be what was good for Harry and not something that would help Deacon. "Could you excuse me for just a moment—"

"Not so fast. We should talk. This fundraiser was a brilliant idea. It certainly squashes those rumors of you becoming some sort of recluse. I've never seen the estate look better. And you, well, it's remarkable. If I hadn't seen you in the hospital, I'd never believe the extent of your injuries."

"The plastic surgeon did an amazing job," Deacon murmured tightly.

"Indeed. And this event is a great chance to get you back in the swing of things. Everyone seems to be having a great time."

"My assistant gets the credit. This fundraiser was her brainchild." It wasn't until the words were out that he realized Gabrielle was no longer his assistant. She was… well, they no longer had any sort of official relationship, but it sure didn't feel that way to him when he saw that other guy hanging all over her. Where had she disappeared to?

"This assistant, she sounds like a miracle worker,"

Harry said. "Perhaps I should try to steal her away from you."

The forced smile slipped from Deacon's face. "I don't think so."

"Well then, I'll get straight to the point of my calls. I have a part in a movie that I think you'd be perfect for—"

"No."

"No?" The agent's mouth gaped. "But surely you want to get back to work."

"I am working. I'm finding that I like being behind the camera more than I like being in front of it."

"So the rumor is true?"

"Yes. I'm starting to back some movies, and I'll see where things go from there."

The agent nodded as he digested the information. "If you change your mind, give me a call."

"I don't think that will happen." Deacon had to admit it felt good to know what he wanted in life. And what he wanted most was Gabrielle—even though he couldn't have her.

The agent's eyebrows rose with surprise before his face settled into a smile. "I knew you weren't one to hold a grudge. Glad to hear all of the ugliness is in the past." And then as though the man didn't know what else to say, he said, "Well, I should be moving on. I have other people that I need to speak to."

Deacon didn't say a word, not wanting to waylay the man. After the man moved on, Deacon's gaze scanned the area for Gabrielle. He didn't see her. But there were so many people that she could be anywhere.

He started moving through the crowd, but it was slow going with so many people wanting to greet him. He did the obligatory handshakes and pasted a smile on his face.

But he didn't linger. He needed to find her. He needed to—to what? Make sure she was okay? And then what?

He wouldn't know the answer to that until he caught up with her. He stopped and turned in a circle looking for her. She had to be here. And he wouldn't stop until he found her.

CHAPTER TWENTY

SHE SHOULDN'T BE HERE.

But she couldn't stay away.

To Gaby's surprise, the morning after she'd left the Santoro estate, the complaint against her father had been formally withdrawn. He was free and clear. There was no reason for Gaby to ever see Deacon again—but seeing him was exactly what she had planned.

She owed Deacon an apology. Instead of helping him with this fundraiser, she'd only made things worse for him. *QTR* had issued a series of malicious articles about Deacon. She recalled the morning's headlines on the *QTR* magazine. It was all over the newsstands, grocery stores and internet: Beast Hides from Public & Justice.

It appeared that *QTR* was intent on running a series of damning articles about Deacon. It killed her to read how they'd stolen her words. *QTR* had twisted the facts and made up other things. They'd embarked on an all-out campaign against him. No wonder she hadn't spotted Deacon amongst his guests. The fact that he had even let the fundraiser go forward amazed her.

When he'd banished her from the estate, she'd worried that he would once again hide away in his darkened office and keep everyone outside the tall estate walls. And after those atrocious headlines, she wouldn't blame him if he cut himself off from the outside world.

She didn't care what Deacon said, she knew he had a good heart. She couldn't—she wouldn't—accept that he'd recklessly taken her aunt's life. It had been a horrible accident. End of a very sad story.

She'd been talking frankly with her father—something she should have done before things had gotten out of control. And the fact that her father had agreed to attend the fundraiser with her was the first step on the road to forgiveness, even if her father would vehemently deny it. He said he was only here because Gaby had planned the event. He refused to acknowledge that the event had anything to do with Deacon.

Her gaze scanned the enormous crowd of finely dressed people. Was Deacon really somewhere among them? She had to try and fix things. She at least had to try. She didn't like the way they'd left things.

"Hey—" Newton nudged her "—isn't that the guy that acts in *The Screaming Racers*?"

She hadn't seen the action movie, but she had seen the previews on the television in her father's living room. "Yes, I think it is."

"What do you think he's doing here?"

"Supporting a good cause."

"I don't know. He's a big star. Why would he come here to the beast's lair?"

"Newton, don't start."

"Hey, it's what they called him in the headlines. You know, the story you helped write."

She gave Newton a stern look. "I only agreed to bring you here because you insisted that my father might need help getting around. But we could leave now—"

"Okay. Okay."

He pressed his lips together into a firm line. But his eyes told a different story. If she wasn't careful with him, he would make a scene. She sincerely regretted bringing him. As soon as she placed some tickets in the raffle baskets, she'd gather her father and Newton and they would go.

"Go find my father. You know, the reason you're here?" she said. "I need to go buy some raffle tickets."

"I'm hungry. Maybe we'll get some food." Newton walked away.

With Deacon nowhere in sight, Gabrielle made her way over to the table where they were selling the tickets for the twenty-five elaborate baskets that had been generously donated by area businesses.

Gabrielle couldn't help but smile as she observed all of the people gushing over the beautiful baskets and buying an arm's length of tickets at a time. This event was turning out better than she'd ever imagined. She wished Deacon could find some comfort in knowing that these people were in attendance in spite of the nasty headlines. That had to mean something, right?

With guests still streaming through the gates and the press along the road photographing the event, this was certainly going to give Deacon some positive spin. She pulled her cell phone from her purse. She clicked through to the different social-media sites to find that Deacon's name was trending. And this time, his name was linked with positive news.

Her lips lifted into a broader smile.

She'd done it. She'd kept her word to Deacon. The fundraiser appeared to be a smashing success. But this event wasn't nearly enough to make up to him for the lies that were lining every grocery store checkout and splattered on the internet. If only she could explain properly, maybe he'd believe her.

But where was he? She'd already worked through the crowd of guests and walked the whole way around the estate. And now, she was back where she'd started, in the garden. There had been no sign of Deacon amongst the pink tea roses, the purple climbing roses and the many other varieties of blooms that took root in the impressive garden.

The truth was she shouldn't have left when he'd told her to. She should have...well, she wasn't sure what she should have done. But leaving hadn't been the right answer. Because every minute she was away from him, the gap between them yawned even wider. She hoped it wasn't too wide for her to cross. Because she missed him with every fiber of her body. Life wasn't the same without him in it.

And then she remembered something her aunt had told her way back when she was in elementary school. There had been some trouble between her and another girl. Her aunt's sage advice was that a gentle word or a kind action could be more powerful than the strongest objection or the harshest retaliation. Her aunt had been a gentle soul. And Gabrielle had a feeling that her aunt would understand why she was doing what she was doing with Deacon. Or at least she hoped so.

"Hey, Gaby! Wait!"

It wasn't Deacon.

Her heart sunk a little.

With a forced smile, she turned to find Newton running back over to her again. "I thought you went with my father to find the food."

"Your father found someone to talk to and I decided to bring you a drink."

She realized now that he must have had more than one himself. He lurched toward her, spilling the drink on her bare arm, and then making as if to pat her dry with his free hand, surprising her.

Gaby turned, jerking away from his touch. "Stop. I'm fine…"

It was then that she spotted Deacon. He noticed her at the same time. Newton was still talking, but she was no longer paying attention. Her full focus was on Deacon.

"Excuse me." She moved past Newton and headed straight for Deacon.

Please let him listen to me before he throws me out.

CHAPTER TWENTY-ONE

GABY'S STOMACH SHIVERED with nerves.

As Deacon approached her, she forgot about everyone else around them. In that moment, it was just the two
of them. She started moving toward him. Although the
closer she got to him, the more she noticed the tenseness
of his body and the rigid set of his jaw. She braced herself for a confrontation. She understood how he'd think
that she'd turned against him.

They stopped in front of each other. At the same time,
they said, "I'm sorry."

Gaby's gaze searched his. "Do you mean it?"

He nodded. "I never should have told you to leave
like that."

"And I should have stayed. I need to tell you how
sorry I am—"

"You!" Newton wedged himself between her and Deacon. "You killed her aunt. You should be in jail."

A hush fell over the growing crowd.

"Newton! Stop." Gabrielle saw the pain that his words
had inflicted on Deacon.

Newton turned on her. "How can you defend him?"

Gabrielle's gaze went from Newton to Deacon. If there
were ever a time to be honest with herself and everyone
else, it was now. "I'm defending Deacon because I've

come to know him. I know that he's a good man with a big heart. He would never intentionally harm a person." She turned to Deacon. She stared deep into his eyes. "I know this because I love him."

"You can't. He's a killer." Newton shouted the accusation.

By then a crowd had formed around them. People were pulling out their cell phones and filming the scene. This mess had gone from bad to worse.

"He's my best friend," she countered.

"Don't," Deacon said. "I can defend myself."

"I'm only speaking the truth," Gaby said, feeling very protective of him.

Before Newton could say another word, Gaby's father rolled his wheelchair between them. He turned to Newton. "That's enough."

"But he is a—"

"Hero," her father said.

"What?" Newton stared at her father like he'd spoken another language.

Her father cleared his voice. "I should have said something earlier. The official accident report was released this afternoon. There is irrefutable proof that Deacon is innocent."

"What evidence?" Deacon approached her father.

"I'll admit my protest in front of your place may have been rash, but it garnered a lot of attention." He held up a hand, staving off Deacon's heated words. "Before you say anything, it was that protest and those interviews that brought forward a reluctant witness. They have a video of the accident. It has cleared you, Deacon. My sister was the one that swerved into your lane."

Gaby reached out and took Deacon's hand in hers. She

smiled through her tears. At last this long, hard journey was over.

She turned to Deacon. "Did you know about this?"

He shook his head. "I haven't touched my mail or listened to my voice mails today. I was busy making sure all of your plans for the fundraiser were carried out."

Gaby's father turned to Deacon. "And I owe you a big apology. Instead of accusing you of horrible things, I should have been thanking you." He held out his hand. Deacon hesitated and then he withdrew his hand from Gaby's grasp in order to shake her father's hand. "Gaby tells me that you don't remember much of the accident, but the witness reported that at great risk, you attempted to save my sister."

Deacon visibly swallowed. "I'm sorry for what you've gone through."

"Thank you." Her father's gaze moved to Gaby and then back to Deacon. "As long as you keep my daughter happy, we'll get along just fine."

Gaby glanced around to find that Newton had disappeared. She scanned the crowd for any sign of him. Thankfully she didn't spot him. She hoped he just kept going. The farther away, the better.

When she finally turned back to Deacon, he presented her with a single, perfect red rose. The simple gesture had a profound effect on her heart and love spilled forth.

Gaby lifted up on her tiptoes and looped her arms around his neck. "There's something else I came here to say."

At the same time, they said, "I love you."

As the crowd of onlookers cheered, Gaby leaned into Deacon's embrace. He claimed her lips with a kiss that promised love and happiness.

EPILOGUE

Six months later...

"I NEED TO talk to you." Gabrielle smiled at her new husband in the back of a black limo.

"Really?" The smile he'd been wearing all day slipped from his face. "I wanted to talk to you, too."

"You did?" Gaby sat up straighter. She couldn't imagine what Deacon had on his mind. "Maybe you should go first."

"Wipe that worried look from your beautiful face. Or else I'll have to put up that privacy divider and give you something to smile about." His eyes twinkled with mischief.

She knew exactly what direction her husband's mind had taken and she shook her head as a smile returned to her face. "That will have to wait." When Deacon made a point of pouting, she added, "There's no time. We're almost to the airport."

He nodded in understanding. "As usual, my wife is right."

"Make sure you remember those words the next time we have a disagreement." The lights of the Los Angeles skyline rushed past the window in a blur as their limo headed for LAX. They were hopping a private plane to Fiji. Their honeymoon was going to be a new adventure for the both of them.

"But if we disagree, we get to have make-up sex."

She couldn't help but laugh at her husband's unabashed eagerness. "Do you ever think of anything besides sex?"

"Not when you're around. You've ruined me." He pulled her closer until she was sitting on his lap. Then he closed the divider. "We should probably save Charles from all of this naughty talk. And this way, I can show you what I was thinking about."

He drew her head down to him and claimed her lips with his own. It didn't matter how many times he kissed her, he still made her heart race. His lips moved hungrily over hers, making her insides pool with desire.

She knew where this kiss was headed and it wouldn't leave time for them to talk before the flight. And there were some things they'd put off discussing for too long. It was best to clear the air now before the honeymoon began.

It took every bit of willpower to place her hands on her husband's muscular chest and push back, ending the kiss. "Deacon, wait."

His eyes blinked open and she could read the confusion in his expression. "What's the matter?"

She moved back to the seat beside him. "You're distracting me."

"But in a good way, right?"

"Of course. But we still need to talk."

The color drained from his face. "What's wrong?"

She couldn't help but laugh at the utter look of panic on his face. "Relax. Nothing is wrong."

"You're sure?"

Gaby nodded. "I know we should have talked about this before now, but I was wondering how you felt about children."

"Children?" His gaze narrowed as he eyed her. "I must say I like them. I happened to be one not so long ago."

"Hah! I've seen your six-bay garage with all those sports cars. You're still a kid at heart."

"Busted. But I do make time for business. Speaking of which, remember how I sued *QTR* for that pack of lies they printed about the car accident?"

She nodded. "How's the lawsuit going?"

"It's over. I got the news yesterday, but with the wedding festivities, I didn't want to ruin anything."

Gaby braced herself for bad news. "Did they get it thrown out of court?"

"It never went to court. *QTR*'s board stepped in and between our combined legal teams we hammered out a reasonable deal. The gist of it is they will be revising their editorial guidelines."

Gaby's mouth gaped as she digested the ramifications of the deal. "You mean no more hatchet jobs?"

"Exactly."

"Deacon, that's wonderful." She rewarded him with a kiss, but before it got too heated, she pulled back.

"Why did you stop again? I have a piece of paper that says we must kiss multiple times a day."

She laughed. "I didn't see that on our marriage certificate."

"It's in the fine print."

"Oh. Okay. I'll have to look closer." She smiled. "And did it say anything about how many kids we're supposed to have?"

"No. How many were you thinking?"

"At least one… Since it's already on the way."

For a moment, her husband didn't speak. He didn't move. She wasn't even sure that he was still breathing.

"Deacon, did you hear me?"

"Say it again." His voice lacked emotion and she was

beginning to wonder if he was having second thoughts about having children.

"We're having a baby."

"That's what I thought you said." He lifted her back onto his lap. Then he placed his large hand over her abdomen. "You're going to be a mom."

"And you're going to be a dad."

A big smile lit up his eyes. "I love you."

"I love you, too."

She reached out, placing her hand behind her husband's head, and drew him toward her. She claimed his lips with her own. No matter how old she got to be, she would never tire of his kisses. And she planned to grow very old with this wonderful man by her side.

* * * * *

BEAUTY AND THE BROODING BILLIONAIRE

DONNA ALWARD

CHAPTER ONE

JESS TOOK ONE look at the lighthouse and knew that the search had been worth it. After weeks of wandering, and months before that of her pencils hovering over her sketch pad, the battered white-and-red lighthouse on Nova Scotia's east coast stood firm against the brisk, briny wind.

In some regards she wondered if the lonely structure *was* her. Tall, a bit battered from the winds of life, but still standing.

Her agent was after her to do another show. "Your last one was such a success," Jack had insisted. "An original Jessica Blundon commands top dollar right now."

"You can't rush the muse," she'd replied, deliberately keeping her voice light. "I don't paint to order."

She hadn't been painting at all. Not since Ana's death. Her mentor. Her best friend. The older sister she'd never had. Losing Ana had devastated her and killed her creativity. Her life had suddenly become colorless and empty. No significant other. No children. No best friend.

She'd isolated herself far too much. So after a good year of grieving and moping, she'd decided to stop hiding away and go in search of what her life was going to look like. The best place to start, she figured, was finding her passion to paint again.

And while she didn't "paint to order," she did do this as

her career. Like most creatives, it was impossible to separate what she did from who she was.

The biggest shock had been that when she was finally ready to put brush to canvas, she couldn't. The block had been real and infuriating, until about six months ago, when she'd finally started sketching.

And traveling. She'd left behind the waters of the Great Lakes—Chicago—and gone west, to Seattle first, then San Francisco and down the coast to San Diego. The Pacific had been beautiful, but it wasn't what she was looking for. She was searching for that feeling, right in her solar plexus, that told her when something was just *right*. The Gulf of Mexico hadn't been it, either, though she'd adored her time in New Orleans and along the panhandle. She'd come closer to finding "it" the farther north she'd gone; past the barrier islands in the Carolinas, to the beaches of New Jersey and then the rugged coastline of Maine. On a whim she'd jumped on the CAT ferry in Bar Harbor and headed to Canada. She'd sketched lonely beaches, colorful coastal houses, gray rocks made black by the ocean waves. Trees budding in the mild spring weather. All lovely. But nothing that had felt inspiring. Nothing that created the burn to create.

Her sketchbook was full of drawings, but the lighthouse before her? It was that punch-to-the-gut feeling, and she relished the trickle of excitement running through her veins. "This is it, Ana," she murmured. "It's time."

The brisk wind off the ocean tossed her hair around her face and bit through the light cotton shirt she wore. May was definitely not Nova Scotia's warmest month, even though the sun shone brightly and warmed a spot between her shoulder blades. She needed to get a different vantage point. The angle here was too sharp. But the lighthouse stood on a bluff jutting out toward the sea, and the only path to it seemed to be from the property before her. And the gate that baldly pronounced Private Property—Do Not Enter.

"Private property," she grumbled, peering over the metal barrier. She couldn't see the house from here, and the drive led to the left while the lighthouse was off to the right and then south. Lips set, she swung her bag over her shoulder and put her foot on the bottom railing of the gate.

"Not electric." She grinned and then nimbly hoisted herself over the metal railings and landed on the other side.

It didn't take long for her to get a glimpse of the house. It was an imposing but beautiful structure, with gray siding and stonework and what would be marvelous gardens in another month or so. Fledgling hostas, their leaves still tightly furled, and a variety of tulips and hyacinths kept the beds from looking sad and naked. Jess expected that there were other perennials beneath the surface waiting for the summer warmth to wake them. The house had a fantastic panoramic view of the Atlantic coastline, and a sloped lawn led to what appeared to be low cliffs. She wondered if there was a beach below. And she'd like to look, but first she wanted to skirt the property and get to the isolated lighthouse, so she could take some pictures and perhaps make a sketch or two.

The ground was hard and rocky beneath her feet as she set off to the lonely tower. She'd made a friend at the nearby resort, and Tori had told her about the hidden gem, suggesting its semi-neglected state might add to its allure. She hadn't been wrong. The weather-beaten clapboards on the outside were in sad need of fresh paint, and as Jess got closer, she realized that the gray wood was worn surprisingly smooth from wind and salt. There was rust on the hinges of the door, and she wondered if the thing would even open or what she might find inside if it did. Dirt? Mice? Other creatures? She looked way up to the top, where the beacon lay, silent and still. Did it still work?

The lighthouse was full of character and secret stories. Her favorite kind of subject.

After her cursory examination, she pulled out her camera and started taking shots. Different angles, distances, close-ups, and with the Atlantic in the background. The ocean was restless today, and she loved the whitecaps that showed in her viewfinder, and the odd spray from waves that crashed on the rocks below.

After she took the photos, she thought she might like to get a few of the house, too. It was more modern and certainly very grand, but still with that lonely brave-the-elements esthetic that she loved. She swung around toward the property and came face-to-face with a pair of angry eyes. The man they belonged to gave her a real start.

"You're trespassing," he said, his voice sharp and condemning.

He looked like a hermit. It was hard to tell his age, because his hair was shaggy and his beard was in dire need of trimming, but she guessed maybe forty, or a little older. The brown shirt was wrinkled and slightly too big for his lean frame, and he wore faded jeans and worn boots. All in all, he was a little bit intimidating. Not just his looks, but the expression on his face. He was angry, and he wasn't bothering to hide it.

Somehow, though, she found him rather compelling. Rugged and mysterious, and beneath the scruff his looks were quite appealing. She rather thought she'd like to sketch him. And while he was intimidating, he didn't seem...dangerous. Just grouchy.

"I was only on the property for a few minutes. I stayed right along the edge until I got to the lighthouse."

"The lighthouse *is* on my property. I'm assuming you saw the sign, and chose to ignore it."

She didn't have an answer to that, because it was true. Except she hadn't realized that the lighthouse was on his private property. Weren't they usually parkland or municipal or something? How many people owned their very own lighthouse?

She put on her most contrite face. Despite his abrasive manner, it appeared she was in the wrong here, not him. If she wanted to have access to this perfect aspect, she needed to appeal to his…friendly side? If he had one.

"I'm really sorry. I truly didn't realize the lighthouse was part of your property. I'm an artist, you see. I'd heard about it from someone at the Sandpiper Resort, and they assured me it was worth checking out. I wouldn't have trespassed if I had realized I wasn't just, well, cutting across your lot."

He crossed his arms.

Now she was getting annoyed. Had she done anything so very awful that meant he had to be so…disagreeable?

She tried again. "I'm Jessica Blundon." She held out her hand and smiled.

He didn't shake it. Instead, his dark eyes assessed her from top to bottom, making her feel…lacking. One of his eyebrows lifted slightly, a question mark. She held his gaze, refusing to cower. If his goal was to intimidate her, he was failing. Despite his horrible manners, she did not feel the least bit threatened. This dog's bark was worse than his bite, she figured. There was something in his gaze that she responded to. He wanted to be left alone. It wasn't long ago she'd felt the same, so she merely lowered her hand and wondered what was hidden behind the beard and longish hair and grumpy exterior.

"Well, Miss Blundon, you're on private property. I'll

ask you to delete those photos off your camera and go back to where you came from."

Her mouth dropped open. He was actually going to get her to delete her pictures? She closed her mouth and frowned. "Is that really necessary? I mean, it's not like the lighthouse is some giant secret."

"It's my lighthouse, on my property, and I don't want you to have pictures of it." He reached into his pocket and took out a cell phone. "You can delete them or I can make a phone call and have the cops out here."

Now he was being utterly unreasonable, and any curiosity or sympathy she'd felt fled. "I could walk away and take my pictures with me. Unless you're planning to personally restrain me."

She lifted her chin, met his gaze. Something flared there, and nerves skittered along her spine. Not of fear. But of awareness. Mr. Hermit was enigmatic, and no matter how much he tried to hide behind his ragged appearance, he was actually quite attractive. There was something familiar about him, too, that she couldn't quite place.

His gaze dropped to her lips, then back up again to her eyes, and for the first time, his mouth curved in a slight smile. "Good luck," he replied. "I know your name and I know you're at the Sandpiper. Not too hard to tell the RCMP where to look."

He'd call the Mounties. He'd really do it, over a few stupid pictures. She lifted her camera and glared at him. "Fine. I'll delete the damned pictures." Her heart broke a little bit just saying it. She needed them. The first true inspiration she'd had in two years...darn it. She held his gaze and got the sense he wasn't bluffing.

"You could just give me the memory card."

"I don't think so. It wasn't blank when I got here. I'll

delete the ones I took just now but that's all. And you're being a jerk."

He shrugged. "I've been called worse."

Jessica switched to view mode and with growing frustration started deleting all the beautiful pictures she'd already taken, all the while calling him worse in her mind. He was being completely unreasonable. She toyed with the idea of keeping one or two, trying to hide them from him, but then figured why bother. When she looked up, he held out his hand.

"Oh, for Pete's sake," she muttered, taking the strap off her neck and putting the camera in his hands.

He scrolled through, appeared to be satisfied, and handed it back.

"Thank you. You can leave now."

Her cheeks flared at being so readily dismissed. She shoved the camera into her tote, fuming. He hadn't even offered his name when she'd introduced herself.

She met his gaze. "For the record, you didn't have to be so rude."

Then she swept by him. She was only a few feet away when she thought she heard him say, "Yes, I did." But when she looked over her shoulder, he was standing with his back to her, looking out to sea.

She hurried on, but when she got to a curve in the property, she turned back. He was still standing in the same spot, looking angry and lonely and lost.

She reached for her camera and took one hurried shot, then scurried back to the gate.

Bran sensed when she was completely gone, and let out a low breath.

Solitude. All he wanted was solitude. For people to leave him alone. The months of pretending in New York had taken their toll. He'd lost himself in his grief, only pulled out occasionally by his best friends, Cole and Jeremy. There'd even been times when he'd smiled and laughed. But then he'd gone home to the reminders of the life he'd once had, the one he'd been on the cusp of having, and he'd fallen apart. Every. Single. Time.

When he'd started to self-medicate with alcohol, he'd known he had to make a change. At first it had been just beer, and in the words of his grandmother, "it's not alcoholism if it's beer." He'd used that for a long time to justify his overindulgence. But when he'd graduated to Scotch, and then whatever alcohol was available, he'd known he was in trouble. He needed to sell the brownstone and get away from the constant reminders. Get his act together.

Jennie would be so angry to know that he'd resorted to alcohol to cope. And so he'd thrown out all the booze, because Jennie's memory deserved better.

The house in Nova Scotia was damned near perfect. Sometimes Jeremy and his new wife were close by, providing him with the odd company to keep him from transitioning from eccentric to downright crazy. No one knew him here, or if they did recognize his name, they didn't make a big time about it. He had groceries delivered to the house. Couriers delivered anything he could buy online...there wasn't much shopping nearby anyway. He spent hours staring out at the sea, trying to make sense of everything. Wondering how to stop caring.

Wondering if he'd ever be able to write again.

The one downside was the stupid lighthouse. In the beginning, it had been an incentive to buy. It was interesting and unusual, and he'd liked the idea of owning it. What he hadn't counted on was the foot traffic, skirting his prop-

erty and solitude with cameras and picnic blankets and…
He shuddered. At least once a week he found a condom on
the ground. It wasn't so much the idea of it being the site
for romantic trysts. He could appreciate a romantic atmosphere. But heck, would it be too much to ask for people
to pick up after themselves?

Today he'd seen the reddish-blond head, and he'd had
enough. The moment she'd pulled out her camera and
started taking photos, he was ready to put on his boots.
But when she turned to take a picture of the house? That
was the clincher. He valued his privacy far too much. So
far reporters hadn't found him, as they had in New York.
But it was only a matter of time. She didn't seem like a
journalist or a paparazzo, but he couldn't be sure.

He watched a gull buffeted by the wind and sighed. She
was right; he'd been a jerk about it. And part of that was
because she'd been trespassing, and the other part was because he'd immediately realized how pretty she was. Early
thirties, he'd guess, with blue eyes that had golden-green
stripes through the irises, making them a most unusual
color that deepened when she got angry, as she'd been
with him when he'd demanded she delete her pictures. A
dusting of freckles dotted her nose, pale, but enough that
it made her look younger than she was. But there were
shadows there, too. And the fact that he'd been curious at
all set him on edge.

He started back to the house, turning over the encounter in his mind. Jessica Blundon, she'd said. The name
sounded vaguely familiar, but he wasn't sure why. Maybe
she was a reporter.

Once inside, he went to his "den," a round-shaped room
on the bottom floor of the house with windows all the way
around. There was a fireplace there for when it was cold

or damp, as it had often been during the end of the winter when he'd moved in. A huge bookcase was near the door, the shelves jammed with a mixture of keepers, books on writing and stories he had yet to read. The furniture was heavy and well-cushioned, perfect for curling up with a book. He picked up his laptop and hit the power button, then started an internet search.

It wasn't difficult to find her. The first hit was her website, and the second was for a gallery in Chicago. Her site had her picture on a press page, but also a catalog of her paintings. He wiped a hand over his face. She was good. Really good. The gallery page brought up a press release from a showing she'd done…nearly two years ago. He flipped back to her site. It didn't appear to have been updated recently.

Had she not been painting all this time? Or had she been secluded away, working on something new?

Something sharp slid through him, and he recognized it as envy. He wasn't sure he'd ever feel whole enough to write again, and his agent had got him an indefinite extension of his contract, with his publisher saying he could turn in a manuscript when he wanted. Hell, at this point his publisher had more faith in him than he did in himself. The only thing keeping him from paying back the advance and killing the deal was that he was in his thirties. What else was he going to do with his life? At least with the open contract, there was something left ahead for him. More than just picking away at his trust fund, and existing.

And here *she* was, with her messy hair and bright eyes and pink cheeks, living life and standing up to the ogre.

Because that was surely what he'd become, and he hated himself for it.

But he was certain he didn't deserve any better.

He lowered the cover of the laptop and set it aside, then picked up his coffee and took a cold sip.

He'd stopped drinking. But nothing else had changed. And that scared him to death.

Jessica looked around the gardens of Jeremy and Tori's house and let out a happy sigh. The property didn't have the wild restlessness of the one with the lighthouse, but the scent of the ocean was strong and the burgeoning perennials added bursts of color. Tori had invited her to dinner, and now they sat outside, listening to the ocean and having tea. Tori held her three-week-old baby in her arms, the tiny bundle making small noises as she slept. Jessica held back the spurt of jealousy. She'd had a chance at a husband and family once, and had blown it. She'd been all of twenty-four and had wanted to travel and paint and not settle down yet.

He hadn't waited. Broken heart number one.

Now she was in her thirties with no relationship on the radar. She'd started to accept that a partner and family was not in the cards for her. It seemed that everyone important in her life always picked up and left in one way or another, and after a while a heart got tired of taking all the risks and never reaping the rewards.

It didn't stop her from getting wistful and broody around Tori's newborn, though. And when Tori asked if she'd hold the baby while she popped inside for a light blanket, Jessica had no choice but to say yes.

Little Rose was a porcelain doll, with pale skin and thick lashes and a dusting of soft, brown hair. Her little lips sucked in and out as she slept, and she smelled like baby lotion. Jess cradled her close, looking down at her face and marveling at the feel of the warm weight in the crook of her arm. She did like babies. A lot.

When Tori came back, Jess held out her hand for the blanket, unwilling to give the baby up just yet. "She's comfortable here and it'll give you a break."

"You mean I'll get to drink my tea while it's hot?"

Jess chuckled. "Exactly." She tucked the crocheted blanket around the baby and leaned back in the chair. "Thank you again for asking me to dinner. The food at the inn is lovely, but a home-cooked meal was very welcome."

"It wasn't anything fancy."

They'd had salad, grilled chicken and some sort of barley and vegetable side dish that had been delicious. Jeremy was now inside, catching up on some work while they enjoyed the spring evening.

"It was delicious. Besides, I was hungry. Someone made me angry today, and I went for a run on the beach after to burn off some steam."

Tori leaned forward. "Angry? Who? Not one of the staff, I hope."

Tori had resigned her position at the Sandpiper Resort, but she was still close with the staff and popped in on occasion to help with events or answer any questions the new assistant manager had. That was how Tori and Jess had met, and they'd ended up chatting and then sharing lunch on the resort patio.

"No, not staff. You know the lighthouse you told me about? I went to see it. Get some pictures...it's gorgeous, just like you said. I got that tingly feeling I haven't had in a really long time. And then the owner showed up. Man, he was a jerk."

She expected Tori to express her own form of outrage, but instead her eyes danced. "So you met Bran."

"You know him? Like, personally?"

"He's Jeremy's friend."

Jess lifted an eyebrow. "You might have warned me.

What an ogre. Hard to imagine him being friendly to anyone."

Yet even as she said it she recalled the flash of vulnerability in his eyes. And while his hair was in major need of a haircut, it had been thick and wavy, a rich brown tossed by the sea breeze. Roguish.

"Bran's been through a lot. He just moved here in February, too. The house is lovely, isn't it?"

"I didn't get to see much of anything. I took some pictures of the lighthouse, and then he stomped out and growled at me and made me delete all the photos I'd taken."

Tori frowned. "He's usually not quite that grumpy."

"He was downright rude." She sighed. "That lighthouse was it. I got the rush I get when I'm particularly inspired. If I could have kept one photo, I could have at least started a sketch."

Except she did have one photo. The one she'd taken of "Bran," now that she knew his name. Facing the ocean. She'd looked at it after her run, and had felt his loneliness.

Something else jiggled in her memory. "You said his name was Bran?"

"Short for Branson." Tori leaned forward. "Do you want me to take her now?" She held out her hands for the baby.

"She's asleep and fine here as long as you're okay with it."

"Are you kidding? When she's sleeping I get to relax." She sat back in her chair. "I just don't want to take advantage."

Jessica turned the name over and over in her mind. Branson. The dark hair, the eyes...

"Branson Black," she said, her voice a bit breathy. "That's him, isn't it? The author?"

Tori frowned. "He keeps a very low profile here. No one in town really knows who he is."

"Of course. It'd be like having Stephen King as your neighbor."

Tori laughed. "Not quite. He's not that famous."

Jess tucked the blanket closer around the baby. "He's pretty famous. And he hasn't published anything since—"

She halted. She remembered the story now. Since his wife and infant son had died in a car crash.

It all came together now. His isolation. Desolation. Growling to keep people away. He was buried in grief, a feeling she could relate to oh, so well. A pit opened in her stomach, a reminder of the dark days she'd had after Ana's death. And a well of sympathy, too. How devastated he must be.

She met Tori's gaze and sighed. "It was in the news."

Tori nodded. "I don't want to betray a confidence, you understand. But yes, he's been struggling with his grief."

"And values his privacy. I understand now." And her frustration melted away, replaced by sympathy.

"Do you?" Tori's eyes were sharp. "Because he's one of the best men I know. He's one of the reasons Jeremy and I are together."

Jess stared into the flickering fire. "A few years ago I lost my mentor and...well, the best friend a person could have. I'm just now starting to paint again. So yes, I get it. Grief can destroy the deepest and best parts of us if we're not careful."

Silence fell over the patio for a few minutes. Then Tori spoke up. "I'm sorry about your friend. And I agree with you. Which was why I sent you over there in the first place."

Jess's head snapped up. "You did?"

Tori nodded. "He needs someone to stir him up a bit. Looks like you did."

Jess wasn't too sure of that. But her heart gave a twist,

thinking of what he'd lost, what he was suffering and how alone he must feel. Because she'd been there. And she'd come out the other side.

He hadn't. And that made her sorry indeed.

CHAPTER TWO

BRAN HAD BEEN up for a walk at dawn, made himself break-fast, had thrown in a load of laundry and was now left with most of the day stretching before him. Each day he had the same ritual. Walk, eat, some sort of menial chore. Check email. Anything to procrastinate so he wouldn't spend hours staring at an empty document. He got through those daily rituals just fine, but the moment he opened up a new file on his laptop, he froze.

He wrote mysteries, and right now, anything dealing with a murder and victims was too much. Even though Jennie and Owen had been in a highway accident and not victims of violence, he just couldn't deal with the idea of dead bodies. The grief was too much. His memory was too vivid.

Instead, he went upstairs and out on the balcony. The fresh air bit at his cheeks, carrying the tang of the ocean as the sky spread blue and wide above him. The lighthouse stood sentinel at the corner of the property, and he shoved his hands in his jeans pockets, thinking of yesterday and the woman who'd shown up uninvited.

She was right. He'd been a jerk. Right now he didn't know how to be anything else. But he was slightly sorry for it. Maybe would be more sorry if she'd been hurt by his gruffness. Instead, she'd been annoyed, and her eyes had sparked with it. It was hard to be sorry for that. She had beautiful eyes, annoyed or not.

He'd been standing there for twenty minutes when a movement caught his eye, just off the shore. He frowned. Was that a boat? He squinted; the sun glinted off the water in blinding flashes, but yes, there was definitely a boat out there, maybe a few hundred yards off the coastline. Certainly no farther. The sea was still rough, and he watched the boat bob and rock, at the mercy of the waves.

Foolish person. The boat couldn't be more than maybe fifteen, sixteen feet. On a calm day, and with a skilled pilot, a boat like that could fare pretty well in open water. He'd certainly gone fishing in his and had no trouble at all. But today wasn't calm. The surf had been high since the storm earlier in the week, and whoever was at the wheel wasn't looking very competent, either. He frowned, and turned to get his binoculars from downstairs. When he returned, the boat was closer to shore, and still bobbing as it drifted.

He lifted the binoculars, focused in, and cursed.

What in hell was she doing? Foolish woman! Out there in a boat, camera around her neck, trying to take stupid pictures! Had he not made his point? He ran his hand through his hair and lifted the binoculars once more. A rolling wave hit the boat sideways, throwing her off balance. She fell, and his heart froze for a few moments as she disappeared from view. Had she hit her head? Was she okay? He held his breath until he saw her struggling to stand again. She turned the craft into the waves, and he hoped to God that she was going to give it some gas and get out of there. But she didn't. She wanted her pictures too badly. As she lifted her camera again, another heavy wave crested and knocked her to the side, while water splashed over boat and woman. If she wasn't careful, she'd be knocked overboard. Or worse…she'd be swept in toward the jagged rocks at the point. The lighthouse was there for a reason, after all.

Another wave swamped the boat and panic settled in his gut. He took off the binoculars and raced down the stairs, out the front door, and to the natural steps leading to his beach and the private dock. It took only a few moments for him to throw on a life vest and start the engine of the boat that was only slightly bigger than hers. He drew away from the dock and opened the throttle as he made his way toward her, his heart pounding as the boat lifted and bottomed out with each rolling wave. If she wasn't swept overboard, she was going to hit the rocks, and neither outcome was particularly appealing. The water was freezing, and while he was confident in his piloting skills, he wasn't so sure about his rescue ones. The only option was to get her out of there.

He got close enough to see that Jessica's delicate pale skin was even paler, her eyes wide with fear. Her jaw tightened as she saw that he was behind the wheel, and she waved him off. "I've got this!" she called. "Go away!"

His fear disintegrated and anger took its place. "Are you kidding me?" He pulled as close as he dared without danger of them crashing together. "You're either going to fall overboard or run into those rocks! Do what I tell you."

Her face flattened. "No man is going to tell me to—"

He swore, and loudly, and Jessica's mouth clamped shut in surprise. "I'm going to tow you back," he shouted. "No arguments. Now shut up and let me help."

When she didn't argue, he figured she'd either finally seen common sense or was too scared to do otherwise. It took several minutes for them to secure her boat to his, with the ominous cliffs of the point coming ever closer. Bran gritted his teeth and pushed the throttle forward, taking up the slack between the two boats as the motor labored to take them both into the oncoming waves and away from shore. Jessica, to his relief, had finally done what he'd told her and was sitting obediently in the captain's seat. The chop smoothed out as they got closer to the tiny cove sheltering his beach, and once they got close to the dock, he stopped, put down his anchor and pulled Jessica's boat close enough he could board. She stood, avoiding his gaze, and stepped away from the wheel.

He stepped in just as a wave sent her off balance and crashing into him.

She was damp from spray, and yet warm and soft as he caught her in his arms and their bodies meshed together awkwardly. Bran put his hands on her upper arms to steady her and push her away. But the damage was done. Her gaze caught his and her cheeks—already rosy from the wind and water—reddened. His gaze dropped to her full, pink lips and his irritation grew. It was bad enough she was a thorn in his side…it was too much that she was also adorable. She bit down on her lip, and he nearly groaned. Adorable wasn't quite the right word. Infuriating and… sexy, dammit.

He pushed his way around her. After disconnecting the towrope, he guided her little boat into his dock and secured it. He left her on the wooden platform and, ignoring the freezing temperatures, dove into the water. Perhaps it would help cool his temper, which was still raging.

The icy shock definitely cleared his mind. He wasted no time climbing the little ladder into his craft, then started the engine and guided it in to the dock. Soaked and shivering, he jumped out and glared at Jessica, who was standing on the dock, looking quite chastised and embarrassingly repentant.

He would not let that get to him. He would not. He focused on tying the knot and not on her frightened face and big eyes.

"Get your things and come to the house," he ordered, and he didn't wait to see if she followed or not. She would if she had any sort of sense at all.

But he didn't check; he heard her feet scrambling up the stone steps behind him. He hurried to the house and stripped off his shirt the moment he got in the door. Within five minutes he'd dumped his wet clothes in the tub and had on warm, dry jeans. He was walking toward the front door with his sweatshirt in his hand when he stopped short.

She'd come inside, just into the foyer, and stood staring at him and his bare chest. Her cheeks blossomed an awkward shade of pink, and she bit down on her lip as he shoved his arms in the sleeves and pulled the shirt over his head. But something strange threaded through him at her silent acknowledgment of...what? Attraction? Awareness? What a ridiculous thought.

He opened the door and guided her outside again, then put a set of keys in her hand. "Where did you get the boat?"

She cleared her throat, and the awkwardness dissipated as they were back on topic. "Cummins's, about a mile from the resort."

He knew the location. "Take my car and drive there. I'll take the boat back. Then I'll drop you at the resort and that's that."

"Branson, I..."

His gaze snapped to her. "How do you know who I am?"

She didn't answer, and he held back a sigh of frustration. It had to have been Tori or Jeremy. "It doesn't matter. Take the car."

He stalked off to the dock again. Damn woman was nothing but trouble.

It took thirty minutes to get to Cummins's boat rentals, and Jessica was already there, her backpack slung over one shoulder. Bran held on to his anger as he turned the boat over to John Cummins, then followed Jessica back to where she'd parked his car. He got in the driver's side and immediately hit his knees on the steering wheel; she'd moved the seat forward. Held back another curse word as he adjusted it, and turned onto the road leading back to the Sandpiper.

He never spoke to her once.

She never spoke to him, either.

The drive was short, and he dropped her in front of reception. Then, and only then, did she speak.

"Thank you," she said quietly, and backed away from the door, as if afraid to say more.

He didn't answer. She shut the door, and he put the car in gear and steered back onto the main road.

But a hundred yards up the road, he pulled over to the side and gulped for air as the shakes finally set in.

The shakes had held on for a long time, part of an anxiety attack that had been utterly debilitating. When he'd been good to drive again, he'd eased his way home, parked the car and had stood at his front door for ten solid minutes, knowing he should go inside, unsure of what he wanted to do when he was in there. The urge for Scotch was strong, so it was just as well he didn't have any. He didn't want to be alone, but the idea of having company was repulsive. The adrenaline in his body told him to pace; the idea of lying down on his long sofa and avoiding everything held similar attraction.

She could have died. Died! For being utterly foolish.

It was just a damned lighthouse. There were dozens along the coast. She could pick another one.

If he'd let her keep her pictures yesterday, this never

would have happened. And if she'd been hurt, or worse, today, that would have been his fault.

Like he didn't already have enough guilt. It was bad enough he had Jennie and Owen on his conscience. The last thing he wanted was to add to the tally of people he'd failed.

In the end he went inside and sat on the sofa, staring at the unlit fireplace. It didn't take a genius to figure out that his fear and anger were all tied up in Jennie and Owen, and how he hadn't been able to save them. Or how his selfishness was responsible for them being on the road in the first place. Jennie hated driving from their place in Connecticut into the city, but he'd been too busy to drive home to see them.

All his life he'd promised himself he'd be different from his father, who had always been too busy working to spend time with his wife and son. He'd promised himself he'd be there, and present, and cherish every moment so his kid would never feel alone or unloved. And he'd failed spectacularly.

Since he was too busy to go home, Jennie had been going to surprise him with a midweek visit while he was doing promo for his latest book.

And they'd never made it.

Jessica probably hated him. He certainly wasn't overly keen on her at the moment. But she was alive, and he'd take that as a win.

And hopefully that would be the last he'd see of her. Surely, after today, she'd learned her lesson.

Jessica felt like a complete and utter fool.

An online course and a few fun rides on the lake years ago, and she'd considered herself suitably experienced to be piloting a boat on rough waters. To Cummins's credit, he hadn't been keen on renting her the boat, but she'd assured him it was a short trip and she'd be fine. And she had been, at first. Until she got near the point at Bran's place.

She'd wanted to get the pictures and get gone. But the waves had been bigger than she'd expected, and more than once she'd hung over the side and retched. The crosscurrent had made everything more difficult, and one particular roll had knocked her down, her shoulder ramming against the fiberglass side.

It still hurt, but not as much as her pride.

She looked at the bruise forming on her shoulder and sighed, then gently put her arms in a soft sweater and pulled it over her head. The moment she'd seen Branson coming toward her, she'd been relieved and then embarrassed all at once. She didn't need rescuing, for Pete's sake. She'd never needed rescuing. She was very good at picking up when things went wrong and starting over. She'd done it when her adoptive parents had divorced. When her mom had died. When she'd lost jobs in the days before she could make a living with her art. After her horrible breakup. Even Ana hadn't rescued her...not really. She'd just appeared, ready to be a friend, a confidant, a professional mentor. She had made Jessica's life richer, but she hadn't saved it.

Today Jessica felt as if Branson Black had literally saved her life. She'd been reckless—not unlike her. But she'd got in over her head, and he'd come to her rescue. He hadn't been pleased about it, either. He hadn't even grunted when she said thank you when he dropped her off.

Twice now she'd got off on the wrong foot with him. Instead of sneaking photos from the water and never having to deal with him again, she'd made it more obvious than ever that she was a pain in his neck.

And for that, she needed to apologize.

She had no idea how to do that, but she'd come up with something. And kill him with kindness if she had to.

Room service sounded like a perfect idea, so she ordered and then took the memory card from her camera and popped it into her laptop. When she opened up the directory and brought up the first picture, she sighed. It was out of focus, but not too bad. But there were only two or three that were even close to being useful. Then the lens got wet and every single picture was blurred and smudged.

All of that for nothing. She'd only accomplished making him hate her even more. Tomorrow she would apologize. And then she'd find another lighthouse. Or something else that sparked her creativity and gave her the burn to create again. In the meantime she'd keep working, because nothing helped get the muse back in business like being ready for her.

CHAPTER THREE

BRAN WAS DRINKING coffee on his deck when he saw someone coming through the stand of trees toward his driveway.
He shifted over to the side so he'd be less conspicuous.
Maybe it was Tori, or Jeremy, though they usually called
first. It took only ten seconds for him to realize it was
Jessica. Again? Frustration burned with the coffee in his
mouth. Hadn't she caused enough trouble? What the heck
was it about his lighthouse that was so intriguing, anyway?

But instead of turning toward the lighthouse, she headed
straight for his front door.

Something twisted in his gut. He watched as she drew
closer, carrying a paper sack in her arms, her sunshiny
hair glinting in the morning sun. There was something so
pure about her, so bright and light. He waited out of sight
for her to go to the door; heard the knock echo both below
him and through the house.

He should answer. Yesterday he'd been so angry and
hopped up on adrenaline and fear that he hadn't said anything to her other than snapping at her to take his car to
the boat rental. Both their encounters had been antagonis-
tic, but last night, as he'd sat in the twilight, he'd realized
that yesterday's foolish actions could have been avoided
if he'd been nicer at the start and let her keep her photos.

Because he felt that responsibility, he was trying not to

be too angry with her. Letting go of his anger left room for other feelings, though. Ones he truly wasn't ready for nor desired. At the very least, discomfort at the sheer amount of time she was in his thoughts at all.

She knocked again. He should go down. And yet the idea of company, of small talk…what would he say? It was different when it was Jeremy or Cole or even Tori. And when he was out in public and didn't have to actually have conversations of any consequence. It was a hello and thank you to the cashier at the market. A thank you to the lady at the post office. What would they say…especially after yesterday?

In the end, he hesitated long enough that she abandoned the door and started back down the drive, only without the paper bag.

Whatever she'd brought with her, she'd left for him. An olive branch? And he was up here like a coward. While he wasn't feeling social, he didn't like that idea. There was nothing to be afraid of. At least today, no one was in any danger.

He stepped to the railing. "Miss Blundon."

She turned around and looked up, shading her eyes with her hand. "Oh! You're up there!"

Did she have to sound so delighted by the discovery? Surely seeing him wasn't exactly a pleasure. Not after the way he'd treated her.

"If you'll wait a few moments, I'll be right down."

"Of course." She smiled at him, a bright reward in his otherwise bleak day.

The whole way down the stairs he wondered what he was doing. He'd moved here to get away from people. To… work through his feelings without any burden of expec- tation. And now he was going to open the door to a red-headed sprite with eyes that snapped and a bright smile. As if yesterday had never even happened.

He'd say thank you for whatever was in the bag and send her on her way.

When he reached the door, she'd retrieved the bag and held it in her arms again, and met him with the same bright smile.

"Good morning!" she said, holding out the bag. "A peace offering for getting off on the wrong foot. Feet. Whatever. Twice."

Her babbling shouldn't have been charming. He instinctively reached for the bag, then regretted it because it meant automatic acceptance. He couched it in the crook of his arm, aimed a level stare at her and said, "Peace offering, or repentance for yesterday's shenanigans?"

Her eyes crinkled at the corners when she laughed, making her look adorable. "Both." She lifted an eyebrow, just a little. "But yes, peace offering. Because you were also mean, Branson Black."

He chuckled, the sound unfamiliar to him, and he fought to take it back but it was too late. Her grin widened.

"Mean?"

"Yes," she asserted firmly. "Mean. So I brought you some things to maybe help with that."

He looked in the bag. He could see a bottle of wine, a few packages of snacks, a pound of coffee and a mug. "What's all this?"

With a pleased expression, she said, "I figured you're either stressed and need a drink, are grouchy from hunger, or undercaffeinated." She hesitated, then added, "Yesterday notwithstanding. That was terrible judgment on my part, and I'm sorry."

He was charmed. He couldn't help it. Particularly because she was blunt and right. He had been mean. And yesterday she had shown terrible judgment.

"You're still after my lighthouse."

She sobered. "There are no strings attached to this gift. I didn't listen to you, and yesterday I acted impulsively. I could have been in danger, and you went to great trouble to make sure I was okay. This really is just a thank you."

He didn't want to like her, but he did. She was so up-front. And she didn't tiptoe around him, like anyone else who knew who he really was. He stepped back and opened the door wider, a silent invitation. He didn't always have to be rude. And she'd apologized, which he appreciated.

Truthfully, his ogre status was getting hard to maintain. It wasn't his normal way. It was just his way of punishing himself.

She stepped inside and halted in the foyer. "Now that's something. I didn't have a chance to tell you yesterday, but this—" she swept her arm out wide "—this makes a statement."

A table sat in the middle of the open space, while the hardwood staircase wound around it, forming a column that went to the top of the house. A skylight there beamed sunlight into the entry, a natural spotlight on the flower arrangement on the pedestal table.

"It does give some wow factor," Bran admitted.

"It sure does. This is a gorgeous place. Airy and roomy."

"Since you've only been three feet inside the foyer, would you like the twenty-five-cent tour?"

Did he really just say that?

"Sure. I promise to keep my camera in my tote bag this time."

He looked over, and her face held an impish expression that made his lips twitch. "Ha ha. Come on. I'll put this in the kitchen first."

He led her through the expansive downstairs. The kitchen was spacious and modern, and while he'd furnished one of the large living rooms, he'd left the other, the one closer to the den, unfurnished. She made appropriate sounds of approval at his den, and then they went upstairs, where she gave a cursory glance at the bedrooms and then sighed at the ensuite bath, which had a stunning view of the water. "Oh, man," she murmured, stepping inside. "A Jacuzzi tub with an ocean view. All you'd need is a book and a glass of wine and you'd be in heaven."

He was treated to a vision of what that might look like; her pale skin surrounded by bubbles and damp tendrils of hair down her neck…a long, wet leg and flushed cheeks from the heat of the bath. He tried, unsuccessfully, to shake the image from his mind. A better idea would be to get her out of his house. Or at least out of the upstairs.

She turned to him then and put a hand on his arm. "I have a confession to make. I figured out who you were after my first visit here. Now I kind of understand why you were so angry. I know I violated your privacy. I really did just come to say that I'm sorry. For everything, Mr. Black."

He hated being called Mr. Black. It reminded him of his father, who had insisted on it from nearly everyone. The only person he'd ever heard call him Peter was his mother. And it had always been Peter, and never Pete. "Branson," he replied, taken aback by her honest little speech. "And I was rude. You're right. I didn't have to be such an ass."

She laughed. "Thanks for the tour, but I should probably get going."

She slid by him, trailing a scent of something that reminded him of lily of the valley.

It really had been a peace offering, then. She hadn't pressed her case about the lighthouse. Hadn't asked him a thing about his books or his family…and what happened was no secret. It had been all over the internet and made it to several print publications. The one good thing about being an author was that his face was less recognizable than other celebrities. Clearly it hadn't escaped her notice, though.

Then again, she was somewhat of a celebrity herself, at least in the art world. Or so it would seem.

"Miss Blundon?"

She turned around and smiled. "If I have to call you Branson, you have to call me Jess."

"Jess." It suited her. "About yesterday... I own part of the blame. If I hadn't been such a jerk, you wouldn't have had to rent a boat. What I'm saying is...if you want to take some pics of the lighthouse, that would be okay."

The way her face lit up made him glad he'd said it. Her eyes sparkled, and her smile was wide and free and full of joy. How long had it been since he'd felt such an unfettered, positive emotion?

Not even at Jeremy and Tori's wedding had he felt so light. Their wedding had been a happy, wonderful occasion, but bittersweet for Bran. He'd been remembering his own wedding day years earlier.

But this was simpler. Granting a small favor, really, and it felt good.

"Really? I'd love that! Would it be possible to do a few sketches while I'm here?"

How could he say no now? Suddenly he realized he'd put himself in an awkward position. He'd thought a few pictures wouldn't hurt. But he wasn't sure he wanted her hanging around.

Her smile faded, and she put a hand on his arm. "I'm sorry. If it's too much, just say so."

The warmth of her hand seeped into his skin. Her fingers were strong, elegant and slim, like a pianist's, and unadorned with any rings or nail polish. Was he enjoying the contact a little too much?

"A few sketches would be okay," he answered, then cleared his throat. "I won't jump down your throat if I see you at the lighthouse, okay?"

She squeezed his arm. "You mean I have permission to access it?"

He had no idea why he was going along with this, other than the fact that he knew he'd been horribly grouchy the day before, and he didn't like that about himself. "Yes, that's what I mean."

Her gaze softened. "Thank you," she said quietly. "I've had such a hard time lately, and this is the first place that's really fired up my creativity. It means more than you know."

He could relate. He hadn't written a word in nearly two years. But he merely nodded as she turned away and started down the stairs. He followed closely behind, not too closely, though. And wondered at the strange feeling settling in the middle of his chest. It was pleasure mixed with anxiety, an odd combination of enjoying the contact while feeling like it was a foreign sensation.

Had he been hiding away too long?

He walked her to the door, feeling more unsure of himself with each step. When they reached the threshold, she opened the door and stepped outside, then turned around to face him.

"I know this probably sounds presumptuous and odd, but do you think we could be friends?"

He chuckled dryly. "That is not what I expected you to say."

She shrugged. "Just to clear the air, I read the news. I'm very sorry for your loss, and I understand that it takes time to recover from something like that. I lost someone very special to me around the same time."

He swallowed around the lump that had suddenly appeared in his throat. "Thank you."

"And I just started painting again. So just so you know, giving me access to the lighthouse actually means a lot. There were times I thought I'd never feel that passion again, but here I am." She spread her arms wide.

She didn't say that he'd get there too. Didn't give assurances that all he needed was time. Simply said that it meant a lot to her. He appreciated that more than she could know. He'd just about had it with the well-meaning but empty platitudes.

"You're welcome," he replied, his voice rough.

There was a pause while he searched for the right way to say goodbye. She shifted her weight to her other hip and then smiled again. "Okay, so I'd better go. Have a good day, Branson."

"You too. And thank you for the peace offering." He attempted to smile back and saw her eyes widen. Wow. Did he really smile so rarely that it came as a complete surprise?

"Okay...bye, then." She took a step backward, then gave a little wave before turning away from him and heading across the lawn toward the bluff and the red-and-white sentinel standing guard.

He shut the door, then went to his den. The broad expanse of windows gave him a perfect view, and he watched as she picked her way over rocks and bumps, her footsteps sure and light. She pulled out her camera and started snapping, and after a while put it away and pulled out a sketch pad. A half smile on his face, he shook his head as she picked a large rock for a seat, plopped herself on it and started to draw.

Then he sat down and opened his laptop. Stared at the screen for a few minutes, then opened his browser.

He wasn't quite ready. But for the first time since losing Jennie and Owen, he felt that someday he might be.

Jess hadn't planned to stay at the Sandpiper so long, and when Tori offered up her boathouse as an alternative place to stay, Jess snapped it up immediately. The building was adorable, with a warm and welcoming red door, tons of natural light, the coziest of galley kitchens and a single bedroom. The bunk beds inside had a small double on the bottom and a single on the top, so she put her clothes in the tiny dresser and made herself comfortable on the mattress with the cheery comforter sporting nautical designs in navy, red and white.

According to Tori, she and Jeremy had considered making it a vacation rental. But they were waiting to do that since Tori's time was taken up with being a brand-new mom. Jess stared up at the bottom of the bunk above her and let out a happy sigh. She'd take this over a hotel room any day.

After a twenty-minute nap, she got up and went to the kitchen to make a cup of tea. While it was steeping, she looked around the tiny living room and examined the light sources. Sketching wasn't a big deal. If she wanted to paint, she had different requirements for light and space. A few adjustments and she'd moved some of the furniture, pushing it closer to the wall. The wicker rocking chair found a new home on the sweet white-railed porch, and she wondered if Tori would be amenable to taking out the coffee table altogether. Then it would be just about right.

But she wasn't ready to start painting yet. Today she'd started some preliminary sketches that she liked but wasn't crazy over. Carrying her tea, sketch pad and pencils, she went to the porch and sat in the afternoon sun, sipping and contemplating. She turned the page over and started something different. Just the very edge of the lighthouse intruded on the right-hand side of the paper; and then, just to the left of center, she started moving her pencil, beginning an outline of a man, hands in his pockets, staring out to sea.

There was something captivating about him. She wanted to say that it wasn't because of his celebrity, but now that she knew, it kind of was. She'd read one or two of his books...figured he'd released something like ten now, maybe a dozen. Mysteries and procedurals, where she couldn't wait to turn another page and was afraid to at the same time. She admired a brain like that, so willing to wander into the darkness and face it unflinchingly, and with such detail. Now, having met him, and knowing he was grieving, she had another impression. In all his books, there was still a thread of hope through them. The bad guy always got what was coming to him. The main characters always came through with a happy ending.

He didn't get his happy ending, though. She knew how that felt. Broken hearts, crushed dreams. Jess had never quite had the family she'd always wanted. And as she made sweep after sweep on her pad, she saw the outline of a broken man coming through.

She didn't notice the time until the sun went behind the trees, dimming her light. She'd been working for hours, and she tilted her neck, working out a creak. With a sigh she picked up her phone and checked her messages. There was one from Tori, inviting her up for drinks later. She checked the time...inviting her for drinks in twenty minutes, to be exact. She'd worked throughout the late afternoon and what normally would have been dinner. She went inside, closing the red door behind her, and opened the fridge. She wasn't about to have drinks on an empty stomach, so she took out a container of hummus and nibbled on some crackers and veggies. Her hair was tucked in a bun and held there with a pencil, but she didn't really care. It was Tori and Jeremy, and they seemed like the most laid back people she'd ever met. On went her flat sandals, a quick smooth over her flowy skirt, and she was off along the gravel path to the main house.

Branson's car was in the driveway and she hesitated, wondering if Tori had asked him to join them. They'd made peace yesterday, but she wasn't sure she was ready for couples drinks and a social call where he was concerned. She nearly turned back when Tori's voice called her name. She couldn't turn around now and pretend she hadn't heard. Her careless hair and slightly wrinkled skirt would have to do. And she could fake her way through small talk, couldn't she?

"Hi!" she called out, skirting the house and heading to the backyard patio. Clearly this was where the action was in the Fisher house. She shivered; it was only May, and she hadn't thought to bring a sweater.

"Hi yourself," Tori offered. "I'm out here grabbing Rose's blanket. I left it out earlier. Come on inside."

Grateful to be going inside for the visit, Jess let out a breath and held the door as Tori went in, her arms full of baby and blanket. Jeremy was at the island pouring drinks. "Hey, Jess," he said. "Glad you could come up."

"Jess?"

She turned around abruptly. Bran was there, at the end of the hall, staring at her. Oh, Lord. He hadn't known she was invited. Her face heated and then together they stared at Tori, whose eyebrows lifted in an expression of innocence.

"What? Jess is staying in our boathouse so she can

paint. And you haven't been over in a week. What's the big deal?"

Bran leveled his gaze on her. "Because you set it up, Miss Innocent."

Great. He had no desire to be there with her. And she wasn't exactly comfortable, but she wouldn't have put it precisely that way. Then again, her initial encounters with Branson had demonstrated his usual manner was blunt.

Jess stared at both of them, then over at Jeremy, who cracked open a can of tonic water. "Don't look at me," he said, pouring the fizzy liquid into a glass.

Tori kept the innocent look on her face. "What? You guys can be civil, right? Lord, it's not like I set you up on a blind date or something."

Except it felt like it. Jeremy pressed a glass of merlot into her hands with a murmur of, "Humor her." The glass of tonic and lime went to Tori. "Bran?" he asked. "What are you having?"

"That tonic will be fine. I'm driving, after all."

Huh. That was surprising. She admired his zero tolerance attitude. "I'm lucky I just have to walk down the path," she said, trying to lighten the awkward atmosphere. "The boathouse is perfect, Tori. I was wondering though if there's somewhere I could put the coffee table? The living room is perfect for me to work."

"Of course!" Tori sat on the sofa and Jess sat beside her, and they immediately started chatting about the boathouse, the decorations and Jess's future plans for it. It was a good distraction from glancing at Bran the whole time, who was still looking rather hermit-like, but with a pressed shirt and his hair tucked behind his ears. The first time they'd met, she'd thought him to be in his forties, but now she thought it was probably younger. Midthirties, maybe. She tried to imagine him with a man bun and nearly laughed out loud. That wasn't for Bran.

He was too… She frowned. *Too much* was all she could seem to come up with. Jeremy said something and Bran chuckled, a low, rough vibration that reached in and ignited something in her belly. Oh, no. This was not a good thing. He was far easier to dismiss as a grouchy old ogre. She didn't actually want to like him. Or feel the stirrings of, if not attraction, curiosity. She was after his lighthouse. Nothing more. Even if she had started to sketch him earlier today.

Jeremy got up and refilled her wineglass and she settled back down into the sofa, relaxing more. She had friends, of course she did. But over the last few days she had thought back to those relationships. Some were lifers. Some had been relationships of utility, for a time only and then moving on or drifting apart. Some had been intense and brief, leaving her an empty vessel at the end. She listened to Jeremy and Branson and heard that rusty laugh again… They had been friends since they were boys. Jeremy drew her and Tori into the conversation with tales from Merrick Hall, the prep school he and Bran had attended together. Before long they were laughing, and Jessica was wondering about the third best friend, Cole, who sounded like the instigator of the bunch. How wonderful it must be to have friends like that. Like she'd been with Ana. There were times she just missed her so much.

She was just lifting her glass to take a sip when Bran's gaze reached over and held hers. Unlike their other meetings, this time his eyes were warm and hypnotizing, his lips holding the tiniest bit of humor, slightly hidden by his beard. Her body responded; there was something untamed about him that drew her in. Which sounded silly, of course.

He was anything but uncivilized. Perhaps it was just his restless energy. Whatever it was, she couldn't look away.

Tori appeared with some crudités and crackers, and Jess averted her eyes and instead focused on fixing a cracker with soft cheese and red pepper jelly. It was delicious, and since she'd missed having a real meal at dinnertime, a welcome addition to her stomach after two glasses of wine. When baby Rose woke and needed attending, Jess felt it was time to make her excuses and head home. Tori would be wanting to settle the baby and get some rest.

Bran seemed to agree, because he stood and collected glasses from the coffee table. "Thanks for having me over," he said, taking them to the kitchen.

"It's good for the hermit to come out of his cave once in a while."

Jess couldn't help it. She snorted as she carried dirty plates to the sink. Tori grinned and Jeremy gave Bran a slap on the back.

"Hey, I get out." Bran aimed a sharp look at Jess, a teasing glint in his eye. "I mean two days ago is a prime example."

"Branson," she said firmly, wishing he wouldn't tell this story. But Tori and Jeremy were staring at them both, and Branson smiled. She really wished he wouldn't do that. His smile was devastating.

"What happened?" Jeremy took the bait.

Jess attempted a preemptive strike. "Branson gave me a lift to the resort from the boat rental place, that's all." She pinned Bran with a "please don't do it" glare.

"What were you doing at the boat rental place?"

"I'd rented a boat."

"But what was Bran doing there?"

He lifted his eyebrows and grinned again. "Come on, Jessica. It's a good story."

"It's embarrassing."

"Hey, you laughed at the story about my underwear earlier. Fair's fair."

He was right. She'd giggled at the antics of the boys at boarding school, while sympathizing with the children they'd been, finding love and acceptance among strangers rather than at home. She was going to say he'd been thirteen at the time, but she also knew Tori was not going to let them leave without him spilling the beans. She sighed and capitulated. "Fine."

She shouldn't have worried. It became crystal clear that Bran was a born storyteller. Tori rocked Rose in her arms and Jeremy stopped putting dishes in the dishwasher as Bran told the tale with suspense in all the right spots, a dash of humor here and there, and without making her sound utterly stupid. Even she was caught up in it, and she was the subject! He finished with, "So I gave her the car and I took the boat back to Cummins's, and then dropped her off at the resort."

Tori shook her head. "What an adventure!"

Jess folded her hands. "Well, all's well that ends well. Rather than see me risk my own neck again, Branson let me take some pictures of the lighthouse, so I don't anticipate any new nautical mishaps for a good long while."

"You brought me food. What was I going to say?"

She laughed. "You could have kicked me off your property like you did the first day. Or ignore me altogether."

"Ignoring you would only have made you do something crazier."

She suddenly realized that Jeremy and Tori were watching them with amused expressions. "And on that note, I think it's time I headed to the boathouse. Thank you both for inviting me up."

"Don't be silly. We're friends now. You can stay in the

boathouse as long as you need. You can be our vacation rental trial run. And the door is always open. It's nice having you around."

"I'd better head out too," Bran said. "New parents need their sleep."

He said it easily, but Jess caught a glimpse of something on his face, a tension around his mouth that hadn't been there before. He and Jeremy were best friends. It had to be a painful reminder to see his friend happily married with a new baby, when Bran had had those things and lost them.

"I'll be in touch about the property for Cole," Jeremy said, oblivious to Bran's expression. "You can help me with that if you like. Something new just came on the market that might be perfect."

"Sounds good," Bran said.

He followed Jess to the front door, and they waved goodbye to their hosts. She expected him to head to his car while she took the path to the boathouse, but he fell into step beside her.

"What are you doing?"

"Walking you home."

She sighed. "It's not necessary. I'm not in danger of capsizing on my way to the boathouse."

"No, but you also didn't turn a light on."

Darn, he was right. The boathouse loomed in the darkness, and she could make out the form of the porch, but she hadn't turned on the outside light.

"The light attracts bugs," she explained.

He chuckled. She wished he would stop doing that. It made her insides all warm and tingly.

Their feet made soft crunching noises on the graveled path. Jess could hear the sound of the ocean shushing against the sand, and somewhere nearby, in a tall tree, an owl hooted. She sighed, loving the solitude and peace of this place. "That's a great horned owl," she said softly. "Who cooks for you?"

"What?"

"Listen to his call. *Who cooks for you?*"

The owl hooted again, and Bran murmured, "Well, I'll be damned."

She smiled in the darkness. It took only another few moments and they were at the porch of the boathouse. "I didn't lock the door," she said, "so I don't need to see the lock. Thank you for walking me, though."

"You're welcome."

"Branson?"

It sounded odd, using his first name, but after yesterday's rescue, it hardly seemed necessary to call him Mr. Black.

"Yes?"

His voice was husky in the dark. She held in a sigh.

"You are a wonderful storyteller. I was so afraid you were going to throw me under the bus in there. But you didn't. You made it sound like some great adventure. Even I was waiting to hear what happened next, and I was there."

"Thanks."

She put her hand on his arm. It was firm and warm beneath her fingers. "What I'm trying to say is…don't give up."

Silence fell between them for a few moments, and Jess found herself looking into his dark gaze. The shadows only lent to the intimacy of the moment, and briefly she wondered if he were going to kiss her.

But then the moment seemed to pass, and she took her hand off his arm. She'd said enough, and hopefully had given him something to think about. "Good night," she whispered, then went inside and shut the door.

CHAPTER FOUR

FOR THREE DAYS Branson watched as Jessica sketched at the lighthouse. After the first day, he left the gate open so she wouldn't have to walk so far. He'd spent his time doing some research. Not for a book, but on the lighthouse he now owned. He wanted to know more about the history of it, and so he'd dug into Google, visited the local library and accessed the provincial archives. The lighthouse was over a century old, made defunct after World War II, and most importantly, he'd found a book from the seventies with ghost stories and local lore at the library that he found most intriguing. His lighthouse had a history, with enough mystery to have his mind turning a plot over and over in his mind.

"You are a wonderful storyteller," she'd said. The compliment had taken him by surprise. He wasn't even sure why he'd felt compelled to recount the incident at all; maybe to prove to Jeremy that he wasn't the hermit everyone said he was. Maybe because he'd missed it. Or maybe just because he'd enjoyed the evening so much, and seeing the gleam in Jessica's eyes.

Her eyes were rather extraordinary.

He took his glass of iced water upstairs and went out on the balcony. He could see the point so clearly here, and Jess had started bringing a folding chair rather than perching on a rock to do her sketching. He'd been watching her for a few hours now, wondering if she'd put sunscreen on her fair skin; the spring sun was still capable of delivering a sunburn even though the temperatures were cool, particularly near the water. After a while he wondered if she'd eaten anything all day. He certainly hadn't seen her put her work aside to break for lunch. Did she get a crick in her neck sitting like that, as he did when he sat at his computer too long?

And why was he standing here thinking of all these questions?

It was going on two when he emerged from the house carrying a plastic bag in lieu of any sort of picnic basket. The wind buffeted his shirt and the chill reached inside him, even as the sun warmed the top of his head. Jessica didn't hear him approach until he was a handful of steps away from her, then she looked up and a smile lit her face. It had been an unconscious response, he realized, and the idea that she'd been glad to see him sent a spiral of warmth through his body.

It was only some lunch. Nothing major. He didn't need to feel…guilty. They were friends. Maybe not even friends. More like *friendly*.

"Hi," she greeted, putting down her pencil. "What brings you out here?"

He lifted his hand. "Food. I don't think you've eaten, and the last thing I need is you fainting and falling off a cliff and me having to rescue you again."

She laughed, that light, easy sound he'd enjoyed the other night, too. He even smiled a little in response.

"I promise I would not faint. Or fall off a cliff. I'm made of tough stuff. But I am hungry. What time is it?"

"Nearly two."

"Oh, my." She stretched her neck, first lifting her face

to the sky, then leaning it toward her right shoulder. "I had no idea."

Bran lifted the bag. "It's not much, but I thought you could use a bite."

"That's very kind of you."

He handed her the bag and then moved away, turning to face the house again.

"Aren't you going to join me?"

He shouldn't want to. That he did—very much—was exactly why he shouldn't. He turned back to face her and hesitated, long enough for her to nod at the flat rock nearby. "There's room for both of us there, and I'll share."

A part of him said, *What would it hurt?* while a second part reminded him that Jennie and Owen would never again have picnics on a cliff on a spring day.

Jessica got up from her seat and tucked her sketch pad and pencils away in her bag, then grabbed the lunch bag and went to his side. "You have that hermit look on your face again. What is it?"

"I shouldn't be here."

"Why?"

She asked the simplest and hardest questions.

Then she reached down and took his hand. "Is it because it feels too much like living again?"

He pulled his hand away. "Stop it. Stop trying to get into my head."

She didn't get upset. Didn't get mad or sad or indignant. That might have been easier. Instead, she just looked at him, her face open and honest and dammit, compassionate. "I'm sorry." Her voice was quiet and sincere. "You have to get through this on your own time. Thank you for the lunch. It's very thoughtful."

He started walking back to the house. Got about fifty feet and turned back, his stomach churning. She was sitting on the rock, peering inside the bag and looking lonely. He'd snapped at her when she hadn't deserved it. "Yes," he called out, and she lifted her head. "Yes, because of that."

Jessica nodded, then shifted over and patted the rock beside her. "The invitation is still open, and I'll mind my own business."

He doubted that. And the odd thing about it was that he wasn't sure he wanted her to. There were so many feelings bubbling inside him, feelings he hadn't been able to share with his family, or even with Jeremy and Cole. He could just imagine the looks on their faces if he shared his deepest thoughts. Those thoughts were pretty dark. But how long could he hold them inside?

Slowly, he made his way back to her and sat on the rock, resting his elbows on his knees. "Here," she said, taking half the chicken sandwich he'd made and handing it to him. "Eat half. There's too much in here for me anyway."

He took the sandwich and took a bite. She did the same, and after she chewed and swallowed, she lifted her face to the sun again, drinking it in. He stared at the column of her neck and had trouble swallowing his bite of sandwich.

When she lowered her chin, he took another bite and moved his focus to the sea spread out before them. True to her word, she didn't say anything. Just ate the lunch he'd prepared—the sandwich, some sliced apples and a couple of cookies he'd had in the pantry—and drank the water bottle full of lemonade he'd put inside.

She took a drink and then offered it to him. He accepted, took a long pull of the sweet and tart liquid, and then handed it back.

"Your lemonade is very good." She smiled as she offered the compliment, and then bit into a chocolate chip cookie.

"Thanks."

She grinned. "After your stories last night, I kind of thought you might have servants to help with things like picnic packing."

Bran angled her a sideways glance, and realized she was attempting to lighten the mood by teasing him. "Oh, my parents still do. The perks of an affluent childhood— never having to lift a finger."

"Or have the satisfaction of accomplishment?"

His lips dropped open in surprise. "Yes, I suppose." He pondered for a moment. "I guess that's the difference between entitlement and actual achievement, isn't it?"

"There's something rewarding about self-sufficiency."

Jess's lips set in a line as she said it. He wanted to ask her what she meant, but was afraid of either of them prying too deeply into past issues. Instead, he turned to the topic at hand, and gestured toward her bag with her sketching materials.

"Your drawings are coming along okay?"

She nodded. "I'm having so much fun. It's a combination of things, I think. The location is simply amazing. But I also think I finally got to a place mentally where I am ready to create again. It feels like the magic happens from both things coming together at the same time. Just the sketching is giving me so much joy."

He hesitated for a long moment, then said, "Do you ever feel guilty for being happy?" He couldn't look at her, but he felt her gaze on him. Nerves churned in his belly just asking the question. Not that he was happy. He wasn't. But could he go through his whole life like this? Did he want to?

"You mean do I feel guilty moving on after grieving someone so close to me?"

He nodded, unable to speak. It seemed they were going to get into the difficult subjects anyway.

"Not now. But I did for a long time. I felt as if I didn't deserve to be happy. That I somehow owed it to Ana to be miserable. And so I was." After a pause she added, "It's a hell of a way to live. I did the same after my mother died, though it was different. My parents divorced when I was ten. I guess I just... I don't know. Didn't feel as emotionally safe with my family as I did with my best friend. She'd never given me a reason to doubt. Besides, I think we grieve different people in different ways."

Another few moments of silence, and then she spoke again. "And I didn't lose my spouse and my child. I can't know what you're going through, Branson. I just know that someday you should be happy again, and not feel as if you're betraying them by moving on."

Tears stung the back of his eyes. She had spoken in a plain manner, with truth and gentleness, and said words that not even his best friends could manage. They tried to bring him back to the world of the living, but they didn't talk about the grief. It was painful relief to be able to do so.

"It's been two years. Owen would have been three now. We might have had more children. And I can't remember..." He swallowed heavily, fighting tears. "I can't remember the exact sound of his voice when he said *Dada*. Why can't I remember that?"

He didn't realize he was actually crying until Jessica put the bag aside and shuffled over, putting her arms around him. Then he noticed the wetness in his beard and on his cheeks. He was mortified to be falling apart in front of her, but he was helpless to stop it.

"It's okay," she said, rubbing his back. "Every single thing you feel and say is okay. There is no one way to grieve and no timetable."

He sniffed and rubbed his hands over his face. "I'm so

sorry. A week ago I was yelling at you and now I'm bawling all over you."

"Don't apologize. I get it. It's probably easier with someone you don't know." Her hand still made circles on his back, and it felt warm and reassuring. He'd been so touch starved. He should move away, but he wasn't ready to yet. She rested the crest of her cheek on his shoulder for a moment. "When Ana died, it was like all the light went out of everything. She was my rock and my best friend. She'd seen me through creative slumps and successes. Through relationships that came and went…she was my person. When I lost her, I lost my anchor and my compass all at once. But eventually I realized that she would be so angry with me for not living.

"It wasn't like flipping a switch, you know? It wasn't like I decided to live again and just started doing it. I had to take baby steps. I stumbled a lot. I pushed through when joy was just not showing up. But happiness is a little like creative inspiration. Sometimes we can't sit around and wait for it to show up. Sometimes we need to go looking for it. Or at least put ourselves out there so we can grab pieces of it when it rushes by."

"I don't know how to do that."

"You will. Something will snag in your brain, and you'll feel the urge to write it down. Or little snippets will come to you, and you'll write a bit and hate it, maybe, but little by little it'll happen. And when it does, you mustn't feel guilty about it."

"Is that how it's been for you?"

She nodded against his shoulder. "At first I started little random sketches. Then I thought I'd travel around and try to get back in the groove again. This past week, here? I finally feel energized and excited to work on something. And I know Ana would want me to."

"What happened to her?"

Jessica paused, then sighed, a sorrowful sound that made him want to hug her back. "She had cancer. One day she was fine. The next day she had stage four pancreatic cancer. In less than three months she was gone."

He could hear the grief in her voice, and he reached over and put his hand over hers. "I'm sorry."

"Thank you."

They sat, comfortable with quiet, for a few minutes. Then Jessica leaned away, taking her arms from around him, letting out a sigh. "It really is beautiful here. So wild and untamed."

Gulls swooped overhead, and Bran let the sun soak into his skin as the dull roar of the ocean on the rocks below filled his ears. "It can be lonely," he admitted. "And comforting at the same time."

"I get that," she agreed. She looked over at him. "You okay now?"

He nodded. "I am. Sorry I got all emotional."

"You don't have to apologize to me," she replied. Then she smiled. "Though I do think this qualifies us as actual friends now."

His gaze dropped to her lips. He shouldn't be thinking it, but he wasn't sure she was the kind of woman he could ever be just friends with. It was probably good she was just here for a short time.

"Friends," he echoed. "You're sure?"

"You brought me lunch. We shared stuff. Pretty sure that makes us friends." She leaned back onto her arms. He smiled as he looked over at her. She was so artless. Now she was sunning herself like a lizard on a rock. He did like her. Very much.

"Well, then," he answered, and adopted a similar posture. They sat for several minutes, until the sun went under

a cloud and the wind took on a chilly bite. "I should probably pack up for the day," Jessica said on a sigh. "I'm going
to lose the best light."

"How much longer are you staying on the South Shore?"

She shrugged. "I don't know. A month? Two? Tori and
Jeremy have said I can rent the boathouse for as long as I
need. I'm going to start painting soon."

There was a hesitation in her voice that told him maybe
she wasn't quite ready yet, but he wasn't going to call her
on it. As she said, it took baby steps. If she was finding
joy, he was happy for her.

And maybe one day he'd find joy, too.

Jessica pressed the cell phone to her ear and let out a sigh.
"I know, Jack. I know. It's been a long time. But I don't
want this to be rushed. For God's sake, I haven't even
started the actual paintings."

His voice was sharp and clear. "Sure, but you're excited.
I can tell. And we can set up a showing now for fall. I just
need the commitment from you."

She pinched the top of her nose with two fingers.
"That's too fast. The fact that I'm even working again is a
blessing. I don't want to add the pressure of a show when
I might only get one decent painting from this summer.
I'm sorry Jack, but the answer's no."

He softened his voice. "Hey, I know you're scared.
Coming back is hard. The world just needs more Jessica
Blundon art. You're going to be back in Chicago by the
fall, right?"

"I was planning on it. I can stay here for a few months,
but I do have to go home sometime."

"Then let me do some asking around. We might be able
to work something really innovative without booking an
actual show. An exclusive, a handful of paintings maybe.

Tie it in with something else. Just say you'll stay open to possibilities."

She laughed a little. "I always stay open to possibilities. And you are too coercive for your own good, Jack."

"Which is why I'm your best agent." Affection and teasing came over the line, and she relaxed a bit. "I don't want to stifle your creativity with pressure, but I also don't want you to miss out on opportunities. I'll be in touch."

"All right."

"Love you, kiddo."

Her eyes stung a little from the easy declaration. "I love you too, Jack. Thanks for not bailing on me."

"Never. Chat soon."

She hung up the call and sighed. The idea of having a showing in the autumn was exciting, but she was sure she wouldn't be ready. While she was ready to work, and even enthusiastic, there was no guarantee that every single work would be ready to show. For now she wanted to create and just revel in the process again. Feel the brush in her hand, the pressure of the bristles on canvas like a beautiful, private language only she could understand. The colors and the smell of paint and turpentine, acrid and as much a scent of home to her as bread baking or apple pie. The scrape of the palette knife. The process was the essence of who she was. She didn't care about shows or accolades. Right now feeling like herself again was all she wanted to focus on.

The rest would come. In time.

She was late getting to the lighthouse because of Jack's call, and the wind was particularly brutal, whipping her hair out of its braid and lifting the corners of her sketch pad. She clipped them down and tried to ignore the gusts that slapped at her, instead focusing on the door of the lighthouse. It was beautifully scarred, the rusty hinges crooked but strong enough that the door didn't droop. It looked as if it hadn't been used in ages, maybe decades, and the battered boards seemed almost like a fingerprint of what time had wrought.

At the foot of the door, just to the side, was a small clump of daisies, stubbornly blooming against the elements and in the rocky soil. Jessica dashed her pencil across the paper, capturing their proud, resilient heads. She smiled, and wrote along the bottom right corner, *Marguerite*. It was the French word for *daisy*, and it felt right.

"Good afternoon."

She jumped, grateful that her soft pencil hadn't been against paper. Bran stood just beside her and behind, his hands in his pockets. "Sorry," he said. "I didn't mean to scare you."

"It's so windy I didn't hear you." She rolled her shoulders. "I've been admiring the daisies. Pretty stubborn to be blooming amid all this salt and rock."

He looked over her shoulder at her sketch. "You like the door."

"It has character. And secrets."

To her surprise, a smile spread across his face. "Are you interested in finding out what some of those secrets are?"

"What do you mean?"

He took a key from his pocket. It was big and old, and she wondered if it would still work. "It works," he said, as if reading her mind. "I had the building inspected before I closed the purchase. The structure is old, but it's sturdy."

Excitement bloomed in her chest. "Of course I want to see inside!" She gave him some side-eye. "Unless it's overrun with mice. In which case I'm not too keen."

"Fair enough. And I haven't been inside either, by the way. First sign of rodents, we're out."

She stood up and tucked her sketch pad away. "Are you kidding? You haven't gone in, not once? You've been here since…"

"February," he supplied. "And it is damned cold here in February. Now though… I'm curious. I thought you might be, too."

"I am. I've never been inside an actual lighthouse before."

This one was small compared to many, but she was interested to see what surprises and treasures were inside. Bran went to the door and fiddled for a while, jiggling the key in the lock. "I wonder if the salt rusted the lock?" he mused, but then the key seemed to find home and turned over with a solid click.

The hinges creaked as he pushed the door open.

She followed behind, stepping into the hollow-sounding space that closed out the sound of the wind. The bottom of the lighthouse was simply a large, single room. An old army cot was against one wall, with a wool blanket heavy with dust covering the mattress. There was a table and chairs there, too, and an oil lantern—empty—sitting on the table. A space jutted out from the otherwise square base of the lighthouse, and a wood stove was in the corner, the flue vented out through the top of the addition. When Bran went to examine it, she stopped him. "Don't," she said quickly. "I promise I'm not usually a wimp, but I have visions of that stove either being full of mice or that birds have made a nest in there."

He chuckled and stepped back. "I'll explore that on my own, then."

"Thank you." She shuddered. She hated mice, and she also hated the thought of a bird flying out of the iron stove and getting trapped in the room.

"It's pretty plain, isn't it?"

She wandered over to the army cot, pushed up against the wall. What a lonely spot. "Was there ever a lighthouse keeper?"

He nodded. "The lighthouse was made defunct in the late forties, after the war. But before that there was. And one before him. Back to 1893, when the lighthouse was built. There was a house, too, but it burned in the twenties, apparently."

She was intrigued. The light in the room was dark and gloomy, thanks to a lack of windows. A sparse amount of sunshine traveled down to the bottom level from a singular window above, along the staircase that led to the actual lamp. She went to the staircase and looked over at him. "I'm lighter. I'll go first and make sure it's sound."

"Please be careful."

She smiled in reply and turned her attention to the rough steps leading to the top. The spiral staircase was narrow, but solid, and Jessica held on to the handrail as she climbed up...and up...and up, Branson's footsteps close behind. She reached a trapdoor at the top, and with a little help from Branson, released the closure and pushed it open.

Light poured in, brash and cheery, along with a gust of cool air. Apparently the windows at the top were not airtight, and the wind gusted around the structure, whistling eerily through the cracks.

Jessica had never been a big fan of heights, but she couldn't deny the view was spectacular. She could see for miles—up and down the coast, and also inland, to where the main road cut through the trees and clearings where other houses were built. None of them were as grand as Bran's.

"Wow," Branson said, standing close behind her. There wasn't much room in the top, and she could feel the warmth of his body near her back. "It's tiny. But look at the size of the lamp."

She looked. "I can't even see a bulb or anything. Is there one?"

"I think it's so old it might have been a lantern. And all these lenses. Cool, right?"

It was cool. It was one of the neatest things she'd ever seen. And the lenses...so many angles and slivers of light and texture. She wished she'd brought her camera. Wondered if Bran would let her come in here again. She thought about the challenge of painting simply *light*. Tingles ran down her arms and she turned to him. "I need to paint this. Look. It's all glass and angles and light and can you imagine what it would look like on canvas?"

His gaze locked with hers, and the power of it slammed into her. They were utterly alone, at the top of an abandoned lighthouse, and the intimacy of the moment was too strong to be ignored. His gaze dropped to her lips briefly, and a slow burn ignited low in her pelvis...attraction. Desire. She tried to push it away. She had no business being attracted to him, especially after their rather personal conversation earlier in the week. He certainly wasn't in any headspace to return any attraction.

"Do you want to go outside?" His voice was rough as he backed away and moved toward a small door leading to the 360-degree platform.

She inhaled a deep breath and accepted the distraction gratefully. "Yes, but I don't trust that railing."

"Me either. It's probably rotted. Stay close to the building."

She followed him out, watched as he gingerly stepped on the platform. Despite its age, the wood seemed mostly sound. She stayed close to the wall, buffeted by the wind until they reached the other side of the lighthouse, which was sheltered and afforded a view that went miles down the coast. The water sparkled so brightly it hurt her eyes, but her chest filled with the fresh, salty air, and she felt a freedom she hadn't felt in a long, long time.

She turned and saw Bran watching her, and she smiled, feeling a connection with him that was new. He smiled back, surprising her, and stepped closer. Her heart hammered at his nearness. A pair of gulls screeched, their cries swallowed by a gust of wind.

"Bran," she murmured.

His gaze tangled with hers, dark, complicated. She shouldn't want him to be nearer. Should suggest they go back inside. Should say she was cold or something…but the truth was she wasn't cold and she didn't want to go back inside and she wanted to sink her hands into his rich mane of hair and feel his beard against the soft skin of her face. Oh, Lord. They had just said they were friends. Now she wasn't so sure.

And she'd called him by a shortened version of his name. Not Branson, but Bran. It seemed too intimate and yet suited him perfectly.

"Jess," he answered, also shortening her name, and all the delicious tension ratcheted up a notch.

He lifted his hand, cupped the back of her head and drew her close. She had barely caught her breath when he dropped his mouth to hers, and she wasn't sure she could still feel her feet.

His lips were full and soft, and his tongue tasted of coffee as it swept inside her mouth. Oh, the man could kiss. Her toes were practically curling in her sneakers as his wide hands drew her up and held her against him even as she melted. Instinctively she reached out and grabbed his shoulders, holding on, fingers gripping his shirt. He shifted, letting her down a little, his hand dropping to the hollow of her back, and she did what she'd wanted to do for days. She slipped her hands into the thick mass of his hair, luxuriating in the soft fullness, the untamed wildness of it.

He groaned. She shifted her weight and…

Her foot went through a board.

She cried out, losing her balance. Branson tore his mouth from hers and pulled her firmly into his arms, his face full of alarm. "Not as sturdy as we thought," he said, backing up a few steps away from the weak spot. Jessica hadn't even had time to be afraid. One moment she'd been kissing him; the next she'd been yanked against his body while his face paled.

She looked over the railing. It was a long, long way down. Dizzying, even. If both her feet had gone through… she would have fallen straight down to the rocky ground below.

"Let's get back inside," he said firmly, leading her back the way they'd come, opening the door and practically shoving her inside. Once he'd secured the door again, he let out a breath. "Okay. That was unexpected."

She didn't know if he meant the near accident or the kiss, and she wasn't about to ask him. Both events had her feeling off balance and speechless.

"I'm fine, really," she assured him, startled by his still-pale face while her heart pounded from the adrenaline. "It was just one foot."

"We shouldn't have gone out there at all. Shouldn't have…" His stormy eyes caught hers. "I shouldn't have kissed you. I'm sorry. I don't know what came over me."

Her feelings were momentarily hurt. He was apologizing for kissing her, as if she hadn't been there, just as involved as he. He wasn't solely responsible. She lifted her chin. "Are you sorry because you regret it or sorry because my foot went through the wood? Just asking if I should take this personally or not."

His lips fell open as he stared. "Take this personally? Jess, you could have fallen. A fall like that would have killed you."

His face was so tortured right now that her heart squeezed. Considering his past, of course this was upsetting. But she stepped a bit closer, enough that she could put her hand on his forearm. "What I'm asking is if this is about the danger or if you think kissing me was a mistake."

He didn't answer. She watched as he swallowed, his throat bobbing with the effort as she slid her hand to his wrist and twined her fingers with his.

"Kissing me isn't wrong, Bran," she said softly. "It's just a kiss. I liked it."

His thumb rubbed over hers. She was sure he didn't realize he was doing it, but it did strange things to her insides. "You shouldn't say things like that."

"Why? We're adults. Kissing is…kissing." She tried a flirty smile, unsure of how it really looked, figuring she probably appeared awkward. But she was trying. She wanted to keep this light. And she wanted to kiss him again. There was nothing wrong with that, was there?

So she eased herself even closer and lifted her other hand to his face. His eyes closed as her thumb rubbed over the crest of his cheekbone, a soft caress to a man who appeared to need it desperately. She wondered how long it had been since he'd been touched. If there'd been anyone since his wife's death…considering how he hid himself away, she somehow doubted it. Was what just happened the first physical intimacy he'd had in two years?

"Branson," she whispered, and his eyes opened. "Please kiss me again. Please."

There was a pause where she didn't think he was going to, and then he dipped his head and touched his lips to hers.

It was different from the kiss outside, which had been windswept and turbulent and unexpected. This was gentle, deliberate, decimating. Jess leaned into him as he folded her into an embrace, and kissed her with a thoroughness that left her breathless and wanting more.

But more was too much, at least for today. So she contented herself with the kiss, the nuances of it, the way he delved deeply and then retreated to nibble at the corner of her mouth, stealing her breath. The way his broad hand curled around the tender skin of her neck, where her pulse drummed heavily. How his body was solid and warm and unrelenting in all the right places, while his lips were soft and persuasive.

She was the one to break away finally, a bit overwhelmed by her own feelings and desires. If it were up to her, they'd christen the lighthouse right here and now, or perhaps dash over the rocky knoll to the house and find their way to his bed. Those desires were natural and exciting, but it was different with Bran. He wasn't the type to sleep with a woman impulsively, or to simply slake a thirst. Not after what he'd been through. So she stepped away, bit down on her lower lip, hoping to memorize his taste, and took a deep, yet shaky, breath.

"You're some kisser," she said, trying a smile. "Please don't apologize for that."

He turned away and faced the windows, looking out over the ocean, and cleared his throat. She smiled a little to herself as she recognized the moment for what it was. She wasn't the only one aroused from that kiss. Secretly, she was glad that stopping was difficult for him, too.

"You're not so bad yourself," he replied, his voice rough. "But—"

"Don't say but," she interrupted. "Let's just leave it as a very nice moment between two very nice people, with no regrets or expectations."

He turned his head to look at her. "Is that possible?"

"I think so. Besides, you're not ready. I'm not stupid, Bran."

He nodded. "We should go back down. The afternoon's getting on."

He opened the trapdoor, and Jess started down the stairs. They were plunged into darkness again as he shut the door, blocking out the light. The small window partway up gave them a sliver of grayness to navigate by, and then they reached the bottom. Branson opened the door and Jess stepped outside into the blustery wind, while he followed and locked the door behind him.

She shouldered her bag and gathered up her gear. Without asking or offering, Bran carried her folding chair and one of her bags to her car, which sat at the end of the lane—she still didn't park at the house. Didn't feel it would be right.

They were nearly to her car when she let out a breath and said what had been on her mind for the last ten minutes. "Bran?"

"Yeah?"

"You weren't thinking of…her, were you? Your wife? When we were kissing?"

And then she held her breath. She could understand him not being ready. Could understand if she was the first sexual contact he'd had since losing Jennie. But she did not want to be a stand-in. Bran didn't have much of a poker face. She peered up at him, hoping she could tell if he were lying.

He didn't look at her, but faced straight ahead. "No," he said firmly. "No, I was not thinking of her when I kissed you."

She should have been relieved. But the underlying anger in his voice killed whatever joy she might have felt.

Because maybe he hadn't been thinking of his dead wife. But he wasn't happy about it, either. And that left her exactly nowhere.

CHAPTER FIVE

BRAN DIDN'T GO to the lighthouse anymore. He had no problem with Jessica setting up there, and he sometimes caught glimpses of her, but he didn't watch from the balcony or take her food or ask if she'd like to go inside.

He'd kissed her, for God's sake.

He poured himself another coffee and wandered through the kitchen, aimless. He'd wanted to be a hermit, to go somewhere isolated and alone to work things out in his head. And it had been fine for a few months. He'd popped into Jeremy's on occasion, and Tori made sure he wasn't too solitary. He hadn't come to any conclusions, but at least he'd been able to stop pretending that he was okay. He didn't have to go through the motions for anyone. And if he wanted to fall apart, he was free to do so without being watched by friends, colleagues and even the press.

Now he was getting a bit of cabin fever. Maybe it was the June weather. The days were warmer and things were really starting to grow. Tulips and daffodils had come and gone in his perennial beds, and the hostas were showing their broad, striped leaves. Now other perennials he couldn't name were sprouting in his flower beds, along with weeds. There was some kind of leafy plant growing in a clump behind the house that he had no idea what to do with.

He could garden, he supposed. Just because he never had didn't mean he couldn't.

But not today. Today was bleak and rainy, a gloomy cover of cloud hanging over the coast while rain soaked into his green lawn. He looked at the lighthouse and wished the light was there, flashing into the distance. Instead, it just looked cold and neglected.

There was the section of platform where Jessica's foot had gone through, scaring him to death.

The railing that wasn't safe, either. How easily she could have lost her balance and gone through it. His heart seized just thinking about the possibility.

The hand holding his coffee paused halfway to his lips as a scene flashed into his head.

A scene. With characters, and danger and a question only his writer's brain could answer. *Did she fall or was she pushed?*

Excitement zipped through his veins. He took his coffee and headed straight for the den and his laptop. This time when he booted up, he didn't bother opening email or his browser. He went right to his word processing program and started typing.

When he looked up later, two hours had passed, his coffee was cold, his brain was mush and he was equal parts relieved and scared.

He could still write.

He could maybe move on.

And he was still carrying guilt with him. Only this time he didn't want to feel guilty for doing something that used to be as natural to him as breathing.

After saving the document, he heated his coffee in the microwave, looked at the time and grabbed a muffin from a plastic container on the kitchen counter. He'd missed lunch but he didn't care. He'd written. Maybe not a lot, but it was a start. And he was standing in his kitchen with two-hour-old coffee, a just-okay blueberry muffin and no one to share his excitement with.

He could call Jeremy, but Jeremy worried too much and would tell Tori, who would ask too many questions in her quest to be helpful. Besides, he wasn't sure either of them would truly get it. He thought about Cole, who totally understood loss and moving on, but who was a workaholic who scheduled his recreation time like part of his to-do list. Bran wasn't close with his own family, and the last people he wanted to talk to about making this kind of a step were his in-laws. They loved him. He loved them. But their relationship was so painful now, tinged with grief and regret. They hadn't spoken since he'd moved into the house.

He picked up his phone and sent a text instead. It said simply:

I wrote today!

There was no immediate answer, so he finished his muffin, pondering more about the kernels of the story he'd begun. Right now he had only a scene. He wasn't even sure who the villain was, or the story question. There was no outline, no solid plot. But there was something. There was a victim and a suspicious death, and that was definitely something to a mystery writer.

His phone vibrated on the countertop, making a loud noise in the silence. He picked it up and saw it was Jess, replying to his text.

That's wonderful! Happy for you!

And she truly was. He knew because she understood.

His thumbs paused as he tried to come up with a suitable response.

It is because of you. I have a dead body at the bottom of the lighthouse. Not sure if she was pushed or if she fell. All because you scared the heck out of me last week.

The phone vibrated in his hand.

I'm trying not to be alarmed by any of that. Seriously, congrats on catching a glimpse of your muse. Give her time to come back to you slowly. Accept what she offers you. Soon you will be good friends again.

His heart warmed. She had such a way of putting things, of seeing the good side, of offering hope. And that was something he hadn't expected to have for a very long time.

Still, she was right about one thing the other day. Writing a scene was one thing. Moving forward on a personal level was something he was not ready for. Her question had rocked him to the soles of his feet. No, he hadn't been thinking of Jennie when he'd kissed Jess. And that had hurt him deeply. He didn't ever want to forget the woman he'd loved. The mother of his child.

He didn't want to fall in love again, either. If he'd learned anything, it was that life was precious and nothing was guaranteed. He'd loved Jennie, loved their son with all his heart. He'd promised to do better for them than his father had done for him. And then he'd done the exact same thing: he'd put work ahead of his family. And the consequences were devastating. He never wanted to go through that again.

Which brought his thoughts around full circle to Jess. He liked her. A lot. And there was no denying he was attracted to her. That kiss the other day had awakened something in him that had been dormant for too long. It was a good thing that she was just here for the summer. Someone passing through his life, not sticking around. There was a little bit of safety in that, after all. The confusing thing was how to proceed. Should they be friends? Could they be friends without being physical? Could they be physical without falling in love? Because the last thing he wanted to do was set up unreasonable expectations.

Bran figured he was probably overthinking, so he pushed the thoughts aside and went out to the lighthouse instead. He walked around the perimeter, examined the ground around the base, looked up at the platform high above. Brow furrowed, he took the key and went inside, then lugged the single mattress up the stairs, trying to ignore the dust and probably mold that had settled into it. Once outside, he gingerly felt his way to the railing, making sure not to get too close. And then he tipped the damp and heavy mattress over the edge, seeing where it fell.

A person would be heavier, but the placement at the bottom was what he was after.

He went inside, shut the trapdoor and timed how long it took him to get back outside and to where the "body" lay. Satisfied, he dragged the mattress back inside and left it on the floor in a puff of dust.

It really was a shame that it was in such disrepair. Had the previous owners not cared? The house was three thousand square feet of elegance and had been lovingly cared for. The lighthouse, full of history, was a derelict.

Maybe he could be the one to restore it.

Energized, he trotted back to the house. First, he wanted more words. There were some adjustments that needed to be made in the scenes he'd just written. And after that, he'd start researching restoration.

He didn't need to think about Jessica Blundon at all. He just needed something to keep him occupied, and this was perfect.

Jess spent one more week sketching at the lighthouse, but Bran never came out anymore. She didn't even see him on his balcony, or in his gardens. It was as if he was deliberately avoiding her ever since they'd shared that kiss. Or kisses, rather. There'd been two. One impulsive. The other not. He wasn't pleased about either.

Now she had started painting, and while she missed sitting out in the sunshine, she was enjoying her time in her makeshift studio with the familiar smells and tools around her. Her loft in Chicago was bigger, but this suited her just fine. She had only to take a few steps to make a cup of tea or something to eat. The ocean was outside her door. And while she didn't want to overstay her welcome, Jeremy and Tori had become friends and she saw them often. Baby Rose was growing each day, and Tori was starting to look slightly more rested as she got more sleep. Jeremy doted on her in a way that was so sweet it made Jess's heart hurt.

She'd never had a love like that. She'd loved, sure. But each time that particular blossom had bloomed, it had ended up wilting, too, until there was nothing left but to move on. She tried not to overthink it. Ana had always said that there was no one good enough. That no one understood what it meant to be a creative. Or they were jealous of her talent. Compliments all, but lonely just the same. And each time a relationship ended, a little bit of hope for a family of her own died, too.

But she could live a fulfilled life just the same. It was all about being happy with what you had, rather than spending too much time wishing. Wishing just led to disappointment.

Right now she was working on her first painting, start-ing small, working from the sketch she'd made of the door and the daisies beside it. She wanted to do a whole series here, not just of the lighthouse but of the whole experience of being on the South Shore.

But she missed Bran. She'd be lying to herself to deny it.

A week passed. The end of June approached and she worked long hours, taking time only for walks and meals. She spoke to her agent and negotiated with Tori to stay at the boathouse until the end of August. Then she, her sketches and paintings would head back to Chicago. She could finish there in her own studio.

Finally, on a Friday night, Tori asked her up to the house for dinner. Jess pressed her phone to her ear and asked the tough question. "Is Branson going to be there?"

"No," Tori replied. "He's gone to Halifax for something. It's just us. And I'm not even cooking. Jeremy is stopping for fish and chips on the way home."

Her stomach growled. That sounded so good… "Okay, then. Let me clean up and I'll be there. What should I bring?"

Tori laughed. "Yourself?"

"How about wine? Or can you have any?"

"I can sneak a glass. I've got enough milk expressed to feed Rose. That would be lovely."

So Jessica washed up, changed into a simple floral maxi dress, twisted her hair into a messy topknot and grabbed not only a bottle of pinot grigio but a basket of early-season strawberries. They'd make a simple dessert after their takeout meal.

When she arrived at the house, Tori was outside in the backyard, putting plates on the patio table while Rose kicked and played in a playpen covered with a fine mosquito net. "Are the bugs bad?" Jess asked, handing over the wine.

"No. I'm just overly cautious, I think, and hate the thought of an itchy bite on Rose's delicate skin. To be honest, I just love eating dinner outside. Unless it's raining, we eat out here nearly every night."

"You guys are the cutest."

Tori beamed. "Do you think? Wait'll I tell Jeremy. 'Cutest' isn't something he's used to being called."

They went into the kitchen briefly and Tori put the wine in the fridge to chill, then put the berries on a shelf. "You know, six months ago I was living in a tiny little house and working at the Sandpiper. It's hard to believe this is my life now. I'm so lucky. I'm so *happy*."

They went back outside, sitting in the shade next to Rose's playpen. "How did you and Jeremy meet, then? He's from New York, right?"

"Connecticut originally." She reached inside the netting and handed Rose a ring with keys on it. The baby shook her fist and the keys rattled, making her even more excited. "He came here on business last summer and stayed at the Sandpiper. Two weeks later he was gone." She met Jess's gaze. "When he came back at the end of November, he discovered I was pregnant."

"Oh, wow." Jess sat back in her chair. "So you got married?"

Tori laughed. "If only it were that simple. But we did in the end. After we fell in love with each other. And now here we are. We're going to split time between here and New York. Jeremy's actually looking for a place for us on Long Island. He'll commute in to work. And he has a flat right by Central Park."

Three residences and all of them pricey. "I didn't realize he was so rich."

"Neither did I. He and Bran and Cole are all loaded. I call them the Billionaire Babies."

Jessica coughed. "Did you say Billionaire Babies?"

Tori nodded. "You didn't know?"

"I knew Branson was successful, but a billionaire?"

Rose started to fuss so Tori took her out of the playpen and sat her on her lap. She straightened her little dress as she chatted. "Oh, most of his money is family money. To be honest, I don't think their childhoods were great. Lots of money, not much love and high expectations."

A billionaire. A freaking billionaire. And yet he was living proof that money was no guarantee of happiness. He'd lost the people most important to him. No money could protect him from that. The conversation they'd had during their picnic came back to her. She'd teased him about servants... but she'd only been teasing. He'd been serious. Of course he'd had servants. Hot embarrassment slid into her cheeks.

"Does it change things?" Tori asked.

"What do you mean?"

Tori rubbed Rose's back and a little burp came out, making them laugh. Tori cuddled her close but then leveled her gaze on Jess. "Knowing he's rich. Does it change how you feel about him?"

Jess frowned. "Why would it? I couldn't care less about his bank balance. Besides, I barely know him."

Tori was quiet for a long moment, and Jess felt her cheeks warm. "Are you sure?" Tori asked.

"Sure about not caring about his money, or sure about barely knowing him?"

"About not knowing him," Tori said. "I believe you about the money. To be honest, I found it a little intimidating at first."

Jess sighed. She did, too. She did just fine on her own, and was successful in her own right. But she wasn't megarich. "It doesn't matter either way. He's still grieving for his wife and son. Even if I were interested, he's not."

"So nothing's happened? Nothing at all?"

Tori sounded so hopeful. And Jess had never been one to kiss and tell, but she hadn't really had a girlfriend since Ana. She missed having someone to confide in, and Tori knew Bran better than most. Would it hurt to get someone else's perspective? Was she overthinking all of this or getting it wrong? Because she certainly hadn't been able to get him off her mind.

"We kissed," she admitted, the heat in her cheeks now a burning flame. "But just one time, really. He hasn't spoken to me since."

Tori leaned forward, her eyes flashing. "Oh, that's wonderful news!"

Jess laughed in spite of herself. "How do you reckon? I mean, we're not speaking." Besides the text about writing again, she thought to herself. But that didn't really count.

"Bran wasn't even leaving the house. Jeremy was so worried. The fact that he kissed you? Major progress." Suddenly her face fell. "Oh, I'm sorry, Jessica. I didn't take into account how you were feeling about it. Are you doing okay?"

She sighed. "Yeah, I'm okay. I mean…it was pretty great. But I could tell he was mad at himself after, you know? So it didn't really end well."

"Well, something happened to him to light a fire beneath his butt. He told Jeremy he was going to Halifax for a few days to look into restoration of the lighthouse. He said it's in rough shape, and he wants to fix it up."

Jess sat up straighter. "Are you kidding?"

"Not at all."

Jess was gutted. The lighthouse was beautiful as it was, strong and scarred. Granted, the platform at the top could use repairs, and it was dirty inside, but restoration? For what purpose? It would be covering up all its character. It would be as if he were erasing anything that smacked of the two of them together. And that stung. Even if it didn't go anywhere, she could take a nice memory away from that afternoon. She certainly didn't feel the need to paint over it.

In fact, the whole encounter had enhanced her approach to the paintings. Imbued her with a new emotion that would only be beneficial.

She was still stewing when Jeremy came through the house to the backyard through the house, carrying a huge paper bag in his hands. "Someone call for dinner?"

The smell of fries and fish filled the air, and Jess's stomach rumbled again. She was hungry, and what Bran did with the lighthouse was his business, wasn't it? She had absolutely no say. She had her sketches. Branson Black could do whatever he liked. And now she knew he had the money to do it. Despite the big house and beautiful car, she'd had no inkling he was so wealthy. He wasn't flashy about it. She'd give him that much.

Jeremy laid out the meal, and Jessica went inside to get the wine and the corkscrew that Tori had put on the island. When she went back outside, Jeremy was holding Rose and Tori was filling her plate with food. It was so perfectly domestic. She wondered if Bran had experienced these moments with his wife and baby. Surely he had. And she could understand how a person might not come back from a loss like that.

She was sympathetic. But it didn't mean she was willing to be…disposable.

Pasting on a smile, she took a takeout container and emptied it onto her plate. It certainly smelled delicious. Jeremy put Rose in her playpen again and worked on opening the wine. She'd stumbled onto the sticking point that had been nagging at her ever since that day at the lighthouse.

He'd treated her as if she was disposable. And maybe he was angry at himself. But there was no question she'd felt cast aside, and that hurt. After going through most of her life feeling invisible, being seen and discarded hurt even more than not being noticed at all. This was why she didn't put herself out there anymore. It just wasn't worth it.

But she wasn't going to let it ruin her evening, so she shook some vinegar on her fish, picked up her fork and dug in. It was perfectly flaky, the tartar sauce creamy and flavorful, and there was a plastic dish of coleslaw for them to share. The conversation turned to other things, namely Jeremy's search for a property for the third in their trio, Cole, who wanted something he could use as a corporate retreat. So far not much had turned up on Jeremy's radar.

When the meal was over, Jess carried the dirty dishes back to the kitchen and returned to the table with the carton of freshly washed berries. As the evening cooled, they talked and Jess had another glass of wine while Tori gave Rose a prepared bottle.

Jess was barely over thirty, but the family scene had her biological clock ticking madly tonight. When Rose was finished eating, she took her from Tori's arms to give her a break and to get baby snuggles. She hadn't thought about wanting children a whole lot, but spending time with Rose these past weeks had made her wonder. She smelled so good; like milk and baby lotion and fresh cotton. The fact that the baby settled so easily into her arms made her feel motherly and strangely competent. It took no time at all before Rose's little lashes were resting on her cheeks and her lips opened slightly, slack in slumber.

She was such a sweet little thing. And for the first time in years, Jessica let herself really yearn for what she didn't have. What she might never have. And she held on tight.

CHAPTER SIX

THE SUN WAS setting and Jeremy had just lit the citronella torches when the slamming of a car door echoed through the still evening air. Jess frowned and looked over her shoulder, but couldn't see anything. A few moments later, Tori met her gaze and nodded. *Bran*, she mouthed, and Jess swallowed tightly. She was still thinking about the kiss, and thinking about him restoring the lighthouse. She bit down on her lip. She couldn't escape the notion that he was fixing it because he wanted to essentially cover up what had happened between them. A fresh coat of paint and some new lumber would erase a lot, wouldn't it?

"Good evening, Bran," Tori said softly. "Come on in and have a seat. You want a drink?"

"Naw, I'm good for now." He came into the circle and nodded at Jess, his gaze settling on her and the baby in her arms. "Jessica. I didn't know you'd be here."

Or else he wouldn't have come. She summoned her pride. "Likewise."

He hesitated, but then sat. "Sorry. I didn't mean that the way it sounded."

Her cheeks heated and she let out a breath. "It's okay. No biggie."

Jeremy jumped into the middle of the awkwardness.

"So, Bran. What brings you by? How was the trip to Halifax?"

"Good." Bran smiled, and it transformed his face. Jess realized she'd hardly ever seen him smile, and that when he did she forgot just about everything in her head. His face completely changed, relaxing and opening more, while his soft lips curved beneath his beard.

The beard that had tickled her chin and neck not long ago. She pushed the thought away.

"You're really going to change the lighthouse?" Jess asked, trying hard to keep censure out of her voice. She had no claim to it. Her creative "tingles" held no weight when it came to what he chose to do with the lighthouse It didn't mean she had to be happy about it.

He nodded. "Yeah. It's in pretty rough shape. I honestly think it's been neglected for decades. First we're going to make it safe. Then we'll worry about cosmetics."

"You don't think all the changes will erase its character?"

"If I leave it as it is, it'll rot away. I don't want it to disappear."

"Not to mention how it might work against resale value," Jeremy pointed out, lifting his glass as he sat in a padded chair. "Sometimes selling points become liabilities real fast."

Jess's gaze met Bran's. "You're thinking of selling already?"

When he shook his head, she was relieved, though she couldn't say why. Her life wasn't here, and there was nothing really between them anyway. Why should she care if he stayed or not?

"No," he answered firmly. "I don't plan on selling for a while. Even if I go back to New York eventually, this is a great place to retreat to, you know?"

"What made you decide to take on the lighthouse, anyway?" Tori asked.

"A discovery that the platform and railing at the top aren't safe." He didn't look at her this time, but his smile had vanished. "Half the boards are rotted. The lamp is fine and won't be used again anyway, but I've got someone coming out to have a look at the foundation and make sure that structurally we're sound. It's been neglected. It's a beautiful piece of history that's mostly been abandoned. At least maybe I can be a better steward to it."

She wanted to be angry or at the very least annoyed that he was going to paint over the battle scars the building had sustained over the years. There were stories there. Stories he should appreciate as a writer. But it was hard to argue with wanting to take care of something and cherish it.

"I think I got used to its weathered look," she said quietly.

Now he looked at her, his gaze inscrutable. "I know. But it's about safety. The last thing I want is for someone to get hurt."

She couldn't look away. He said it while looking directly in her eyes. And the moment on the platform spun out in her mind—the wind, the moment her foot went through the rotten board and the instant freezing fear, and the feel of his strong body against hers as he held her tight.

He might be able to walk away from their kisses that day without any problem, but she couldn't.

She was smart enough to realize that she was falling for Branson Black, the most unavailable man she'd ever met.

Dammit.

Rose squirmed a bit in her arms, and she finally broke eye contact. "Shh…" She adjusted the weight of the baby in an effort to keep her settled, but Tori got up and came to retrieve Rose. "Her naps in the early evening are getting shorter. Which is a blessing for me. Now she'll stay up until about eleven, and sleep through until five. It feels like absolute heaven."

Jess's arms felt cold and empty without the baby, a thought she didn't want to delve too far into. Instead, she smiled and got to her feet. "I really should go anyway. I'm up early these days to work. But thank you once again for dinner. I'm going to have to have you down to the boathouse for a meal soon."

"That would be lovely!" Tori snuggled a fussy Rose against her shoulder.

Of course Jess didn't quite know where she was going to seat everyone, now that the main floor space was transitioned into a studio. But no matter. They'd figure it out. Maybe it would turn into a picnic on the beach.

Bran stood as well. "I'll walk you home," he said.

Jeremy laughed. "Sure, bro. It's like a hundred yards to the boathouse. You're not fooling anyone."

Jess blushed and Bran stared at his friend. "Shut up, Jer," he said mildly. But Jeremy merely chuckled and didn't say anything more. Jess was cluing into the fact that Bran was a still-waters-run-deep kind of guy, and that when he spoke, people generally listened. It was a trait that could be frustrating but that she admired, too.

This time when they reached the boathouse she invited him in. "Why don't you come in for a bit? It's still early."

He stepped inside and took off his shoes, leaving them on the tiny mat by the door.

"You know, I've never been in here," he mused, peeking ahead. "It's tiny but kind of cozy."

"I think it's somewhere between six and seven hundred square feet. Single bedroom, bathroom, living room, small kitchen. But as a getaway, it's sweet." She led him through to the living room and smiled as his eyes widened. Her easel was set up, and a small covered table held brushes, paint, palette knives and an apron that was smattered with a rainbow of colors. To her it was the most comforting sight in the world. To him, it must look like chaos.

"Wine? I have white and red. I might have a beer in here somewhere."

"None for me. I'll take water if you have it."

She looked at him closely. Realized she'd never actually seen him have a drink other than lemonade or coffee, which he seemed to drink constantly. "I have sparkling."

"That'd be great."

She went to the fridge for the bottle and poured some into a glass with ice, then handed it to him. "Do you mind if I do?" she asked, motioning toward the half-empty bottle of red on the counter.

"Of course not." He smiled at her. "So this is your studio."

"For now. It's a lot smaller than my place in Chicago, but it suits my needs better than I ever expected."

She poured some wine into a glass and turned to him. "I was only going to stay a week or two, you know. Move on like I've been doing for months. And then Tori offered me this place...and it's been wonderful. The peace and quiet. The cute towns and scenery. I understand why you chose it to..." She paused, feeling suddenly awkward. "Well, to regroup, I suppose. Or recharge. I know it's working for me."

"Yeah." He hesitated a moment, then said, "Are you upset about me restoring the lighthouse? I know you've used it as inspiration."

Jess took a sip of her wine. "I was at first. For a few reasons that were nothing but selfish. But what you said about being a steward is right. And so is safety. I'm so sorry I scared you that day."

"It wasn't your fault."

She gestured to the front door. "Do you want to sit outside? There's more room."

"Sure."

The little porch gave a glimpse of the water, and as evening settled around them, they sat in the Adirondack chairs and let the soft sound of the waves soak in. He sipped his water; she savored the wine and let out a happy sigh. The sky turned shades of lilac, peach and pink, a natural palette that filled Jess's soul with comfort.

"It's beautiful tonight."

"Yeah. There's something about the ocean that just calms me and energizes me at the same time."

He let out a long sigh. "It soothes. The sea just is. It crashes and rolls, it waves and breaks and chases the sand. Twice a day it moves in, then retreats, leaving treasures behind. When our world is small and filled with worries, the ocean is endless and constant."

She shouldn't have been surprised at his being poetic; he was a writer after all. But the description touched her just the same. "Is your world small and filled with worries, Bran?" She'd held her breath as he spoke, but now let it out slowly.

"Not as much as it used to be. The sea has worked its magic on me, too."

"I'm glad."

"And so have you."

Her breath stopped. "Me?"

He looked over at her, his eyes black in the growing twilight. "Yes, you. I'm sorry for the way I acted that day." She didn't need to ask which day he meant. "I was feeling guilty, and mad at myself, and I took it out on you. You did nothing wrong, Jess."

She held his gaze. "Neither did you, Bran. You just weren't ready for it. But it wasn't wrong." She reached for his hand. "I might be overstepping here, so please don't be angry when I say very bluntly that you are not married to her anymore."

His throat bobbed as he swallowed, then he squeezed her fingers. "I know. But I'm in that spot where I feel as if moving on means I'm forgetting her."

"You'll never forget her. Allowing yourself to have a life and move on doesn't mean forgetting."

"In my head I know that. But that day, I reacted. I reacted when I kissed you and I reacted when I put you in your car to leave. It was wrong and I owe you an apology."

"Accepted. And I'm thrilled you're writing again."

She thought he would pull his hand away, but he kept his fingers twined with hers and she tried not to think too much about it.

"Me, too. It's slow going, but it's a start. I haven't said anything to anyone else, though. I don't want to set up expectations."

"Not even your agent?"

"Not yet. I want to have a solid start before I talk to him about it. It's early days. But one of the reasons I went to Halifax was to visit the archives and do a little digging."

"And did you find out anything interesting?"

"Lots. Like rumors of U-boats off the coast in the forties. The presence of spies during the war. It's feeding my muse, and she's been hungry a long time."

"Looks like this place is kind of key for both of us. Two lost souls, huh?"

"I'm not feeling so lost right now."

His dark gaze had her insides fluttering again, so she got up and held out her hand. "Can I get you a refill?"

Slowly, ever so slowly, he pushed himself up from the chair. He was so tall, and in the dark, with his beard and hair, he looked intimidating and dangerous. But not truly dangerous…more enigmatic and sexy.

"I can get it."

He took the glass and went inside while Jessica let out a long, slow breath. She was not immune to him in any way. She'd been prepared to be angry with him about the restoration. To let it be the thing that kept him at arm's length. Instead, he'd stated his reasons and the distance evaporated. Every time she set up some sort of block, he knocked it down with ease.

She was here only for the summer. He was not for her. And she seemed to lack the willpower to push him away.

He returned with a full glass and instead of sitting, went to the railing and looked out over the sloping lawn and shrubs to the beach below. "You wanna walk?" he asked.

A moonlight walk on the beach? Could she possibly say no?

"That would be lovely," she whispered.

He drank his water and put the glass down on the arm of the wooden chair, and then held out his hand. She took it, hoping he couldn't tell that hers was shaking. What a ninny she was, trembling over holding hands at her age. It wasn't like she hadn't ever been in love and he was some sort of first. He was just…different.

Like now, with his hair blowing back from his face in the ocean breeze. He'd left his sandals inside her door and his feet were bare as they approached the silky white sand. She tugged on his hand to stop him for a moment while she slipped off her Vans and let her toes sink in, the sand still warm from the day's sun.

He still had her hand. She swallowed tightly and kept her fingers tangled with his. Admitting that she'd been lonely was hard. She considered herself strong and self-reliant. She always had been, with a good dose of obstinacy thrown in for good measure. But she'd needed this, she realized. Even more so since she lost her best friend. She needed contact and intimacy. Clearly Branson Black was not Mr. Right. But he was doing a pretty good job being Mr. Right Now.

"I never imagined soft white sand like this up here," she said, her steps lazy and squishy in the thick sand. "I always imagined it farther south. In the clear waters of the Caribbean. But this is amazing."

He was quiet for a few moments, then lifted his chin and drew in a deep breath of sea air. "I met Jennie in Nova Scotia. Not here. On the other side of the province. I decided to take a road trip and drove north through Maine, took the ferry from New Brunswick to Digby, and ended up on the Fundy coast. She was working the summer doing marine research. My plans to travel to Prince Edward Island and Cape Breton just disappeared. Once I met her, that was it."

"She was from here?"

"No, she was on some university grant summer research program with Boston University. I was still living in Connecticut. For nine months we drove back and forth and saw each other on weekends. And once she graduated I asked her to marry me."

"You were young."

He nodded. Breakers swept over the sand, brushing their feet, and Jess mulled over the fact that he was telling her about his wife while they were holding hands. Still, she wasn't going to interrupt. She was curious, and she got the feeling this was not something he talked about often.

"We were, though she was younger than me. We ended up with a two-year engagement and pulled out all the stops for the wedding." He looked over at her. "I would have been happy with the courthouse, but if you knew Jennie..." His smile was sad. "I wanted to give her everything she desired. And I could, so I did."

"She was lucky to have you, Bran." Jess squeezed his hand as they kept taking lazy steps up the beach.

"Was she? Because I got caught up in myself and didn't cherish her enough. I have regrets, Jessica. More than you know."

She stopped and pulled on his hand, making him stop too as she looked up into his face. "I think whenever someone dies, we all have regrets of some sort. You loved her. Maybe you weren't perfect, but you loved her. That's so clear to see in the way you talk about her."

"I did." He sighed. "Jennie was my home. The warm, loving space I didn't have as a child. And I blew it. I was angry about the accident for a long time, and then the sadness threatened to pull me under. Now I'm wanting to start living again, and it feels so strange to be doing it without her. Without our baby, too. God, he was the sweetest thing." His voice thickened and he cleared his throat. "I hope you never have to go through anything like that in your life. I wouldn't wish it on my worst enemy."

He turned and they started walking again, while Jess's thoughts were in turmoil. She'd had her share of loss; not just Ana but of her adopted mother, too. Her dad was still around but had remarried, and they weren't that close. And while her life growing up had been okay, she'd always wondered about her birth parents. She knew nothing about them.

"I was adopted when I was two. I don't have memories of before, but I know that CPS stepped in and removed me from my home when I was a year old. After my parents divorced I stayed with my mom. And then she died several years ago. I was nearly engaged once, but he didn't want to wait for me. So I guess we all have something. You're holding on to regrets. I think I'm just used to the people I love not sticking around."

"Damn. I'm sorry. I mean, I'm not particularly close with my family. My dad is a workaholic and a bit… I don't know, cold. And my mom is okay, but we've never been a tight family. Still, I know they're there."

"And they sent you off to boarding school."

"Yeah, but you know what? I met my best friends in the world. It ended up being the best thing that could have happened. Cole and Jeremy became my family."

She smiled a little. "You certainly seem to have good memories."

"The best." He sighed. "You know, my life's been a bit charmed. Yeah, I lost Jennie and Owen, but we loved each other. I'm blessed to have had that, I guess."

They'd stopped again, and she turned to face him and put her arms around his middle, wrapping him in a hug. What a bittersweet blessing, to have found perfection and to lose it so young.

"Hey," he said softly, and his wide, warm hand came to rest on the middle of her back.

She sniffled. "Sorry. I just thought you needed a hug. Or that I needed to give you one."

"It's okay. You can hug me."

And his other arm came around her and hugged her back.

Bran drank in the scent of her hair, something soft and floral that mixed with the salty tang of the sea. She was so warm, and so very, very generous. What she'd said about her childhood was surprising. He'd imagined her having this warm and picture-perfect family, completely well-adjusted and loving. But she'd had her share of heartbreak, too, and yet she still found a way to be…open.

It took a certain strength to be able to do that. And something special to make him respond to it, after months of numbness.

Jennie would have liked her. It should feel odd to have such a thought, but somehow it wasn't. Jennie had had that sweetness wrapped in strength, too.

It felt so good to be held.

He pulled her closer against him, let his hand glide over her back, touching warm skin. God, so good, the touch of another human being. She responded, slipping her hands beneath the hem of his T-shirt, and he could feel the gentle marking of her fingernails on his back. He groaned with pleasure, moving his hand down her ribs, his thumb grazing the tender skin between breast and waist through the soft material.

"Bran," she whispered, and his body came alive.

He lowered his head and nuzzled at her ear, pleased when goose bumps erupted on her skin. She tilted her head, and he touched his lips to the soft skin of her neck, up to her jawline, over to her lips, which were slack and waiting for him. The kiss was a wild and wonderful thing, full of passion and acknowledgment of their attraction. She stood up on tiptoe and wrapped her arms around his neck; he lifted her up off her toes and held her flush against his body as he plundered her mouth. Her hands sank into his hair and his pulse leaped. If he wasn't careful, he was going to lay her down on the sand right here and now. At Jeremy's house. He understood now why his lighthouse was the perfect spot for a tryst. A little ocean, some moonlight, add a lot of desire and things had a way of happening.

Her chest heaved with her breathing, and he placed his hand over her heart. He was shocked to discover she wasn't wearing a bra as her small, firm breast pressed against his hand.

His control was on shaky ground.

So he lifted her up in his arms, cradling her close, and started walking toward the water.

He was nearly to his knees when Jessica figured out what he was doing. She pushed against him and started to laugh and protest at the same time. "Bran! No! You are not going to throw me in the water!"

He grinned. "Throw? No. But we need to cool off, and there's only one way I can think of to do that."

She struggling against him some more, but suddenly she was laughing too, and the sound filled his heart with something that felt...joyful. Water splashed up over his knees as the waves rolled in. It was cold; there was definitely going to be some temperature shock. But nature's equivalent of a cold shower was in both their best interests right now.

"Bran!" she exclaimed, as a wave rose up and touched her bottom, making her arch against him.

He laughed, the sound rumbling in his chest before erupting into the evening air. His shorts were wet now, and another step had them in up to his waist. "Ready?" he asked.

"No!" She squealed and twisted in his arms, laughing the whole time. "You are not going to drop me into the ocean. You are not—"

He took one more step, then let her go with a splash. And then he dove under, hoping to cool his jets.

When he surfaced about ten feet away, Jessica had come up and was still spluttering and wiping her hair away from her face. She looked so indignant that he burst out laughing. The look she turned on him was positively venomous, and then she started toward him. When she was five, maybe six feet away, she started splashing him, the water hitting him in the face and he had to stop laughing to keep from getting a mouthful. Instead he turned, stepped toward her and yanked her close, where she couldn't splash anymore.

"You. Are. Incorrigible." She was still laughing but said the last word on a sigh. He kept his arm around her and she kicked up from the bottom, pointing her toes up through the surface. "I can't believe you did that."

"Me either." He let her go, and they bobbed around in the water for a few minutes. His cargo shorts were heavy and his T-shirt uncomfortable, and his legs were already starting to go numb from the cold. Still, he found it hard to be sorry. It had been so long since he'd done anything impulsive or...or fun. Kissing Jessica and then taking a plunge in the Atlantic had been both.

Her dress billowed around her, moving with the waves as she ran her fingers through her hair, which was far darker now that it was wet. It made her skin glow in the moonlight, and her eyes shone at him. Quick as anything, she ducked under the water, the tips of her toes giving a little splash like a mermaid. When she surfaced, she was several feet away, standing hip deep in the water.

The fabric of her dress clung to her skin, highlighting every curve and point, and his mouth went dry. Perhaps a dunking in the sea hadn't been the best plan after all.

Sex would be a mistake. For both of them. Wouldn't it?

To distract himself, he swam out until he started to get tired, and then turned to come back. Jess was treading water a few hundred yards away, as if waiting for him. He swam in, and then they went to shore together. The exertion had helped expend some of his restless energy, and when they got to the shore, they hurried out of the water and onto the beach.

"Come up to the boathouse and towel off. You must be freezing."

No more than she was.

The slow, meandering walk of earlier was replaced by quick steps in the sand, and a shorter angle to the path leading away from the beach. Jessica stopped and grabbed her shoes, and when she stood he noticed her lips were blue from cold. He was shivering, too. The days had been summerlike, but the nights were still chilly and being soaking wet made it even worse. In the space of a few minutes, they were at the boathouse. He stood on the mat while she disappeared into the bathroom and returned with two big, fluffy towels.

She scrubbed her hair and rubbed it over her arms and legs. He did the same. And wished her dress wasn't quite so see-through. It wasn't helping his resolve to keep things nonsexual.

"You're freezing," she said, looking up at him. "Let me put your things in the dryer."

"I don't exactly have anything to change into."

Suggestion swirled around them, but Jessica was the one to break the moment. "I have a blanket. I know it's not optimal, but you can't go home like that. Unless you want to go to Jeremy's and ask for a change of clothes."

He lifted an eyebrow. "No, thanks. He'll ask too many questions."

"Well, then. Hang on."

She disappeared into the bathroom and came out again with another towel and a soft blanket. She handed him the towel first. "You can put this on like a skirt, to cover your...sensitive bits." Her cheeks flushed. "And then wrap the blanket around you."

He grabbed at the hem of his T-shirt and swept it over his head, though it stuck to his shoulders as he pulled it off. He dropped it on the floor with the first towel, and when he saw her owlish expression at his bare chest he paused with his fingers on the button of his shorts.

Her cheeks were ruddy now and she turned away. "I'll just go change and then put my stuff in with yours."

A laugh built in his chest as he took off his shorts and secured the towel away from his…what had she called them? Sensitive bits. The blanket was large enough that he wrapped it around himself like a cape. When she emerged from the bedroom, she gathered up his wet clothes and scuttled off to the laundry room. He heard a few beeps and then the low hum of the dryer.

When she came back out, she stopped in the kitchen and put water in her kettle. She'd changed into yoga pants and a soft sweatshirt with paint stains on it. Her hair was starting to dry a little, with bits of natural curl framing her face. He felt like an idiot standing there in a towel and blanket, but what the hell. Nothing about their relationship so far had been ordinary or exactly comfortable.

She looked over at him and laughed. "You look silly."

"I feel silly."

"How about that drink now? I have some Scotch. It might warm you up."

He met her gaze. "I don't drink anymore."

Her face changed. First there was surprise, followed swiftly by embarrassment. Then a growing realization and acceptance. She'd been at his house. To Jeremy's for drinks, but he'd never partaken in anything alcoholic. He didn't make a big deal of it, but he could see her putting the pieces together.

In her blunt fashion, she met his gaze and asked, "Are you an alcoholic?"

CHAPTER SEVEN

BRAN SHRUGGED AS he considered her question. "I don't know. I mean, I don't know if there's an actual criteria I would meet or anything. What I do know is that I was self-medicating to deal with my grief, and I stopped." He hesitated, then decided to be completely honest. "Jennie would be pretty angry with me if she knew I'd turned to alcohol as a coping mechanism."

"What took its place?"

"Getting out of New York. Long walks on the beach. And there were times it was really hard. But I don't keep any in my house, and it makes it easier."

Her lips dropped open and an expression of dismay darkened her face. "Oh, Bran. I gave you a bottle of wine that first day for stress. I'm so sorry."

He waved it away, and nearly dropped the blanket. "Don't be. You didn't know. I've still got it. You're welcome to it sometime when you're visiting."

Her blue eyes touched his. "Will I be visiting?"

It was hard to draw breath. This was the moment where they were maybe becoming a thing. Maybe not sex. Maybe not ever sex. But agreeing to spend time together rather than finding ways not to or chalking it up to coincidence. He nodded slightly. "If you want to."

Her voice was soft. "I'd like that."

He was in danger of moving closer to her again, what with her soft voice and big eyes. "Can we sit down somewhere? I'm feeling kind of ridiculous here."

"Of course!" Her eyes sparkled as she looked at him. "If you can make it around the drop cloth, there's a decent sofa."

He took a look at her current painting as he went by. It was the lighthouse, a full rendering of it, with the soft colors of a sunrise taking shape behind. She was so talented. Even partially completed, the painting seemed to breathe, have a life of its own. "This is beautiful, Jess."

She turned and smiled, then gestured toward the sofa. "Thank you. I'm playing with some colors with that one, and so far I'm liking it."

They sat on the sofa, the plush cushions soft and comfortable. Jess tucked her feet up underneath herself, relaxed in the corner of the sofa. It was a bit more difficult for him to find a comfortable spot, what with the towel and the blanket. When he finally got situated, she was grinning broadly.

"Don't make fun of me," he said, but his voice held a trace of humor.

"Hey, you were the one who decided to go for the swim, not me."

A sigh escaped his lips. "Only because we were getting too close to..."

His words trailed off. To what? Making a mistake? Making love? Both phrases made his chest tighten. He opted for humor. "To getting naked on Jeremy's beach."

She coughed and laughed at the same time. "Oh, can you imagine if they'd seen..."

He met her gaze evenly. "That dip was my equivalent of a cold shower. I like you, Jess. We have chemistry." She made a sound that was the equivalent of "yeah, we sure do." He held the blanket tightly in his fingers. "I'm not sure sex is in our best interests right now."

She nodded. He wished he didn't notice how full her lips were when they were open just that little bit. Or how her eyes glowed, the little tiny striations of gold and green in the blue making him think of the water at the edge of the lake at Merrick. Or even how her chest rose and fell anytime things heated up between them. Even now, just talking about it and not touching. He was so attuned to her.

Her throat bobbed as she swallowed. "Because of Jennie."

"Yeah. It wouldn't be fair to you."

"Tell me about her, Bran."

He broke eye contact and looked away. Across the room was a matching love seat and one of the pillows was out of place.

But she edged over closer to him and put her hand on his blanket-covered knee. "You need to talk about her. There's no judgment here, Bran. Just talk. Tell me what she was like. Tell me why it's so hard." She squeezed his knee. "I can put on some coffee if you want."

He debated. It was strange thinking about telling the woman you'd almost had sex with about your dead wife. And yet not so strange thinking about telling Jess. Besides, if she knew everything, maybe this horrible, wonderful attraction between them would be nonexistent, and he wouldn't have to worry about making a mistake.

"I don't need coffee," he murmured, resting his hands on his knees. The hem of the towel cut into his pelvis, but he didn't care.

He'd already told her about how he and Jennie had met. But the last year of their marriage...everything had changed.

"The year or so before they died was really different for

us," he began. "Owen had been born, and Jennie was such an amazing mother. Like Tori, you know? Loving and caring and tired and fun. She'd spend hours counting his toes and making him laugh. Or just sitting in a rocking chair with him while he slept, wanting to hold on to those first baby days forever." Emotion rose in a wave and he fought it back, not wanting his voice to crack as they spoke.

"Does seeing Tori make it worse for you?" she asked softly.

"Sometimes. It just hurts, seeing Rose grow and knowing that one day soon she'll start having the milestones that Owen never had. But it's not their fault, and he's my best friend. I can't stay away, you know? That's not fair."

She nodded and put her hand on his back, rubbing reassuringly, just like she'd done that day of their picnic on the rock. "But it still hurts."

"Yeah." He took a deep breath. "My career had really taken off by then. My eighth book had just released, and it was a big deal. It hit the lists in its first week, and there was a bunch of appearances set up." He frowned. "I let it go to my head a little bit. I had to be here, there. Signing books. Doing interviews. I'd gone to our apartment in the city for a few weeks to tackle it all, planning to go home on the weekend in between. But another opportunity came up and I was so tired that I stayed in the city." He tried not to think about the argument he'd had with Jennie about not going home that weekend. She'd been 100 percent right about how he was losing sight of his family.

"The next week Jennie decided to surprise me by driving up from Connecticut. We'd fought about me not being home, and we didn't fight often so it felt so very wrong and off. I had no idea what she was planning until I got the call from the police." His chest cramped so much it nearly made him lose his breath. "I was listed as next of kin, our address the one in New Haven. By the time they reached me, the accident had been cleared and their bodies at the hospital."

His voice finally broke. "I can still see them there, Jess. She was cut up bad. But Owen…he looked like he'd just gone off to sleep. God, I pray he was sleeping and never felt anything. I hope it was all so fast that neither of them suffered or knew what was happening." The well of emotion threatened to strangle him. "They shouldn't have been on the road that night. And they wouldn't have been, if I'd been less full of myself and had gone home as we planned. All she wanted was for us to spend time together as a family, and I was too damned important and busy."

Jess's hand was still rubbing his back. "You blame yourself."

"Of course I do!" he snapped, then let out a breath. "She was my wife. He was my son. The two most important people in the world to me, and I let them down so badly. It should have been me."

"You don't feel you deserve to live."

"No! Yes. I don't know." He shifted away from her hand. "That's the thing, Jess. For a long time, I didn't want to live. And now I do, and I'm left wondering if that makes me a horrible person."

Jess was quiet for a long moment. She finally let out a long breath and angled her body toward him. "When Ana got sick, I was so damned angry. But I didn't cause her cancer. You didn't cause that accident. It was an accident, and they happen."

"But she wouldn't have been on the road at all if I had just gone home like she'd asked."

"And maybe you would have had an accident going home. Would you want Jennie to feel like if she just hadn't asked you to come home that you'd still be alive?"

"Of course not."

"She made a choice, Bran. She could have waited until the weekend. She could have taken a different route, left at a different time. Ana might not have had cancer. What I'm saying is…to think any of this is actually within our control is so flawed. But we look for explanations and blame so we have somewhere to put our grief."

She sniffled and Bran realized she was crying. He wasn't, not this time, but she was, and seeing the wetness on her cheeks and the redness of her eyes nearly undid him. She was so beautiful, inside and out. And he was so very unworthy.

He pulled her close. "You loved her very much."

"More than anyone ever in my life, I think. Even the guy I thought I was going to marry."

"Were you *in* love with her?"

She lifted her head sharply, looked into his eyes. "Oh… no. Not that way."

He chuckled and his arm tightened around her. "Are you surprised I asked?"

"A little. Would it matter to you?"

He shook his head and lifted his shoulders in a shrug. "Why would it? It takes all kinds of love to make the world go round. I never assume anything."

She pushed away and turned on the sofa, sitting with her legs crossed, but she still held his hand. "You know, I didn't expect you to surprise me more than you already have tonight, but you just did." A sweet smile touched her lips. "And every time you surprise me, I like you a little bit more."

She shouldn't like him. It made things harder. And yet he found himself rubbing his thumb over her wrist in a comforting gesture. He could still see the trails tears had made on her cheeks. "I'm sorry you lost her," he said quietly. "She sounds like a wonderful woman."

"She was. And I'm sorry you lost Jennie and Owen. But we're alive, Bran. You and me. Alive and we have lives to live. You can't punish yourself forever. I can't be sad forever."

"Jess…"

"And I feel most alive when I'm with you."

If she kept it up with that soft voice and her big eyes, he was going to have to go for another dip in the sea. He should look away. But he couldn't. Her gaze held him prisoner, his breath shortened as the moment drew out. He was still holding her hand; meanwhile the towel and blanket were feeling rather constrictive.

"I'm not relationship material, Jess. You need to know that. I have nothing to offer someone in that way."

Had she somehow moved closer? "I don't recall asking for a relationship. Or any sort of promises," she whispered. "I don't want them, Bran. I'm here for a matter of weeks, and then I'm going back to my life." She lifted her other hand and cupped his jaw. "Besides, I'm trying this thing where I live in the moment."

In this moment he knew exactly what he wanted. But she asked him first.

"Stay with me," she murmured.

He swallowed around a lump in his throat, his heart pounding with what he was sure were equal measures of arousal and fear.

But he didn't have time to think. Jess shifted and slid one leg over him, so that she was straddling him and he was having serious doubts about the reliability of the towel. She kissed him softly, on the crests of his cheeks, the corners of his eyes, the spot just above his lower lip, until he could hardly breathe. In less than a moment he lifted his arms, sending the blanket cape falling to the side as he wrapped her in a tight embrace. And then they kissed, long, slow, deep, until his brain was swimming with nothing but the feel of her, the scent of her skin, soft and salty from the sea.

When the sofa grew uncomfortable, Jess slid off his lap and held out her hand. He knew what she was asking. Knew it might be a mistake. But he also knew he had never wanted something so badly. This feeling alive thing was addictive, and he needed another hit. There was one thing standing in his way, though. And it was something he'd never risk.

"Jess, I'm not prepared."

Her cheeks pinkened delightfully, but she shook her head. "It's okay. I've been on the pill for years."

He put his hand in hers and stood, his towel falling away.

Jess tried not to stare, but Bran was standing naked in her living room. Tall and lean, with a small scar on his lower right abdomen, and a soft dusting of hair from his chest down to his navel. She wanted this. But the fierceness with which she wanted him was unfamiliar, and gave her a moment's pause.

Then she met his gaze and he lifted a single eyebrow. She tugged on his hand, leading him past her easel and canvas to the small bedroom and the bottom bunk.

"There's not a lot of head room," she whispered, catching her breath when he came up behind her and his body grazed hers.

"I'm not planning on standing up." His voice was low and seductive, warm at her ear. "Unless you want to."

Oh, my.

Jess took a deep breath and pulled off her hoodie. She

still wasn't wearing a bra, and the night air made goose bumps rise on her skin. Wordlessly she shimmied out of her yoga pants, and once she was naked, Bran reached out and pulled her close.

She was afraid. Not of him. But of being overwhelmed.

But he took his time, kissing her, touching her with light strokes, lighting her on fire and making her melt at the same time. His skin was warm on hers, and she marveled at the intimacy of the feeling, skin on skin. When her knees grew weak and he laid her down on the mattress, his eyes found hers in the dim moonlight cast through the window. "Okay?" he asked.

Tears pricked her eyes and she blinked them away. He was so considerate. So gentle. So…everything.

"More than okay," she assured him.

His gaze held hers, his eyes widening for a moment as they came together, key into lock. Jess felt a pang in her heart, the bittersweet knowledge that she'd fallen for a man she couldn't have, or could have but only for a little while.

But living in the moment meant embracing the moment, and she was determined to do that. So she reached up and looped her hand around his neck, pulling him down for a kiss. If she couldn't have Branson as her love, she could at least have him for her lover. And when their breathing finally slowed and the sweat dried from their skin, she had no regrets.

Jess shifted beneath the blanket, trying not to wake Bran. The sun was barely up, and the light in the bedroom was watery and dim. But it was enough that she could make out his features completely. The bit of hair that was in a tangle on the pillow. His lips, open slightly as he slept, and the way he linked his fingers together over his belly. She liked that the most, as it seemed like a cute little quirk individual to him. He was a back sleeper. She was usually a sprawler, but sprawling was impossible in a bed this size and shared with a man of his build.

They were both naked under the covers. His clothes were still in the dryer, and she was on the inside of the bed, closest to the wall, and hadn't gotten up to pull something on after…

After.

Her chest cramped, in both delicious memory and delightful anticipation. He'd been a thorough, attentive lover. There'd been a moment where something threatened to overwhelm her, and maybe him, too. Their eyes had met and their smiles faded. In that moment sex had become more than just sex. It had become his first time since Jennie. She was sure of that. And for her…

It had been connection. Bone-deep, in-the-blood connection with another human being. For all her live-in-the-moment Zen-ness, deep connections, trust…those were rare occurrences. It was why losing Ana had hurt so badly.

People didn't tend to stay in her life. But this time there was no danger of that. She was going into this with the knowledge and understanding that in a matter of weeks, they'd both be moving on. No surprises, no being blindsided, no one hurt. Bran let out a sigh and something soft and sentimental wound through her at the sound. A smile touched her lips. This summer would be one of healing, for both of them if they were lucky. And they'd be able to look back on this as the summer they made their way back to the living, with fond memories.

Bran stirred and shifted to his side, then his eyes slowly opened. She met his gaze evenly, the smile still on her lips. "Good morning," she whispered.

"Good morning." His cheeks colored a little and she loved that he was blushing right now, just a hint of pink above his beard.

"You okay?" Mornings-after could be awkward. Things were different in the light of day. Last night they'd been swept up in each other, but now...now they had to navigate the dynamic.

He nodded slightly, then shifted his arm and said, "Come here."

She shifted over and curled in next to his side. His skin was soft and warm, and the smattering of hair on his chest tickled her breasts.

His arm tightened around her. "I'm okay. You?"

She nodded, her cheek rubbing against his shoulder. "Me, too. I was afraid it might be...awkward."

He chuckled, a low sound that moved his chest and made her smile. "It is, a little. I'm very out of practice with mornings-after. But..." He moved his head so that he was looking down at her, and she tilted up her chin. "We've been fairly gentle with each other so far. I figure if we can keep doing that, we're okay."

"Except, you know, when you kicked me off your property."

A smile lit his face. "Yeah, except then. And when I saved you with my boat. I didn't say you weren't a pain in my ass."

She laughed, then they grew quiet again. She was thinking about how their friendship had evolved when her stomach growled loudly in the silence.

"Someone is hungry."

"I have eggs and sourdough bread. Maybe even some bacon. You want breakfast?"

"I would. But it means not sneaking away before Jeremy has a chance to see my car."

She pushed away and rested on her elbows so she could see him better. "That would bother you, huh."

"Him knowing? Not that, exactly. It's more the questions to follow." He lifted an eyebrow. "I hate when people want me to explain myself."

"I have an answer for that."

"Do tell."

She grinned. "Practice saying this phrase—*It's none of your business.*"

Bran's face straightened into a serious expression. "It's none of your business."

"Nope. Not convinced. Try again."

This time it was accompanied by an angled eyebrow. "It's none of your business."

"Better. Let's practice some more. Hey, Bran, how's the new novel coming?"

He grinned. "It's none of your business."

"What's it about? Come on, you can tell me that."

Firmer this time: "It's none of your business."

"Good! And wow. You spent the night with Jess. Are you sure that was a good thing?"

He rolled slightly and placed a kiss on her naked shoulder. "Oh, I'm very sure it was a good thing," he replied, his voice husky.

"Tsk-tsk. That's not the right answer."

"Yes, it is," he murmured, running his fingers through her hair. "But it's none of Jeremy's business, or Tori's either." He kissed her, long and slow, and then slid out from beneath the covers and left the bedroom, presumably heading toward the dryer and his clothes.

Her body was still humming from the power of that kiss, though. He was very, very good at it.

She slipped out from beneath the sheets and pulled on underwear and last night's yoga pants and top. She'd shower later, before she had to make the trip to Halifax to pick up more supplies.

Branson was in the kitchen, already boiling water for making coffee in her French press, his shorts and T-shirt wrinkled from being in the dryer overnight, but looking entirely scrumptious. She let him work his magic—clearly he knew his way around coffee—and dug out eggs, and bacon she bought at the farmer's market. She put the latter to fry in a cast iron pan, then set to work slicing sourdough bread for toast.

The scent of bacon and coffee filled the air and she smiled up at Bran, who'd found her mugs and had poured her a cup of coffee. It was nice having him here, though it played havoc with her heart a little. She was not sticking around. It wouldn't be good to get used to this kind of domestic scene, would it?

Bran took over toasting the bread while Jess drained the bacon and then cracked eggs into the pan. "How do you like your eggs? Over? Yolks hard or soft?"

"Over and just set."

Just like she preferred hers.

Soon they were seated at her tiny table, with bacon, eggs, and pots of butter and jam between them for the toast. "Delicious," Bran said, chewing on a strip of bacon.

"Big breakfast is one of my favorites," she admitted. "Sometimes I even like having breakfast for dinner."

He laughed. "Me, too. Only with pancakes."

"Mmm... Or waffles."

She spread raspberry jam on her toast and took a bite. "So. What's on your agenda for today?"

He shrugged. "Changing my clothes. Going over some of the stuff from yesterday, with the restoration and stuff. You?"

"Actually, I think I'm the one heading to Halifax today.

I want to visit a shop there for more supplies. I've only been there once since arriving. To be honest, I could stand a little city life for a day. As much as I love all this nature, I miss people sometimes. The vitality of it."

Bran was quiet for a moment, took a sip of his coffee, then looked her in the eye. "What if I went with you? We could make a day of it. You could pick up your supplies, and we could go for dinner someplace nice downtown."

"Like a date?"

Again, he shrugged. "If you want to call it that. We could just call it hanging out."

It did sound lovely. A couple of hours drive on a beautiful summer day, an errand or two, and then a fine dinner… She hadn't done that in a long time. Especially with company. She'd spent the last several months traveling alone, and she'd enjoyed it, but she couldn't deny it was a lonely existence.

"You're welcome to come along."

"Do you want me to drive, or take yours?" He lifted an eyebrow. "If we take mine, you can have some wine with dinner. I'm happy to be your designated driver."

It was a generous offer, but she already felt a little odd, considering he wasn't drinking at all. "I don't need wine," she said, popping the last crust of toast into her mouth.

"You say that, but the place I have in mind has a very good wine list. And it doesn't bother me, Jess. Truly."

She took his plate and stacked it on her own. "Then I accept. It sounds like a very nice day, and since my cooking is plain at best, a dinner out sounds lovely."

"Perfect." He pushed away from the table and then checked his watch. "It's nearly eight. Jeremy will have noticed my car by now. Time to answer the inevitable questions, and head home for a shower. What time should I pick you up?"

She pondered for a moment. "Eleven? It would give me a couple of hours to work before we go."

"Sounds perfect."

She took the dishes to the sink, and when she turned back again, there was an odd moment where they stood and stared at each other.

"Okay. So the awkward exit is a thing," he said, then took a step forward and kissed her on the cheek. "Thanks for last night," he murmured, his lips close to her ear. "I'll see you in a few hours."

She nodded, feeling a little breathless.

And then he was gone.

Jess stared at the door for ten seconds, then shook herself into action. First, work. Then, a shower.

And then, the rest of the day with a man who could never really be hers.

CHAPTER EIGHT

BRAN RETURNED AT just past eleven o'clock. He'd left without encountering Jeremy, nor was there any questioning text message from either him or Tori. They either hadn't noticed his car, or they were minding their own business. If he were a betting man, he'd say they had slept in and missed his exit. Because Jeremy wouldn't hesitate to put in his two cents.

This time, instead of parking in the main driveway, he pulled in next to Jess's car. She came outside and shut the door behind her, and his breath caught a little.

He wasn't supposed to be feeling this way. Not now. Maybe not ever. And yet he wasn't going to cancel their plans. It was just a summer thing. He wasn't going to fall in love, so that wasn't an issue. And they were both clear on that, weren't they? She was leaving to go back to Chicago. Why shouldn't they combat some of their loneliness with each other?

Jess wore a pretty little dress with a light blue background and tiny pink flowers, with cute little blue sandals on her feet. She looked as fresh and pretty as a spring morning, with her sunny hair shining and grazing the tips of her shoulders in soft waves. A bag was slung over her shoulder, a pastel-colored tapestry kind of thing that suited her completely. "Have you been waiting?" she asked, descending the two steps to the graveled walk.

"Only for a few minutes. You look very nice." He moved to the passenger side to open her door. Lord, she smelled delicious, too. Like sweet peas softened by hints of vanilla.

"Thanks." She smiled up at him. "No paint-stained jeans and tees for me today. If we're going to dinner, I wanted to dress up a little."

She looked him up and down too, as he held open the door. "You also look very nice."

He needed a haircut, but there hadn't been time. But he'd trimmed his beard and put aside jeans and tees for dress pants and a button-down shirt in off-white.

"Well, let's hit the road," he suggested, and watched the long length of her leg as she slid into the car and he shut the door behind her.

They drove to Halifax in just under two hours. The highway traffic was light, and they only hit one small section of construction. Bran used the car's GPS to navigate his way to the art supply store Jess had picked, and went inside with her as she browsed and made her purchases. They stowed everything in his trunk, and then he suggested a walk in the popular public gardens.

The sun was bright, and there was a light breeze as they made their way to the entrance. "It's a beautiful day," she said, letting out a happy sigh. "This was such a good idea, Bran."

"The gardens will be packed, but I hear they're beautiful. If you like flowers."

She patted her bag. "I'll make a confession. I brought a small sketch pad with me."

He laughed. Laughing was so easy with her, particularly when she looked up at him with a twinkle in her eye. "Of course you did."

"Don't tell me you don't always have a notebook with you."

He angled a wry look in her direction. "Of course I don't." Then after a moment, he added, "I voice record on my phone."

But he wasn't interested in dictating now. He just wanted to spend the afternoon with her, in the early summer sun, and live in the moment.

It was miles better than living in the past.

The garden was heavy with tourists and what appeared to be a couple of bus tour groups. As they entered the ornate iron gates, a strange amphibious vehicle approached the intersection, loaded with tourists and a guide narrating local history. They sent up a strange cry of "ribbit-ribbit" as they passed, and then Bran chuckled. "The Harbor Hopper," he said, nudging her and pointing. "Want to go? From the look of it, it's one of those land and sea tour things."

"Oh, my," she replied, laughing as the vehicle pulled away, the guide changing topic. "I'm not sure I'm dressed for that."

"I'm sure you wouldn't fall in." He took her hand in his. "But if you did, I'm a strong swimmer."

"One ocean rescue is enough for me." She pushed up her sunglasses. "Oh, Bran. You were right, this is gorgeous."

They wandered along the paths, meandering slowly around all the different flower beds, examining species of tree and shrub and bloom. Couples posed for pictures and selfies on a small stone bridge, and Jess kindly offered to snap photos of a couple on their honeymoon. The smell was absolutely heavenly: fresh-cut grass and the heavy, sweet scent of lilacs; rhododendrons in various shades of purple, the size of cars, were in full, showy bloom, and the annual flower beds offered bright rainbows of colors. They ambled in the shade and stopped for Jess to take out her pencils and sketch a laburnum tree, the yellow chains of flowers reminding Bran of a sunshine-hued wisteria.

They stopped again and sat on a bench near the pond. A middle-aged man fed the ducks on the bank, and Bran was happy to sit and watch as Jess worked away, her pencil strokes brisk and confident. A tiny replica of the *Titanic* floated on the water, and Bran considered telling Jess the city's connection to the disaster, only he didn't want to interrupt her.

She was in another world when she sketched. Her focus was razor sharp, and nothing escaped her notice as her gaze darted between subject and paper.

He was happy to people watch. He leaned back on the bench, crossed an ankle over his knee, and watched the dynamics between parents and children, old and young, couples on dates and those who seemed to have been together for a long time. They were the ones who didn't have to hold hands to show intimacy; it was in their relaxed body language and the easy way they touched each other in passing, speaking of a comfort and devotion that pricked at Bran's capricious contentment. Strangers wandered together, name tags stuck to their shirts from some sort of guided tour. They were smiling and polite as they talked to each other, pointing out blossoms and reading the species signs dotted throughout the garden.

A father and son left the pathway nearby, the boy holding his dad's hand as they picked their way over the grass toward a handful of ducks near the water's edge. "Dada, ducks!" the boy exclaimed. Bran guessed he was maybe three. He swallowed thickly. Owen would be about the same age now, if he were alive. Would he have liked ducks? Held Bran's hand, maybe in Central Park on Saturdays?

Watching the two of them play by the water, the way

the father patiently kept the boy from the edge, or pointed out all the different colored feathers from each species, warmed his heart. The ache was bittersweet; he was sure he would never quite get over losing his child. But it hurt less today.

Jess looked over at him, put her hand on his knee. "They're sweet, aren't they?"

He nodded, unable to tear his eyes away. "He's a good dad."

"You can have it again someday, you know," she offered gently. "When you're ready."

Bran tore himself away from the father and son scene and met her gaze. "No," he said quietly. "I can't. I can't go through that again. But I'm getting to a place where I'm okay with it."

"Then maybe you'll get to a place where you'll consider it again, too. You never know."

But he shook his head. "No," he repeated. "I know. I had my shot at a family, and I won't chance going through this hell again."

The pink in her cheeks deepened. "I'm sorry," she murmured. "I didn't mean to press."

"You didn't. It's just…there's not much I'm sure of. But that's one thing I am. And I've made my peace with it."

The father and son had moved on, skirting the pond. And Bran got up from the bench, ready to move on, as well.

Jess shoved her sketch pad into her bag and hurried to catch up with Bran, who was starting down the path toward the middle of the gardens. She hadn't meant to upset him, but clearly she had. She should have known better than to bring up fatherhood. It was still too raw for him. At the same time, she'd never been more sure that their relationship was destined for a dead end. He really didn't want a family again, and she did. Being with him, and being around the Fishers had shown her that she did want children of her own. And a partner to share life with. And yet something held her back from saying the words out loud. She could tell Bran all about life not giving guarantees, but she also understood why a person wouldn't want to set themselves up for potential heartbreak.

After all, she'd been doing it for years.

And still there was Bran to consider. It would be easier to end things right now. Probably smarter, too. But she didn't want to. Not yet.

"Hey, wait up," she called, trotting to catch up to him. When she did, she took a deep breath and matched her steps to his. "You gonna be okay?"

He nodded. "Yeah. I'm okay."

"I overstepped, Bran. I really am sorry."

He reached down for her hand, a reassuring gesture that touched her heart. "I know you are. And don't worry about pressing me. It's good for me. It helps, even when it makes me grumpy."

Forgiven, she kept her hand in his as they made their way to the large gazebo that was the centerpiece of the gardens. People milled around, and there was a line at a small building to their left, which appeared to house public bathrooms and a small café, complete with ice cream. The large patio area was full of people enjoying the sweet, cold treat. "You want some?" Bran asked.

"Do you?" She wasn't really hungry, even though they hadn't had lunch. The big breakfast had been super filling, but could she really pass up ice cream in the park?

"A small one? It looks delicious."

They detoured into the building and waited in line for the hand-paddled treat. When they got to the front of the line, she chose blueberries and cream for her flavor.

Bran went for a more sedate maple walnut, and then they emerged out into the bright sunshine again.

"Let's find a place to sit," he suggested. "Someplace with shade. I don't want to be responsible for you getting a sunburn."

She was sure the sun had already left a bit of a burn on her shoulders. Her pale complexion meant she burned easily, and she hadn't thought to bring sunscreen today. "How about up there?" She pointed to the top end of the garden, where there was an open area bordered by benches and leafy trees. There was even a chess table adding character to the area.

"Perfect."

Her ice cream was starting to melt by the time they got to the benches, and they picked one that was shaded and would remain so as the sun shifted. For several minutes they ate in comfortable silence. Despite the earlier tension, Jess couldn't remember the last time she'd been so comfortable with someone. They didn't need to talk. Didn't need to fill up the space with empty words that meant nothing. She finished her ice cream, and he finished his, and he took their garbage to a nearby trash can. When he came back, he put his arm along the back of the bench, and she relaxed against him, her head resting in the curve of his shoulder.

"People watching," he said softly. "I love people watching."

"Ana and I used to make up stories about people," she offered, a smile touching her lips. "Like that woman there." She nodded toward a woman several yards away, sitting on an identical bench and reading. "What's her story, do you think?"

Bran tapped a finger to his lips. "She's waiting for

someone, but he's late. He's always late, so she brings a book so she doesn't look as if she's waiting."

"Well, that's sad. Why does she have to be waiting for a man, anyway?" She lifted her eyebrows. "I think she's single. Maybe she's just broken up with someone because she wants to be put first. So she's putting herself first and spending an afternoon exactly how she wants—in the gardens in the sunshine and with a good book."

"The heroine of her own life."

"You bet." She grinned up at him. "Do you always go for the sad and tragic?"

"Waiting for someone isn't exactly tragic."

"I don't know. Waiting for someone who is chronically late and doesn't care enough to show up on time... I mean, if someone loves you, they should be impatient. Like they can't wait for that moment when they see you again. A thirst that needs to be quenched."

He laughed and squeezed her shoulder a little. "Are you sure you're not a writer?"

"I'm an observer," she answered. "Okay, tell me another one."

He looked around for a moment, then nodded. "That old gentleman there." The man in question was walking slowly along the path with the aid of a cane. A cap shielded his eyes, and he wore a long-sleeved shirt and pants even though the day was hot. "He comes here every day to walk. He used to come here with his wife, but she's no longer with him. But it doesn't matter to him. He's not sad. He walks and he remembers, and he's thankful for the years they had together. And when he gets home to his little apartment, he tells her picture about everything he saw. Because she's still with him."

She loved the wistful picture he drew with words. "You're a romantic, Branson Black. Don't deny it."

He shrugged. "I suppose I can be. When I'm not murdering people and creating horrible villains."

"Everyone has a little darkness inside them. It's all about the choices."

He was quiet for a few moments.

"I saw the darkness for a while, Jess. I'm not gonna lie."

"I know, sweetheart. I know."

"It's not so dark lately, though. I have you to thank for that."

Her heart warmed, and a tingly sensation wound its way from her chest down to her belly. Sometimes she wished she didn't have this visceral reaction to him, and other times she reveled in it. Today he'd made it clear that he wasn't interested in anything serious, wasn't looking to have more children or a family. Where did that leave her? She wanted those things. Maybe not right this minute, but eventually. Hoping for him to change was a sure path to disappointment. This summer—these few weeks—were all they would have together. She wanted to cherish them, but to do so she had to remind herself that she could not fall in love with him, and she had to live in the moment.

Could she do that? Because if she couldn't, she should walk away right now.

She looked up at him. He'd closed his eyes and lifted his face to the sun that filtered through the leafy canopy.

As if he could sense her gaze, he said, "You should sketch. You know you want to."

She did, so she leaned forward and retrieved her sketch pad. But it wasn't flowers or trees or strangers that she drew. It was him, and the angle of his jaw, the crisp edges of his lips, his soft eyelashes, and the way his unruly hair touched his shoulders when his head was tipped back.

She wasn't in love, but she wouldn't lie and say her heart wasn't involved. Of course it was. Her pencil moved quickly across the paper, then she reached for another with a softer lead. She wanted to capture the unguarded moment as best she could before he opened his eyes and caught her.

The sketch was rough but there was something in it she liked. It wasn't perfect, but the sweeping strokes captured an urgency and energy that surprised her.

Bran opened his eyes, squinting and looking at her. She turned the page over and smiled up at him, hoping he hadn't seen the sketch. She wanted it just for her.

She wanted to have something to remember him by when their time together was over.

As, of course, it would be.

CHAPTER NINE

HE TOOK HER to dinner at a seafood restaurant in the city's downtown core. While she went for a seafood pasta, he ordered steak and an appetizer of mussels in a garlic cream sauce. Best of all was the history of the place, which had its beginnings as a school, then as a mortuary, particularly during the time of the *Titanic* sinking and a massive explosion that had leveled the north end during the First World War. Jess listened raptly as Bran told her what he knew of the place, and then grinned when he said it was haunted.

"Do you really believe in that stuff?" she asked, taking a sip of the fine semi-dry white she'd ordered.

"Of course I do. Don't you?"

She shrugged. "I don't know. I mean, I think it's possible. I just haven't experienced anything that would, you know, make me really believe."

After a moment of hesitation, she looked up at him. "Have you ever, you know, seen a ghost?"

He furrowed his brow and picked at his potato for a few moments. "No? I mean, not actually seen a ghost. But I've felt things that I can't really explain."

She held her breath as she asked, "You mean Jennie?"

He sighed and met her gaze, his eyes sad. "You know, at times I kind of wish Jennie would show up. I'd like to see her again. And then as soon as I think that, I realize that if she did, it'd scare me to death. I don't know what I'd do. Or say."

And make it harder to let go, Jess thought, but she kept the words locked inside.

They changed the subject and chatted over the magnificent dinner, and even though Jess was stuffed, she agreed to share a serving of lemon tart. It was after eight when they finished and made their way back to his car. It would be ten before they reached home, and just dark, as the days were long. Jess was determined now not to return to the maudlin subject of his wife; it had dampened the mood earlier and while she had no problem being an ear for his thoughts, twice during the day she'd felt as if there was a third person on their date. It seemed Bran was determined, too, because he'd reverted back to his easy manner as he opened the car door for her, and closed it solicitously before getting in on the driver's side. Once behind the wheel, he hesitated, then reached for her hand.

"Thank you for allowing me to tag along today. It was nice, don't you think?"

Yes, it had been nice. Despite the conversation getting heavy at times. She'd enjoyed his company, but something had been missing. So nice was a perfectly adequate word.

"What's wrong?" he asked quietly. He hadn't yet started the car, and the silence around them was heavy.

She shifted in her seat and looked over at him. "Did things get weird today? Are you having regrets?"

His eyes warmed. "No, I'm not. I'm sorry if I got moody. It's just that…well, for a long time, that moodiness was a constant. Lately not so much." He squeezed her fingers. "Lately I've found myself enjoying things. I forget to be sad. So when those moments creep in, I'm not ready for them." He smiled a little. "I think it's a good thing, really. Forgetting to be sad. Maybe someday I actually won't be sad at all."

She squeezed his hand back. "Thank you for telling me," she said softly. "I wondered if I'd done something wrong."

"No, nothing," he assured her, and then leaned over the seat and kissed her gently. "You are lovely and sweet and strong." He kissed her again, and she melted a little, leaning into the soft and seductive contact. "You're just what I need, Jess."

Her heart slammed against her ribs as she opened her mouth and led him to a deeper kiss. Desire darkened the sweetness of it, like rich chocolate over marshmallow. He let go of her hand and threaded his fingers through her hair, and she moaned against his lips as his strong fingers massaged the back of her head.

He pulled away, a little reluctantly, she thought, and stared down at her. "We're in a car in broad daylight," he said, his voice a bit rough. "Put a pin in this until we get home?"

"It's a long drive," she said.

"We could spend the night in the city. Drive back in the morning."

The suggestion came as such a surprise she was temporarily dumbstruck. Finally she managed a weak, "Bran…"

"Order room service for breakfast."

Never in her life had she ever rented a hotel room for sex. And yet the two-hour drive seemed interminably long, and the idea of spending the night in a hotel was exciting. His gaze held hers and the tension in the car leaped. "Bran," she said, trying for a low note of caution. Instead that single syllable—his name—came out with a breathy sort of yearning. "I think… I want to…"

Oh, dear.

He turned the car on and pulled out of the spot, navigating a few streets until he reached the hotel she'd noticed earlier, across from the gardens. He parked in the underground garage, and without looking at her, got out and came around to open her door.

She grabbed her tote bag while a rush of feelings swept through her body. Excitement. Arousal, for sure. Anxiety. Were they rushing things? Was this really a smart idea?

"Relax," he whispered, taking her hand as they made their way into the hotel and to the front desk. Within moments he'd secured them a room and was guiding her to the elevator.

As they waited for the elevator, Bran took her hand. Jess swallowed against a nervous lump in her throat. Were they really doing this? Last night had been one thing. They'd been in her place, talking and snuggling after a make-out session on the beach. It had seemed…a logical progression of events. This was different. The bell dinged and the doors opened, and Bran guided her inside. She let out a long slow breath and asked herself a sudden question.

What would Ana do?

Jess bit down on her lip. Ana wasn't here. But Ana had lived life until the last moment, and she'd undoubtedly tell Jess to grab what happiness she could while it lasted. Jess chanced a look over at Bran, and he looked back at her, unsmiling, his dark eyes gleaming. None of the intensity in the car had been lost, and she got a thrill seeing the desire in his eyes.

No one was guaranteed another day. Look at Ana. Look at Jennie. You had to grab each day and its precious, fleeting moments.

The doors opened and they stepped out, then hesitated while Bran scanned the plate on the wall with arrows to room numbers.

They were off again, down the hall, stopping in front

of a door, waiting while he let them in and shut the door behind them.

Jess had a glimpse of a king-sized bed covered in white and gold linens, and matching draperies on either side of an elegant desk. It was more luxurious than even Bran's room at his house, but the moment after the door shut, the sheer opulence of the room was forgotten. Bran's mouth was on hers, his hands were on her waist and she was swept entirely away into a sea of sensation.

CHAPTER TEN

BRAN WOKE WITH light streaming through the window. He checked the clock beside the bed: five forty. The days were incredibly long at this time of year. Last night, before they'd fallen asleep, sated, it had still been daylight. He'd slept straight through, dreamless. He regretted that he hadn't awakened in the night, simply to make the hours last longer.

Jess was breathing slow and deep beside him, her face turned toward him, her hair strewn on the white linen of the pillowcase. She was so beautiful, with her sunrise-colored hair and delicate lips. An unfamiliar tenderness washed over him. The sex was fantastic, but it was more than that. They were friends.

He wondered if that friendship would be ruined now that they'd slept together. Certainly, after the summer, their relationship would be over. And yet he'd miss her. She understood him in a way that was so…well, easy.

Yes, he was going to miss her.

She shifted and rolled to her right side, so that her back was to him. It was early to wake her, so instead he slid closer, gently putting his arm over her waist and snuggling in, spoon-style. He closed his eyes and drank in the scent of her hair and the light musk of her skin. For two years he'd slept alone. The last two nights he'd had Jess with him, and it would be too easy to get used to her there. Spending time with her was one thing. Having fun was fine. But he wouldn't use her as a tonic for his loneliness, and he wouldn't get too used to her.

Last night had been impulsive and exciting, but they couldn't make a habit of this, could they?

But reality was hours away, and he wanted to absorb every moment he could. So he closed his eyes and imprinted the moment on his memory, until she woke up.

He didn't mean to fall back asleep, but when he opened his eyes again, Jess was facing him with a soft smile on her face.

"Good morning."

"Hi," he answered. Her foot slid along his calf, just a light caress, but it instantly brought his body to attention. "Sleep well?"

"Too well," she laughed. "I think I got more than a full eight hours. I don't remember the last time that happened."

He wiggled his eyebrows, and she laughed again. Maybe keeping it light was the way to go.

"I think we wore each other out."

She blushed, and he loved it.

A piece of hair had fallen over her cheek, and he reached out and tucked it back behind her ear. "So, what do you think? Room service?"

"Why not?"

"What do you like?"

This time she wiggled her eyebrows, and he laughed. Lord, she was such a ray of sunshine. "Everything," she answered.

His brain took a direct trip back to last night, and his body wasn't far behind. But while they'd been a bit crazed and frantic, he didn't want to assume this morning would be a continuation. As much as he would like it to be. He pushed the thoughts aside as best he could and rolled to the night table, where he grabbed the folder containing the in-room dining guide. A few minutes later he'd ordered a veritable feast, due to be delivered in thirty minutes.

She sat up, the sheets tucked under her arms, covering her breasts. "So…uh…want to shower before breakfast?"

He swallowed tightly. "Together?"

There was that blush again. The air of innocence around her was enchanting. She didn't need to ask again; they made their way to the luxurious bathroom and spent five minutes cleaning up and fifteen finding mind-blowing pleasure. After they'd caught their breath and dried with the fluffy towels, they dressed in the hotel-provided robes and waited for their meal.

When it came, he watched as she loaded her plate with French toast and fruit and bacon, then drizzled on enough maple syrup that it puddled under everything. He liked her so much. Liked just about everything about her. But as they shared a laugh over her love of the syrup, he realized something important.

He didn't love her. Or at least, he wasn't in love with her. It came as a huge relief. He didn't want to love again. And they were having fun, weren't they? A summer fling.

He bit into his omelet and frowned. Jeremy and Tori had a summer fling and look at them now. But that wouldn't happen to him. Jess was on the pill, and so there wouldn't be a surprise baby popping up. Even so, perhaps he'd be wise to stop at a pharmacy and grab some condoms just in case. There was no harm in doubling up, was there?

"You okay, Bran?" Jess's light voice interrupted his thoughts. "You look like you disappeared for a moment."

"I'm perfect," he replied, feeling on surer ground now. "This is delicious. And so are you."

She blushed and he grinned. "What?" she asked, tilting her head a bit in that adorable way she had.

"You blush a lot, and I like it."

The pink color deepened. "I blush at everything, so there."

"Mmm-hmm." He stood and leaned over the table to get a taste of her maple-sweet lips. "I still like it."

After breakfast they dressed in their clothes from the day before, and Bran dropped the key at the desk before they made their way to the parking garage. In no time, they were back on the highway and headed home. Bran's heart felt lighter than it had in years, and he tapped his fingers on the steering wheel in time to the music playing through the speakers. Jess told him about her agent wanting to set up a showing in the fall, and how much she was enjoying painting again. Truthfully, Bran couldn't wait to get home and open his laptop. He wasn't going to push, but he felt the urge to write, and he wanted to strike while the iron was hot. He'd always been a disciplined writer, working consistently but also riding a wave of inspiration when it hit.

It seemed no time at all that they arrived at Jeremy's, and he parked behind her car at the boathouse. He helped her take in her packages from the art store, and then hesitated on the threshold. "So, I'll see you soon?"

She nodded. "You know where I am." Her smile was sweet. "I'll be here, painting."

"Good." He reached out and pulled her close again, kissing her lightly. "I had a really great time," he murmured against her mouth.

"Me, too."

He left her standing there on the porch, and found himself whistling as he slid behind the wheel of his car and backed out of the lane, heading home once more.

* * *

Jess changed out of her dress and into more comfortable clothes—denim capris and a T-shirt—then organized her new supplies and studied the painting she had been working on for a week. She was happy with how it was progressing, and she spent an hour and a half working on it, trying to focus. But something wasn't quite right.

She stepped back and thought for a moment, and then, to her surprise, she rushed forward and removed the canvas from the easel and replaced it with a fresh one.

Something else was calling to her right now. She pulled out the photo of the first day, and then the sketch she'd done, and knew she had to paint it. The one with Bran looking out to sea.

For a moment she rolled her eyes and let out a sigh. Two nights with a man and suddenly he was her subject? And yet, she'd been drawn to that moment time and again over the last few weeks. The loneliness telegraphed in his body language, in the gray sea beyond him and the weary lighthouse. A thread of excitement wound through her as she started the process of turning canvas to art. She forgot the time, forgot to eat, forgot everything but the work until there was a knock on her door.

She checked her watch, shocked to discover it was almost four in the afternoon. She removed her apron as she made her way to the door, and opened it to find Tori on the other side, a frown immediately replaced by a relieved smile as she saw Jess in the doorway.

"Oh, good, you're all right!" Tori slipped into the boathouse, leaving Jess feeling off balance. She'd been so swept up in work that the interruption had her head trying to catch up.

"All right?" she parroted, following Tori into the main room.

"I stopped by yesterday and you didn't answer."

"Oh, is that all?" Jess laughed a little. "I went into Halifax for supplies."

Tori's brow wrinkled. "You did? But your car was here. And I texted, too. Gosh, I hope I got the right number."

Jess felt the heat creep up her neck. She hadn't even checked her phone since yesterday afternoon. She'd been utterly preoccupied—first with Bran and then with work.

"How did you get to Halifax?" Tori asked, and the heat reached Jess's ears.

"Oh, um, Branson had some things to do so we went together. No biggie." She smiled widely. "And it saved me from having to navigate the city. Bran's much more familiar."

Tori's face sobered. "You and Bran, huh?"

Oh, Lordy. She had such a horrible poker face. "Yeah, well, we get along okay now." A memory slid into her brain, of his face in the shower this morning, and she struggled to breathe. "At least he doesn't hate me anymore."

"Oh," Tori said, "no danger of that. He walked you home the other night."

"It's no big deal," Jess replied. And hoped beyond hope that Tori hadn't seen his car yesterday morning.

"Well, I'm hoping Jeremy and I didn't make a mistake." She rested her hand on the countertop. "We kind of pushed you two together, you know? Bran needed someone to shake him up a bit. But…" She peered into Jess's face. "It's more than shaking up, isn't it?"

Jess had to make light of this. She really didn't want Tori to butt in, or start asking more detailed questions. For one, she didn't know how she'd answer. The last two nights had been amazing, but they'd also shaken her more than she wanted to admit.

"I promise you have nothing to feel badly about. I like

Bran, he likes me, and sometimes we spend time together without fighting." Indeed. "Really, Tori, it's no big deal."

"So you're just enjoying each other's company?"

Jess let out a relieved breath. "Yes, that's exactly it."

Tori tapped her finger on her lips. "Hmm. Okay. I'm going to shut up now because I don't want to pry too deeply. I just…well, we love Bran, and I like you a lot, Jess. Jeremy and I don't want to see either of you hurt."

The words were heartfelt, so Jess relaxed a little and motioned toward the tiny table and chairs. "Listen, sit down for a bit and let me get you a drink."

Tori did sit, and as Jess went to the fridge, she called out, "So where's Rose this afternoon?"

"Sleeping. Jeremy's home and working in his office, with the baby monitor next to him." Jess turned around and saw Tori smiling. "I love her to bits, but going somewhere, even for thirty minutes, without a baby and the requisite gear is so nice."

"You didn't venture far," Jess teased. "Soda water okay? I have some flavored stuff. Lemon lime or grapefruit."

"Ooh, grapefruit, please," Tori replied. Jess retrieved two cans, opened them and poured them over ice before returning to the table. She sat across from Tori and tried to relax, though she was still feeling odd about the whole thing. She wasn't accountable to anyone, but the night away was still more of a secret than anything, for the simple reason that she wanted to avoid questions.

"You started a new painting," Tori said, staring at the white canvas. "What's this one?"

"Actually, it's from a photo I took the first day. Bran was looking out over the point, and he seemed so lost and lonely. The image hasn't left me alone, so I figure it's time to get started on it."

Tori's voice was soft. "You really care for him, don't

you? Oh, Jess. I'm afraid we really did goof. I don't want to see you fall for him, only to get hurt."

The consideration was genuine, and Jess patted Tori's hand. "It's fine. We like each other but neither of us is after anything serious. We've talked about it, Tori, so truly, don't worry. I'm going to paint to my heart's content, and at the end of the summer I'm going to head back home to my life. Besides, Bran is not in a relationship place. He's still too hung up on his wife."

"I never knew her. Jeremy says she was lovely, though, and that they were very happy."

"Hard to compete with that." She took a sip of her soda water. "Not that I want to. Still, we enjoy spending time together. That's all there is."

And the sex, she thought, but didn't say. She and Tori had become friends but weren't quite close enough to be confidants of that sort.

"So you aren't falling in love with him?"

"Of course not."

Jess said the words with confidence, but she knew deep down it wasn't strictly true. No matter how often she repeated the words to herself—summer romance, short-term fling—she couldn't erase the sight of Bran while they were making love, the intense expression on his face as he gazed into her eyes as if no one else existed. He was an extraordinary man, smart and sexy and deep, sometimes grouchy and other times sweet, and a man who knew how to love a woman with all his heart. Of course she was falling for him. Her head was in the clouds, and there was going to be an awful thud at the end. The difference was this time she wasn't going to be blindsided. She saw it coming and could prepare.

And yet, she looked at Tori and said, "Men like Bran

don't come along often. I'd be a fool not to spend whatever time I can with him. Even knowing the outcome."

Tori nodded and looked down in her glass, and looked up again, her eyes bright as if she might cry. "I felt the same way about Jeremy." Her voice was soft and dreamy. "And I was fine after he left, mostly. Until he came back. You're right, though. Bran isn't ready for anything serious. As long as you know that, and you're having fun... more power to you."

"I appreciate you caring, Tori, I do. But I've got this."

"Of course you do. You're a strong woman. I think that's why Bran likes you. None of those men are the kind who like pushovers."

"I think that's a compliment."

Tori laughed. "The best kind. Now, I'd better get back up to the house. I truly am glad you're okay. I was worried you'd got sick or something."

"I'm absolutely fine," she replied. "But thank you for caring." At least Tori hadn't realized that Jess hadn't returned home until this morning. The conversation had been personal enough without that information being out in the open.

After Tori left, Jess made an early dinner since she'd missed lunch. She checked her email on her phone; no texts from Bran. That was okay. After the past forty-eight hours, maybe he needed time to process everything. She certainly did.

Because she was falling for him, no question. But he didn't need to know that. And neither did Tori.

CHAPTER ELEVEN

BRAN LOOKED UP from his laptop and squinted. Ever since his return from Halifax, he'd either been embroiled in research, or working on the opening chapters of the new book. It had felt wonderful working again. The words weren't quite flowing, but they were there, ready for him to pluck out of his brain and put them on the page. Now the story had a basic outline, he had pages full of notes and his master document had the better part of two full chapters written.

Not long now, and he'd call his agent and tell him the good news. Maybe send him some pages. But right now, the light was dimming and he'd been working the better part of sixteen hours.

He checked the date on the bottom right corner of the screen. Was that correct? Had he been back from Halifax for three days already? And he hadn't heard from Jess. Not once. Nor had he texted.

He hit the save button and slumped back in his chair. He wasn't sure what to do about Jess, really. To say he wanted her was an understatement. Having sex again had been amazing…she was a good lover, sweet and generous and passionate. Their nights together had been wonderful, but he'd stayed quiet for two reasons. One, he'd gotten the bug to write and he wanted to catch the words while they were there, no longer out of reach. And two, it would be very easy to get wrapped up in her. Spending a few days regaining his equilibrium seemed like a good idea, especially after their dash to the hotel. That wasn't his usual style. There was a "can't keep my hands off her" edge to his feelings, and it was strange.

She was different from Jennie, and he was so glad. He still hadn't forgotten the way she'd asked if he'd been thinking of his wife when he'd kissed her. He wasn't into looking for a substitute. That wouldn't be fair to Jess, or to him.

But she hadn't called him, either. And that made him wonder if she was having second thoughts.

It wasn't something he wanted to talk about over the phone, so he closed his laptop, changed his shirt and drove over to the boathouse.

The porch light was off, but light poured from the windows onto the stone path leading to her door. It was nine at night; was she up working this late? Perhaps she'd been painting just as much as he'd been writing.

Then the sound of laughter filtered out through the open window, and he hesitated. She had company?

Maybe he should do this another time.

He hesitated for a full ten seconds, then he heard Tori's laugh and Jeremy's low voice, and then another round of laughter. Something unfamiliar swept over him, and he realized it was loneliness. Not the welcome, self-imposed kind he'd reveled in for the last few years, but the kind that longed to be a part of something warm and fun. Before he could change his mind, he stepped up onto the porch and knocked on the door.

Jess answered, her face alight with laughter as she stood with the door open. "Well, hello, stranger."

"Hi," he said quietly, a little off balance by how happy

he was to see her face. It had been what, three days? And he'd missed her terribly.

"Come in. Jer and Tori are here. And little Rose is asleep."

In that much noise? He wasn't sure how it was possible. Owen had always awakened at anything over normal speaking level.

He stepped inside and took off his sandals, padding to the kitchen in his bare feet. Jeremy and Tori were sitting at the round table, with cards in their hands.

"We're playing cribbage," Jess explained. "Tori taught us how. Jeremy is about to get skunked."

He had never played the game in his life, and stared at the oddly shaped board with different colored pegs in various spots. "Oh."

"We're almost done this game," Tori said, taking a sip of what appeared to be sparkling water. "Come on in and watch the carnage."

"There's sparkling water and ginger ale in the fridge. Help yourself, Bran. And chips on the counter."

The small gathering was very different from social occasions he'd gone to as a member of the Black family. No one ever helped themselves, or sat as an odd man out during a game of cards while munching on chips straight from the bag. Instead, it reminded him of days spent at Merrick, playing poker with the guys, drinking contraband beer and pooling snacks.

He'd loved those days. Missed them.

So he helped himself to a ginger ale and grabbed the bag of chips and pulled up a fourth chair to watch. Tori deftly dealt five cards to each player and put one on the table, though he wasn't sure what it was for. Then each of them studied their cards and removed one from their hand, adding it to one on the table.

"All right. Jess, your go."

Branson didn't ask questions, just watched as they took turns laying cards and occasionally moved their pegs on the board. Jess's brow wrinkled each time she considered her play, and he thought she looked adorable. Jeremy sat back in his chair in an indolent posture, very reminiscent of his body language in school. And Tori sat straight and kept an easy expression on her face. He bet she'd be good at poker.

When all the cards had been played, they counted points in some weird format that had something to do with fifteens and runs. Jess had a dozen points, putting her within a few of Tori. There was laughter when Jeremy had four points, keeping him short of the line that had an S beside it. And Tori moved only six. Apparently the four extra cards were hers, too, but to Jess and Jeremy's glee, contained no points.

"One more hand," Jess said, "and this time the crib is mine."

He grabbed a handful of chips and watched.

Jeremy laid a seven after Jess, which gave him two points, putting him one shy of the skunk line. Another round he announced "thirty-one for two" and it put him over, which caused a victorious whoop. "What happens if he doesn't cross?" Bran asked.

"You lose double," Tori replied, grinning. "You just snuck over, Jer."

They continued. Jess played a card and gave a yelp of triumph as she moved three points, so close to Tori and ever closer to the final hole on the board.

At that moment the sound of a baby crying interrupted the game. Jess frowned. "Darn, I'm sorry. I think I woke her."

"It's all right. She'll be fine until we finish this hand."

But Bran looked at Tori and noticed that her relaxed

face now had the shadow of tension around her eyes. Tori played a card, and then it was Jess's turn; Rose's crying got louder.

"We can pause the game," Jeremy said. "It's no big deal."

Bran tamped down the apprehension building in his chest and stood. "You guys finish. You're nearly done. I'll go get her."

He walked to the bedroom with heavy steps, totally unsure of himself but knowing he needed to do this sometime. Rose was two months old and he had yet to hold her, even though Jeremy and Tori had named him her godfather. The cries reminded him of a little lamb, bleating with distress. After taking a deep breath, he stepped into the room, went to the bed and scooped her up from the pillow barrier that Tori had set up, even though Rose was nowhere near old enough to roll over yet.

The moment he cradled her against his chest, her cries changed to whimpers. She was so tiny and warm, and he could hear her sucking on her fist as he tucked the light blanket close around her. She smelled like baby lotion and the combination of milk and diapers, and the familiarity of it snuck in and pierced his heart. But there was more than pain there now. There was emptiness but also something more, something warm and glowing that crept in around the corners. Memories that were bitter but also sweet. Her soft, downy head nuzzled into his neck and his throat closed with emotion, tears stinging the backs of his eyes.

"Hello, Rosie. I'm your godfather." He kept his voice low and soothing, and he rocked back and forth a bit as he used to with Owen when he'd been fussy. The cranky noises eased into something that was half-slurp and half-coo, and he closed his eyes and rested his cheek against her.

"You want your mama, huh? Let's go find her."

He reentered the kitchen, and the room suddenly quieted at the sight of him with the baby in his arms. Cards were forgotten in hands as Jeremy's eyes widened and Tori…ah, damn, Tori gave an emotional sniff, and he found his own emotions raw and hovering right at the surface.

Then Jess was there, getting up from her chair and pasting on a smile. "Oh, there's my girl! Look at her all sleepy and snuggly." She went to Bran and didn't take Rose from him, but put her hand on the baby's back. "Tori, do you want me to change her?"

Jess's interference seemed to jolt the others into action, and Tori put down her cards. "Oh, sure, that'd be great! I can get a bottle ready while you do that. Thanks, Jess."

"It's okay. I know where your bag is."

She retrieved a diaper and wipes from the diaper bag in the kitchen, and then motioned for him to follow. He did, following her into the bedroom, where she put down a soft flannel blanket and then took Rose from his arms.

"Unless you want to do the honors?" she asked.

"I, uh…"

She looked up at him, a blinking Rose in her arms. "Baby steps?"

He nodded, unable to say anything more. But he watched as she deftly undid Rose's soft pajamas, changed her diaper and dressed her again, talking softly to the baby the whole time.

"You're very good with her," he observed, his emotions once again riding very close to the surface.

"I like babies." She picked up Rose and set her on her arm. "Isn't that right, sweetie?" And then she met Bran's eyes. "I'd like to have my own someday. But that option hasn't really presented itself. And I'm not at the point where I'm prepared to take things into my own hands."

"You'd like a family, then."

She nodded. "I would. Figuring out how that would fit into my life is another story."

With Rose tidied and dressed, there was no reason to linger, and Jess headed back to the kitchen. But Bran hesitated a moment.

She wanted a family. Babies of her own. If he'd ever thought that this could work between them at all, the idea just died a quick death. He never wanted to do that again. No matter how sweet Rose was. Or how adorable Jess's children would be, with their sunrise hair and blue-green eyes, and a healthy dose of freckles.

Back in the kitchen, he watched while Jess, Jeremy and Tori played out their final hand. Jeremy was over the skunk line, and Jess gave Tori a run for her money, but Tori won by three small points. Rose was in Tori's arms, the bottle braced up so she could eat, and Jeremy pegged the last points for his wife.

"Well," Tori said, sitting back. "That was fun. You're a fast learner, Jess."

"You're a good teacher. Another drink? Anyone want more snacks?"

"We should probably be going," Jeremy said, looking at Bran briefly.

Bran wanted to say that there was no need, that he hadn't come for a specific reason, but the truth was, he had. To test the waters, so to speak. Hoping that Jess's silence wasn't her being angry at him. That she'd been just as busy as he had.

"Yes, and once Rose is fed, she'll go back to sleep. If I can put her in her crib for the night, I might get some good sleep, too."

"Or, you know. Pay attention to your husband."

"Or that." Her grin was teasing but their gazes held, and Bran knew that look. They were so in love. Despite having a baby, they were still in the stage of not getting enough of each other.

He looked at Jess, whose cheeks had gone pink as she picked up dirty glasses from the table.

A few minutes later, Tori and Jeremy said their good-byes and the house was quiet again. Bran cleared his throat. "I'm sorry I interrupted tonight. I should have called first."

Jess put the glasses in the small dishwasher and shrugged. "It's fine. We were just playing some cards. Tori hasn't gotten out a lot since Rose was born, and doesn't want to leave her with a sitter yet. I think Jeremy was getting a little worried."

She closed the dishwasher and turned to face him. "Was Jennie like that? How old was Owen before you got a sitter?"

He frowned and turned away. "Don't ask me things like that."

But she stepped forward. "Was tonight the first time you held Rose?"

"Jess. Stop." His voice was firm. "I didn't come over to talk about babies, okay? I just… I realized that it's been three days and I didn't call, and I was feeling like a heel about it."

She stopped and stared at him, angling her head a bit as if trying to puzzle him out. "I didn't call you, either."

"Why?"

She looked over at her small living room and then back at him. "To be honest, I needed some time to think. And I've been painting. A lot."

He let out a breath and some of the tension tightening his body. "I've been writing, too."

"I guess our trip was inspiring." Her eyes lit with a bit of the fire he loved, and he was transported back to the hotel room. The way she looked, tasted, sounded.

"So…"

"So I'm not the kind of woman who has to be called hours after being dropped off. I'm not that insecure, Bran. And we both agreed this is not...a real relationship. We want different things. Besides, I have no claim on you or your time. I told myself I was just going to enjoy what time we had."

Her words should have made him feel better, as they essentially let him off the hook. But somehow they didn't, and he couldn't pinpoint why.

"Had," he said quietly. "Past tense?"

"That's up to you." She moved forward. "It got to be too much for you, didn't it?"

"I don't know." He paused and ran his hand through his hair. "It's just a lot. I'm dealing with a lot. You're the first woman I've been with since Jennie. And yeah, tonight was the first time I've held Rose. I'm moving back into the world of the living, but it's hard. I'm not sure I have it in me to navigate...nuance. With a relationship."

She nodded as if she understood completely, but how could she?

"Would it help if we set ground rules?"

He gestured to the small table and chairs. "Can we sit to discuss this? I feel weird standing here, as if we're facing off."

She obliged him by taking a seat, but angled her chair so that their knees bumped slightly. It helped that she was touching him, actually. Like an anchor to keep him grounded, when he could very easily be overwhelmed.

He could still smell the scent of baby, and his brain remembered a past life he couldn't access anymore. And never would again.

If anything, the past month had taught him that he could move forward without them.

"We both agreed this is a summer thing. That I'll be

going back to Chicago and my own life, and you'll be here or wherever else you call home." She folded her hands in her lap. "And since we really do like each other, I think we also agree that there might be a little bit of fear that we'll get too attached to each other."

"Like?" He lifted an eyebrow.

She smiled gently. "Okay, more than like. I care about you, Bran, and I think you care about me. And neither of us wants to get hurt, or be responsible for hurting the other person."

"True."

"So, ground rules. I'll go first. No more overnights."

He blinked. He'd thought she was going to say no sex, but she'd said no staying over. He nodded, thinking of how the intimacy of waking up together made things so much more complicated. "Agreed." Then he added a condition of his own. "No declarations."

"Declarations?"

Bran wasn't sure how to word this one. "I mean, we care about each other. But we both agree that this isn't going to turn into love. I'm not ready for that and like you said, we want different things. So no declarations of love."

"Absolutely. No danger there."

It made him pause for a moment, how quickly she'd said "no danger there." Again, he knew he should be relieved, so why was there this nagging feeling that something was off?

He pushed the feeling aside and ticked off another one on his fingers. "Space to create, and no getting upset when either of us is unavailable because we're working."

She grinned at him. "That's an easy one."

"Maybe. But not for a lot of people. Not everyone gets it."

"Canceling plans is fine, but the courtesy of a call is nonnegotiable. That's just being polite."

"Deal. Or at least… I'll try. I've been known to lose track of time. Anything else?"

She studied him for a long moment. "We agree that we can add to the ground rules as needed if and when things come up we didn't think of tonight."

It was odd, setting rules for something as simple as a casual relationship, but Bran also knew that setting the rules now meant their relationship would stay casual, which was what he wanted. What they both wanted.

He let out a sigh. "Does this feel weird to you?"

And then she laughed, that light, musical sound that he enjoyed so very much, and he smiled, too. The awkwardness and tension of the evening fell away, and she leaned forward, putting her hand over his. "Of course it does. But we both feel the need to protect ourselves, and Bran, I needed to be honest. The only way this is going to work is if we're honest with each other."

Something undefinable flickered behind her eyes, and he briefly wondered what it was, but then she got up from her chair and went to stand in front of him. "And now," she whispered, "will you please kiss me? Because I've been dying for you to for over an hour."

CHAPTER TWELVE

SETTING GROUND RULES seemed to be working. Jess was an early bird, so she was up early each morning, sketching and painting, and usually touched base with Bran when she broke for lunch. Some days they'd venture into the nearby town for errands; sometimes she drove to his house and they spent the day on the beach below his low cliffs, dipping into the ocean and soaking in the sun.

They made love on a blanket in the sand, and in his enormous bed. One evening there was a thunderstorm and the power went out, and so they gathered all the candles he had and put them around the bedroom, making love to the sound of the rain.

She loved his house. Even though it was big, it wasn't cold. No expense had been spared, and sometimes they cooked dinner together in his vast kitchen, which was much better equipped than the boathouse. One afternoon he wrote in his den, and she pulled a book out of his bookcases and read. And because that first day she'd mentioned the Jacuzzi, she arrived one evening to find a bath drawn and a glass of wine waiting from the bottle she'd gifted him, so she could soak and watch the ocean through the windows. It had felt incredibly extravagant and surreal. Even more surreal when he'd held her towel when she got out...

But she didn't stay over, and he didn't stay at the boathouse, either.

It should have been absolutely perfect.

Bran and Jeremy's friend Cole came to town and stayed at Bran's, which put a bit of a kink into their social plans. And yet Jess thought it lovely when she saw the two of them together. Cole was tall and fair, with a magnetic personality and an energy that was contagious—something that had a positive effect on Bran. He smiled more and laughed often, and Jess got a glimpse of the man he used to be. She already thought him pretty amazing. But this…it was different. For a little while, it seemed as if the weight of the world was off his shoulders, particularly when he, Cole and Jeremy were all together. She remembered what he'd said—that they were family.

Today they were all going to an island offshore to look at property. The whole island, in fact, with the exception of ten acres that was owned by someone else. Cole was considering buying it and turning the mansion into a corporate retreat that he could use for business. Jess tried not to be awestruck when she realized that she was accompanying three billionaires on a shopping spree worth what they were calling a steal—nearly seven million dollars.

The five of them were making a day of it, or at least the better part of a day. Tori's mother was coming to stay with the baby, and it was Tori's first day away from Rose for more than an hour. As she and Bran met the others at the wharf, Jess could tell that Tori was both excited to be going along, and anxious about leaving Rose. She put an arm around Tori's shoulders and gave her a squeeze. "It'll be all right, Mama," she said with a smile. "Grandmas need a chance to spoil babies anyway."

Tori smiled back. "I know. It's just first time nerves. I've got to do it sometime."

Cole had rented a boat for his stay, a fast and luxurious Boston Whaler docked at a nearby marina. The island itself wasn't far outside the bay, but it was only accessible by boat or, Cole explained, by the helipad on-site. Tori looked at Jess and shook her head. Neither of them was used to such luxury, and Jess grinned up at Bran as he sat beside her. "Helipad, huh? Does Cole have his own helicopter?"

Bran shook his head. "Naw. He just charters when he needs to."

Jess's and Bran's definition of *need* seemed to vary, but today she didn't care. Today she was free and ready for fun. How often did one get to visit a private island, anyway?

Cole piloted the boat, and it wasn't long before they were at the island. Instead of docking right away, Cole took them all the way around. Jess got a glimpse of an enormous house with well-trimmed grounds sloping toward the water; the west side had more of a rocky shoreline but the east side had a beautiful sandy beach, similar to the one at Jeremy's, and what looked to be white, soft sand like that by the Sandpiper Resort. The dock was at the southern tip of the island. An ancient fishing boat was already docked, as well as a smaller craft.

Jeremy got off first, and held out his hand to help Tori and then Jess, with Bran and Cole following. "The other Realtor will be at the house. But there should be a golf cart up there—" he pointed to a garage-type structure at the top of the path "—that we can use to get to the main house."

Jess followed the direction of his finger and noticed not only the garage, but a large house behind it. "That's not the main house, is it?"

He shook his head. "Nope. There's about ten acres that's owned by another party. The house is hers. The rest of the island, about eighty acres or so, is what's for sale."

Interesting. Jess hung back and waited for Bran, and

together they walked side by side behind the others. "Your friend is seriously going to buy his own island," she said incredulously.

Bran nodded. "Looks like it. He's right. It's a steal. Besides, Cole's changed a lot in the last year. He tries not to show it, but he has."

"How so?"

"He took over his father's businesses when he was only twenty-three. He's accumulated more since, and I've never seen anyone work so hard or play so hard. It caught up with him and while he won't come right out and say so, I think he hit some burnout. He stepped away for a few months."

"He's okay now?" She looked up ahead. Cole was talking energetically with Jeremy and Tori, his hands gesturing wildly. It was impossible to imagine him slowing down, let alone grinding to a full stop.

Bran nodded. "I think so. But this place…it's different. He doesn't want it to simply acquire something new and shiny. He wants to use it to help executives and companies. Corporate retreats. Team building events. That sort of thing. It's not very Cole, but people change when life kicks them in the ass."

"Like it changed you."

"Cole and I grew up in the same world. We wanted for nothing, but that came with heavy expectations. My parents never wanted for me to be a writer. It was a waste of my time, they said. For a kid who supposedly had every privilege, it felt very much like I was in a cage. Until I got to Merrick and found Cole and Jer. So when my life went sideways, it wasn't all my money or status that got me through it. It was those two."

He looked over at her. "You've been kicked, as well. But you know, quite often we're better people for it."

She wondered at that, really. She knew he'd do anything

to turn back the clock and redo that night two years ago. But if he also liked the changes that had happened this summer, that was something huge. "Are you happy, Bran?"

They stopped for a moment and he faced her. "I'm happier than I've been in a very long time, and it's unexpected. I have you to thank for that."

He leaned down and placed a gentle kiss on her lips. She was stunned; while it was no big secret that she and Bran were spending time together, for him to make such a gesture while they were with his friends felt huge.

"Come on," he said. "We need to catch up or we'll miss our ride."

They climbed on the golf cart, squeezing three of them on the bench seat in the back, and Jeremy drove them past the farmhouse and down a long lane, clear to the other side of the island. The land vacillated between green forests and meadows with waving grass and wildflowers, wild and untamed. But before long the landscape turned into landscaped lawns and gardens, and a grand house appeared.

Cole turned around from the front of the cart and grinned. "Twelve thousand square feet. A dozen bedrooms, eight bathrooms, a kitchen that's a chef's dream and hopefully a room I can convert into a boardroom-type meeting room. What do you think?"

Jess grinned. "It's ginormous!" It was more the size of a hotel than a house.

Cole laughed. "I don't do things halfway. Didn't Bran tell you that?"

She nodded, still grinning. "He did."

The Realtor was waiting for them, and Jess and Bran once again brought up the rear as they were taken on a tour of the house. Jess had never been in anything like it, and was absolutely dazzled. There were indeed twelve bedrooms, each beautifully appointed with gleaming wood furniture and expensive linens. The bathrooms had marble counters and gold fixtures; three had Jacuzzi tubs and there was a sauna downstairs, next to the fully equipped exercise room. A theater room with a large projector screen and theater seating made Jess's eyes goggle.

Back upstairs, the Realtor showed them the addition on the back that held an indoor heated pool. The kitchen was huge, with double stainless-steel refrigerators and a large range with spider burners as well as double wall ovens. There was a small dining area, and then a large adjoining room with a table for at least twelve. To go with the bedrooms, Jess supposed.

One of the large rooms off the foyer could be turned into the meeting room Cole wanted. The other had a conversation pit, and a grand piano in front of tall, gleaming windows.

It was easy to see that Cole was in love with the place, and he and Jeremy kept their heads together, discussing details. Tori took out her phone and called home to check on Rose, and Bran caught Jess's eye and pointed outside. "Come on," he said quietly. "Let's explore outside."

"I'd like that."

The sun was bright and cheery as they stepped out of the grand house. "Oh, it's amazing," she said, "but too big for me."

"I know. But for what he's intending to do with it? It's perfect."

"Probably." She peered up at him. "I think for me it's… not really a home. It doesn't have that homey kind of feeling about it."

Bran studied her for a moment. "Do you feel that way about my house?"

She took his hand, and they started to walk across the plush lawn. "Not really. Yours is different. With yours, it *can* be cozy and welcoming and have that vibe. The possibility is there. I don't know how else to explain it."

"What would it take for it to be that way?"

The answer came to her mind so quickly it left her speechless. *Children*, she thought. *Family. Love.*

She couldn't say those things, so she simply answered, "Healing."

He tugged on her fingers and turned her toward him. "I'm trying."

Her heart squeezed at the honest confession. "I know. And you're doing just fine." She slid closer, wrapping her arms around him and nestling close to his strong, wide chest. "And along the way, you've been healing me, too. For what it's worth, I've loved every moment in your house, from the first time I walked in and saw you with your shirt off."

His arms cinched tightly around her, pulling her close as he laughed. His breath was warm on her hair as they hugged, his body tall and strong and the kind a woman could lean on when she wanted. The brisk wind off the ocean buffeted their bodies, but they stood firm against it, holding on to each other, the moment touching Jess's heart more than any of their more intimate moments. He pulled back a bit and cupped her face in his hands, his smile replaced with a look of wonder. "You've changed everything," he said roughly, and brought his lips down on hers for a kiss.

It was a hell of a time for her to realize she'd broken the ground rules. She'd gone ahead and fallen in love with him. But she wouldn't say it. Not and ruin what they had, when it was so fleeting to begin with.

Bran tried not to think about that kiss as he strolled along the beach with Jess. She stopped now and then to pick up shells, and took off her shoes to dip her toes in the cool water, the light breakers ruffling over her feet before creeping up on the sand and then retreating again. Her hair had come out of its bun and whipped around in the stiff breeze, and her laugh carried to him, making his heart hurt and yearn for things he couldn't have.

He'd seen her feelings on her face even if she hadn't said the words. She had turned away and laughed, running for the beach, but the distraction didn't quite work. He'd seen it, the way her lips fell open the slightest bit with words unsaid and the soft vulnerability and surprise in her eyes. He didn't want to say goodbye to her, not yet. The summer was just coming into its own. There was a good six weeks they could have together if they didn't let emotions get in the way. So thank God she hadn't said what had been written all over her face.

A gull cried overhead, circling above them. He could just pretend it had never happened, that's all. No declarations of love. That was the rule. And despite his suspicions, she hadn't broken it.

Cole, Jeremy and Tori joined them briefly, then as a group they left the beach and made their way back to the golf cart for the return trip to the dock. Bran remained quiet as Cole admitted that he was putting in an offer, and talked excitedly about his plans.

Back on the mainland, Jeremy offered Jess a drive home since they were going to the same place anyway, and that meant Cole and Bran drove back to his house together. Bran was quiet on the way back, until they were nearly at his house. Cole broke from his monologue about the island property and frowned at Bran.

"You know, I wasn't expecting you to have fallen in love this summer."

Bran's head swiveled so fast he nearly put the car in the

ditch. "What? I'm not in love. Don't be ridiculous." He chuckled tightly, as if to show how ludicrous of an idea it was, and focused on the road.

But Cole's expression was grim as he continued to stare at Bran. Bran kept glancing over, until Cole finally said, "Dude, it was written all over your face today. You light up when she's around."

"Lighting up is not love, dumbass. It's enjoying some-one's company."

"You know, I'd be tempted to say, 'if you say so,' but I'm not, because this is serious, Bran. I want to be happy for you. But I'm not sure you're ready, and she seems like a great person. She doesn't deserve to be hurt."

Bran's temper flared. "If you think Jess and I haven't talked about it, you're wrong. Both of us have our eyes wide open."

And then he thought of the way she'd looked at him today, and his heart stuttered.

They turned onto his lane and made their way into the garage. The doors echoed in the silence, and Bran opened the door from the garage to the house.

Maybe Cole would let the matter drop.

"Hey, listen. Jeremy and I have been talking about it, too. We're both concerned for you. He said your car has been there overnight. And that you guys went to the city and spent the night earlier this month."

Heat rushed through Bran's chest as irritation flared again. "That is no one's business but ours."

"You're right."

"And it's just sex."

Cole started laughing, putting his hand on the island in the kitchen to brace himself. "Oh," he said, catching his breath. "Bran, you're a horrible liar. I've known you for most of your life. You don't do casual sex. You don't get with a woman without your heart being involved. Brother, you are lying to yourself."

Bran opened his mouth to speak, but Cole held up a hand. "Hey, don't get me wrong. Losing Jennie and Owen was such a horrible, horrible thing, and you deserve to move on and be happy again. I just… I find myself feeling protective of you. I don't want you to get hurt."

Those last words took the heat out of Bran's anger. Cole was a workaholic and he played hard—when he made time for it. But of the three of them, he was the most protective. Like the big brother of the group. As much as no one wanted to admit it, Cole was the glue that bound them together.

And Cole was always there for them…even when he wasn't taking care of himself.

Bran let out a breath. "I can't love her, Cole. There's no danger of that. But I care about her a lot. She's fun and full of life, and she doesn't let me get away with anything. I'm actually writing again, which is a total surprise and a massive relief. But she lives in Chicago. I live here and in New York. We both agreed that this is a temporary thing where we just enjoy each other for the time we have. Because life is short."

Cole went to the fridge and took out two cans of soda. He handed one to Bran and then snapped the top on his own and leaned against the counter. "Okay," he said quietly, "okay. Maybe that's true. But Bran, it's okay if you fall in love with her. You know that, right? I'm worried about you, but it's not *wrong*."

A pit opened up in Bran's stomach as he looked at his friend. How could he make Cole understand when he was finding it hard to understand himself? He wasn't even sure he was capable of being in love. And the look on Jess's face today scared him to death. Not so much because she loved him but because he couldn't feel that way in return.

"I can't, Cole." His voice was low and rough. "My heart won't let me. Maybe it would be easier if I could. Right now I'm trying to look at all the positives. I'm not hurting so much. I'm getting out, I'm writing again. Anything more is a lot to ask for."

"Yet up until she showed up in your life, you weren't doing any of those things. Doesn't that say something to you?"

Bran let out a sigh of resignation. "Yeah," he said, looking past Cole and out at the backyard. "It tells me she deserves someone who can give her a lot more than I can."

And in that moment, he knew he had to stop what was between them.

CHAPTER THIRTEEN

JESS POURED HERSELF some orange juice and tried to decide if she wanted yogurt and berries this morning or something a little more comforting, like toast with butter and jam. She was feeling rather out of sorts after yesterday. The trip to the island had been fun and she'd enjoyed it, but she wasn't so sure about her latest revelation.

She didn't want to be in love with Bran. Up until yesterday, she'd been able to logic her way out of it. But then there was that moment. The moment he'd kissed her, however, something had shifted. Something profound and deep and joyful and sad and terrifying all wrapped up in one ball of emotion.

She loved him, and she wasn't sure if she should break it off now for the sake of self-preservation, or if she should give herself these final weeks as a gift, no matter the end result.

She really wished Ana was here to give her advice and ask her the right questions. Tori was a good friend. Jess had other friends in Chicago. But none like Ana.

A wave of grief threatened to swamp her, so instead she reached for her pillbox, which contained her vitamins and birth control. She stared at the little plastic strip with surprise. How was it that she was on her two sugar pills? It meant she'd get her period anytime. She went to her bedroom to get the next month's supply out of the drawer and put it in the little sleeve. So much had changed since her last cycle. It had literally been only a little over a month since she'd met Bran. Her whole world had been turned upside down.

She was just eating her yogurt when her phone buzzed. It was a text from Bran, explaining that Cole was in town for only a few more days and they were going to spend some time together, but he'd be in touch by the weekend. That was that, then. She'd have time to think and make some decisions before seeing him again.

And in the meantime, she'd paint. There was nothing that helped her work through her problems like putting her heart on canvas.

By Saturday Jess was starting to panic.

She was three days into her new pack of pills and she hadn't had a period at all. Granted, being on the pill made them lighter, but usually on her second sugar pill she started, like clockwork. She laid in bed, staring at the bunk above her, trying not to freak out over the fact that she might be pregnant. Because she'd replayed every detail of her nights with Bran, and had discovered that the morning after their hotel stay she hadn't taken her pill at all. She'd missed it completely. It shouldn't make a difference, but it could. They'd had room service, and she'd come home and had been so distracted that she was sure she'd missed her pill and her vitamins.

She couldn't be pregnant. Oh, Lord, what a mess that would be. She wanted children but not this way. Not with a man who didn't want any. Not on her own with no support. She didn't know how to be a mother.

She threw off the covers. Okay, so that might be putting the cart a long way before the horse. She really couldn't do anything until she took a test. Maybe she just missed for whatever reason. And if it was positive, then she'd figure things out. One step at a time.

The drive to the pharmacy didn't take that long, and Jess figured there was no point in waiting and putting off something that wouldn't change the outcome. So she took one of the tests out of the box and into the bathroom she went. Then she came out and made coffee while waiting the three minutes suggested.

When she went back in and looked at the stick, she let out a huge breath.

Negative.

Her hand shook as she dropped the test in the trash can and sat on top of the toilet for a moment, trying to make sense of her feelings. There was relief, of course, because this was so not the right time and even though she was in love with him, Bran wasn't the right man no matter how much she might want him to be. But there was also disappointment. She thought of all the times she'd held Rose, snuggled her close, and how she longed for her own family. Those feelings were there, too. At least the result had clarified much of her thoughts. She and Bran wanted different things. They were just fooling themselves with ground rules and flings and whatever else. He was a good man. They might even be good for each other. But that didn't mean they had a future.

She was just fixing her coffee when there was a knock on the door and then it opened, as she'd left it unlocked as she usually did during the day. Bran came through the door, a small smile on his face, and a paper bag in his hand. "I went to the bakery," he said, holding up the bag. "And got chocolate croissants."

She wasn't ready for this conversation, so she smiled

back and kept it light. "I just made coffee. I'll get you some."

"Sounds good. How've you been?"

What a loaded question. She hesitated and then said, "All right. Has Cole gone back to New York?"

"He left last night."

She handed him a mug. "You had a good visit though, huh?"

Bran nodded. "We did. We caught up about a lot of stuff. This island project of his…it's pretty cool."

"So he's going to do it?"

"Yeah, I think so." Bran's grin was genuinely wide now. "Who knew? The three of us went to school together, live within an hour or so of each other, and now have second homes here in Nova Scotia. You'd almost think we were brothers."

Her heart melted at the genuine affection in his voice. "You are, in all the ways that count. I think it's lovely."

"Thanks. Hey, got any milk or cream for this?"

She'd forgotten he liked his coffee light, and before she could move he'd gone to the fridge, making himself at home as he had the last several times he'd visited. But when he turned around, his face dropped and she realized she'd left the pregnancy test box on the counter.

He put the mug down very quietly.

"Bran, I—"

"Are you pregnant?"

The way he said those three words sent her heart straight to her feet. He made it sound as if the world were truly ending. The last time she'd heard that exact tone, Ana had taken her hand and said, "I have cancer."

Bran was so repulsed by the idea that it wasn't just undesirable. It was a world-ending scenario.

She wanted to say something, but the words wouldn't

come together in her mind, let alone out of her mouth. Bran's lips tightened and he picked up the box. "You told me you were on the pill. I bought condoms to double up. And now you're pregnant? I told you I don't want more children. I was very, very clear about that."

His voice wasn't angry. It was worse. It was surgically precise, almost emotionless. She understood he didn't want more kids. She understood that came from grief and that it was his right. He'd been honest from the start. But she also knew that it had taken two of them, and right now it certainly felt as if any blame would have fallen on her, rather than be shared, and that made her angry.

Her voice shook as she replied. "If I were pregnant, we would both bear responsibility. But I'm not, so don't worry, Branson. You're off the hook. You can start breathing again."

"Oh, thank God."

He sounded so relieved that tears stung the backs of her eyes. "Would it have been so bad?" she snapped. "Would me being pregnant be the worst thing in the world to happen?"

He stepped back at the vitriol in her voice. "No. The worst thing in the world to happen is losing a child."

Dammit. Silence fell, harsh and thick. Of course it was. She wasn't that insensitive, even though she'd lashed out. "I'm sorry, Bran. Of course you're right. I didn't mean to…" She didn't know what to say after that. "Look, I'll be honest with you. The night we stayed in Halifax… I forgot to take my pill the next day. I didn't have my period this week on schedule, so I got tests this morning just in case."

"But you're not pregnant."

"No." She lifted her chin a little. "But I think this whole thing, the idea with the ground rules, the summer fling with us going our separate ways with a smile was a little disingenuous on both our parts. I don't think this is going to work anymore."

He blinked. Opened his mouth to say something, then shut it again. Then opened it again, and hesitated. "Jess, I like being with you. You've brought me back to life, you see? I'm writing. I'm looking toward a future rather than drifting aimlessly. We don't have to break it off. We can revise the ground rules—"

"No," she said, firmer now. "No, we can't. Bran, there are two things you don't want. You don't want more children, and you don't want to fall in love. But you see, I do want children someday. And I fell in love. I know that's breaking a rule, but I also know it's a deal breaker anyway. I'm in love with you, and I can't go through the rest of the summer pretending I'm not, only to break up at the end after I get in even deeper." She tried to ignore the catch in her voice. "I don't want to be left again, so we have to do this now."

"Jess," he whispered, running a hand over his face.

"Tell me you haven't been thinking the same thing. In the beginning you couldn't wait to rush over here, to steal moments together. But after the trip to the island earlier this week, you sent one text saying you were hanging with Cole. The three of you are tight, but you guys didn't come over here, and you certainly didn't steal away for a stolen hour. You're scared. So let's be honest, okay? I can't see you anymore. It's too hard."

"Yeah, I've been thinking the same thing. So what? Listen, we don't have to have sex…"

The tears behind her eyes sprang forward and trickled down her cheeks. "Is that what it's been to you? Sex? I don't believe it. Oh, Lord, Bran, this goes so much further than sex. It's about my heart, don't you see? Just being with you, holding your hand, listening to your voice…it all does stuff to me. Intimacy isn't all about the bedroom."

"I know that. Do you think I don't know that? Don't you think that's what I miss about Jennie every day?"

It was his turn to snap, and she swallowed against the growing lump in her throat. It was always going to come down to Jennie, wasn't it? Maybe he didn't compare her to his dead wife when they were together, but he certainly wasn't over her. He didn't want to love again, couldn't love again, because he couldn't let Jennie go.

She couldn't do this anymore. "I'm going to give Tori and Jeremy my notice and go back to my loft in Chicago. My agent is clamoring to do a showing, and I have more than enough work to keep me busy. And you have a book to write."

He came around the counter and took her hand, then lifted his other hand and wiped a tear off her cheek with his thumb. The contact felt so wonderful and sad. After today she wouldn't hear the sound of his voice again, or feel the pad of his thumb, or be able to run her hands through his shaggy locks. She'd be going back to Chicago alone, to the loft she'd shared with Ana, fighting against emptiness all over again. For the briefest of moments, she wished the test had been positive just so she'd have company in that huge empty space. A baby wouldn't leave her. And Bran wasn't leaving her, either. But she was quickly learning that it didn't matter who did the leaving. It all hurt.

"I don't want us to leave things this way," he whispered. "Not angry and hurting. What we've been to each other deserves more than that."

It did, except she was having a hard time moving past the sound of his voice and the hard lines of his face when he'd seen the test box. It left a sour taste that she couldn't quite wish away.

"It does hurt. But I'll be fine. I always am, you see. And we did have a good time, we truly did. It's just time."

He nodded. "Can I kiss you one more time?"

Her heart hadn't actually broken during the whole conversation. She'd been hurt and she'd been angry, but she hadn't actually felt the moment where the ground seemed to disappear beneath her feet and left this sense of…emptiness. But now…she knew it was for the best, and yet she wanted him to tell her that she was wrong; that he had fallen in love with her too and they could work it out.

She'd always been a stupid dreamer like that.

Her lips trembled as he bent his head and touched his mouth to hers, then pressed his forehead against hers for a long moment while his hands gripped her upper arms.

"I'm sorry," he whispered. "I'm sorry I can't give you what you want."

He let her go and turned away, and without looking back went through the door, down the steps and to his car.

Every cell in her body begged her to go after him and tell him it didn't matter.

But it did matter. And it was for the best. Because she deserved someone who loved her unreservedly.

And that wasn't him, no matter how much she wanted it to be.

CHAPTER FOURTEEN

BRAN VENTURED OUT to the lighthouse to survey the latest work. It was coming along nicely, now that the restoration had begun. The foundation had been sound, but there'd been work to do at the top, including replacing the platform and making everything airtight. The door was replaced with a replica of the old one, and fresh paint would go on early next week.

The biggest change, however, was the addition of windows on the bottom level. Now when he went inside, beams of light lit the interior, making the empty space bright and cheery.

Except nothing was very cheery at all.

He ran his finger over the top of the woodstove, remembering the day Jess had been here and she'd cautioned him not to open the stove door in case there were mice. He smiled a little at the memory, but sadness made his heart heavy. He missed her. His days had gone back to the routine of one after another, little variation, too much time on his own.

The writing was there now, at least, and he'd sent off an opening and general synopsis to his agent, who'd responded with relief. Bran wasn't a lot of things, but he was still a writer, thank God. Even if the sunshine seemed to have disappeared from his life, he was back in the land of the living.

It just seemed so very bland and pointless without her.

Despondent, he went back to the house and made himself a coffee, then wandered to the den. He booted up his laptop and then, missing her more than usual, opened the browser and went to her website.

It had been updated.

She had a show opening in late October in Chicago. A recent photo showed her laughing, her face alight with happiness and her sunshiny hair gleaming. It hit him right in the gut. Of course she was happy. He was glad. But he was resentful, too. That she'd clearly moved on and he was still…here. Moping half the time and writing the other.

But this was what he'd wanted. What he'd chosen.

His attention was diverted by a car coming up the driveway—Jeremy's Jaguar. Bran closed the window and shut the laptop, preparing himself for a visit. Cole would be closing on the island property soon, and then the three of them had made a promise to spend a weekend after the possession date, a guys' weekend with some deep-sea fishing, maybe some rounds of pool in the games room, and unhealthy food like chicken wings and pizza. Bran was looking forward to it.

Anything to be able to stop thinking about her all the time.

He opened the door for Jeremy, and immediately had a moment of alarm. The man looked like he'd hardly slept. His hair stuck up on one side, and his eyes were red.

"What's happened?" Bran asked, his heart freezing.

"Rose is sick. She's in Halifax at the children's hospital right now, but I've just spent twenty-four hours there and came home to get stuff to take back. Except… I can't go in the house, Bran. I didn't know where else to go."

Bran took a deep breath. While memories threatened to overwhelm him, he pushed them aside. His best friend needed him, and Bran knew the fear and shock Jeremy was going through. "Is Tori okay?"

Jeremy nodded. "She's fine. Still at the hospital. We didn't want to leave Rose alone, and there was no way I was going to be able to tear Tori away, so…"

His voice trailed off, weak and shaky.

"It's okay. You need to pick up what, clothes? Toiletries? Maybe some food for Tori, so she keeps eating?"

Jeremy nodded, his expression one of exhaustion and misery. "Yes, all of those things."

"I'll help." He put his hand on Jeremy's shoulder. "You don't have to do this alone, okay?"

Jeremy nodded. "I'm sorry, bro. I know this is hard for you—"

"Not as much as it used to be. I'm okay. I can deal. Promise."

He realized it was true as he grabbed his wallet and keys. Three months ago—even two—he would have run in the other direction. Not now. He took Jeremy's keys from him and drove them over to the house, then waited while Jeremy gathered clothes and personal items. Bran walked over to the sofa and paused, staring down at a little yellow bunny on the cushions. He remembered that bunny. Jess had bought it during one of their trips to the market.

Things were suddenly very quiet, so Bran braced himself and made his way upstairs to check on his friend. He found Jeremy in the nursery, sitting in a rocking chair and holding a blanket in his hands. He wasn't crying, but Bran knew that meant nothing. He was hurting on the inside, and he was scared.

"Do they know what's wrong with her?" Bran finally asked, keeping his voice as calm as possible.

"Measles. Something about how she could have picked them up at her last checkup, but she's too little for the vaccine yet." His tortured gaze met Bran's. "Babies can die from measles, Bran."

"I know. But she's at the hospital and getting great care, right?"

Jeremy nodded.

"Okay. So let's put this stuff in the car and get to Halifax so you can give Tori a break. All right?"

Jeremy nodded. "Yeah. Yeah, let's go."

As Jeremy got up, Bran noticed a framed picture on the wall. It was a sketch, and one of Jess's, he was sure of it. Of Rose, in a little bonnet, bundled up and in presumably Tori's arms. A lump formed in his throat. That precious little girl, who smiled and gurgled at her father's silly faces, who looked at her mother so adoringly, who had studied him with such wide-eyed curiosity the night of the card game as he'd picked her up for the first time.

His best friend would not lose his daughter the way he'd lost Owen.

They packed the two bags in the car, and Bran offered to drive so Jeremy could rest. They had barely hit the highway when Jeremy fell asleep, and Bran was glad of it. He'd likely been awake all night, worrying about Rose and Tori. Bran remembered one time when Owen had got a cold and struggled to breathe so much. There'd been sleepless nights, but he'd also hated to see Jennie so exhausted and worried.

Bran found his way to the children's hospital and pulled into the parking garage, waking Jeremy as he rolled down the window for the parking stub. "We're here, buddy."

"I didn't mean to sleep. Sorry."

"Don't be. You needed the rest. Come on, I'll go in with

you. Is there someplace inside where we can grab you and Tori some food? Coffee?"

Jeremy nodded. "Yeah. I don't know if Tori will eat, but..."

"Tea," Bran suggested. "She drinks tea a lot, right? Get her tea and a sandwich she can pick at. It's your job to make sure she takes care of herself. And you can't do that if you don't look after yourself, too."

"I'm fine."

"Humor me."

They spent precious minutes picking up sandwiches and drinks, and then Bran carried the overnight bags in his hands as Jeremy hit the elevator button taking them to the correct floor. Bran's pulse accelerated as they headed for the isolation unit; he hated hospitals, and the memories bubbled to the surface simply from the sounds and the smell that was so peculiar to hospitals. But he carried on, knowing that for months Jeremy had been there for him, and it was his turn to repay the favor.

Poor little Rose was in isolation since she was so contagious. Once they arrived, Tori came out, shedding her mask and gown. She looked like hell. Her hair was pulled back in a ponytail, and there were dark circles under her eyes. She appeared to have slept in her clothes, but the relief on her face when she saw Jeremy lit up the room. Bran felt a strange emotion wash over him. It was like just being in the same room together made everything okay. He'd felt that not long ago, with Jess. She hadn't had to do anything but be there and smile, and the world was forever changed.

He was forever changed.

He put the bags down and went forward to give Tori a hug. "Hello, little mama," he said softly, giving her a squeeze. "How's she doing?"

"They're giving her fluids through an IV and stuff to bring down her fever. We just keep hoping there aren't complications like—" she took a breath, swallowed, got herself together again "—like encephalitis."

"She's a tough cookie. And Jeremy has food for you."

"I'm not hungry."

"Then save the sandwich for later and drink some tea. He got mint, the kind you like."

She looked up, and Jeremy was holding out the paper cup. "I got a large. You need to look after yourself too, honey. You haven't slept."

"Neither have you."

He smiled a little. "I slept in the car while Bran drove."

Bran peeked into the room and clenched his teeth. He couldn't see anything, but he imagined poor little Rose, blotchy and red, sleeping while an IV was taped to her, delivering fluids and medication. No little one should have to go through such a thing.

Tori sat down and peeled the top back on the tea. The scent of peppermint filled the air. "I don't want to be out here too long. I keep thinking she has to know that we're there. I've been singing to her."

"Of course she knows you're there." Bran sat down next to Jeremy, and reached for the bag of sandwiches. "Here, you two. Seriously, eat something. And while you're doing that, I'm going to book you a hotel room nearby. Even if you have to sleep in shifts, it'll give you a base until she's able to go home. You can get some good rest and have a hot shower."

"Bran, you don't have to do that."

He leaned forward and met Jeremy's eyes, and finally said something he should have said long ago. "When I needed you, you were there. Bullying me into eating and sleeping and showering. Sitting with me. This is a very small thing, Jer. Let me do it for you."

Jeremy nodded. "Okay."

"Do you need anything else? Is there anything I can do?"

"Not right now. Thank you, Bran."

He excused himself and went to a nearby lounge to make accommodation arrangements, giving Jeremy and Tori time alone. His thumbs hovered over the keypad, knowing he should send the message and afraid to all the same. He hadn't had contact with Jess since that day at the boathouse when they'd called it quits.

Still, she'd want to know.

Before he could reconsider, he typed rapidly.

Jess, just letting you know that Rose is in the hospital in Halifax with the measles. I'm here with Jeremy and Tori. Bran.

He sat back in the chair and replayed that morning in his mind. He'd been such an ass. Handled things all wrong just because seeing the pregnancy test box had scared him out of his wits. He'd known they had to break it off, but not like that. He'd wanted to explain that she deserved so much more. That she was wonderful and needed someone who could give her all of himself. Give her the family she wanted. And Lord, not ask her to take on so much baggage. Instead, he'd jumped down her throat and it had just been…awful.

He regretted that more than anything. That their beautiful friendship had ended with harsh words and hurt feelings. It seemed their relationship deserved a better ending.

His phone vibrated in his hand, and he looked at the screen. Jess had replied.

Oh, no! Is she okay? I'll call Tori. She must be so distressed.

There was a pause, and then another quick message.

I appreciate you telling me, Bran.

He didn't know what to say after that. Anything would either be too much or not enough. He tucked the phone back in his pocket and sat for a long time, replaying old thoughts in his head. Some made sense but others...others did not. What did that mean for his future? Could he truly go through life with a couple of friends and a laptop for company?

He'd missed her every single day.

Eventually he made his way back to the unit. Tori was leaned against Jeremy's shoulder, her eyes closed and breathing deep.

"I'll go so she can rest."

"Stay a minute. She'll sleep for a while now. The tea helped her relax."

They kept their voices low, and Jeremy adjusted a little so that the angle of Tori's neck was a little gentler. Then he looked up at Bran. "You and Jess. What happened?"

Bran swallowed. Thought about how happy he'd been just to see her impersonal text minutes earlier. "I wasn't ready. And she had a pregnancy scare."

"Oh, man. That sent you running for the hills, huh."

"Considering the current situation, I'm not sure you want to talk about Owen."

Jeremy nodded slowly, but then met Bran's eyes. "I'm a wreck, it's true. That little girl...and her mother...they changed my life. I can't imagine...no, that's not true. I can imagine, and it scares me to death. So I think I understand. Yours isn't just imagination. You've lived through it and would rather do anything than go through it again."

That Jeremy understood so completely came as a relief. "Yeah. There's just one problem, Jer."

"What's that?"

"I'm in love with her."

Jeremy let out a huge breath. "Well, doesn't that make the cheese more binding."

They both laughed a little.

"I couldn't admit it when she was here. I mean it when I say I wasn't ready. I wasn't over Jennie. I don't know if I'll ever be over Jennie. How is that fair?"

Jeremy frowned. "I'm not sure this is ever anything you are 'over.' I think it's a decision to leave it in the past, and be brave enough to embrace a future. It's a big thing."

"It's a huge thing. She wants a family, Jer. And she should have one. You've seen her with Rose. She loves that little girl. She should have babies of her own if that's what she wants. And I just don't know."

"All love carries risks."

"I know."

"And rewards. But only you can decide where that balance lies. If being without her is easier than taking the risk, then you know letting her go was the right thing."

"But if it's not?"

Jeremy shrugged. "You have to sort that out on your own. All I'm going to say is that I loved Jennie, but Jess had a way of making you smile that was just…different. There's no question in my mind that she fell in love with you."

Tori shifted and he moved with her, smoothing her hair off her face while she slept on. Bran marveled at the tenderness he saw in his friend's expression.

"Love changes a person, you know?" Jeremy looked away from his wife's face and smiled. "It made me a better man. It made me want things I didn't feel worthy of asking, but somehow…she makes it right. You found it once, Bran. If you are lucky enough to have found it a second time, think long and hard before letting it slip away."

CHAPTER FIFTEEN

JESS HAD NEVER been so glad for air-conditioning in her life.

Chicago was stifling. A late July heat wave was making things miserable, and she cringed to think of her power bill with how much her AC was running, but at least she was comfortable. Most of the time.

Living alone had never been this difficult. Ana had been the one to move into the loft with her, taking the second bedroom and bringing her boundless energy and kindness with her. After she'd gone, it had been hard to live in the apartment without hearing Ana's voice, singing in the shower, or the way she'd stay up on Saturdays watching old movies.

But this loneliness was different. Because it wasn't the loft that was quiet and lonely, it was her whole life. It was like taking one of her paintings and suddenly only seeing it in black and white. There was a vibrancy missing that she knew had one cause: Bran.

She missed him. It seemed impossible; they'd been together such a short time. But time didn't matter. What was time, anyway? Measurable in months, days, hours, minutes…and yet it moved slowly and quickly. Her time in Nova Scotia had been too short, and now her days were too long. And yet the clock ticked on at the same pace.

So she worked. She buried herself in it, putting all her

feelings and thoughts and longings and regrets on canvas. It was the neglected door and the determined daisies, the lighthouse strong and sure, and the waves and wind that battered it relentlessly. It was a long, white beach that stretched on forever, and a man standing on a bluff overlooking the ocean, lost.

Her agent had seen most of what she'd done and raved over it. Jess had come away from the meeting glad he was happy, but personally caring little about the commercial appeal of it and more concerned with the process.

The only thing she could think to do was paint him out of her heart. So far she wasn't succeeding.

Had she been wrong to leave? Should she have given him more time? Maybe. Though in her heart she knew staying would have just prolonged the inevitable.

A quick glance at the clock on the microwave showed just after one o'clock, so she decided it was as good a time as any for a break. She turned on the kettle to make coffee. She'd picked up some bagels at the market a few days ago, so she popped one in the toaster. A bagel with cream cheese would suffice for lunch.

The kettle had just boiled and she'd poured the water into the press when a knock sounded at the door.

She frowned. A courier, maybe? She certainly wasn't expecting anyone. She padded to the door in her bare feet and peeked through the hole to see who was there.

Bran.

Her paint-stained fingers flew to her mouth. What was he doing here? Her first thought was that something had happened to Rose. Oh, God, she hoped not. But would he fly all the way here to deliver that news?

The only other option was that he was here for her. And that was...unbelievable. Considering how they'd left things.

She opened the door, curiosity getting the better of her.

His gaze swept over her, top to bottom to top again, and a smile bloomed on his face. "You look wonderful," he said. His voice held a note of reverence that touched her deeply, and she bit down on her lip. And in the next moment she was in his arms, in the middle of the biggest bear hug she could ever remember.

It was a shock and confusing as heck, but she went with it, because it was so damned good to see him again and hold him close. The scent that was uniquely Bran—soap and aftershave and sea air. How could he smell like the sea after sitting on a plane?

"You feel so good," he said close to her ear, sending shivers down her body. "God, I've missed you."

He loosened his hold and she leaned back so she could see his face, trying not to be so glad to see him. "What are you doing here? Is Rose okay?" He'd cut his hair, she noticed. Not super short, but the shaggy locks were tamed and his beard was precisely trimmed. It was sexy as anything.

"That little bean is just about perfect. She's very close to rolling over."

Oh, bless him. He called Rose a little bean. Why did he have to be so…everything?

She wilted in relief. "Okay, good. Because I thought for a minute you'd come to tell me that…" She hesitated. "I'm sorry. I shouldn't bring stuff like that up."

"No, it's okay. She was really sick, but she's okay now. Full recovery. And that's not why I'm here. But maybe we could go inside and close the door? It's hot as blazes out here, and you're letting all your lovely cool air out."

He wasn't wrong, so she stepped back and once they were clear of the threshold, shut the door. It was a relief to be out of the midday heat.

"Do you want coffee? I just made some. It's likely to

be strong now. I poured the water in my press the moment you knocked."

"Coffee sounds great."

She led the way to the kitchen, which was about a quarter of the size of the one in his house and still held a small dining set. Heart pounding, fingers trembling, she got two mugs out of the cabinet and then pushed down the plunger in the press, pouring strong brew in each cup.

She looked up at him. "There's milk in the fridge."

His gaze held hers. Coffee and milk had been the catalyst on that last fateful day. But now he calmly went to the refrigerator, took out a carton of milk put it on the counter.

"I'm sorry, Jess. For all the things I said that day."

"Me, too. I mean... I knew we had to end, but that wasn't how I wanted it to happen."

"Do you think it ever would have been parting with a kiss and a fond farewell and a 'thanks for the memories'?" he asked. He came a step closer. "Because I think it was always going to be messy. I'm not sure it can be avoided when two people love each other."

She was holding out his mug for him to take when he said those words, and suddenly she couldn't move. Her hand started to shake. He reached out and took the mug and then set it down on the table.

"You heard me right. You said you loved me that day, and I did not. I didn't think I could. I thought it was impossible. But the truth is, I was already in love with you and too scared to admit it to myself. It was easier to say I'd never love anyone again. There was protection in it."

"You weren't ready. I knew that. It's why I had to go."

"I know, sweetheart. I know."

This wasn't happening. He wasn't here, in her kitchen, saying all these wonderful things. Panic threaded through her veins. She'd thought she'd known what she wanted.

But it turned out she didn't know anything. Oh, how smug she'd been.

"What changed?" she asked, trying and failing to keep the tremor out of her voice.

"Rose. And Jeremy. And me being a lonely, grumpy man whose closest relationship is with his laptop. And I wouldn't even have that if it weren't for you." He took her hand. "Come, sit. Let me explain, and then you can decide what you want to do with me."

Oh, she knew what she wanted to do with him. That hadn't changed. But this was about more than their physical compatibility. It always had been.

He held her hand as she across from him. "When Rose got sick, Jeremy came for me. He was a wreck. He's my best friend. Of course I was going to be there for him. And walking into that hospital made me face a lot of things. But it also helped me realize that I've healed a lot. Jennie and Owen—they're a part of my past that will always be in my heart. But I can't keep living there. It's not living at all, and after I met you, I discovered I actually do want to live again."

"Oh, Bran…"

"And then Jeremy gave me a bit of a talking-to. And I've been thinking for a while now about what I want my life to look like. I've come to the conclusion that I don't much care, as long as you're in it."

Tears threatened to spill over. "You really mean that."

"I do." He squeezed her fingers. "Loving again terrifies me, I'm not gonna lie. But being without you scares me more. I never thought I'd ever find this again. That there'd be someone I couldn't live without." He hesitated a moment, licked his lips and then said, "You told me once that the people that you loved had all left you. When I remembered that, I realized why you sent me away that day. You walked away first so I wouldn't, didn't you?"

The tears did spill over then. It was the secret wound she'd only ever shared with two people—him and Ana. And Ana was gone now. She nodded. "I suppose I did." She sniffled and wiped her fingers over her cheeks. "God, I'm sorry. I don't mean to cry."

"It's okay. I hurt you. We hurt each other because we were scared. I'm still scared, Jess. But I'm here. And I'm staying, if you'll have me."

Silence fell in the tiny kitchen. "What do you mean, staying?"

He reached out and cupped her cheek tenderly. "I mean, you get to decide. You have a life here. I can write anywhere. I have a place in New York and the house in Nova Scotia and wherever you want to be, that's where we'll go. All I need is an internet connection, a supply of coffee and you."

He was offering her everything. She loved this loft, but she loved a lot of things. And there was still one thing they hadn't talked about. A very big, very important thing.

"What about children?"

He met her gaze evenly. "I miss being a father. It's going to scare me to death, but, yes. Yes, to a family. I look at Jeremy and Tori, and it's something that's missing in my heart. I'll always have a spot for Owen. But I won't love our babies any less, Jess."

Now he really was giving her everything. She stood and went over to him, sitting on his knees, wrapping her arms around his shoulders as she started to cry for real. He was here. He loved her. He wanted babies. And Bran… she knew in the deepest parts of her heart and soul that he was not the kind of man to leave once he'd promised to stay. Not if he had any choice in the matter. And life didn't have guarantees, did it?

But it certainly had wishes and dreams come true.

"Do you know what I want the most?" she said, holding him close.

"What?"

"I want to go home."

EPILOGUE

THE CHICAGO AIR had lost the summer heat, and the breeze was now cool and brisk in the first week of November. Bran held Jess's hand as they entered the gallery, and then gave her a kiss as Jack rushed over and took her away to do artisty things. Bran knew the drill; he'd done the same during signings and events, and he was thrilled to see Jess enjoying so much success.

She was so beautiful tonight, in a long black dress that hugged her curves and her hair up in the topknot he'd come to love so much. Her freckles were hidden by makeup, and her lips were a pretty shade of pink. She'd told him, back in the hotel room, that she'd forbidden the esthetician from using false eyelashes. He'd laughed and kissed her, nearly ruining the careful makeup job.

There'd be time enough for that later.

Instead, he accepted a rare glass of champagne and took his time wandering through the gallery. The collection was small but beautiful; he was so stinkin' proud of what she'd accomplished. And these paintings would always be special to him. It was like a visual diary of how he'd fallen in love with Jess. Or as she was known tonight, *the* Jessica Blundon.

There were three paintings in black and white that he thought were stunning. One was of the reflectors of the lighthouse lamp, and so very different from her other works. A second one was a fishing boat, tied to a dock. And the third made him catch his breath. It was him. Standing on the bluff by the lighthouse, looking out over a rough sea. He looked so…lonely. Bereft. He understood why she'd done it in black and white.

An arm slid through his, and she pressed up against him. "Hello, handsome."

"Hello, famous artist. This one…wow, Jess."

"I took a pic of that the first day, when you kicked me off the property," she said softly. "Something about you just drew me in. I never believed you were an angry old troll."

He snorted and laughed, and looked down at her. She shared an impish smile with him that made him warm all over.

The last months had been nothing short of amazing. Jess had gone back to Nova Scotia with him, staying at his house, and he'd turned the lighthouse into a studio for her. He'd finished the draft of his book, and they were making a stop in New York on the way home so he could meet with his agent and editor. He'd sold his brownstone there that he'd shared with Jennie, and that had been hard, but Jeremy was going to hook them up with a new property that was just for them.

Life was moving forward, and he was happy.

Unlike the man in the painting. But instead of being sad, it made him realize how far he'd come, thanks to the love of the wonderful woman at his side.

"Come with me for a moment," she said, removing her arm from his and reaching for his hand instead. "There's something I want you to see."

She led him to the other side of the gallery, where a lone painting was displayed. He stopped and stared. It was the same painting—with him on the bluff—but it was in full color, rich and vibrant. The sea wasn't angry; the waves were joyous and playful, and the grass and flowers waved in bright sunlight next to a pristine white lighthouse. Before and after.

But what truly made it different was that he wasn't alone in this one. A woman was beside him. She was beside him, in a flowy dress and her hair up and…

And in between them was a small child, holding on to their hands.

"I was going to call this one *Dreams*," she said. "And then I decided it was something else."

"What?" he asked, his throat tight and his heart full.

"Future."

He stepped closer. The little silver plaque beneath it had *Future* inscribed. And there was a tag on it that said "Not for sale."

"Jess?"

"I'm not selling this one. It's our future, Bran."

He stared into her eyes. "Are you saying…"

She put her hand to her still-flat stomach, but a smile broke out on her face and he swore she lit up like a candle.

"I took the test last week. Barely, but yes, I'm pregnant."

He started to laugh. He couldn't help it. It was a joyful expression of happiness and disbelief, mostly that he could be this lucky. "It's funny?" she asked, raising an eyebrow.

"It's unbelievable," he confirmed, and pressed a quick kiss to her lips. "Look, I was going to do this whole big thing after your showing, but I think this is the right time." He reached into his suit jacket and took out a blue box. "I love you, Jess. I don't know that I believed in angels until you showed up at my lighthouse, being all sassy and beautiful. But if there are angels, you're mine. Will you marry me?"

She nodded. He put the ring on her finger, then pulled her close, amazed and awed that their baby was between them right now.

Jeremy was right after all. Not everyone got lucky a second time around. Now that he had, he was never going to let her go.

* * * * *

CLAIMED IN THE ITALIAN'S CASTLE

CAITLIN CREWS

To the fairy tale heroines who didn't get
to be princesses.

CHAPTER ONE

This door you might not open, and you did;
So enter now, and see for what slight thing
You are betrayed... Here is no treasure hid,
No cauldron, no clear crystal mirroring
The sought-for Truth, no heads of women slain
For greed like yours, no writhings of distress;
But only what you see... Look yet again:
An empty room, cobwebbed and comfortless.
Yet this alone out of my life I kept
Unto myself, lest any know me quite;
And you did so profane me when you crept
Unto the threshold of this room tonight
That I must never more behold your face.
This now is yours. I seek another place.

　　　　　　　—Edna St. Vincent Millay, *Bluebeard*

HER SISTERS WERE in a dither.

This was not an unusual state of affairs. Petronella and Dorothea Charteris had never met a molehill they couldn't make into the Alps. Angelina, the younger sister they preferred to exclude from anything and everything, usually ignored them.

But as Angelina slipped through the servants' passageway this evening, racing to change for dinner after another long day of hiding from her family in this petri dish they called their home, she paused. Because she could hear the rise and fall of her sisters' voices a little too well, and they weren't discussing one of their usual topics—like why they were cruelly sequestered away in the family mausoleum as their youth and vitality slipped away...

Because it never occurred to them to leave and make their own way, as Angelina planned to do, when they could sit at home and complain instead.

"We shall be slaughtered in our sleep!" Petronella screeched.

Angelina paused, there on the other side of the paper-thin wall of the drawing room, because that sounded extreme. Even for the notably dramatic Petronella.

"It will be me, I am sure of it," Dorothea pronounced in the trembling tones of an Early Christian Martyr. Her happy place, in other words. "He will spirit me away, and no. No, Petronella. Do not attempt to make this better." Angelina could hear nothing that suggested Petronella had attempted anything of the kind. "It will be a sacrifice—but one I am prepared to make for the sake of our family!"

Angelina blinked. Dorothea preferred to talk about sacrifices rather than make any, in her experience. What on earth was going on?

Petronella wailed, then. Like a banshee—a sound she had spent a whole summer some years back perfecting, waking everyone round the clock with what their mother had icily called *that caterwauling*. That had been the summer Petronella had wanted to go on a Pilates retreat to Bali with the loose group of pointless women of indiscernible means she called friends—when she wasn't posting competing selfies on social media. Petronella had claimed the screams had nothing at all to do with Papa's refusal to fund her trip.

"Everything is blood and pain, Dorothea!" she howled now. "We are *doomed*!"

That sounded like the usual drama, so Angelina rolled her eyes. Then, conscious that time was passing and her happiness was directly related to remaining invisible to her stern mother, she hurried along the passage. She took the back stairs two at a time until she reached the family wing. Though it was less a wing and more the far side of the once great house that everyone pretended had not fallen into ruin.

Charming, her mother liked to say stoutly whether or not anyone had asked. *Historic.*

Angelina was well aware that in the village, they used other words. More appropriate words. *Rundown,* for example. She had once pretended not to hear the grocer's wife refer to the once-proud Charteris family estate, nestled in what bits of the French countryside her father hadn't sold off to pay his debts, as *"that crumbling old heap."*

Though it had never been made clear to her whether the woman referred to the house or Angelina's father.

Either way, while her sisters flounced about screaming and carrying on about everything from the lukewarm temperature of their thin soup at lunch to the lack of funds for the adventures they wished to take with their far flashier friends—because they wished to perform it on social media, not because they had an adventurous bone in either one of their bodies—Angelina had spent another pleasant afternoon practicing piano in the conservatory. A room not a single member of her family had been inside in the last decade, as far as she knew. Mostly because there was nothing there any longer. Just the old piano and Angelina, who far preferred the company of Bach, Mozart, and Beethoven to her sisters.

She had nurtured grand dreams of leaving the family entirely and going off to Paris when she hit eighteen. Or anywhere at all, as long as it was elsewhere. But there had been no money for what her father had sniffed and called her "vanity project."

There had been money for Petronella's Year of Yoga, as Angelina recalled. And for Dorothea's "art," which had been two years in Milan with nothing to show for it but some paint smudged on canvases, a fortune spent on wine and cafes, and a period of dressing in deeply dramatic scarves.

But that was a long time ago. That was when Papa had still pretended he had money.

"Of course there's no money for you to *play piano,*" Dorothea had scoffed. "When Petronella and I have scrimped and saved these past years in the vain hope that Papa might throw us a decent debutante ball. Ironically, of course, *but still.*"

Angelina had learned early on that it was better not to argue with her older sisters. That was a quick descent into quicksand and there was no getting out of it on one piece. So she had not pointed out the many problems with her eldest sister's statement. First, that Dorothea was thirty and Petronella twenty-six—a bit long in the tooth for debutante balls, ironic or otherwise. And second, that there was no point in pronouncing oneself a debutante of any description when one was a member of a rather shabby family clinging desperately to the very outskirts of European high society, such as it was.

Her sisters did not like to think of themselves as shabby. Or clingy, come to that.

Even if it was obvious that the house and family were not *in* a decline. The decline had already happened and they were living in the bitter ashes that remained.

She slipped into her bedchamber, staring as she always did at the water damage on her bare walls. Her ceiling. All the evidence of winters past, burst pipes, and no money to fix it. Her mother claimed that the family's reliance on the old ways was a virtue, not a necessity. She waxed rhapsodic about fires in all the fireplaces to heat the house, no matter how cold it got in this part of France. She called it atmospheric. *It is our preference,* she would tell anyone who even looked as if they might ask. *A family custom.*

But the truth was in the cold that never lifted in this place of stone and despair, not even in the summertime. The house was too old, too drafty. It was June now and still chilly, and the picked-bare rooms and stripped walls didn't help. Slowly, ever so slowly, priceless rugs disappeared from the floors and paintings from their hooks. Family heirlooms no longer took pride of place in the echoing rooms.

When asked, Mother would laugh gaily, and claim that it was high time for a little spring cleaning—even when it was not spring.

The more time Papa spent locked up his office, or off on another one of those business trips he returned from looking grim and drawn, the more the house became a crumbling patchwork of what had once been a certain glory.

Not that Angelina cared. She had her piano. She had music. And unlike her sisters, she had no interest at all in scaling the heights of society—whether that was bright young things who called themselves influencers, who Petronella desperately emulated, or the dizzy heights of the European once-nobles who turned Dorothea's head.

All she wanted to do was play her piano.

It had been her escape as a child and it still was now. Though more and more she dreamed that it might also be her ticket out of this house. And away from these people she knew only through an accident of birth.

She hurried into the bath attached to her chamber, listening for the comforting symphony of the leaking pipes. She wanted a bath, but the hot water was iffy and she'd spent too much time in the servants' passage, so she settled instead for a brisk, cold wash in the sink.

Because evening was coming on fast, and that meant it was time for the nightly charade.

Mother insisted. The Charteris family might be disappearing where they stood, but Mother intended they should go out holding fast to some remnant of their former grandeur. That was why they maintained what tiny staff they could when surely the salaries should have gone toward Papa's debts. And it was why, without fail, they were all forced to parade down to a formal dinner every evening.

And Margrete Charteris, who in her youth had been one of the fabled Laurent sisters, did not take kindly to the sight of her youngest in jeans and a sweater with holes in it. Not to mention, Angelina thought as she stared in the mirror, her silvery blond hair wild and unruly around her and that expression on her face that the piano always brought out. The one Mother referred to as *offensively intense.*

Rome could be burning in the drawing room and still Angelina would be expected to smile politely, wear something appropriate, and tame her hair into a lady-like chignon.

She looked at herself critically in the mirror as she headed for the door again, because it was too easy to draw her mother's fire. And far better if she took a little extra time now to avoid it.

The dress she'd chosen from her dwindling wardrobe was a trusty one. A modest shift in a jacquard fabric that made her look like something out of a forties film. And because she knew it would irritate her sisters, she pulled out the pearls her late grandmother had given her on her sixteenth birthday and fastened them around her neck. They were moody, freshwater pearls, in jagged shapes and dark, changeable colors and sat heavily around her neck, like the press of hands.

Angelina had to keep them hidden where none of her sisters, her mother, or Matrice, the sly and sullen housemaid, could find them. Or they would have long since been switched out, sold off, and replaced with paste.

She smoothed down the front of her dress and stepped back out into the hallway as the clock began to strike the hour. Seven o'clock.

This time, she walked sedately down the main hall and took the moldering grand stair to the main floor. She only glanced at the paintings that still hung there in the front hall—the ones that could not be sold, for they had so little value outside the Charteris family. There were all her scowling ancestors lined up in ornate frames that had perhaps once been real gold. And were now more likely spray painted gold, not even gilt.

Angelina had to bite back laughter at the sudden image of her mother sneaking about in the middle of the night, spray painting hastily-thrown-together old frames and slapping them up over all these paintings of her austere in-laws. Margrete was a woman who liked to make sweeping pronouncements about her own consequence and made up for her loss of her status with a commensurate amount of offended dignity. She would no more *spray paint* something than she would scale the side of the old house and dance naked around the chimneys.

Another image that struck Angelina as hilarious.

She was stifling her laughter behind her hand as she walked into the drawing room, just before the old clock stopped chiming.

"Are you *snickering*?" Mother demanded coolly the moment Angelina's body cleared the doorway. She looked up from the needlepoint she never finished, drawing the thread this way and that without ever completing a project. Because it was what gently bred women did, she'd told them when they were small. It wasn't about *completion,* it was about succumbing to one's duty—which, now she thought about it, had been the sum total of her version of "the talk" when Angelina left girlhood. "What a ghastly, unladylike sight. Stop it at once."

Angelina did her best to wipe her face clean of the offending laughter. She bowed her head because it was easier and dutifully went to take her place on the lesser of the settees. Her sisters were flung on the larger one opposite. Dorothea wore her trademark teal, though the dress she wore made her look, to Angelina's way of thinking, like an overstuffed hen. Petronella, by contrast, always wore smoky charcoal shades, the better to emphasize her sloe-eyed, pouty-lipped beauty. None of which was apparent tonight, as her face looked red and mottled.

That was Angelina's first inkling that something might actually be truly wrong.

"Have you told her?" Petronella demanded. It took Angelina a moment to realize she was speaking to their mother, in a wild and accusing tone that Angelina, personally, would not have used on Margrete. "Have you told her of her grisly fate?"

Dorothea glared at Angelina, then turned that glare back on Petronella. "Don't be silly, Pet. He's hardly going to choose *Angelina*. Why would he? She's a teenager."

Petronella made an aggrieved noise. "You know what men are like. The younger the better. Men like him can afford to indulge themselves as they please."

"I've no idea what you're talking about," Angelina said coolly. She did not add, *as usual*. "But for the sake of argument, I should point out that I am not, in fact, a teenager. I turned twenty a few months ago."

"Why would he choose Angelina?" Dorothea asked again, shrilly. Her dirty-blond hair was cut into a sleek bob that shook when she spoke. "It will be me, of course. As eldest daughter, it is my duty to prostrate myself before this threat. *For all of us*."

"Do come off it," Petronella snapped right back. "You're gagging for it to be you. He's slaughtered six wives and will no doubt chop your head off on your wedding night, but by all means. At least you'll die a rich man's widow." She shifted, brushing out her long, silky, golden blond hair. "Besides. It's obvious he'll choose me."

"Why is that obvious?" Dorothea asked icily.

Angelina knew where this was going immediately. She settled into her seat, crossing her ankles demurely, because Mother was always watching. Even when she appeared to be concentrating on her needlepoint.

Petronella cast her eyes down toward her lap, but couldn't quite keep the smug look off of her face. "I have certain attributes that men find attractive. That's all I'm saying."

"Too many men, Pet," Dorothea retorted, smirking. "He's looking for a wife, not used goods."

And when they began screeching at each other, Angelina turned toward her mother. "Am I meant to know what they're talking about?"

Margrete gazed at her elder two daughters as if she wasn't entirely certain who they were or where they'd come from. She stabbed her sharp needle into her canvas, repeatedly. Then she shifted her cold gaze to Angelina.

"Your father has presented us with a marvelous opportunity, dear," she said.

The *dear* was concerning. Angelina found herself sitting a bit straighter. And playing closer attention than she might have otherwise. Margrete was not the sort who tossed out endearments willy-nilly. Or at all. For her to use one now, while Dorothea and Petronella bickered, made a cold premonition prickle at the back of Angelina's neck.

"An opportunity?" she asked.

Angelina thought she'd kept her voice perfectly clear of any inflection, but her mother's cold glare told her otherwise.

"I'll thank you to keep a civil tongue in your head, young lady," Margrete snipped at her. "Your father's been at his wit's end, running himself ragged attempting to care for this family. Are these the thanks he gets?"

Angelina knew better than to answer that question.

Margrete carried on in the same tone. "I lie awake at night, asking myself how a man as pure of intention as your poor father could be cursed with three daughters so ungrateful that all they do is complain about the bounty before them."

Angelina rather thought her mother lay awake at night wondering how it was she'd come to marry so far beneath her station, which seemed remarkably unlike the woman Angelina knew. Margrete, as she liked to tell anyone who would listen, and especially when she'd had too much wine, had had her choice of young men. Angelina couldn't understand how she'd settled on Anthony Charteris, the last in a long line once littered with titles, all of which they'd lost in this or that revolution. Not to mention a robust hereditary fortune, very little of which remained. And almost all of which, if Angelina had overheard the right conversations correctly, her father had gambled and lost in one of his numerous ill-considered business deals.

She didn't say any of that either.

"He's marrying us off," Petronella announced. She cultivated a sulky look, preferring to pout prettily in pictures, but tonight it looked real. That was alarming enough. But worse was Dorothea's sage nod from beside her, as if the two of them hadn't been at each other's throats moments before. And as if Dorothea, who liked to claim she was a bastion of rational thought despite all evidence to the contrary, actually *agreed* with Petronella's theatrical take.

"We are but chattel," Dorothea intoned. "Bartered away like a cow or a handful of seeds."

"He will not be marrying off all three of you to the same man," Mother said reprovingly. "Such imaginations! If only this level of commitment to storytelling could be applied to helping dig the family out of the hole we find ourselves in. Perhaps then your father would not have to lower himself to this grubby bartering. Your ancestors would spin their graves if they knew."

"Bartering would be one thing," Dorothea retorted in a huff. "This is not *bartering*, Mother. This is nothing less than a guillotine."

Angelina waited for her mother to sigh and recommend her daughters take to the stage, as she did with regularity—something that would have caused instant, shame-induced cardiac arrest should they ever have followed her advice. But when Mother only stared back at her older daughters, stone-faced, that prickle at the back of Angelina's neck started to intensify. She sat straighter.

"Surely we all knew that the expectation was that we would find rich husbands, someday," Angelina said, carefully. Because that was one of the topics she avoided, having always assumed that long before she did as expected and married well enough to suit her mother's aspirations, if not her father's wallet, she would make her escape. "Assuming any such men exist who wished to take on charity cases such as ours."

"Charity cases!" Margrete looked affronted. "I hope your father never hears you utter such a phrase, Angelina. Such an ungrateful, vicious thing to say. That the

Charteris name should be treated with such contempt by one who bears it! If I had not been present at your birth I would doubt you were my daughter."

Given that Margrete expressed such doubts in a near constant refrain, Angelina did not find that notion as hurtful she might have otherwise.

"This isn't about marrying," Petronella said, the hint of tears in her voice, though there was no trace of moisture in her eyes. "I've always wanted to marry, personally."

Dorothea sniffed. "Just last week you claimed it was positively medieval to expect you to pay attention to men simply because they met Father's requirements."

Petronella waved an impatient hand. The fact she didn't snap at Dorothea for saying such a thing—or attempting to say such a thing—made the prickle at Angelina's nape bloom into something far colder. And sharper, as it began to slide down her spine.

"This isn't about men or marriage. It's about *murder*." Petronella actually sat up straight to say that part, a surprise indeed, given that her spine better resembled melted candle wax most of the time. "We're talking about the Butcher of Castello Nero."

Invoking one of the most infamous villains in Europe—maybe in the whole of the world—took Angelina's breath away. "Is someone going to tell me what we're talking about?"

"I invite you to call our guest that vile nickname to his face, Petronella," Margrete suggested, her voice a quiet fury as she glared at the larger settee. "If he really is what you say he is, how do you imagine he will react?"

And to Angelina's astonishment, her selfish, spoiled

rotten sister—who very rarely bothered to lift her face from a contemplation of the many self-portraits she took with her mobile phone—paled.

"Benedetto Franceschi," Dorothea intoned. "The richest man in all of Europe." She was in such a state that her bob actually trembled against her jawline. "And the most murderous."

"Stop this right now." Margrete cast her needlepoint aside and rose in an outraged rustle of skirts and fury. Then she gazed down at all of them over her magnificent, affronted bosom. "I will tolerate this self-centered spitefulness no longer."

"I still don't know what's going on," Angelina pointed out.

"Because you prefer to live in your little world of piano playing and secret excursions up and down the servants' stairs, Angelina," Margrete snapped. "This is reality, I'm afraid."

And that, at last, made Angelina feel real fear.

It was not that she thought she'd actually managed to pull something over on her mother. It was that she'd lived in this pleasant fiction they'd all created for the whole of her life. That they were not on the brink of destitution. That her father would turn it all around tomorrow. That they were ladies of leisure, lounging about the ruined old house because they chose it, not because there were no funds to do much of anything else.

Angelina hadn't had the slightest notion that her mother paid such close attention to her movements. She preferred to imagine herself the ignored daughter.

Here, now, what could she do but lower her gaze?

"And you two." Margrete turned her cold glare to the other settee. "Petronella, forever whoring about as if giving away for free what we might have sold does anything but make you undesirable and useless. Wealthy heiresses can do as they like, because the money makes up for it. What is it you intend to bring to the table?"

When Petronella said nothing, Mother's frosty gaze moved to her oldest daughter. "And you, Dorothea. You turned up your nose at a perfectly acceptable marriage offer, and for what? To traipse about the Continent, trailing after the heirs to lesser houses as if half of France doesn't claim they're related to some other dauphin?"

Dorothea gasped. "He was Papa's age! He made my skin crawl!"

"The more practical woman he made his wife is younger than you and can afford to buy herself a new skin." Margrete adjusted her dress, though it was perfect already. Even fabric dared not challenge her. "The three of you have done nothing to help this family. All you do is take. That ends tonight."

Angelina found herself sitting straighter. She was used to drama, but this was on a different level. For one thing, she had never seen her sisters ashen-faced before tonight.

"Your sisters know this already, but let me repeat it for everyone's edification." Margrete looked at each of them in turn, but then settled her cold glare on Angelina. "Benedetto Franceschi will be at dinner tonight. He is looking for a new wife and your father has told him that he can choose amongst the three of you. I am not interested in your thoughts or feelings on this matter. If he chooses you, you will say yes. Do you understand me?"

"He has had six wives so far," Petronella hissed.

"All have died or disappeared under mysterious circumstances. *All,* Mother!"

Angelina felt cold on the outside. Her hands, normally quick and nimble, were like blocks of ice.

But deep inside her, a dark thing pulsed.

Because she knew about Benedetto Franceschi. *"The Butcher of Castello Nero,"* Petronella had said. Everyone alive knew of the man so wealthy he lived in his own castle on his own private island—when the tide was high. When the tide was low, it was possible to reach the *castello* over a road that was little more than a sandbar, but, they whispered, those who made that trek did not always come back.

He had married six times. All of his wives had died or disappeared without a trace, declared dead in absentia. And despite public outcry, there had never been so much as an inquest.

All of those things were true.

What was also true was that when Angelina had been younger and there had still been money enough for things like tuition, she and her friends had sighed over pictures of Benedetto Franceschi in the press. That dark hair, like ink. Those flashing dark eyes that were like fire. And that mouth of his that made girls in convent schools like the one Angelina had attended feel the need to make a detailed confession. Or three.

If he chooses you, came a voice inside her, as clear as a bell, *you can leave this place forever.*

"He will choose one of us," Petronella said, still pale, but not backing down from her mother's ferocious glare. "He will pick one of us, carry her off, and then kill her. That is what our father has agreed to. Because he thinks that the loss of a daughter is worth it if he gets to keep this house and cancel out his debts. Which man is worse? The one who butchers women or the man who supplies him?"

Angelina bit back a gasp. Her mother only glared.

Out in the cavernous hallways, empty of so much of their former splendor, the clock rang out the half hour.

Margrete stiffened. "It is time. Come now, girls. We must not keep destiny waiting, no matter how you feel about it."

And there was no mutiny. No revolt.

They all lived in what remained of this sad place, after all. This pile of stone and regret.

Angelina rose obediently, falling into place behind her sisters as they headed out.

"To the death," Petronella kept whispering to Dorothea, who was uncharacteristically silent.

But it would be worth the risk, Angelina couldn't help but think—a sense of giddy defiance sweeping over her—if it meant she got to live, even briefly.

Somewhere other than here.

CHAPTER TWO

WHEN A MAN was a known monster, there was no need for posturing.

Benedetto Franceschi did not hide his reputation.

On the contrary, he indulged it. He leaned into it.

He knew the truth of it, after all.

He dressed all in black, the better to highlight the dark, sensual features he'd been told many times were sin personified. Evil, even. He lounged where others sat, waved languid fingers where others offered detailed explanations, and most of the time, allowed his great wealth and the power that came with it—not to mention his fearsome, unsavory reputation—to do his talking for him.

But here he was again, parading out like *l'uomo nero*, the boogeyman, in a crumbling old house in France that had once been the seat of its own kind of greatness. He could see the bones of it, everywhere he looked. The house itself was a shambles. And what was left of the grounds were tangled and overgrown, gardeners and landscapers long since let go as the family fortune slipped away thanks to Anthony Charteris's bad gambles and failed business deals.

Benedetto had even had what was, for him, an unusual moment of something like shame as he'd faced once more the charade he was reduced to performing, seemingly preying on the desperation of fools—

But all men were fools, in one form or another. Why not entertain himself while living out what so many called the Franceschi Curse?

The curse is not supposed to mean you, a voice inside him reminded him. *But rather your so-called victims.*

He shrugged that away, as ever, and attempted to focus on the task at hand. He had little to no interest in Anthony Charteris himself, or the portly little man's near slavering devotion to him tonight. He had suffered through a spate of twittering on that he had only half listened to, and could not therefore swear had been a kind of "business" presentation. Whatever that meant. Benedetto had any number of fortunes and could certainly afford to waste one on a man like this. Such was his lot in life, and Charteris could do with it what he liked. Benedetto already failed to care in the slightest, and maybe this time, Benedetto would get what he wanted out of the bargain.

Surely number seven will be the charm, he assured himself.

Darkly.

His men had already gathered all the necessary background information on the once proud Charteris family and their precipitous slide into dire straits. Anthony's lack of business acumen did not interest him. Benedetto was focused on the man's daughters.

One of them was to be his future wife, whether he liked it or not.

But what he liked or disliked was one more thing he'd surrendered a long time ago.

Benedetto knew that the eldest Charteris daughter had been considered something of a catch for all of five minutes in what must seem to her now like another lifetime. She could have spent the last eight years as the wife of a very wealthy banker whose current life expectancy rivaled that of a fragile flower, meaning she could have looked forward to a very well-upholstered widowhood. Instead, she had refused the offer in the flush of Anthony's brief success as a hotelier only to watch her father's fortunes—and her appeal—decline rapidly thereafter.

The possibilities of further offers from wealthy men were scant indeed, which meant Dorothea would likely jump at the chance to marry him, his reputation notwithstanding.

Unlike her sister, the middle daughter had shared her favors freely on as many continents as she could access by private jet, as long as one of the far wealthier friends she cozied up to were game to foot the bill for her travels. She had been documenting her lovers and her lifestyle online for years. And Benedetto was no Puritan. What was it to him if a single woman wished to indulge in indiscriminate sex? He had always enjoyed the same himself. Nor was he particularly averse to a woman whose avariciousness trumped her shame.

Of them all, Petronella seemed the most perfect for him on paper, save the part of her life she insisted on living in public. He could not allow that and he suspected that she would not give it up. Which would not matter if she possessed the sort of curiosity that would lead her to stick her nose into his secrets and make a choice she couldn't take back—but he doubted very much that she was curious about much outside her mobile.

The third daughter was ten years younger than the eldest, six years younger than the next, and had proved the hardest to dig into. There were very few pictures of her, as the family had already been neck deep in ruin by the time she might have followed in her sisters' footsteps and begun to frequent the tiresome charity ball circuit of Europe's elite families. What photographs existed dated back to her school days, where she had been a rosy-cheeked thing in a plaid skirt and plaits. Since graduating from the convent, Angelina had disappeared into the grim maw of what remained of the family estate, never to be heard from again.

Benedetto had already dismissed her. He expected her to be callow and dull, having been cloistered her whole life. What else could she be?

He had met the inimitable Madame Charteris upon arrival tonight. The woman had desperately wanted him to know that, once upon a time, she had been a woman of great fortune and beauty herself.

"My father was Sebastian Laurent," she had informed him, then paused. Portentously. Indicating that Benedetto was meant to react to that. Flutter, perhaps. Bend a knee.

As he did neither of those things, ever, he had merely stared at the woman until she had colored in some confusion, then swept away.

Someday, Benedetto would no longer have to subject himself to these situations. Someday, he would be free...

But he realized, as the room grew silent around him, that his host was peering at him quizzically.

Someday, sadly, was not today.

Benedetto took his time rising, and not only because

he was so much bigger than Charteris that the act of rising was likely to be perceived as an assault. He did not know if regret and self-recrimination had shrunk the man opposite him, as it should have if there was any justice, but the result was the same. And Benedetto was not above using every weapon available to him without him having to do anything but smile.

Anyone who saw that smile claimed they could see his evil, murderous intent in it. It was as good as prancing about with a sign above his head that said *LEAVE ME ALONE OR DIE*, which he had also considered in his time.

He smiled now, placing his drink down on the desk before him with a click that sounded as loud as a bullet in the quiet room.

Charteris gulped. Benedetto's smile deepened, because he knew his role.

Had come to enjoy it, in parts, if he was honest.

"Better not to do something than to do it ill," his grandfather had often told him.

"If you'll c-come with me," Charteris said, stuttering as he remembered, no doubt, every fanciful tale he'd ever heard about the devil he'd invited into his home, "we can go through to the dining room. Where all of my daughters await you."

"With joy at their prospects, one assumes."

"N-naturally. Tremendous joy."

"And do you love them all equally?" Benedetto asked silkily.

The other man frowned. "Of course."

But Benedetto rather thought that a man like this loved nothing at all.

After all, he'd been fathered, however indifferently, by a man just like this.

He inclined his head to his host, then followed the small man out of what he'd defiantly announced was his "office" when it looked more like one of those dreadful cubicles Benedetto had seen in films of lowbrow places, out into the dark, dimly lit halls of this cold, crumbling house.

Once upon a time, the Charteris home had been a manor. *A château,* he corrected himself, as they were in France. Benedetto could fix the house first and easily. That way, no matter what happened with his newest acquisition, her father would not raise any alarms. He would be too happy to be restored to a sense of himself to bother questioning the story he received.

Benedetto had played this game before. He liked to believe that someday there would be no games at all.

But he needed to stop torturing himself with *someday,* because it was unlikely that tonight would be any different. Wasn't that what he'd learned? No matter how much penance he paid, nothing changed.

Really, he should have been used to it. He was. It was this part that he could have done without, layered as it was with those faint shreds of hope. All the rest of it was an extended, baroque reconfirmation that he was, if not precisely the monster the world imagined him, a monster all the same.

It was the hope that made him imagine otherwise, however briefly.

This was not the first time he'd wished he could excise it with his own hands, then cast it aside at last.

The house was not overly large, especially with so much of it unusable in its current state, so it took no time at all before they reached the dining room on the main floor. His host offered an unctuous half bow, then waved his arm as if he was an emcee at a cabaret. A horrifying notion.

Benedetto prowled into the room, pleased to find that this part of the house, unlike the rest with its drafts and cold walls despite the season, was appropriately warm.

Perhaps too warm, he thought in the next moment. Because as he swept his gaze across the room, finding the oldest and middle daughter to be exactly as he'd expected, it was as if someone had thrown gas on a fire he could not see. But could feel inside of him, cranked up to high.

The flames rose higher.

He felt scalded. But what he saw was an angel.

Angelina, something in him whispered.

For it could be no other.

Her sisters were attractive enough, but he had already forgotten them. Because the third, least known Charteris daughter stood next to her mother along one side of a formally set table, wearing a simple dress in a muted hue and a necklace of complicated pearls that seemed to sing out her beauty.

But then, she required no embellishment for that. She was luminous.

Her hair was so blond it shone silver beneath the flickering flames of a chandelier set with real candles. Economy, not atmosphere, he was certain, but it made Angelina all the more lovely. She'd caught the silvery mass back at the nape of her neck in a graceful chignon that he longed to pick apart with his hands. Her features should have been set in marble or used to launch ships into wars. They made him long to paint, though he had never wielded a brush in all his days.

But he thought he might learn the art of oils against canvas for the express purpose of capturing her. Or trying. Her high cheekbones, her soft lips, her elegant neck.

He felt his heart, that traitorous beast, beat too hard.

"Here we all are," said Anthony Charteris, all but chortling with glee.

And in that moment, Benedetto wanted to do him damage. He wanted to grab the man around his portly neck and shake him the way a cat shook its prey. He wanted to make the man think about what it was he was doing here. Selling off a daughter to a would-be groom with a reputation such as Benedetto's? Selling off an angel to a devil, and for what?

But almost as soon as those thoughts caught at him, he let them go.

Each man made his own prison. His own had contained him for the whole of his adult life and he had walked inside, turned the key, and fashioned his own steel bars. Who was he to cast stones?

"This is Benedetto Franceschi," Charteris announced, and then frowned officiously at his daughters. "He is a very important friend and business partner. *Very* important."

Some sort of look passed between the man and his wife. Margrete, once a Laurent, drew herself up—no doubt so she could present her bosom to Benedetto once more. Then again, perhaps that was how she communicated.

He remained as he had been before: vaguely impressed, yet unmoved.

"May I present to you, sir, my daughters." Margrete

gestured across the table. "My eldest, Dorothea." Her hand moved to indicate the sulky, too self-aware creature beside the eldest, who smirked a bit at him as if he had already proposed to her. "My middle daughter, Petronella."

And at last, she indicated his angel. The most beautiful creature Benedetto had ever beheld. His seventh and last wife, God willing. "And this is my youngest, Angelina."

Benedetto declared himself suitably enchanted, waited for the ladies to seat themselves, and then dropped into his chair with relief. Because he wanted to concentrate on Angelina, not her sisters.

He wanted to dispense with this performance. Announce that he had made his choice and avoid having to sit through an awkward meal like this one, where everyone involved was pretending that they'd never heard of the many things he was supposed to have done. Just as he was pretending he didn't notice that the family house was falling down around them as they sat here.

"Tell me." Benedetto interrupted the meaningless prattle from Charteris at the head of the table about his ancestors or the Napoleonic Wars or some such twaddle. "What is it you do?"

His eyes were on the youngest daughter, though she had not once looked up from her plate.

But it was the eldest who answered, after clearing her throat self-importantly. "It is a tremendous honor and privilege that I get to dedicate my life to charity," she proclaimed, a hint of self-righteousness flirting with the corners of her mouth.

Benedetto had many appetites, but none of them were likely to be served by the indifferent food served in a place like this, where any gesture toward the celebrated national cuisine had clearly declined along with the house and grounds. He sat back, shifting his attention from the silver-haired vision to her sister.

"And what charity is it that you offer, exactly?" he asked coolly. "As I was rather under the impression that your interest in charity ball attendance had more to do with the potential of fetching yourself a husband of noble blood than any particular interest in the charities themselves."

Then he watched, hugely entertained, as Dorothea flushed. Her mouth opened, then closed, and then she sank back against her seat without saying a word. As if he'd taken the wind out of her sails.

He did tend to have that effect.

The middle daughter was staring at him, so Benedetto merely lifted a brow. And waited for her to leap into the fray.

Petronella did not disappoint. Though she had the good sense to look at him with a measure of apprehension in her eyes, she also propped her elbows on the table and sat forward in such a way that her breasts pressed against the bodice of the dress she wore. An invitation he did not think was the least bit unconscious.

"I consider myself an influencer," she told him, her voice a husky, throaty rasp that was itself another invitation. All of her, from head to toe, was a carefully constructed beckoning. She did not smile at him. She kept her lips in what appeared to be a natural pout while gazing at him with a directness that he could tell she'd practiced in the mirror. Extensively.

"Indeed." His brow remained where was, arched

high. "What influence do you have? And over what—
or whom?"

"My personal brand is really a complicated mix
of—"

"I am not interested in brands," Benedetto said, cutting her off. "Brands are things that I own and use at
will according to my wishes. The purpose of a brand
is to sell things. Influence, on the other hand, suggests
power. Not the peddling of products for profit. So. What
power do you have?"

She shifted in her chair, a strange expression on her
face. It took him a moment to recognize it as false hu-
mility. "I couldn't possibly say why some people think
I'm worth listening to," she murmured.

Benedetto smiled back, and enjoyed watching the
unease wash over her as he studied her, because he
was more the monster they thought he was than he
liked to admit.

Especially in polite company.

"Pretty is not power," he said softly. "Do you know
how you can tell? Because men wish to possess it, not
wield it. It is no different from any other product, and
like them, happily discarded when it outgrows its useful-
ness or fades in intensity. Surely you must know this."

Petronella, too, dropped her gaze. And looked uncertain for the first time since Benedetto had walked
in to the dining room.

He was not the least bit surprised that neither of
the Charteris parents intervened. Parents such as these
never did. They were too wrapped up in what they had
to gain from him to quibble over his harshness.

But he hardly cared because, finally, he was able to
focus on the third daughter. The aptly named Angelina.

"And you?" he asked, feeling a coiling inside of him, as if he was some kind of serpent about to strike. As if he was every bit the monster the world believed he was. "What is it you do?"

"Nothing of consequence," she replied.

Unlike her sisters, Angelina did not look up from her plate, where she was matter-of-factly cutting into a piece of meat he could see even from where he sat was tough. They had given the choice cuts to him and to themselves, of course. Letting their children chew on the gristle. That alone told him more than he needed to know about the Charteris family. About their priorities.

Perhaps the truth no one liked to face was that some people deserved to meet a monster at the dinner table.

"Angelina," bit out Margrete, in an iron voice from behind a pasted-on smile and that magnificent chest like the prow of a ship.

"I spoke the truth," Angelina protested.

But she placed her cutlery down, very precisely. She folded her hands in her lap. Then she raised her gaze to Benedetto's at last. He felt the kick of it, her eyes blue and innocent and dreamy, like the first flush of a sweet spring.

"I play the piano. Whenever I can, for as long as I can. My other interests include listening to other people play the piano on the radio, taking long walks while thinking about how to play Liszt's *La Campenella* seamlessly, and reading novels."

Her voice was not quite insolent. Not *quite*. Next to her, her mother drew herself up again, as if prepared to mete out justice—possibly in the form of a sharp slap, if Benedetto was reading the situation correctly—but he lifted a hand.

"Both of your sisters attempt to interact with the outside world. But not you. There's no trace of you on the internet, for example, which is surpassingly strange in this day and age."

There was heat on her cheeks. A certain glitter in her gaze that made his body tighten.

"There are enough ways to hide in a piece of music," she said after a moment stretched thin and filled with the sounds of tarnished silver against cracked china. "Or a good book. Or even on a walk, I suppose. I have no need to surrender myself to still more ways to hide myself away, by curating myself into something unrecognizable."

Petronella let out an affronted sniff, but Angelina did not look apologetic.

"Some would say that it is only in solitude that one is ever able to stop hiding and find one's true self," Benedetto said.

And did not realize until the words were out there, squatting in the center of the silent table, how deeply felt that sentiment was. Or was that merely what he told himself?

"I suppose that depends." And when Angelina looked at him directly then, he felt it like an electric charge. And more, he doubted very much that she'd spent any time at all practicing her expression in reflective glass. "Are you speaking of solitude? Or solitary confinement? Because I don't think they're the same thing."

"No one is speaking about solitary confinement, Angelina," Margrete snapped, and Benedetto had the sudden, unnerving sensation that he'd actually forgotten where he was. That for a moment, he had seen nothing but Angelina. As if the rest of the world had ceased to exist entirely, and along with it his reality, his responsibilities, his fearsome reputation, and the reason he was here...

Pull yourself together, he ordered himself.

The dinner wore on, course after insipid course. Anthony and Margrete filled the silence, chattering aimlessly, while Benedetto seethed. And the three daughters who were clearly meant to vie for his favor stayed quiet, though he suspected that the younger one kept a still tongue for very different reasons than her sisters.

"Well," said Anthony with hearty and patently false bonhomie, when the last course had been taken away untouched by a surly maid. "Ladies, why don't you repair to the library while Signor Franceschi and I discuss a few things over our port."

So chummy. So pleased with himself.

"I think not," Benedetto said, decisively, even as the older daughters started to push back their chairs.

At the head of the table, Anthony froze.

Benedetto turned toward Angelina, who tensed—almost as if she knew what he was about to say. "I wish to hear you play the piano," he said.

And when no one moved, when they all gazed back at him in varying degrees of astonishment, outright panic, and pure dislike, he smiled.

In the way he knew made those around him...shudder.

Angelina stared back at him in something that was not quite horror. "I beg your pardon?"

Benedetto smiled wider. "Now, please."

CHAPTER THREE

"ALONE," ADDED THE TERRIBLE, notorious man when Angelina's whole family made as if to rise.

He smiled all the while, in a manner that reminded Angelina of nothing so much as the legends she'd heard all her life about men who turned into wolves when the moon was high. She was tempted to run to the windows and see what shape the moon took tonight, though she did not dare.

And more, could not quite bring herself to look away from him.

Angelina had not been prepared for this. For him.

It was one thing to look at photographs. But there was only so much raw magnetism a person could see on the screen.

Because in person, Benedetto Franceschi was not merely beautiful or sinful, though he was both.

In person, he was volcanic.

Danger simmered around him, charging the air, making Angelina's body react in ways she'd thought only extremes of temperatures could cause. Her chest felt tight, hollow and too full at once, and she found it almost impossible to take a full breath.

When he'd singled her out for conversation she'd responded from her gut, not her head. And knew she'd handled it all wrong, but only because of her mother's reaction. The truth was, her head had gone liquid and light and she'd had no earthly idea what had come out of her mouth.

Nothing good, if the pinched expression on Margrete's face was any guide.

Still, disobedience now did not occur to her. Not because she feared her parents, though she supposed that on some level, she must. Or why would she subject herself to this? Why would she still be here? But she wasn't thinking of them now.

Angelina wasn't thinking at all, because Benedetto's dark, devil's gaze was upon her, wicked and insinuating. A dare and an invitation and her own body seemed to have turned against her.

He wanted to hear her play.

But a darker, less palatable truth was that she wanted to play for him.

She told herself it was only that she wanted an audience. Any audience. Yet the dark fire of his gaze worked its way through her and she knew she wasn't being entirely honest. The yearning for an audience, instead of the family members who ignored her, wasn't why her pulse was making such a racket, and it certainly wasn't why she could feel sensation hum deep within her.

She could hardly breathe and yet she stood. Worse, she knew that she *wanted* to stand. Then she turned, leading him out of the dining chamber, careful not to catch her sisters' eyes or sneak a glance at her worryingly, thunderously quiet father on her way out.

Angelina tried to steel herself against him as she moved through the murky depths of the house, certain that he would try to speak to her the moment they were alone. Charm her into unwariness or attempt to disarm her with casual conversation.

But instead, he walked in silence.

And that was much, much worse.

She was so aware of him it made her bones ache. And it took only a few steps to understand that her awareness of him was not based on fear. Her breasts and her belly were tight, and grew tighter the farther away they moved from the dining room. Deep between her legs she felt swollen, pulsing in time with her heart as it beat and beat.

Helpless. Hopeless.

Red hot and needy.

The house brought it all into sharp relief. It was dimly lit and echoing, so that their footsteps became another pulse, following them. Chasing them on. Angelina was certain that if she looked at the shadow he cast behind them, she would see not a man, but a wolf.

Fangs at the ready, prepared to attack.

She could not have said why that notion made her whole body seem to boil over, liquid and hot.

She walked on and on through a house that seemed suddenly cavernous, her mind racing and spinning. Yet she couldn't seem to grasp on to a single thought, because she was entirely too focused on the man beside her and slightly behind her, matching his stride to hers in a way that made her feel dirty, somehow.

It felt like a harbinger. A warning.

She was relieved when they reached the conservatory at last, and for once didn't care that it was more properly an abandoned sunroom. She rushed inside, shocked to see that her hands trembled in the light from the hall as she picked up the matches from the piano bench, then set about lighting the candles on the candelabra that sat atop her piano.

Because her parents only lit a portion of the house, and this room only Angelina used did not qualify.

But then it was only the two of them in the candle-light, and that made the pulse in her quicken. Then drum deep.

Especially when, overhead through the old glass, she could see the moon behind the clouds—a press of light that did not distinguish itself enough for her to determine its shape. Or fullness.

Angelina settled herself on the piano bench. And it took her a moment to understand that it wasn't her pulse that she could hear, seeming to fill the room, but her own breathing.

Meanwhile, Benedetto stood half in shadow, half out. She found herself desperately trying to see where the edges of his body ended and the shadows began, because it seemed to her for a panicked moment there that there was no difference between the two. That he was made of shadows and inky dark spaces, and only partly of flesh and bone.

"We have electricity," she felt compelled to say, though her voice felt like a lie on her tongue. Too loud, too strange, when his eyes were black as sin and lush with invitation. Everything in her quivered, but she pushed on. "My parents encourage us to keep things more…atmospheric."

"If you say so."

His voice was another dark, depthless shadow. It moved in her, swirling around and around, making all the places where she pulsed seem brighter and darker at once.

She sat, breathing too heavily, her hands curved above the smooth, worn keys of this instrument that— some years—had been her only friend.

"What do you want me to play?"

"Whatever you like."

She did not understand how he could say something so innocuous and leave her feeling as if that mouth of his was moving against her skin, leaving trails all over her body, finding those places where she already glowed with a need she hardly recognized.

You recognize it, something in her chided her. *You only wish you didn't.*

Angelina felt misshapen. Powerful sensations washed over her, beating into her until she felt as if she might explode.

Or perhaps the truth was that she wanted to explode.

She spread her hands over the keys, waiting for that usual feeling of rightness. Of coming home again. Usually this was the moment where everything felt right again. Where she found her hope, believed in her future, and could put her dreary life aside. But tonight, even the feel of the ivory beneath her fingers was a sensual act.

And somehow his doing.

"Are you afraid of me, little one?" Benedetto asked, and his voice seemed to come from everywhere at once. From inside her. From deep between her legs. From that aching hunger that grew more and more intense with every second.

She shifted on the bench. Then she stared at him, lost almost instantly in his fathomless gaze. In the dark of the room with the night pressing down outside. In the flickering candlelight that exposed and concealed them both in turn.

Angelina felt as if she was free falling, tumbling from some great height, fully aware that when she hit the ground it would break her—but she couldn't look away.

She didn't *want* to look away.

He was the most marvelous thing that had ever happened to her, even if he really was a murderer.

She didn't know where to put that.

And again, she could hear her own breath. He leaned against the side of the piano, stretching a hand out across the folded back lid, and her eyes followed the movement. Compulsively. As if she had no choice in the matter.

She would have expected a man so wealthy and arrogant to have hands soft and tender like the belly of a small dog. She wouldn't have been surprised to see a careful manicure. Or a set of garish rings.

But his hand was bare of any accoutrement. And it was no tender, soft thing. It looked tough, which struck her as incongruous even as the notion moved in her like heat. His fingers were long, his palms broad.

And she could not seem to keep herself from imagining them touching her skin, cupping her breasts, gripping her bottom as he pulled her beneath him and made her his.

When a different sound filled the room, she understood that she'd made it. She'd gasped. Out loud. And that darkness he wore too easily seemed to light up with a new kind of fire she couldn't read.

"I'm accustomed to having my questions answered," he said in a quiet tone, but all she heard was menace.

And she had already forgotten the question, and possibly herself. So she did the only thing she could under the circumstances.

Angelina began to play.

She played and she played. She played him melodies that spoke of her dreams, her hopes, and then the crushing storm of her father's losses. She played him stories of her confinement here and the bitter drip of years in this ruined, forgotten place. Then she played him songs that felt like he did, impossible and terrifying and thrilling all the same.

She felt caught in the grip of his unwavering, relentless gaze. And the notes that crashed all around them, holding them tight even as they sang out the darkest, most hidden parts of her.

And while she played, Angelina found she couldn't lose herself the way she usually did.

Instead, it was as if she was found. As if he had found her here, trapping her and exalting her at once.

So she played that, too.

She played and played, until he stepped out of the shadows and his face was fully in the candlelight.

Fierce. Haunted. Sensual.

And suffused with the same rich, layered hunger she could feel crashing around inside of her.

For a long time, while the music danced from her fingers into the keys and then filled the room, it was as if she couldn't tell which one of them was which. His hands did not touch her body, and yet somehow they were all over her. She could feel the scrape of his palm, the stirring abrasion of his calloused fingers.

And she explored him, too, with every note she coaxed from her piano. They were tossed together in the melody, tangled, while the music tied them in knots and made them one glorious note, held long and pure—

When she stopped playing, for a moment she couldn't tell the difference.

And then the next, his hands were on her.

His beautiful, terrible hands, for real this time.

He sank his fingers into her hair, pulling it from her chignon—and not gently. And her whole body seemed to bloom. His face was over hers, his mouth as grim as his eyes were hot. And then he bent her back at an angle that should have alarmed her, but instead sent a thick delight storming through her in every direction.

He feasted on her neck like the wolf she half imagined he was, teasing his way around those sullen, moody pearls she wore.

I need, she thought, though she could not speak.

The more he tasted her flesh, the more she felt certain that he stole her words. That as his mouth moved over her skin, he was altering her.

Taking her away from here. From herself. From everything she knew.

He shifted then, spreading her out on the piano bench. She lay down where he put her, grateful to have the bench at her back. Then he lowered himself over her, the dark bespoke suit he wore seeming blacker than pitch in the candlelight. He skimmed his wicked hands down the length of her body, moving his way down until he wrenched the skirt of her shift dress up to her waist.

It didn't occur to her to object.

Not when every part of her wanted to sing out instead, glory and hope alike, and no matter that this man was not safe. There was no safety in staying where she was, either. There was only disappointment and the slow march of tedious years, and Benedetto felt like an antidote to that.

He touched her and she felt as if she was the piano, and he was making her a melody.

She threw her arms over her head and arched into him.

Then she felt his mouth, again. She heard his dark laugh, desire and delight. He tasted the tender flesh of her inner thigh and she could not have described the sounds she made. She could only *feel* them, coming out of her like an echo of those same songs she'd played for him.

When she could feel the harsh beauty of them in her fingers, she realized that she was gripping his strong shoulders instead.

"Angelina," he said, there against her thigh where she could feel her own name like a brand against her skin. In the candlelight that danced and flickered, she lifted her head and found herself lost in his gaze with only her own body between them. "Are you afraid of me?"

"Yes," she lied.

He laughed, a rich, dark sound that crashed over her like a new symphony, louder and more tumultuous by far.

Then he shifted, pulled her panties to one side, and licked deep into the center of her need.

And then Benedetto Franceschi, the Butcher of Castello Nero, ate her alive.

He made her scream.

She bucked against him, crying out for deliverance but receiving nothing but the slide of his tongue, the faint scrape of his teeth. A benediction by any measure.

And when she died from the pleasure of it—only to

find she lived somehow after all, shuddering and ruined and shot through with some kind of hectic glee—he pulled her to her feet, letting her shift dress do what it would. He sank his hands into her hair again, and then this time, he took her mouth with his.

Sensation exploded in her all over again, hotter and wilder this time.

The madness of these melodies. The glorious terror of his possession.

The dark marvel of it all.

His mouth had been between her legs, and the knowledge of that made her shake all over again. She pulsed and shook, and she was too inexperienced to know what part of the rough, intoxicating taste was him, and which part her.

So she angled her head and met him as he devoured her.

Angelina felt debauched and destroyed. As ruined as this house they stood in.

And why had she never understood that the real price of a ruin like this was the sheer joy in it?

The dark, secret joy that coursed through her veins, pooled between her legs, and made her arch against him as if all this time, all these years, her body had been asleep. Only now had it woken up to its true purpose.

Here. With him.

Like this.

He kissed her and he kissed her.

When he finally lifted his mouth from hers, his grin was a ferocious thing. Angelina felt it inside her, as if she was made fierce, too, because of him.

And she had never known, until this moment, how deeply she wanted to be fierce.

"If you marry me," he told her, in that dark, intense voice of his, "you can never return here. You will no more be a part of your family. You will belong to me and I am a jealous, possessive creature at the best of times. I do not share what is mine."

Angelina hardly felt like herself. There was too much sensation coursing in her and around her, she couldn't tell if it was the music she'd played or the way he'd played her body in turn, but she couldn't seem to worry about that the way she should.

The way a wiser woman would have, with a man like him.

"Is that a warning or promise?" she asked instead.

"It is a fact."

And her skirt was still rucked up. She felt uncomfortably full in the bodice of her dress. She could not tell which was more ravaged and alight, the aching center of her need between her legs or her mouth.

But the candlelight made all of that seem unimportant.

Or perhaps, whispered a voice inside her, *it is not the light that seduces you, but the dark that makes it shine.*

"If I marry you," she said, because she was already ruined, and she wanted things she was afraid to name, "I want to live. I don't want to die."

And then, for the first time since they'd walked away from her family and into this chilly, barren room, it occurred to her to worry about the fact that he was a man with six dead wives. She was all alone with him and everyone believed he was a murderer.

Why did something in her want to believe otherwise?

His mouth was a bitter slash. His eyes were much too dark.

For the first time, Angelina wanted to cover herself. She felt cold straight through.

If she could have taken the words back, she would have. If she could have kept him from touching her, she—

But no. Whatever happened next, his mouth on her had been worth it.

"Every one of us must die, little one," Benedetto said, his voice a mere thread of sound. It wound through her and then flowered into something far richer and more textured than fear, making Angelina shudder as if he was licking into her molten core again. "But we will do so in the way we live, like it or not. That I can promise you."

CHAPTER FOUR

A MONTH LATER, Angelina woke up to the sound of hammering, the way she had almost every morning since that first night.

The only difference was that today was her wedding day, like it or not.

Construction on the old house had begun immediately. Benedetto had made good on his promise with crews arriving by truckload at first light. Since then, day after day, the hammering fused with that pulse inside her, until she couldn't tell whether her heart beat inside or outside of her body.

It had been the longest and shortest month of her life.

Her sisters veered between something like outrage and a more simple, open astonishment. And sometimes, when they remembered themselves, a surprising show of concern.

"You must be careful," Petronella had said very seriously, one evening. She'd come and interrupted Angelina in the conservatory, where Angelina played piece after piece as if the piano was telling stories to keep her alive. And as long as she played she would be safe. Night after night, she played until her fingers cramped, but nothing eased that ravaged, misshapen feeling inside of her. "Whatever happens, and whatever he does to you in that castle of his, you must not react."

"I didn't think you knew where the conservatory was." Angelina blinked at her sister in the flickering candlelight. Outside, a bloated summer moon rose over the trees. "Are you lost?"

"I'm serious, Angelina," Petronella snapped, scowling, which felt more like her sister than this strange appearance and stab at worry. "One dead wife could be an accident. The second could be a terrible tragedy. I could even *maybe* think that a third might be a stroke of very bad luck indeed. But six?"

Angelina slammed her hands on the keys, the discordant jangle of noise sounding a great deal like she felt inside. As if her ribs were piano keys she'd forgotten how to play.

Maybe that was what getting married was supposed to feel like.

"I don't need you to remind me who he is," she said.

Another slap of noise.

Petronella looked different in the candlelight. Younger. Softer. She lifted her hand, almost as if she intended to reach over and stroke Angelina with it. But she thought better of it, or the urge passed, and she dropped it to her side.

"I really did think he would choose me," she said, softly.

And when Angelina looked up again, Petronella had gone.

Dorothea was far less gracious. If she was worried about her younger sister, the only way she showed it was in an officious need to micromanage the trousseau that

Benedetto was funding for his new bride along with everything else.

"If he's a murderer," Angelina had said tightly one afternoon, after Dorothea made her try on armful after armful of concoctions she'd ordered straight from atelier in Paris on Angelina's behalf, "do you really think that choosing the right selection of negligees will save me?"

"Don't be ridiculous," Dorothea tutted, bustling about Angelina's bedchamber as if she'd never sat on a settee wailing about her impending death. "You know how people like to talk. That's all it is, I'm certain. A series of tragic events and too many rumors and innuendos."

"I hope you're right," Angelina had said.

But Dorothea's only response had been to lay out more soft, frilly things for Angelina to try on.

And it was a strange thing indeed to know that her life had changed completely—to understand that nothing she knew would be hers any longer, and soon— when for thirty days, only the trappings of her life changed. The manor house slowly returned to its former glory. Her father laughed again. Margrete looked less stiff and tense around the eyes.

But Angelina still woke in her same old bed. She still timed her breakfast to avoid the rest of the family, and then set off for her long morning walk, no matter the weather. She still played the piano for hours, alone in the conservatory.

If it weren't for the endless hammering, she might have been tempted to imagine that she'd made the whole thing up.

Then again, every time that Benedetto visited—a

stolen evening here, a day or two there—the balance in Angelina's family...shifted.

Because she was shifting, she thought as she lay in her bed at night with her hands between her legs, not sure if she wanted to sob or scream out all the wildfires he'd lit inside her. With that dark gaze. With the things he did to her when they were alone. His mouth, his fingers. And always that dark, seductive laugh.

She had always thought of a seduction as something...quicker. The mistake of an evening. Something hasty and ill-considered that would take time and space to repent.

But Benedetto taught her many lessons about time. And patience.

And the exquisite torture of anticipation.

The only thing Angelina had ever wanted was her piano and a place to play it. She had been certain she knew herself inside and out. But this man taught her—over and over—that there were banked fires in her she hardly understood.

Dark, greedy claws that dug in, deep, whenever he touched her and when he did not. Red and terrible longings that made her toss and turn when she wanted to sleep.

This hunger that made her run to him when she knew full well she should have run the other way.

"Such a pretty, needy little thing you are," he murmured one evening.

Like all the nights he came here, there had first been the awkward family dinner where he'd demonstrated his mastery over her father, then cowed her sisters and mother into uncharacteristic silence—usually with little more than a lift of one dangerous brow. When her mother and sisters repaired to the drawing room, leaving her father to his solitary port, Benedetto would usher Angelina to the conservatory.

It was the same every time.

That long, *fraught* walk through a house only half-alive. The sound of his footsteps mingled with hers. The humming, overfull silence stretched out between them and echoing back from the walls. Her breath would change as they moved, and she was certain he could hear it, though he always remained behind her. And he never spoke.

She told herself she marched toward her own, slow execution. She walked herself off the plank.

But the truth she never wished to face was that the closer they got to the conservatory, the quicker her steps. The quicker her breath.

And oh, how molten and hot her blood ran in her, pooling between her legs with a desperate intent.

Because inside that room, who knew what might happen?

He always made her play.

And then he played her, always making her scream and arch and shake. Always his wicked fingers, his clever mouth, tasting her, tempting her.

Training her, something in her whispered.

"Is this how you murder them all?" she asked one evening, a scant week away from their wedding.

Benedetto had laid her out on the chaise that had appeared one morning, along with all kinds of furniture throughout the *château*. It was as if the house was a visual representation of her own femininity, and she could see it grow its own pleasure. Lush and deep.

Paintings reappeared. Priceless antiques took their

places once again. There were updates everywhere, light where there had been darkness, the cobwebs swept away and cracks plastered over.

She'd forgotten herself, with her skirts tossed up and his head so dark between her thighs.

She'd forgotten herself, but she remembered with a jolt when she shifted and caught a glimpse of them in the fogged-up windows that surrounded them on all sides.

Benedetto was so big, tall and strong, and she was laid out before him, splayed wide like an offering. He was eating her alive and she was letting him, but she should never have let herself forget that the pleasure he visited upon her untried body was a weapon.

Everything about this man was a weapon only he knew how to use.

"I didn't mean that," she managed to gasp out while her heart galloped inside her, lust and fear and that same dark ache fusing into one.

She tried to pull her legs closed but his broad shoulders were between them, and he did not move. He lifted his head and his night-black eyes bored into her. He pressed his palm, roughened and huge, against the faint swell of her abdomen.

And something about the pressure made a new, dangerous heat uncurl inside her.

"What do you know of marriage?" he asked, and his voice was as dark as the rest of him, insinuating and dangerous.

She could feel that prickle that was as much longing as it was fear sweep over her body, leaving goose bumps in its wake.

"I have never been married before."

Angelina didn't know why she was answering him so prosaically. When she was as he liked her, still dressed for dinner but with her skirts around her waist, so she was bared only to him. Bared and wet and aching again.

Sometimes she thought the aching might actually kill her, here in this house before she had the chance to leave it, and that notion made her want to sob out loud.

Other times, she hoped it would.

Benedetto shifted his weight so that he held himself up on one crooked elbow. He let his hand drift from her abdomen to her secret, greedy flesh.

"Put your hands above your head," he told her, and she knew it was an order. A command she should have ignored while she still could, but her arms were already moving of their own accord. Lifting over her head so that her back arched and her breasts pressed wantonly against the bodice of the old dress she wore.

She knew he liked that. She knew a lot of the things he liked, by now. He liked her hair free and unconfined, tangled about wherever he lay her. He liked to get his fingers in it so he could guide her head where he wanted it. Particularly when he kissed her, tongue and teeth and a sheer mastery that made her shiver.

"Tell me what you know of men, Angelina," he said now, stroking the bright need between her legs, though he had already had her sweating, shaking, crying out his name.

This time, when her hips began to move, he found her opening. And he began to work one of those blunt, surprisingly tough fingers into her depths of her body.

She felt the stretching. The ache in her intensified.

Her nipples were delirious points, and every time she

breathed, the way her breasts jarred against the fabric of her bra made her want to jerk away. Or move closer.

"I have never spent much time with men," she managed to pant out. "I had a piano tutor, a boy from the village, but I learned all he had to teach me long ago."

"Did you play for him as you play for me?" Benedetto asked, his voice something like a croon—but much, much darker. "Did you open your legs like this? Did you let him slip between your thighs and taste your heat?"

And even as he asked those questions, he added a second finger to the first. He began to stroke his way deep inside her, and the sensation made it impossible to think. Impossible to do anything but lift her hips to meet him, then try to get away, or both at once.

His hand found a rhythm, but her hips took convincing.

"N-No…" She wasn't sure what, precisely, she was saying *no* to. His fingers plunged, withdrew. Then again. And again. A driving, relentless taking. "No one has ever touched me."

"Not even you?" he asked. "Late at night, tucked up beneath your covers in this tomb of a house? Do you not reach down, slip your fingers into all this molten greed, and make yourself shudder into life?"

Angelina was bright red already. But the flash of heat that he kindled within her swept over her until she was making a keening, high-pitched cry. Her hips finally found their rhythm, thrusting against him wildly as her head fell back.

And she thrashed there, not sure how anyone could survive these little deaths, much less the bigger one that waited for her.

Not sure anyone should.

"Look at me," Benedetto ordered her.

She realized she didn't know how much time had passed. How long she had shaken like that, open and exposed. It took her a long while to crack open her eyes. She struggled to sit up because he was sitting too, regarding her in his typically sinful and wicked way.

Angelina couldn't tell if it was shame or desire that worked inside of her, then.

Especially when he held her gaze, lifted the fingers he'd had inside her, and slowly licked them clean.

She heard herself gasping for breath as if she was running. If she was running to escape him, the way she knew she should. She could crash through the windows into the gardens that her parents had let go to seed, and were now manicured and pruned. She could race into the summer night, leaving all this behind her.

She could save herself and let her family do as they would.

But she only gazed back at him, breathing too heavily, and did not move an inch to extricate from this man who held her tight in his grip—though he was not touching her at all.

"I want you desperate, always," he told her, his voice that same, serious command. "I want you wet and needy, Angelina. When I look at you, I want to know that while you look like an angel, here, where you are naked and only ever mine, you are nothing but heat and hunger."

"Do you mean…?"

"I mean you should touch yourself. Taste yourself, if you wish. I insist. As long as you are always ready for me."

She understood what he meant by *ready* in a different way, now. Because it was one thing to read about sex. To read about that strange, inevitable joining. She understood the mechanics, but was not until now, so close to her wedding night, that she understood that it would be far more than merely *mechanical*.

Benedetto's head tilted slightly to one side. "Do you understand me?"

"I do," she said, and his smile was dark.

"Then I do not think, little one, that you need to worry overmuch about murder."

That was the last time she'd seen him.

She pushed herself upright in her bed this morning, her head as fuzzy as if she'd helped herself to the liquor in the drawing room when she didn't dare. Not when she had Benedetto to contend with and needed all her wits about her.

And it shocked her, as she looked around her room, that there was a lump in her throat as she accepted the reality that this room would no longer be hers by the time the sun set.

Her bedchamber had already undergone renovations, like so much of the house had in the past month. It already looked like someone else's. Plush, quietly elegant rugs were strewn about the floors, taking the chill away. She'd forgotten entirely that once, long ago, there had been curtains and drapes and a canopy over her bed, but they were all back now.

He'd given her back her childhood so she would know exactly what she was leaving behind her when she left here today.

She got up and headed to her bathroom, walking gingerly because she could feel the neediest, greediest part of her ripe and ready—just the way he wanted her. But she paused in the doorway. Because she could no longer hear the symphony of the old pipes.

And when she turned on the water in her sink, it ran hot.

Angelina ran herself a bath and climbed in, running her hands over her slick, soapy skin. Her breasts felt larger. Her belly was so sensitive she sucked in a breath through her teeth when she touched it.

And when she ran her hands between her legs, to do as he'd commanded her, she was hotter than the water around her.

Then hotter still as she imagined his face, dark and knowing, and made the water splash over the sides of her tub onto the floor.

But too soon, then it was time to dress.

Margrete bustled in, her sisters in her wake like sulky attendants. And for a long while, the three of them worked in silence. Petronella piled Angelina's hair on top of her head and pinned in sparkling hints of stones that looked like diamonds. Dorothea fussed with her dress, fastening each of the parade of buttons that marched down her spine. Margrete called in Matrice, the notably less surly housemaid now that there was money, and the two of them packed Angelina's things.

Petronella did Angelina's makeup. She made her younger sister's face almost otherworldly, and did something with her battery of brushes and sponges that made Angelina's eyes seemed bluer than the summer sky.

Matrice left first, wheeling out Angelina's paltry belongings with her.

And there was no need to keep her hiding place a secret now, so Angelina let her mother and sisters watch as she walked over to the four posts of her bed, unscrewed one tall taper, and pulled out her grandmother's pearls.

Her sisters passed a dark look between them while Angelina fastened the dark, moody pearls around her neck and let the weight of them settle there, against her collarbone.

And then her mother led her to the cheval glass.

The dress had arrived without warning two weeks before the wedding. Angelina had tried it on and let the seamstress who'd arrived with it take her measurements and make her alterations. The dress had seemed simple. Pretty. Not too much, somehow.

But now there was no escaping the dress or what it meant or what would become of her. She stared into the mirror, and a bride stared back.

The dark pearls she'd looped around her neck looked like a bruise, but everything else was white. Flowing, frothy white, while her hair seemed silvery and gleaming and impossible on top of her head.

She looked like what she was.

A virgin sacrifice to a dark king.

"You must ask him for what you want," Margrete told her, her voice matter-of-fact, but her eyes dark. "A piano, for example."

"He has already promised me a Steinway."

Margrete moved the skirt of the wedding gown this way, then that. "You must not be afraid to make demands, but you must also submit to his." Again, a touch of her dark gaze in the mirror. "No matter what, Angelina. Do you understand me? With a smile, if possible."

Angelina expected her sisters to chime in then, making arch comments about sex and their experiences, but they were silent. She looked in the glass and found them sitting on the end of her bed, looking…she would have said lost, if they had been anyone else.

"I'm not afraid of his demands," she said.

It wasn't until her mother's gaze snapped to hers again that she realized perhaps she ought to have been.

"You must remember that no matter what, you need only call and I will come to you," Margrete said then, as if she was making her own vows.

Angelina could not have been more shocked if her mother had shared sordid details of her own sexual exploits. "I… Really?"

Margrete turned Angelina then, taking her by the shoulders so she could look into her face.

"You're not the first girl to be ransomed off for the benefit of her family," Margrete said in a low, direct voice. "My father lost me in a card game."

There was a muffled sound of surprise from the bed. But their mother did not wait for that astonishing remark to sink in. Margrete lifted her chin, her fingers gripping Angelina's shoulders so hard she was half worried they would leave a mark.

"Life is what you make of it. Some parts are unpleasant, others regretful—but those are things you cannot control. You can always control yourself. You can school your reactions. You can master your own heart. And no one can ever take that from you, Angelina. No one."

"But Papa…" Angelina was turning over the idea of a card game and her severe grandfather in her head. "Papa was not a murderer."

"All men are murderers." Margrete's dark eyes flashed. "They take a daughter and make her a woman whether she wants it or not. They kill a girl to create a wife, then a mother. It's all a question of degrees, child."

And with those words, Margrete took her youngest daughter by the hand and led her down the grand, restored stair to the ballroom, where she handed Angelina off to her father.

The father who had *won* her mother, not wooed her, as Angelina had always found so hard to imagine.

The father who did not look at the daughter he was sacrificing to line his pockets even once as he marched her down the aisle, then married her off to a monster.

CHAPTER FIVE

BENEDETTO TOLERATED THE CEREMONY.

Barely.

God knew, he was tired of weddings.

His angel walked toward him, spurred on to unseemly haste by her portly father, who was practically salivating at the opportunity to hand her over to Benedetto's keeping. Or to her death. That Anthony Charteris had not required Benedetto to make any statements or promises about Angelina's well-being showed exactly what kind of man he was.

Tiny. Puny. Greedy and selfish to his core.

But then, Benedetto already knew that. If Anthony hadn't been precisely that kind of man, he wouldn't have come to Benedetto's notice.

As weddings went, this one was painless enough. There was no spectacle, no grand cathedral, no pageant. The words were said, and quickly, and the only ones he cared about came from Angelina's mouth.

"I do," she said, her voice quiet, but not weak. "I will."

He slid a ring onto her hand and felt his own greed kick hard enough inside that he could hardly set himself apart from Charteris. What moral high ground did he think *he* inhabited?

Soon, he told himself. *Soon enough.*

The priest intoned the words that bound them, and then it was done.

He was married for the seventh time. The last time, he dared to hope, though there was no reason to imagine he could make it so.

There was no reason to imagine this would be anything but the same old grind. The lies, the distrust. In his head he saw a key in a lock, and a bare white room with nothing but the sea outside it.

Oh, yes. He knew how this would end.

But despite everything, something in him wished it could be otherwise. Her music sang in him, and though he knew better, it felt like hope.

Once the ceremony was over and Angelina was his wife, he saw no reason to subject himself to Charteris or his family any longer. With any luck, neither he nor Angelina would ever see any of them again—for one reason or another.

He left Angelina to the tender mercies of her mother and sisters for the last time. He cut through the small gathering, ignoring the guests that Charteris had invited purely to boast about his sudden reversal of fortune, something that was easy to do when they all shrank from him in fear. And when he reached the place where Anthony was holding court, he scared off the cluster around him with a single freezing stare.

"My man of business will contact you," he told his seventh father-in-law with as little inflection as possible. "He will be your point person from now on for anything involving the house or the settlement I've arranged. Personal communications from you will not be necessary. And will no longer be accepted."

"Yes, yes," Charteris brayed pompously, already florid of cheek and glassy of eye, which told Benedetto all he needed to know about how this man had lost the fortune he'd been born with and the one he'd married into, as well. "I was thinking we might well have a ball—"

"You may have whatever you wish," Benedetto said with a soft menace that might as well have been a growl. "You may throw a ball every weekend. You may build a *château* in every corner of France, for all I care. The money is yours to do with as you wish. But what you will not have is any familiarity with me. Or any access to your daughter without my permission. Do you understand?"

He could see the older man process the rebuke like the slap it was, and then, just as quickly, understand that it would not affect his wallet. He did not actually shrug. But it was implied.

"I wish you and my daughter every happiness," Charteris replied.

He raised his glass. Benedetto inclined his head, disgusted.

And then he went to retrieve his seventh wife.

As he drew closer to the little knot she stood in with her mother and sisters, he felt something pierce his chest at the sight of her. Gleaming. Angelic.

All that, and the way she played the piano made him hard.

And that was nothing next to her taste.

Something in him growled like the sort of monster he tried so hard to keep hidden in public. Because people so readily saw all kinds of fiends when they looked at him—why should he confirm their worst suspicions?

"Come," he said, when his very appearance set them all to wide-eyed silence. "It is time to take you to my castle, wife."

He watched the ripple of that sentence move through the four of them. He could see the words *Butcher of Castello Nero* hanging in the air around them.

And whatever he thought of Anthony Charteris, whatever impressions he'd gleaned of these women over the past month, they all paled in unison now.

Because everyone knew, after all, what happened to a Franceschi bride. Everyone knew the fate that awaited her.

For the first time, the things others thought about him actually...got to him.

Benedetto held out his hand.

The Charteris sisters remained white-faced. Their mother was made of stouter stuff, however, and the look she fixed on him might have been loathing, for all the good it would do her.

But it was Angelina who mattered. Angelina whose cheeks did not pale, but flushed instead with a brighter color he knew well by now.

Angelina, his seventh bride, who murmured something soothing in the direction of her mother and sisters and then slid her delicate hand into his.

Then she let him lead her from her father's house, never to return.

Not if he had anything to say about it.

He assisted her into the back of the gleaming black car that waited for them, joining her in the back seat. He lounged there, as the voluminous skirts of her soft white wedding gown flowed in every direction, like seafoam.

Benedetto found he liked thinking of her that way,

like a mermaid rising from the deep. A creature of story and fable.

"Why have you waited to...seal our bargain until our wedding night?" she asked as the car pulled away from the front of the old house that was already starting to look like itself again. Its old glory restored for the small price of Angelina's life.

What a bargain, he thought darkly.

Of course, neither Angelina nor her noxious father had any idea of the bargain he intended to pose to her directly—but he was getting ahead of himself.

And if this time was different—if he had found himself captivated by this woman in ways he did not fully understand and had never experienced before—well. He was sure he would pay a great penance for that, too, before long.

But she was gazing at him, waiting for him to answer her.

"It is customary to wait, is it not?" Because he was happy to have her think him deeply traditional. For now. He watched her, but she did not turn around to watch her life disappear behind her. So she did not see her sisters, clutching each other's hands as they stood at the top of the stairs, staring after her. She did not see her mother in the window, her face twisting. She did not note the absence of her father from these scenes of despair. "Some things have fallen out of favor in these dark times, I have no doubt, but I hope a white wedding will always be in fashion." He allowed his mouth to curve. "Or a slightly off-white wedding, in this case. It is your piano playing, I fear. It undoes all my good intentions."

Angelina looked at him, her blue eyes searching his

face though her own looked hot. "You have had many lovers, if the tabloids are to be believed."

"First, you must never believe the tabloids. They are paid to write fiction, not fact. But second, I have always kept my affairs and my wives separate."

She cleared her throat. "And now? Will you continue in the same vein?"

He picked up her hand, and toyed with the ring he'd put there, that great, gleaming red ruby that shone like blood in the summer light that fell in through the car windows. "What is it you are asking me?"

"Do you conduct your affairs while you're married?" She sat straighter, though she didn't snatch her hand back from him. "Will one of my duties be to look the other way?"

"Are you asking me if I plan to be faithful? Less than an hour after we said our vows before God, man, and your father's creditors?"

"I am. Do you?"

Again, he was struck by how different she was from the rest of his brides—none of whom had seemed to care who he touched, or when. It was as if Angelina had cast a spell on him. Enchanted him, despite everything.

"As faithful as you are to me, Angelina." His voice was darker than it should have been, but it was one more thing he couldn't seem to control around her. "That is how faithful I will be to you in return."

This time he was certain he could see those words, like another set of vows, fill up the car like the voluminous skirts she wore.

"That's easy enough then," she replied with that tartness that surprised and delighted him every time she dared show it. "I have only ever loved one thing in my life. My piano. As long as you provide me with one to play as I wish, as you promised, why shouldn't I keep the promises I made to you?"

He lifted her hand to his mouth, and then, idly, sucked one of her fingers into the heat of his mouth.

"I've never understood cheating," she continued, her voice prim, though he could see the way she trembled. He could taste it. "Surely it cannot be that difficult to keep a vow. And if it is, why make it in the first place?"

"Ah, yes. The certainty of youth." He applied more suction, and she shuddered beautifully. "You know very little of passion, I think. It has a habit of making a mockery of those who think in terms of black and white."

Her eyes were much too blue. "Have you cheated on your wives before?"

And he had expected silence. That was typical. Or if there were questions, this being Angelina who seemed so shockingly unafraid of him, perhaps more pointed questions about murderers or mysterious deaths. Or euphemisms that didn't quite mention either. But not this. Not what he was tempted to imagine was actual possessiveness on her part. He noted that the hand he was not holding was balled into a fist.

Benedetto would have sworn that he was far too jaded for passion to make a mockery of him, and yet here he was. Hoping for things that could never be.

"I have never had the opportunity to grow bored," he replied, deliberately. With no little edge to his voice. "They were all gone too soon."

He watched her swallow hard. He watched the column of her neck move.

He wished he could watch himself and this dance of his as closely.

"You have not told me your expectations," she said, shifting her gaze away from him and aiming it somewhere in front of her. He found he missed the weight of her regard. "You're obviously a very wealthy man. Many wealthy men have staff to take on the position normally held by a wife."

"I assure you that I do not intend to take my staff to my bed."

He saw the lovely red color on her cheeks brighten further but she pushed on, and her carefully even voice did not change. "I'm not referring to your bed. I'm referring to the duties involved in running a great house. Or in your case, a castle."

"You are welcome to engage my housekeeper in battle for supremacy, Angelina. But I warn you, Signora Malandra is a fearsome creature indeed. And jealously guards what she sees as hers."

His bride looked at him then, narrowly. "Does that include you?"

Benedetto shrugged, keeping his face impassive though he was once again pleased with her possessiveness. "She's been with my family for a very long time. You could argue that in many ways, she raised me. So yes, I suppose she does see me as hers. But she is not my lover, if that is what you are asking."

He didn't actually laugh at that. Or the very notion of suggesting such a thing where his housekeeper could hear it.

Angelina managed to give the impression of bristling without actually doing so. "It had not occurred to me that you might install your lovers under the same roof as your wife. Though perhaps, given your infamy, I should anticipate such things."

"I will not do anything of the kind," he drawled, trying to sound lazy enough that the car would not reverberate with the truth in his words. "But whether you believe that or not will be up to you."

"You expect me to be jealous?"

"I'm not afraid of jealousy, Angelina. On the contrary. I do not understand why it is considered a virtue to pretend the heart is not a greedy organ when we can all feel it pump and clench in our chests. Lust starts there. And where there is lust, where there is need and want and longing, there will always be jealousy." He shrugged. "This is the curse of humanity, no? It is better to embrace the darkness than to pretend it does not or cannot exist."

"Jealousy is destructive," she said, again in that matter-of-fact tone he suspected was a product of her youth.

"That depends what you are building," he replied. "And whether or not you find beauty in the breaking of it."

And then he laughed, darkly and too knowingly, as she reddened yet again.

It was not a long drive to the private airfield where his plane waited for them. Once there, he escorted her up the stairs and then into the jet's luxurious cabin.

Angelina looked around at the ostentatious display of his wealth and power and swallowed, hard. "Are my things here? I can change—"

"I think not," he said, with a quiet relish. "You will remain in that gown until I remove it myself, little one."

Again, that glorious flush that made her glow. Her lips fell open while her pulse went wild in her throat. "But... But how long...?"

"We will have a wedding night," he assured her, though wedding nights with him were rarely what his brides imagined. "Were you worried?"

"Of course not," she said.

But she was lying. He could hear the music she played in his head. He could remember all too well those steamy evenings in that barren room that she'd filled with art and longing and her own sweet cries of need and release.

He was entirely too tempted to indulge himself—because he couldn't recall the last time he'd been tempted at all.

Benedetto tilted his head slightly as he regarded her, not surprised when that bright glow crept down her neck. "You have my permission to please yourself as you wish if you find you cannot wait. No need to lock yourself away." He indicated one of the plush leather seats in the cabin. "Pull up your skirts, bare yourself to me, and show me your pleasure, Angelina."

He could hear her ragged breath as she took that in. "I… I can't."

Her voice was barely a whisper.

"Then you must suffer, wife. And you must wait."

And he watched her almost idly as he handled matters of business on the short flight. She sat in her seat as if it was made of nails, shifting this way, and that. Clearly squirming with anticipation, though he supposed she might lie to them both about that. Too bad it was stamped all over her.

He couldn't wait to indulge himself. He, who usually preferred his wedding nights be more theater than anything else.

Why couldn't he stick to the script with this woman?

They landed in Italy on another private airfield not far from the coast where the Franceschis had lived for centuries. He ushered her into another car that waited for them, gleaming in the afternoon sun, but this time he drove it himself.

"We must hurry if we wish to make the tide," he told her.

And the dress she wore barely fit into the bucket seats of the low-slung sports car. But the helpless, needy sound he heard her make when he put the car into gear could only be a harbinger of things to come.

If he let it.

And oh, how he wanted to let it. He had already tasted her—and he couldn't seem to get past that. He couldn't seem to keep his head together when he was near her. He couldn't remember his duties, and that spelled disaster.

He knew all that, and still, all he could focus on was her reaction to his car.

He could imagine the way the low, throaty growl of the engine worked its way through her where she sat. But even if he couldn't, the way she began to breathe— too heavily—told him what he needed to know.

She might not like him. She might want him for the concert piano he'd had made especially for her. She might choose to leave him like all the rest, and soon.

But she wanted him.

Desperately.

There was an honesty in that. And it was new. Completely different from the six who'd come before her.

Benedetto found he was less interested in her sensual suffering than he probably should have been.

"I cannot wait, Angelina," he told her now. "I want

you to lift your wedding gown to your waist, as if we were back in your stark conservatory."

And he could tell the state she was in when she didn't argue. Or stammer. Or even blush again.

He shifted the car into second gear as he raced down the old roads toward the coastline his grandparents had kept undeveloped, even when that had required they fight off "progress" with their own hands, and watched as she obeyed him.

So quickly her hands were shaking.

"Good girl," he murmured when she'd bared all the soft, silken flesh of her thighs to his gaze. He could only glance at all that warm lushness as he drove, faster and faster, but it was enough. It made him so hard he ached with it. "Touch yourself. I want you to do whatever you need to do to come, Angelina. Fast and hard. Now."

She let out a sound that could have been a sob. A moan.

But he knew when she'd found her own heat, because she made a sound that was as full of relief as it was greed.

It made his sex pulse.

And he drove too fast down the coastal road he knew by heart. Then he sped up as he hit the treacherous drive that stretched out into the water that rose higher and higher by the moment as the tide came in and began to swallow it whole.

"Come," he ordered her.

She rocked her hips, making mindless, glorious little sounds. He could hear the greediness of her flesh, and a quick glance beside him found her with her head thrown back and her hands buried between her legs. The summer afternoon light streamed into the sports car, bouncing off the water and making her so bright, she nearly burned.

So beautiful, it cut at him.

So perfectly innocent, it should have shamed him, but it didn't. Not when he wanted her this much.

If he hadn't been a monster already, this would have made him one, he was sure of it.

Benedetto heard her breath catch. Her head rocked back, and he was sure that he could feel her heat as if it was his hands on her, clutched deep in her molten core. That hot rush of sweet, wet fire as she took herself over the edge.

She shook and she sobbed, and he drove faster. There was light and water and his seventh bride, coming on command. And when her sobs had settled into a harsh panting, he reached over. He took one of her hands, and sucked her fingers into his mouth because that heat was all for him. It was his.

She was his, and no matter if that damned them both, he didn't have it in him to stop this madness. He couldn't.

"Open your eyes, Angelina," he told her then, another soft order. "We are here."

That was how he drove her into Castello Nero, the ancestral home of his cursed and terrible clan. Flushed and wanton, wet and greedy, the taste of her in his mouth and that wild, ravaged look on her face.

Welcome home, little one, Benedetto thought darkly.

And then he delivered them both into their doom.

CHAPTER SIX

ANGELINA BARELY HAD the presence of mind to shove her skirts back down, letting the yards and yards of soft white fabric flow back into place. To preserve whatever was left of her modesty.

Though she almost laughed at the thought of modesty after…that. After the past month, after this drive—what was left for him to take?

But, of course, she knew the answer to that.

And imagining what she had to lose here in this place made it difficult to breathe.

The castle keep rose on all sides, the stone gleaming in the summer afternoon light. The sunshine made it seem magical instead of malevolent, and she tried her best to cling to that impression.

But her body felt like his, not hers. Even her breath seemed to saw in and out of her in an alien rhythm.

His, she thought again. Not hers.

Benedetto swung out of the car but Angelina stayed where she was. The drive from the airfield had been a blur of heat, need, and the endless explosion that was still reverberating through her bones, her flesh. Still, she could picture the car eating up the narrow road that flirted with the edge of the incoming tide on what was little more than a raised sandbar. Some of the waves had already been tipping over the edge of the bar to sneak across the road as Benedetto had floored his engine. It was only a matter of time before water covered the causeway completely.

And all the molten heat in the world, all of which was surely pooled between her legs even now, couldn't keep her from recognizing the salient point here in a very different way than she had when she was merely thinking about Castello Nero instead of experiencing it herself.

Which was that once the tide rose, she would be stuck here on the island that was his castle.

Stranded here, in fact.

"How long is it between tides?" she had asked at the family dinner table one night while Benedetto was there, oozing superiority and brooding masculinity from where he lounged there at the foot of the table, his hot gaze on her.

Because she might have already betrayed herself where this man was concerned, but that didn't mean she hadn't read up on him.

"Six hours," Dorothea had said stoutly.

"Or a lifetime," Benedetto had replied, sounding darkly entertained.

She could feel her heart race again, the way it had when she'd been back in the relative safety of her father's house. But it was much different here, surrounded by the stone walls and ramparts. Now that this was where she was expected to stay. High tide or low.

Come what may.

The door beside her opened, and he was there. Her forbiddingly beautiful husband, who was looking down at her with his mouth slightly curved in one corner and that knowing look in his too-dark eyes.

And his hand was no less rough or insinuating when he helped her from the sports car. No matter where he touched her, it seemed, she shuddered.

"Welcome home, wife," he said.

The ancient castle loomed behind him, a gleaming stone facade that seemed to throb with portent and foreboding. It had been built to be a fortress. But to Angelina's mind, that only meant it could make a good prison.

The summer sky was deceptively bright up above. The castle's many towers and turrets would surely have punctured any clouds that happened by. Her heart still beat at her, a rushing, rhythm—

But in the next moment, Angelina understood that what she was hearing was the sea. The lap of tide against the rocks and the stone walls.

She didn't know if that odd giddiness she felt then was terror or relief.

When she looked back at her husband, that same devil that had worked in her the first night he'd come to her father's house brushed itself off. And sat up.

"Why do you call me 'wife' instead of my name?" she asked.

"Did you not marry me?" he asked lazily, giving the impression of lounging about when he was standing there before her, his hands thrust into the pockets of the dark bespoke suit he wore that made him look urbane and untamed at once. "Are you not my wife?"

"I rather thought it was because all the names run together," Angelina said dryly. "There have been so many."

She didn't know what possessed her to say such a

thing to the man who had rendered Margrete Charteris silent. Or how she dared.

But to her surprise, he laughed.

It was a rich, sensuous sound she knew too well from back in her father's conservatory. Here, it seemed to echo back from the ancient stone walls, then wrapped as tightly around her as the bodice of the wedding dress she wore.

"I never forget a name." He inclined his head to her. "Angelina."

Hearing her name in his mouth made the echo of his dark laughter inside her seem to hum.

Benedetto took his time shifting his gaze from her then. He focused on something behind her, then nodded.

That was when Angelina realized they were not, as she'd imagined, alone out here in this medieval keep. She turned, her neck suddenly prickling, and saw an older woman standing there, dressed entirely in black as if in perpetual mourning. The housekeeper, if she had to guess, with a long, drawn face and a sharp, unfriendly gaze.

"This is your new mistress," Benedetto told the woman, who only sniffed. "Angelina, may I present Signora Malandra, keeper of my castle."

"Enchanté," the older woman said in crisp, cut-glass French that did not match her Italian name.

"I'm so pleased to make your acquaintance," Angelina murmured, and even smiled prettily, because Signora Malandra might have been off-putting, but she was no match for Margrete Charteris.

"Come," said Angelina's brand-new husband, once again fixing that dark gaze of his on her. "I will show you to the bedchamber."

The bedchamber, Angelina noted. Not *her* bedchamber.

Her heart, having only just calmed itself, kicked into high gear again.

He did not release her hand. He pulled her with him as he moved, towing her through an archway cut into the heavy stone wall. Then he drew her into the interior of one of the oldest castles in Italy.

She still felt off balance from what had happened in his car, but she tried to take note of her surroundings. *Should you have to run for your life,* something dark inside her whispered. She tried her best to shove it aside—at least while she was in her husband's presence.

Unlike the house where she'd grown up, Castello Nero was flush with wealth and luxury. Benedetto took her down corridors filled with marble, from the floors to the statues in the carved alcoves, to benches set here and there as if the expectation was that one might need to rest while taking in all the art and magnificence.

He laughed at her expression. "Did you expect a crumbling Gothic ruin?"

She blinked, disquieted at the notion he could read her so easily. "I keep imagining kings and queens around every tapestry, that's all."

"My family have held many titles over time," he told her as they walked. Down long hallways that must have stretched the length of the tidal island. "A count here, a duke there, but nobility is much like the tide, is it not? In favor one century, forbidden the next."

Angelina's family considered itself old money rather than new, but they did not speak in terms of *centuries.* They were still focused on a smattering of generations. The difference struck her as staggering, suddenly.

"The castle has remained in the family no matter the revolutions, exiles, or abdications that have plagued Europe," Benedetto said. "Titles were stripped, ancestors were beheaded, but in one form or another this island has been in my family since the fall of the Roman Empire. Or thereabouts."

Angelina tried to imagine what it must feel like to be personally connected to the long march of so much history—and to have a family castle to mark the passage of all that time.

"Did you grow up here?" she asked.

Because it was impossible to imagine. She couldn't conceive of children running around in this shining museum, laughing or shrieking in the silent halls. And more, she couldn't picture Benedetto ever having been a child himself. Much less engaging in anything like an ungainly adolescence. And certainly not here, in a swirl of ancient armor and sumptuous tapestries, depicting historical scenes that as far as Angelina knew, might have been the medieval version of photo albums and scrapbooks.

"In a sense," he replied.

He had led her into a gallery, the sort she recognized all too well. It was covered with formal, painted portraits, she didn't have to lean in to read the embossed nameplates to understand that she was looking at centuries of his ancestors. The sweep of history as represented by various Franceschis across time. From monks to noblemen to what looked entirely too much like a vampire in one dark painting.

Benedetto gazed at the pictures on the wall, not at her. "My parents preferred their own company and my grandfather thought children were useless until properly educated. When my parents died my grandfather—and Signora Malandra—were forced to take over what parenting was required at that point. I was a teenager then and luckily for us all, I was usually at boarding school. It felt like home. I was first sent there at five."

Angelina had never given a single thought to the parenting choices she might make one day, yet she knew, somehow, that she did not have it in her to send such a tiny child away like that. Off to the tender mercies of strangers. Something in her chilled at the thought.

"Did you like boarding school?" she asked.

Benedetto stopped before a portrait that she guessed, based on the more modern clothing alone, might have been his parents. She studied the picture as if she was looking for clues. The woman had dark glossy hair and a heart-stoppingly beautiful face. She sat demurely in a grand chair, dressed in a gown of royal blue. Behind her chair stood a man who looked remarkably like Benedetto, though he had wings of white in his dark hair. And if possible, his mouth looked crueler. His nose more like a Roman coin.

"There was no question of liking it or not liking it," Benedetto said, gazing at the portrait. Then he turned that gaze on her, and she found the way his eyes glittered made her chest feel constricted. "It was simply the reality of my youth. My mother always felt that her duties were in the providing of the heir. Never in the raising of him."

"And did… Did your parents…?"

Angelina didn't even know what she was asking. She'd done what due diligence she could over the past month. Meaning she had Googled her husband-to-be and his family to see what she could find. Mostly, as this castle seemed to advertise, it seemed the Franceschi family was renowned for wealth and periodic cruelty stretching back to the dawn of time. In that, however, she had to admit that they were no different from any other storied European family. It was only Benedetto—in modern times, at any rate—who had a reputation worse than that of any other pedigreed aristocrat.

His mother had been considered one of the most beautiful women in the world. She and Benedetto's father had run in a glittering, hard-edged crowd, chasing and throwing parties in the gleaming waters of the Côte d'Azur or the non-touristy parts of the Caribbean. Or in sprawling villas in places like Amalfi, Manhattan, or wherever else the sparkling people were.

"Did my parents regret their choices in some way?" Benedetto laughed, as if the very idea was a great joke. "How refreshingly earnest. The only thing my parents ever agreed upon was a necessity of securing the Franceschi line. Once I was born, their duties were discharged and they happily returned to the things they did best. My father preferred pain to pleasure. And as my mother was a martyr, if only to causes that suited her self-importance, they were in many ways a match made in heaven."

Angelina's mouth was too dry. "P-Pain to pleasure?"

Benedetto's eyes gleamed. "He was a celebrated sadist. And not only in the bedroom."

Angelina didn't know what expression she must have had on her face, but it made Benedetto laugh again. Then he drew her behind him once more, leading her out of this gallery filled with black Franceschi eyes and dark secrets, and deeper into the castle.

"Why is that something you know about your own

father?" she managed to ask, fighting to keep her voice from whispering off into nothingness. "Surely a son should be protected from such knowledge."

Benedetto's laugh, then, was more implied than actual. But Angelina could feel it shiver through her all the same.

"Even if my parents had exhibited a modicum of modesty, which they did not, the paparazzi were only too happy to fill in the details before and after their deaths. Barring that, I can't tell you the number of times one or other of their friends—and by friends, I mean rivals, enemies, former lovers, and compatriots—thought they might as well sidle up to me with some ball or other and share. In excruciating detail." He glanced down at her, his mouth curved. "They are little better than jackals, these highborn creatures who spend their lives throwing fortunes down this or that drain. Every last one of them."

"Including you?" She dared to ask.

That curve in the corner of his mouth took on a bitter cast. "Especially me."

Together they climbed a series of stairs until they finally made it to a hall made of windows. Modern windows in place of a wall on one side, all of them looking out over the sea. Angelina could see that the wind had picked up, capping the waves in white, which should have added to the anxiety frothing inside her. Instead, the sight soothed her.

The sea carried on, no matter what happened within these walls.

It made her imagine that she might, too.

Despite everything she knew to the contrary.

"This is the private wing of the castle," Benedetto

told her as they walked beside the windows. "The nursery is at one end and the master suite far on the other end, behind many walls and doors, so the master of the house need never disturb his sleep unless he wishes it."

"Your parents did not come to you?" Angelina asked, trying and failing to keep that scandalized note from her voice.

"My provincial little bride." He sounded almost fond, though his dark gaze glittered. "That is what nannies are for, of course. My parents held regular audiences with the staff to keep apprised of my progress, I am told. But Castello Nero is no place for sticky hands and toddler meltdowns. I would be shocked to discover that your parents' shoddy little *château* was any different."

That was a reasonable description of the house, and still she frowned. "My parents were not naturally nurturing, certainly," Angelina said, choosing her words carefully. "But they were present and in our lives."

"No matter what, you need only call and I will come to you," Margrete had said fiercely before the wedding ceremony today. It had shocked her.

But Margrete had always been there. She might have been disapproving and stern, but she'd always been involved in her daughters' lives. Some of Angelina's earliest memories involved reading quietly at her mother's feet, or laboriously attempting to work a needle the way Margrete could with such seeming effortlessness.

It had never occurred to her that she would ever look back on her childhood fondly.

Of all the dark magic Benedetto had worked in the last month, that struck Angelina as the most disconcerting. Even as he towed her down yet another hall festooned with frescoes, priceless art, and gloriously thick rugs.

"You will find a variety of salons, an extensive private library, and an entertainment center along this hall." Benedetto nodded to doors as he passed them. "Any comfort you can imagine, you will find it here."

"Am I to be confined to this hall?"

"The castle is yours to explore," her husband said. "But you must be aware that at times, the castle and grounds are open to the public. Signora Malandra leads occasional tours. Because of course, there is no shortage of interest in both this castle and its occupant."

"But…"

Once more, she didn't know what on earth she meant to say.

Benedetto's dark eyes gleamed as if he did. "Foolish, I know. But far be it from me not to profit off my own notoriety."

He paused in the direct center of the long hall that stretched down the whole side of the castle. There was a door there that looked like something straight out of the middle ages. A stout wooden door with great steel bars hammered across it.

"This door opens into a stairwell," Benedetto told her. He did not open the door. "The stairwell goes from this floor to the tower above. And it is the only part of the castle that is strictly forbidden to you."

"Forbidden?" Angelina blinked, and shifted so she could study the door even more closely. "Why? Is the tower unsafe?"

His fingers were on her chin, pulling her face around to his before she even managed to process his touch.

"You must never go into this tower," he said, and there was no trace of mockery on his face. No curve to that grim mouth. Only that blazing heat in his dark eyes. "No matter what, Angelina, you must never open this door."

His fingers on her chin felt like a fist around her throat.

"What will happen if I do?" she asked, her voice little more than a whisper.

"Nothing good, Angelina." The darkness that emanated from him seemed to take over the light pouring in from outside. Until she could have sworn they stood in shadows. At night. "Nothing good at all."

She felt chastened and significantly breathless as Benedetto pulled her along again. Hurrying her down the long corridor until they reached the far end. He led her inside, into a master suite that was larger than the whole of the family wing of her parents' house, put together. It boasted a private dining room, several more salons and studies, its own sauna, its own gym, a room entirely devoted to an enormous bathtub, extensive dressing rooms, and then, finally, the bedchamber.

Inside, there was another wall of windows. Angelina had seen many terraces and balconies throughout the suite, looking out over the sea in all directions. But not here. There was only the glass and a steep drop outside, straight down into the sea far below.

There was a large fireplace on the far wall, with a seating area arranged in front of it that Angelina tried desperately to tell herself was cozy. But she couldn't quite get there. The fireplace was too austere, the stone too grim.

And the only other thing in the room was that vast, elevated bed.

It was draped in dark linens, gleaming a deep red that matched the ring she wore on her finger. *Like blood,* a voice inside her intoned.

Unhelpfully.

Four dark posts rose toward the high stone ceiling, and she had the sudden sensation that she needed to cling to one of them to keep herself from falling. That being in that bed, with nothing but the bloodred bedding and the sky and sea pressing down upon her, would make her feel as if she was catapulting through space.

As if she could be tossed from this chamber at any moment to her death far below.

Angelina couldn't breathe. But then, she suspected that was the point.

She only dimly realized that Benedetto had let go of her hand when she'd walked inside the room. Now he stood in the doorway that led out to the rest of the suite and its more modern, less stark conveniences.

Perhaps that was the point, too. That inside this chamber, there was nothing but her marriage bed, a fire that would not be lit this time of year, and the constant reminder of the precariousness of her situation.

And between her and the world, him.

"Is this where it happens, then?" She turned to look at him, and thought she saw a muscle tense in his jaw. Or perhaps she only wished she did, as that would make him human. Accessible. Possessed of emotions, even if she couldn't read them. "Is this where you bring your wives, one after the next? Is this where you make them all scream?"

"Every woman I have ever met screams at one point or another, Angelina," he said, and there was a kind of challenge in his gaze. A dark heat in his voice. "A better question is why."

But that impossible heat pulsed inside her, and Angelina didn't ask. She moved over to the bed and as she moved, remembered with a jolt that she was still dressed in her wedding gown. And between her legs, that pulsing desire he had cultivated in her thought it had all the answers already. She ran her hand over the coverlet when she reached it, not at all surprised to find that what she'd seen gleaming there in the dark red linens were precious stones. Rubies. Hard to the touch.

She pressed her palm down flat so that the nearest precious stone could imprint itself there. She gave it all her weight, as if this was a dream, and this was a kind of pinch that might jolt her awake.

Did she want to wake up? Or would it be better still to dream this away?

You keep thinking something can save you, something in her mocked her. *When you should know better by now.*

Angelina's palm ached, there where the hard stone dug into her flesh. And the man who watched her too intently from across the room was no dream.

She already knew too well the kind of magic he could work on her when she was wide awake.

Outside, she could hear the thunder of the sea. The disconcerting summer sky stretched off into the horizon.

But here in this castle filled with the plunder and fragments of long-ago lives, she was suspended in her white dress. Between the bloodred bed and the husband who stood like a wall between her and what remained of her girlhood. Of her innocence.

Whatever was left of it.

And suddenly, she wanted to tear it all off. She wanted to pile all the girlish things that remained inside her into that fireplace, then light a match.

Angelina was tired of being played with. She was tired of that dark, mocking gleam in his eye and that sardonic curve to his mouth. Of being led through a castle cut off from the mainland by a man who trafficked in nightmares.

She'd married him in a veil, but he had peeled it back when he claimed her mouth with his, there in front of witnesses.

She wanted to burn that down, too. No more veils of lace or ignorance.

If this was her life, or what remained of it, she would claim it as best she could.

She pressed her palm down harder on the coverlet, until it ached as much as she did between her legs.

Then Angelina faced the husband she couldn't quite believe was going to kill her like the rest. But she had to know if that was the real dream. Or a false sense of security six other women had already felt, standing right where she was now.

"I don't want to talk about screaming," she said.

He looked amused. "That is your loss."

"I have a question, Benedetto."

She thought he knew what she wanted to ask him. There was that tightening in his jaw. And for a moment, his black eyes seemed even darker than usual.

"You can ask me anything you like," he said.

She noticed he did not promise to answer her.

But Angelina focused on the question that was burning a hole inside her. "Don't you think it's time you told me what happened to the six who came before me?"

CHAPTER SEVEN

"As you wish," Benedetto said. His own voice was a rumbling thing in the bedchamber of stone, like thunder. Though outside it was a mild summer afternoon inching its way towards evening. "If you feel the shade of the marital bed is the place for such conversations."

He did not wish. He would prefer not to do this part of the dance—and he would particularly prefer not to do it with her.

The things he wanted to do with her deserved better than a castle made of unbreakable vows to dead men. She deserved light, not darkness. She deserved a whole man, not the part he played.

His still-innocent angel, who came apart so beautifully while the sea closed in around them. His curious Angelina, who would open doors she shouldn't and doom them both—it was only a matter of time.

His brand-new wife, who thought he was a killer, and still faced him like this.

Benedetto had expected her to be lovely to look at and reasonably entertaining, because she'd showed both at her dinner table the night they'd met. He had developed a deep yearning for her body over the course of the past month.

But he didn't understand how she'd wedged herself beneath his skin like this.

It wasn't going to end well. That he knew.

It never did.

And he had a feeling she was going to leave her mark in a way the others never had.

"Do you do the same thing every time?" she asked, as if she knew what he was thinking.

Benedetto couldn't quite read her, then. It only made him want her more. There was a hint of defiance in the way she stood and in the directness of her blue gaze. The hand on the wide bed shook slightly, but she didn't move it. Or hide it.

And he could see fear and arousal all over her body, perhaps more entwined than she imagined. He didn't share his father's proclivities. But that didn't mean he couldn't admire the things trembling uncertainty mixed with lust could do to a pretty face.

She tipped up her chin, and kept going. "Did you marry them all in bright white dresses, then bring them here to this room of salt and blood?"

It was a poetic description of the chamber, and he despised poetry. But it was also the most apt description he'd ever heard of what he'd done to this room after his grandfather had died. Benedetto had gutted it and removed every personal item, every hint of the man who'd lived and died here, every scrap that a ghost might cling to.

Because that was what he and his grandfather had done together after his grandmother had died, and it seemed only right to continue in the same vein.

And because he was haunted enough already.

"Where else would I bring them?" he asked softly.

"Tell me." Her gaze was too bright, her voice too urgent. "Tell me who they were."

"But surely you already know. Their names are in every paper, in every language spoken in Europe and beyond."

"I want to hear you say them."

And Benedetto wanted things he knew he could never have.

He wanted those nights in that stark conservatory in her father's ruined house, the wild tangle of music like a cloud all around them, and her sweetness in his mouth. He had wished more than once over this past month that he could stop time and stay there forever, but of all the mad powers people whispered he possessed, that had never been one of them.

And innocence was too easily tarnished, he knew. Besides, Benedetto had long since resigned himself to the role he must play in this game. Monster of monsters. Despoiler of the unblemished.

He had long since stopped caring what the outside world thought of him. He had made an art out of shrugging off the names they called him. His wealth and power was its own fortress, and better still, he knew the truth. What did it matter what lesser men believed?

What mattered was the promise he'd made. The road he'd agreed to follow, not only to honor his grandfather's wishes, but to pay a kind of penance along the way.

"And who knows?" his grandfather had said in his canny way. With a shrug. *"Perhaps you will break your chains in no time at all."*

Benedetto had chosen his chains and had worn them proudly ever since. But today they felt more like a death sentence.

"My first wife was Carlota di Rossi," he said now, glad that he had grown calloused to the sound of her name as it had been so long ago now. It no longer made him wince. "Her parents arranged the match with my grandfather when Carlota and I were children. We grew up together, always aware of our purpose on this planet. That being that we were destined to marry and carry on the dynastic dreams of our prominent families."

"Did you love her?"

Benedetto smiled thinly. "That was never part of the plan. But we were friendly. Then they found her on what was meant to be our honeymoon. It was believed she had taken her own life, possibly by accident, with too many sleeping pills and wine."

"Carlota," Angelina murmured, as if the name was a prayer.

And Benedetto did not tell her the things he could have. The things he told no one, because what would be the point? No one wanted his memories of the girl with the big, wide smile. Her wild curls and the dirty jokes she'd liked to tell, just under her breath, at the desperately boring functions they'd been forced to attend together as teenagers. No one wanted a story about two only children who'd been raised in close proximity, always knowing they would end up married. And were therefore a kind of family to each other, in their way. The truth was Carlota was the best friend he'd ever had.

But no one wanted truth when there was a story to tell and sell.

Benedetto should have learned that by watching his parents—and their sensationalized deaths. Instead, he'd had to figure it out the hard way.

"Everyone agrees that my second wife was a rebound," he said as if he was narrating a documentary of his own life. "Or possibly she was the mistress I'd kept before, during, and after my first marriage."

He waited for Angelina to ask him which it was, but she didn't. Maybe she didn't want to know. And he doubted she would want to know the truth about the understanding he and Carlota had always had. Or how his second marriage had been fueled by guilt and rage because of it.

Benedetto knew his own story backward and forward and still he got stuck in the darkest part of it. In the man he'd allowed himself to become. A man much more like his detestable father than he'd ever imagined he could become.

When Angelina did not ask, he pushed on, his voice gritty. "Her name was Sylvia Toluca. She was an actress of some renown, at least in this country, and a disgrace to the Franceschi bloodline. But then, as most have speculated, that was likely her primary appeal. Alas, she went overboard on a stormy night in the Aegean after a well-documented row with yours truly and her body was never found."

"Sylvia," his new wife said. She cleared her throat. "And I find I cannot quite imagine you actually…rowing. With anyone."

Benedetto detached himself from the wall and began to prowl toward her. His Angelina in that enormous white gown that bloomed around her like a cloud, with those dark pearls around her neck and eyes so blue they made the Italian sky seem dull by comparison.

"I was much younger then," he told her, his voice a low growl. "I had very little control."

He watched her swallow as if her throat hurt. "Not like now."

"Nothing like now," he agreed.

She swayed slightly on her feet, but straightened, still meeting his gaze. "I believe we're up to number three."

"Monique LeClair, Catherine DeWitt, Laura Seymour." Angelina whispered an echo of each of their names as he closed the distance between them. "All heiresses in one degree or another, like you. There were varying lengths of courtship, but yes, I brought each of them here once we married. All lasted less than three months. All disappeared, presumed dead, though no charges were ever brought against me."

"All of them."

He nodded sagely. "You would be surprised how many accidents occur in a place like this, where we are forever pitted against the demands of the sea. Its relentless encroachment." He stopped only scant inches from where she stood, reaching over to trace her hand where it still pressed hard against the bejeweled coverlet. "The tide waits for no man. That is true everywhere, though it is perhaps more starkly illustrated here."

"Surely, after losing so many wives to the sea, a wise man would consider moving inland," Angelina said in that surprising dry way of hers that was far more dangerous than the allure of her body or even her music. Those only meant he wanted her. But this… This made him like her. "Or better still, teach them to swim."

"Do you know how to swim?" he asked, almost idly, his finger moving next to hers on the bed.

"I'm an excellent swimmer," she replied, though her color was high and her voice a mere whisper. "I could swim all the way to Rio de Janeiro and back if I wished."

He watched the way her chest rose and fell, and the deepening flush that he could see as easily on her cheeks as on the upper slopes of her breasts.

"I applaud your proficiency," he said. "But I am only a man. I can control very few things in this life. And certainly not an ocean or a woman."

She did not look convinced.

"And your last wife?" she asked, her breath sounding ragged as he began to trace a pattern from the hand on his bed up her arm, lazy and insinuating. "The sixth?"

"Veronica Fitzgibbon." Benedetto made a faint tsking sort of sound. "Perhaps the best-known of all my wives, before marrying me. You might even call her famous."

"More than famous," Angelina corrected him softly as his hand made it to the fine, delicate bridge of her collarbone and traced it, purely to make her shiver. "I doubt there's a person alive who cannot sing at least one of her father's songs. And then she dated his drummer."

"Indeed. Scandalous." He concentrated on that necklace of hers, then. The brooding pearls against the softness of her skin. The heat of her body, warming the stones.

"She lasted the longest. Three months and two days," Angelina whispered.

He made himself smile. "See that? You do know. I thought you might."

"She crashed her car into a tree," Angelina told him, though he already knew. He'd spent two days in a police station staring at the pictures of the wreckage as the authorities from at least three countries accused him of all manner of crimes. "On a mountain road in the Alps, though no one has ever been able to explain what she was doing there."

"There are any number of explanations," Benedetto corrected her. "Most assume she was fleeing me. And that I was hot in pursuit, which makes for a delicious tale, I think you'll agree." He lifted his gaze to hers. "Alas, I was giving a very boring lecture at a deeply tedious conference in Toronto at the time."

"And how will I go, do you think?" she asked, a different sort of light in her blue eyes, then.

He hated this. He had disliked it from the start, though a truth he'd had to face was that he'd found a certain joy in the details. The game of it. The end justifying the means. But here, now, with her and that bruised look on her face and his own heretofore frozen emotions unaccountably involved this time—he loathed it all.

"I have already told you," he said quietly. "We all die how we live. It is inevitable."

"But—"

"A better question to ask," he said quietly, cutting her off, "is why any woman would marry me, knowing these things. These assumptions and allegations that must be true, because they are repeated so often. There must be a fire after all this smoke, no? Why did you say yes, Angelina?"

He watched, fascinated, as goose bumps shivered to life all over her skin. And she shifted, there where she stood. "I had no choice."

"Will we be starting this marriage off with lies?" Benedetto shook his head. "Of course you had a choice. Your father promised me a daughter. Not you in particular. Had you refused to marry me I had two others to choose from."

"My mother made it very clear that none of us were permitted to say no, no matter what."

"That must be it, then." He didn't quite smile. It was too hard, too furious a thing. "But tell me, Angelina, how do you rationalize away the many times you came apart in my hands?"

"I don't rationalize it." Her blue eyes flashed. "I deplore it."

"I don't think you do," he told her, and he moved his hand to her jaw, tilting her head so that her mouth was where he wanted it. "I think you're confusing hunger for something else. But then, you did spend all that time in the convent, did you not? I'm surprised you feel anything at all save shame."

"I have a full complement of emotions, thank you. Chief among them, revulsion. Fury. Disgust."

"I want you too, little one," he said, there against her mouth. "I hear the seventh time is the charm."

She made a tiny little noise, protest and surrender at once, and then Benedetto took her mouth with his.

Because a kiss did not lie. A kiss was not a story told around the world, losing more and more truth each time it was sold to the highest bidder.

There was only truth here in the tangle of tongues. In the way her body shuddered beneath his hands. In the way she pressed herself against him, as if she would climb him if she could.

He could taste her fear and her longing, her need and her hope.

Benedetto tasted innocence and possibility, and beneath that, the sheer punch that was all Angelina.

He anchored her with an arm around her back, and bent her over, deepening the kiss. Taking more and more, until he couldn't be sure any longer which one of them was more likely to break.

She was intoxicating.

Despite all the times he'd done this, there had never been a time that he had wanted a wife like this. Or at all. But then, in all the ways that mattered, she was his first.

That thought made a kind of bitterness well in him, and he pulled away. And then took his time looking at her. Her lips parted. Her eyes dark with passion.

This from the woman who claimed she didn't want him at all. That she had been forced into this.

He rather thought not.

He liked to think he had been, though that wasn't quite true either. He'd had his choices, too.

"Not yet," he murmured, as much to himself as to her.

Because one choice he did have was to treat her the way he'd treated the others. He had already tasted her more than the rest of them, save Sylvia. He had already betrayed himself a thousand times over while in the thrall of her piano.

But she didn't have to know that. And he didn't have to succumb to it here.

And now that they were married, he could get this back on track.

Benedetto let go of her, pleased despite himself when she had to grip the bed beside her to stay on her feet. He picked up the hand she'd been pressing against the bed and could see the indentation of the coverlet's stone on her palm.

He was savage enough to like it.

"What do you mean, *not yet*?" she demanded. "I thought that once we were married—"

"So impatient," he taunted her. "Especially for one forced to the altar as you have been."

If she dared, he could tell, she would have cursed him to his face.

Instead, she glared at him.

"Don't you worry about consummating our marriage." He laughed, though the lie of it caught a little in his chest. "I will take you in hand, never fear. But first, I wish to show you something."

Benedetto turned and headed for the door without taking her hand to bring her with him. And he smiled when he heard her follow him.

He didn't have to turn around and study her face to understand her reluctance. It was entirely possible she didn't know why she was following him. That she was simply as compelled as he was. He hoped so.

It was a good match for this mad yearning he felt inside, when he knew better. A yearning that he was terribly afraid would be the end of him. This innocent, untrained girl could bring him to his knees.

But then, that was a power he had no intention of handing over to her. If she didn't know, she couldn't use it.

He led her out into the master suite, then through a door that led to a separate tower from one of the salons.

Angelina balked at the door, looking around a little bit wildly.

"This is your tower," he told her, sounding almost formal. "You can enter whenever you wish."

"That seems like a lot of towers to remember," she

said, a little solemnly, from behind him. "I wouldn't want to make a mistake."

He looked over his shoulder as they climbed the stairs.

"Don't," he warned her, and meant it more than he usually did. More than he wanted to mean it. "Whatever else you do here, do not imagine that the warning I gave you was a joke, Angelina."

He saw her swallow, hard, but then they were at the top of the stairs. He threw open the door, then waited for her to follow him inside.

And then Benedetto watched as she tried to contain her gasp of joy.

"A piano," she whispered, as if she couldn't believe it. "You really did get me a piano. A Steinway."

"I am assured it is the finest piano on the Continent," he told her, feeling...uncertain, for once. Unlike himself. Did he crave her approval so badly? When he didn't care in the least if the entire world thought him a monster? It should have shamed him, but all he could do was drink in the wonder all over her. "It is yours. You can play it whenever you wish, night or day. And I will give instructions to my staff that you are to be left to it."

There was a look of hushed awe on her face. She aimed it his way, for a moment, then looked back at the piano that sat in the center of the room. When he inclined his head, she let out a breath. Then she ran to the piano to put her hands on it. To slide back the cover, and touch the keys.

Soft, easy, reverent. Like a lover might.

And for a deeply disturbing moment, Benedetto found himself actually questioning whether he was, in fact, jealous of an inanimate object.

Surely not.

He shoved that aside, because he'd been called a monster most of his life and he could live with the consequences of that. He had. It was smallness and pettiness he could not abide, in himself or anyone else. Benedetto hated it in the men who auctioned off their daughters to pay their debts; he despised even the faintest hint of it in himself.

"Play, Angelina," he urged her. And if his voice was darker than it should have been, rougher and wilder, he told himself it was no more than to be expected. "Play for me."

He was married. Again. Every time he imagined he might be finished at last. That it would be the end of this long, strange road. That finally, this curse would be lifted and he would be freed.

Finally, he could bury his grandfather's dark prophecies in the grave where the old man lay.

And every time, Benedetto was proved wrong. He'd almost become inured to it, he thought as Angelina spread her fingers, smiled in that inward, mysterious manner that he found intoxicating, and began to coax something stormy and dark from the keys.

As the music filled the tower he admitted to himself that this time he wanted, desperately, to be right.

He wanted to be done.

He wanted *her*.

It was the way she played, as if she was not the one producing the notes, the melodies, the whole songs and symphonies. Instead, it was as if she was a conduit, standing fast somewhere between the music in her head and what poured out of her fingers.

Benedetto had never seen or heard anything so beautiful.

And he couldn't help but imagine that she could do the same for him and the dark destiny he had chosen to make his own.

Outside, the afternoon wore on, easing its way into another perfect Italian evening.

And his bride played as if she was enchanted, her fingers like liquid magic over the keys. Half-bent, eyes half-closed, as if she was caught in the grip of the same madness that roared in him.

Or perhaps Benedetto only wished it so.

When *wishing* was another thing he had given up long ago.

Or should have.

But everything had changed when he'd walked into that dining room in her father's house and seen an angel where he'd expected nothing more than a collection of wan socialites. He stood against the wall in the tower room, his back against the stones that had defined him as long as he'd drawn breath.

It was easy to pretend that he had been disconnected from this place, shuttled off to boarding school the way he had been, but Castello Nero lived inside him and always had. As a child he'd loved coming home to this place. Endless halls, secret passages, and his beloved grandmother. His parents had always been away, but what did that matter when he could play mad siege games on the rocks or race the tide?

There was a part of him that would always long for those untroubled times. That wished he could somehow recreate them, if not for himself, for a child like the one he'd been too briefly. Maybe that was nothing more than a fantasy. Then again, maybe it was all he had.

He had to take his fantasies where he could.

Because it wasn't long after those dreamy days that he'd understood different truths about this place. These ancient walls and the terrible price those who lived here had paid, and would pay. Some would call it a privilege. Some would see only the trappings, the art and the antiques, the marble gleaming in all directions. Some would assume it was the shine of such things that made the difference.

They never saw any blood on their hands. They never heard the screams from the now defunct dungeons. They walked the halls and thought only of glory, never noticing the ghosts that lurked around every corner.

Or the ghosts that lived in him.

But as Angelina played, Benedetto imagined that she could see him.

The real him.

The music crashed and soared, whispered then shouted. The hardest part of him stood at attention, aching for her touch—and yet feeling it, all the same, in the music she played, here in the tower he had made a music room, just for her.

She played and played, while outside the tide rose, the waves swelled, and the moon began to rise before the sun was down.

That, too, felt like a sign.

And when she stopped playing, it took Benedetto too long to realize it. Because the storm was inside him, then. *She* was. Her music filled every part of him, making him imagine for a moment that he was free.

That he could ever be free.

That this little slip of a woman, sheltered and sold off, held the key that could unlock the chains that had held him all his life.

It was a farce. He knew it was a farce.

And still, when she turned to look at him, her blue eyes dark with passion and need and all that same madness he felt inside him, he...forgot.

He forgot everything but her.

"Benedetto..." she began, her voice a harsh croak against the sudden, bruised silence.

"I know," he heard himself say, as if from a distance. As if he was the man he'd imagined he'd become, so many years ago, instead of the man he became instead. The man he doubted his grandmother would recognize. "I know, little one."

He pushed himself off from the wall and had the same sensation he always did, that the *castello* itself tried to hold on to him. Tried to tug him back, grip him hard, smother him, until he became one more stone statue.

Some years he felt more like stone than others, but not today.

But Angelina sat on the piano bench, her wedding gown flowing in all directions, and her chest heaving with the force of all the emotions she'd let sing through her fingers.

And she was so obviously, inarguably *alive* that he could not be stone. She was so vibrant, so filled with color and heat, that he could not possibly look down and find himself made into marble, no matter how the walls seemed to cling to him.

Benedetto crossed the floor, his gaze on hers as if the heat between them was a lifeline. As if she was saving him, here in this tower where no one was safe. And then he was touching her, his hands against her flushed cheeks, his fingers finding their way into the heavy, silvery mass of her blond hair.

At last, something in him cried.

"What are you doing?" she asked, though there was heat in her gaze.

"Surely you know," Benedetto said as he swept her up into his arms. "Surely your mother—or the internet—should have prepared you."

"Neither are as useful as advertised," she said, her head against his shoulder. And that dry note in her voice gone husky.

He had not planned to take her, as he had not taken the rest. They were offerings to fate, not to him. They were meant to worry over the bed that made his chamber look blooded, like so much stage dressing. They were never meant to share it with him. Not like this, dressed like a bride and at the beginning of this bizarre journey.

But Angelina was nothing like the others.

She never had been.

She was music, and she was light. She was every dream he'd told himself wasn't for him, could never be for him.

And every time he tasted her, he felt the chains that bound him weaken, somehow.

So Benedetto carried her, not down the tower stairs to the master suite, but to the chaise he'd set beneath the windows in this tower room. Because it had amused him to make this tower look as much like the conservatory in her father's shambles of the house as possible, he'd assured himself.

Or perhaps he'd done it because he wanted her to feel at home here, however unlikely that was—but he shied away from admitting that, even to himself. Even now.

He laid her down before him, admiring the way her hair tangled all about her. Like it, too, was a part of the same magic spell that held him in its thrall.

The same spell that made this feel like a real marriage after all.

"Welcome to your wedding night," Benedetto said as he lowered himself over her, and then he took her mouth with his.

Claiming Angelina, here in this castle that took more than it gave.

At last.

CHAPTER EIGHT

ANGELINA FELT TORN apart in the most glorious way and all he was doing was kissing her.

It was the music. The sheer excellence of the piano he'd found for her, and had set up in perfect tune.

She had only meant to play for a moment, but the keys had felt so alive beneath her fingers, as if each note was an embrace, that too soon, she'd lost herself completely.

She still felt lost.

And yet, somehow, she'd been aware of Benedetto the whole time. Her husband and perhaps her killer—though she couldn't quite believe that, not from a man who could give a piano like this as a gift—standing in the corner of the room with his gaze fixed on her.

She would not say that she was used to him, because how could anyone become used to a hurricane?

But she craved that electric charge. The darkness in his gaze, the sensual promise etched over his beautiful face, his clever mouth.

She'd played and played. And she could not have explained it if her life depended on it, as she supposed it might, but the longer she played, the more it was as if her own hands moved over her body. As if she was making love to herself, there before him, the way she had in the car.

Exposed and needy and at his command.

Right where she'd wanted to be since that very first night.

Angelina could hardly contain herself. All she could think of were the many times in this last, red-hot month of waiting and worrying and wondering, when her legs had been spread wide and he had been between them. His mouth. His fingers.

She'd played because her body felt like his already and there was no part of her that disliked that sensation.

She'd played because playing for him felt like his possession. Irrevocable. Glorious. And as immovable as the stone walls of the tower that sang the notes she played back to her, no matter the piece, as sweet and sensual songs.

Benedetto lowered himself over her on the chaise, and she forgot about playing, because he kissed her like a starving man.

Angelina kissed him back, because his shoulders were as wide as mountains and behind him she could see only the darkening sky. And her ears were filled with the rushing sound of the sea waiting and whispering far below.

He was hard and heavy, and this time, he did not crawl his way down her body to bury his head between her legs. This time he let her feel the weight of him, pressing her down like a sweet, hot stone.

And all the while he kissed her, again and again, rough and deep and filled with the same madness that clamored inside her.

Angelina could no longer tell if she was still playing the piano, or if he was playing her, and either way, the notes rose and fell, sang and wept, and she could do nothing about it.

She didn't want to do anything about it but savor it.

Because whatever song this was, it made her burn.

Again and again, she burned.

Only for him, something in her whispered. And that made her burn all the more.

Benedetto tore his mouth from hers and began to move down her body, then, but only far enough to tug on the bodice of her dress. Hard.

He glanced at her, his dark eyes bright and gleaming, and tugged on her dress until it tore. Then he tore it even more, baring her breasts to his view.

And when she gasped at the ferocity, or at the surge of liquid heat that bloomed in her because of it, he laughed.

Benedetto looked at her, his face dark with passion and set fierce like a wolf's, as he shaped her breasts with those calloused palms of his and then took one aching nipple into his mouth.

And then she was a crescendo.

Angelina arched up, not sure if she was fighting him or finding him, or both at the same time. His mouth was a torture and treat, and she pressed herself even more firmly into his mouth. Whatever he wanted to give her, she wanted to take. As much as possible.

His hands moved south, continuing their destruction. He tore her white dress to ribbons, baring her to him. And she thrilled to every last bit of sensation that charged through her from the air on her flesh, or better still, his wicked mouth.

And when he thrust his heavy thigh between hers

even as he continued to hold her down and take his fill of her, she found that gave her something to rock the center of her need against.

Over and over again, because it felt like soaring high into the night.

And when she shattered, tossed over a steep edge as if from the window of this tower to the brooding sea far below, he laughed that same dark, delighted laugh that had thrilled her from the first.

Angelina could feel the laugh inside her, and it only made her shudder more.

When she came back to herself, rising from the depths somehow, he had rolled off of her. Her wedding dress was torn to pieces, baring her to his view completely. That he could see all of her was new, and faintly terrifying. No one had seen Angelina fully naked since she was a small child.

But far more overwhelming was the fact that as Benedetto stood beside her, looking down at the chaise from his great height, he was shrugging out of his own wedding clothes.

In all this time, all throughout this longest month, he had never dislodged his clothing or allowed her to do so.

"Are you horribly scarred?" she'd asked him once, feeling peevish with lust and longing and that prickling fear beneath. She'd been stretched out on her piano bench in the conservatory back home, after he'd buried his face between her thighs and made her scream.

As usual.

Benedetto had only smiled, drawing her attention back to that mouth of his and the things it could do. *"None of my scars are external."*

And now the first stars were appearing in the sky

outside. He blocked them all out and somehow made them brighter at the same time, because he was perfect. He was everything.

She had never seen a naked man in real life. She had never imagined that all the various parts that she'd seen in pictures could seem so different in person. Because she knew what it felt like to be in his arms and she knew what it felt like to taste him in her mouth.

But Benedetto naked was something else. Something better. He looked as if he'd been fashioned by a sculptor obsessed with male beauty, but she knew that he would be hot to the touch. And more, unlike all the marble statues she'd ever seen—many of them here—there was dark hair on his chest. A fascinatingly male trail that led to a part of him she'd felt against her leg, but had never seen.

"What big eyes you have," he said, sounding dark and mocking.

Angelina jerked her gaze up over the acres and acres of his fine male chest, all those ridges and planes that made her fingers itch. To touch. To taste. To make hers, in some way, the way he had already taken such fierce possession of her.

"I understand the mechanics," she confessed. "But still…"

"Your body knows what to do." He came down over her again, and she hissed out a breath because it was so much different, now. Bare flesh against bare flesh. Her softness against all the places where he was so impossibly hard. Everything in her hummed. "And so do I."

And then, once again, she felt as if she was the piano.

Because he played her like one, wringing symphonies out of her with every touch, every brush of his mouth over parts of her body she would have said were better ignored.

He flipped her over onto her stomach, right when she thought that she might simply explode out of her own skin—

And he laughed in that dark, stirring way of his, there against the nape of her neck. Then he started all over again.

Angelina…lost track.

Of herself. Of him. Of what, exactly, he was doing. All she could seem to do was feel.

He slipped his fingers between her legs and stroked her until she shattered and fell apart, but he didn't stop. There was no ending, no beginning. There was only the rise and fall. The fire that burned in both of them and between them, flickering one moment, then roaring to life the next.

And all the while Angelina couldn't seem to get past the feeling that all of this was exactly how it was supposed to be. All of this was *right*.

It was full dark outside when Benedetto turned her over again. He stretched her arms up over her head and finally, finally, settled himself between her thighs. She could *feel* him, a hard ridge of perfect male arousal where she was nothing but a soft melting.

She was shuddering. She thought maybe there was moisture on her face. But all Angelina could care about was the blunt head of his masculinity that she could feel pressing into her.

Not exactly gently. And yet not roughly, either.

It was a pinch she forgot about almost as soon as it happened followed by a relentless, masterful thrust, and then Benedetto was seated fully inside her.

And that time, when Angelina burst into flame and shattered into a million new pieces, each more ragged than the last, she screamed herself hoarse.

Benedetto was laughing again, dark and delirious and too beautiful to bear, as he finally began to move.

And all her notions about piano music and symphonies shattered.

Because this was far more *physical* than she could possibly have imagined. Her body gripped him. He worked himself into her, then out. His chest was a delicious abrasion against hers, she could feel the press of his hipbones with every thrust, and there was heat and breath and so much *more* than the things she'd read in books.

He dropped his hard, huge body against hers and Angelina thought that should smother her, surely. But instead she bloomed.

As if her body was made to be a cradle, to hold him between her thighs. Just like this.

He bent his head to hers and took her mouth again, so that she was being taken with the same sheer mastery in two places at once.

And she understood that there was no place he did not claim her.

Inside and out, she was his.

She could feel that ring of his on her finger and that hard male part of him thrust deep inside her body.

And it seemed to her that her pulse became a chant. *His. His.*

His.

And then, finally, Angelina tore her mouth from his. She gripped the fierce cords of his neck with her hands, and found herself staring deep into his dark, ferocious gaze.

Into eternity, she was sure of it.

His.

And when she exploded into fire and fury, claimed and reborn, he cried out a word that could have been her name, and followed.

Angelina was hardly aware of it when he moved. She came back to herself, disoriented and gloriously replete, as he lifted her up into his arms.

She was aware of it as he carried her down the tower's narrow stair, high against his chest with only her hair trailing behind them. As naked as the day they were born.

Maybe she should have been embarrassed, she thought idly. For she knew full well that just because a staff was unseen did not mean they were not witnessing the goings-on of the house.

But how could she care if there were eyes on them when she felt like this? More beautiful than she ever had been. Perfect in his arms.

Right, straight through.

And so she looped her arms around his neck, rested her head against his shoulder, and said nothing as he took her back to that master suite. She did nothing but *feel* as he carried her into that room she'd seen before that contained only a massive, luxurious tub with a view straight on to forever.

Benedetto put her down carefully beside it so she could hold on if her knees gave way. They did, and he smiled, and then he set about drawing the bath himself. Soon enough, the water was steaming. And the salts he threw in it give the water a silky feel when she dipped her fingers in.

He said nothing. He only indicated with his chin that she should climb into the hot water, so she did.

Then she sat there, relaxing against the sloping side, the warm water like an embrace. The heat holding her the way he had. She thought he would climb in with her, but instead, with a long, dark look she had no hope of reading, Benedetto left her there to soak.

Something curled around inside her, low and deep, so she stayed where she was to indulge it. The water felt too good. She was too warm, and outside the sea danced beneath the stars, and flirted with her. She could not bring herself to climb out.

Angelina didn't think she slept, there in a bathtub where she could so easily slip beneath the water to her death—in a place that hinted at death around every corner. But she was still startled when there were hands on her again, and she was suddenly being lifted up and out of the warm water.

But in the next moment, she knew it was him. And the knowledge soothed her.

It felt like a dream, so she didn't really react as Benedetto wrapped her in a towel and set about drying her himself. She had tied her hair in a knot on top of her head and she could feel the curls from the heat, framing her face, in a way she had never liked—but she did not have the energy to do anything about it.

She blinked, realizing that he had showered. She could smell the soap on him. And all he wore now were a pair of low-slung trousers. Somehow that felt more intimate than his nakedness.

For the first time, Angelina actually felt shy in this man's presence.

The absurdity did not escape her, after the things he'd done to her in her father's house. The things he'd done to her tonight. She should have been immune to him by now. Instead, he toweled her dry and then wrapped her in the softest, most airy robe she had ever felt in her life, and she suddenly felt awkward. Exposed.

She thought he would say something then. The way he looked at her seemed to take her apart, his dark eyes so unreadable and his mouth in that serious, somber line. But he didn't. He ushered her from the room, with a certain hint of something very nearly ceremonial that made her heart thud inside her chest.

"Where we going?" she asked.

And it was times like these, when she was walking next to him—close enough that they could have been hand in hand if they were different people—that she was more aware of him than was wise. How tall he was. How beautiful and relentlessly male.

How dark and mysterious, even though he wore so little.

And she was forced to confront the fact that it wasn't the things he wore that made him seem so dangerous. So outrageously powerful. It was just him.

The master of Castello Nero. The boogeyman of Europe.

Her husband. Benedetto.

"You did not think that was the sum total of your wedding night, I hope." There was the faintest hint of a smile on his hard face. "We have miles to go, indeed."

That didn't make her heart thud any less.

Angelina followed him down the hall inside the

grand suite and noticed that all the doors stood ajar. All the doors in the castle were wide open, now that she thought of it, save the one he'd showed her out in the hallway.

She thought of reinforced steel and heavy oak. Hidden stairs to a secret tower.

And she didn't know why it made her pulse pick up.

"Do you live here now?" she asked. His brow arched, as if to say, *We are here, are we not?* She could almost hear the words and felt herself flush, ridiculously. But she pushed on. "I mean to say, after spending all that time in boarding school. And knowing that your own parents did not spend much time here, from what you said. When did you move back yourself?"

"After my grandfather died," he replied. Not in the sort of tone that invited further comments.

"Were these his rooms?"

But she already knew the answer. She eyed a portrait on the wall of an old man gripping a cane with a serpent's head as its handle, while staring down from his great height with imperious eyes that look just like Benedetto's.

"When I was young," Benedetto said, his voice sounding something slightly less than frozen through, "my grandfather entertained me for at least one hour every Sunday in his drawing room here. He asked me fierce and probing questions about my studies, my life, my hopes and goals, and then explained to me why each and every one of them was wrong. Or needed work."

He stopped at a different door, and beckoned for Angelina to precede him.

"He was a terrifying, judgmental, prickly old man who would have been a king in a simpler time. He was never kind when he could be cutting, never smiled when he could scowl, and I miss him to this day."

Angelina was so startled by the indication that Benedetto had emotions or feelings of any kind that she almost stumbled on her way into the room. And it took her a moment to realize that the reason she didn't recognize it outright as the private dining room she'd seen when she'd first walked into the suite was because it was transformed.

There were candles lighting up the table, and clearly not, as in her parents' house, because of worries about an impending electric bill. Because out in the hallway, lights were blazing. The candles were here to set a mood.

The table was filled with platters of food. And not, she thought she drew closer, just any food. A feast. There were only two table settings, straddling the corner of the highly polished, deep mahogany table, but there was food enough for an army.

"This looks like…"

But she couldn't finish the sentence.

"It looks like a celebration, I hope," Benedetto said stiffly. He pulled out the chair that was clearly meant to be hers, and she almost thought she saw a hint of something like apprehension on his face. Could it be…uncertainty? Her heart stuttered. "I stole you away from your wedding reception. I offer this instead."

And suddenly, Angelina found the world around her little bit blurry. She sat in the chair he indicated, jolting slightly when her bottom found the chair beneath her because she was tender. Gloriously, marvelously tender between her legs.

He had given her a perfect piano and let her play, so

that her introduction to her new life—her new home, her new status, her possible dark fate—was draped in a veil of music.

He had taken her down on that chaise and made a woman of her.

Her chest felt tight because he had made her wedding feast, and her *heart*. Her traitorous, treacherous, giddily hopeful heart beat out a rhythm that was much too close to joy for the seventh wife of the Butcher of Castello Nero.

Angelina could only hope it wouldn't be the death of her.

Literally.

CHAPTER NINE

SHE DID NOT ask him directly if he'd killed his wives.

How they'd died, yes. Not whether or not he was guilty of killing them. Not whether he'd done the dark deeds with his own two hands.

And Benedetto couldn't decide, as they sat and ate the wedding feast he'd had his staff prepare for them, if he thought that was evidence that she was perfect for him or the opposite.

All he knew was that he was in trouble.

That he had already treated her differently than any other woman, and all other wives.

He kept expecting something—anything—involving this woman to be *regular*. Ordinary. But instead, she was incomparable to anyone or anything, and he had no idea what to do with that.

Even now, when she was scrubbed clean, bathed so that all her makeup was gone and her hair was merely in a haphazard knot on the top of her head, she was more radiant than she had been at their wedding ceremony.

And he didn't think he could bear it.

"You look quite angry with your crab cakes," she pointed out in that faintly dry tone of hers. "Or is it the company that does not suit?"

"Tell me about the piano," he said, instead of answering her question. "You are quite talented. Why did you never think to leave that ruin of a *château* and do something with it?"

"I thought of nothing else." And she actually grinned at him. At *him*. "There was no money for necessities, much less ambition."

"I do not understand," Benedetto said, with perhaps more ill-temper than necessary. "Surely your father could have avoided most of the unpleasantness in his life if he had made money from you and your piano. Rather than, say, trying his hand at high stakes card games he was doomed to lose before he walked in the room."

And this woman, this unexpected angel who should never have agreed to become his wife, grinned even wider.

"But to do so, you understand, he would first have to believe that that infernal racket I was forever making could benefit him in some way. Instead, he often asked me why it was I could not entertain myself more quietly while sucking off the family teat, quote unquote. The way my sisters did."

Benedetto couldn't keep his eyes off of her. She was grinning as she waved away her father's indifference to her talent. And while she did, she applied herself to each course of the feast he had ordered with equal abandon.

He liked her hunger. He wanted to feed it.

All her hungers.

"It sounds as if you were kept in a prison," he told her, his voice in a growl. "But you do not seem the least bit concerned by this."

"Because you freed me."

And there was laughter in her voice as she said it. In her eyes, too, making the blue into a sparkle that was brighter than the candles.

A sparkle that faded the longer she gazed at him.

"It is a long, long time indeed since I have been viewed as the better of two options," he said darkly.

"People always tell you the devil you know is better," Angelina said, a wisdom beyond her years where that sparkle had been, then. "But I have never thought so. There's more scope for growth in the unknown. There has to be."

"How would you know such a thing? Did they teach it in the convent?"

Again, her lips moved into something wry. "Ask me in three months and two days or so."

And despite himself, Benedetto laughed.

What was the harm in pretending, just for a little while, that this was real? That it could be precisely what it seemed. No more, no less. Would that really be the worst thing that ever happened?

He suspected he knew the answer. But he ignored it.

When they finished eating, he led her out onto one of the balconies, this one equipped with a fire pit built into the stone, benches all around, and a hot tub on one end with nothing before it but the sea. He could imagine winter nights in that tub, the two of them wound around each other—

But he stopped himself, because she wouldn't be here when winter came.

He watched as she stood at the rail, the sea breeze playing with her hair, making it seem more like spun silver than before.

Or making him feel like spun silver himself, which should have appalled him.

"You look remarkably happy." The words felt like a kind of curse as they came out of his mouth. As if he was asking for trouble. Or tempting fate too directly, standing there beside her. It was as if his heart seized up in his chest, then beat too hard, beating out a warning. "Particularly for a woman who married a monster today."

She turned her dreamy face to his and then his fingers were there, helping the breeze at its work, teasing her hair into curls and lifting them seemingly at random.

"If you think about it," she said softly, "we are all of us monsters. In our hearts, most of all."

"Are you already forgiving me?" Benedetto asked, though it seemed to him that the world had gone still. The tide had stopped turning, the planet had stopped spinning, and there was only Angelina. His last, best wife and her gaze upon him, direct and true, like his own north star. "Don't you think that might be premature?"

"Do you need forgiveness?"

Something inside him crumbled at that. It was a question no one had ever asked him. Because everyone thought they already knew all the answers to the mystery that was Benedetto Franceschi. Everyone believed they were privy to the whole story.

Or they preferred to make up their own.

Over and over again.

"Carlota," he heard himself say. And though he was horrified, he couldn't seem to stop himself. "I should never have married her."

Angelina's gaze moved over his face, but he didn't see the revulsion he expected. Or anything like an accusation. It made him…hurt.

"I thought you had to marry her." She tilted her head slightly. "Isn't that what you said?"

"That was the understanding, but I doubt very much we would have been marched down the aisle with shotguns in our backs if we'd refused." He let go of her hair and straightened from the rail. And no matter how many times he asked himself what he thought he was doing, he couldn't seem to stop. "Still, we were both aware of our duty. I thought she was like me—resigned to our reality, but happy enough to play whatever games we needed to along the way. Because as soon as the line was secure, we could do as we liked. And even before, for that matter. All that needed to happen was that we set aside a certain period of time of strict fidelity to ensure paternity."

"That sounds very dry and matter-of-fact. We are talking about sex and marriage and relationships, are we not?"

"We are talking about ancient bloodlines," Benedetto replied. "Ancient bloodlines require ancient solutions to problems like heirs. And once the deed was done, we could carry on as we pleased. Another grand old tradition."

Angelina blinked. "You do know that science exists, don't you? No need to do the deed at all."

He should have stopped talking. He shouldn't have started. But he didn't stop.

"You must understand, Angelina. Carlota and I knew we were to be married before either one of us had any idea what that meant. We were intended for each other, and everything we learned about the opposite sex we learned in the shadow of that reality. And when it finally came time to do our duty, she suggested we jump right in and get the heir taken care of, rather than messing about with invasive medical procedures we would inevitably have to discuss in the press. We were friends. We were in it together. She rather thought we should handle things the old-fashioned way because it was quicker and easier. Theoretically."

"What did you think?"

There was a certain gleam in her gaze then that reminded him that this was a woman he'd not only married, but had enjoyed for the past month. And just today, had made sob out his name like another one of her symphonies.

Benedetto smiled. "I was young and brash and foolish. I thought that as long as Carlota and I had agreed on all the important things—like the fact neither one of us was interested in fidelity once our duties were handled, hale, and hardy—we might as well."

He could remember Carlota's bawdy laugh. The way she'd smoked cigarettes with dramatic, theatrical flourish. The way she rolled her eyes, speaking volumes without having to speak a word.

I can't cope with having it all hanging there over my head, she'd declared a few months before their wedding. *It will be just be too tedious. Let's get in, get out. Get it done.*

Are we a sports team? Benedetto had asked dryly.

In his memory, he was as he was now. Cynical. Self-aware and sardonic. But the reality was that he'd been twenty-two. Just like her. And he'd had no idea how quickly things could change. Or how brutally life could kick the unwary, especially people like them who thought their wealth protected them from unpleasant realities.

They'd both learned.

"I was so arrogant," he said now, shaking his head. "I was so certain that life would go as planned. Looking back, there were any number of warning signs. But I saw none of them."

"Was she very depressed?" Angelina asked, her eyes troubled.

"Carlota? Depressed? Never." Benedetto laughed. "She was in love."

"With you." Those blue eyes widened. "So you did break her heart when you refused to give up your mistress."

"That is a very boring tabloid story." Benedetto sighed. "Sylvia was my mistress, though I think you will find that when a man is twenty-two years old and dating an actress of roughly the same age, they're just... dating. But no matter, that does not make for splashy, timeless headlines."

"Mistress is certainly catchier," Angelina said quietly.

"Carlota was in love, but not with me," he said, because he couldn't seem to stop doing this. Why was he doing this? Nothing good could come of unburdening himself to her. "He was not of our social class, of course. Her parents would not have cared much if she carried on with him, because everyone could boast about sleeping with the odd pool boy—which is something her mother actually said to me at her funeral. But you see, Carlota wasn't simply sexually involved with this man of hers. She was head over heels in love with him, and he with her. Something I knew nothing about."

And then he hissed in a breath, because Angelina lifted a hand and slid it over his heart.

"It works, Benedetto," she said quietly. "I can feel it."

He felt something surge in him, huge and vivid. Something he could hardly bear, and couldn't name, though he had the terrible notion that it had been frozen there inside him all this time. That it was melting at last.

And the only thing this was going to do was make this worse. He knew that all too well.

"We spent the first few days of our honeymoon as friends, because that was what we'd always been," he gritted out, because he'd started this. And he would finish it, no matter the cost. "But then she decided that we might as well start making that heir as quickly as possible, so we could move on. She went off to prepare herself. Which, because she was in love with another man and had never had the slightest interest in me, involved getting drunk and then supplementing it with a handful of pills."

"You don't think she killed herself," Angelina breathed.

"On the contrary," Benedetto said grimly. "I know she did. It was an accident, I have no doubt, but what does that matter? It happened because she needed to deaden herself completely before she suffered a night with me."

He had never said anything like that out loud before in his life. And he hated himself for doing it now. He wanted to snatch the words back and shove them down his throat. He wanted to insist that Angelina rip them out of her ears.

"Was she truly your friend?" Angelina asked, and he couldn't understand why she wasn't looking at him with horror, as he deserved.

Or with the same resigned bleakness his grandfather had.

"She was," he said, another thing he never spoke about. To anyone. "She really was."

"Then, Benedetto." And Angelina's voice was soft. "You must know that she would never want you to suffer like this. Not for her. Don't you think she would have wanted at least one of you to be free?"

That landed in his gut like a punch.

He wasn't sure he could breathe.

"You have no idea what you're talking about, Angelina. You have no idea the kinds of chains—"

But he cut himself off, because that wasn't a conversation he could have, with her or anyone else. He'd promised. He'd chosen. He gathered her to him instead, then crushed his mouth to hers, pouring it all into another life-altering kiss.

For a moment, he imagined that it really could alter his life instead of merely *feeling* that way. That he could change something. Anything.

He kissed her and he kissed her.

And Benedetto realized with a surge of light-headedness that the taste he hadn't been able to get enough of over the past month, that impossible glory that was all Angelina, was hope.

Damn her, she was giving him *hope*.

He sensed movement in his peripheral vision, so he lifted his head, holding Angelina close to him so he could see who moved around in the dining room on the other side of the windowed doors.

It was Signora Malandra, and he felt himself grow cold as the older woman stared out at him.

She didn't say a word. But then, she didn't need to. Because if this castle was a prison, then Signora Malandra was the jailer, and it was no use complaining about a simple fact.

Angelina didn't see the silent, chilly exchange. Benedetto checked to make sure, and when he looked up again the housekeeper had disappeared.

Taking his fledgling hope with her.

"You don't have to tell me anything further," Angelina told him then. "You don't have to tell me anything at all, Benedetto."

Her face was still so perfect. Her expression still so dreamy. And he knew that she had forgiven him for acts she knew nothing about, even if that was something he could never do himself.

He swept her up into his arms again. And he didn't head for that bloodred bed in the room of stone that might as well have been a stage.

Benedetto shouldn't have done any of the things he'd done with Angelina, but he had. And he wasn't going to stop until he had to. But that only meant he needed to make sure what stolen moments they had were real.

She was the only thing in his life that had ever been real, as far as he could tell, for a long, long time.

He carried her into one of the salons, this one with a fireplace and a thick, soft rug before it. He lay her down and then busied himself preparing the fire.

"I would have sworn that there was no way a man of your consequence would know how to light a fire," Angelina said, laughing again.

And what was he supposed to do with her when she

kept laughing where any other woman would have been crying? Shivering with fear? Barring herself in a bathroom? All things other wives of his had done after Sylvia had died, and with far less provocation.

But then, he hadn't touched any of them.

He looked over his shoulder at her, incredulously, but she didn't seem to take the hint.

"The only reason I know how to do it is because we relied on fires for light and heat in my father's house," she confided. Merrily, even. "Necessity makes you strong or it kills you, I suppose. Either way, not something the great Benedetto Franceschi would ever have to worry about, I would have thought."

He busied himself with the logs. "It was not always in my best interests to alert members of this household as to my whereabouts. I can fend for myself. Inside the walls of the castle, anyway."

"But surely—"

But Benedetto was done talking.

"Quiet, little one," he growled, and then he crawled toward her, bearing her back down beneath him.

And he taught her everything he knew.

How to take him in her mouth. How to indulge herself as if he was her dessert. How to ride him and how to drive him wild by looking over her shoulder with that little smile of hers while he took her from behind.

He was a man possessed, falling asleep with her there before the fire, only to wake up and start all over again.

He could not taste her enough. He could not touch her enough.

As if, if he only applied himself, he could take all

that hope and beauty, all that magic and music, and infuse it directly into his veins.

As if there was more than one way to eat her alive.

As if he could keep her.

And in the morning, dawn crept through the windows, pink and bright. It woke him where he lay stretched out before that fire still.

He had done everything wrong. He knew that.

But that didn't change what had to happen now. It didn't alter in the slightest the promises he'd made. The choices he'd walked into with his eyes wide open, never expecting this. Never expecting Angelina.

Benedetto lifted her up. He tried to steel himself against the way she murmured his name, then turned to bury her face against his shoulder, not quite waking up.

He carried her through the suite, everything in him rebelling as he walked into the bedchamber at last. Outside the windows, he could see the light of the new day streaking over the sea.

It should have been uplifting, but all he wanted to do was rage. Hit things. Make it stop.

He took her to that bloodred bed and laid her in it. He drew the coverlet up, but left her hand exposed, that bloodred ruby marking her as his. And a fortune or two of them surrounding her.

Blood on blood.

He didn't want to leave, but he knew he had no choice if he was to keep his old vow. He handled the hateful practicalities and then he tore himself away. He forced himself out of the bedchamber and refused to allow himself to look back.

But the sight of her was burned into his brain anyway. Blond hair spread out over the pillows like silver filigree, somehow making all that dark red seem less ominous. Cheerful, almost.

As if she really was an angel.

Benedetto took a long shower, but that didn't make it any better. He dressed in a fury, then had another fight on his hands to keep himself from walking back into the bedchamber and starting all over again.

Instead, he stepped out into the hall. He wasn't the least bit surprised to see the figure of his housekeeper waiting there, halfway down. Right in front of the door he'd told Angelina she was never to open.

Inside him, he was nothing but an anguished howl. But the only sound he made was that of his feet against the floor.

Walking toward his duty and his destiny, as ever.

When he reached Signora Malandra, they stared at each other for a quiet eternity or two.

"It is done," Benedetto said, the way he always did.

The older woman nodded, her canny gaze reminding him of his grandfather.

Or maybe that was his same old guilt talking too loudly once again, trying to drown out that tiny shimmer of hope.

"Very well then, sir," she said. She smiled at the door, locked tight, then at him. "So the game begins. Again."

CHAPTER TEN

ANGELINA WOKE UP on the first morning of her married life with a buoyancy inside her chest that she would have said was impossible—because she'd certainly never felt anything like it before.

At first, she was a bit surprised to find herself in that great, blood colored bed. More than surprised—she was taken aback that she had no memory of getting into it. The memories she did have were white hot, stretched out in front of a fire her forbiddingly grand husband built himself. A delicious shiver worked its way over her body, inside and out.

She sat up slowly, holding the bejeweled coverlet to her chest as she looked around. But nothing had changed. The room was still a stark aerie, nothing but stone before her and above her, and the sea outside. Waiting.

But for some reason, what she'd expected would feel like a fall to her death felt like flying instead. Exhilarating. She shoved her hair back from her face, and spent a good long while staring out at the sea in the distance. Blue. Beautiful.

Only as brooding as she made it.

When she swung her legs over the side of the high

bed and found the cool stones beneath her feet, she felt almost soothed. Not at all the reaction she would have expected to have in this room that had scared her silly yesterday.

She took a long, hot shower, reveling in such a modern installation only yards from that medieval bedchamber. And as she soaped herself up, reveling in how new her own skin felt, she thought that Benedetto was much the same as this castle of his. Stretched there between the old and the new and somehow both at once.

Benedetto.

Her heart seem to cartwheel in her chest, and she couldn't help the wide, foolish smile that took over her face at the thought of him. He had taken her virginity— or more accurately, she'd given it to him. First while she played, offering him everything she was, everything she had, everything she hoped and dreamed.

The physical manifestation of the music she'd played for him had been appropriately epic.

She could still feel his hands, all over her flesh. She could feel the tug and rip of her gown as he'd torn it from her, then buried himself inside her for the first time. She still shuddered as images of the darkly marvelous things he'd taught her washed through her, over and over.

And she couldn't wait to do all of it again.

Maybe, just maybe, she could be the wife who stuck.

She was turning that over in her head, thinking about stories that lost more truth in each telling, as she dressed herself in the sprawling dressing room that was filled with clothes that she knew, somehow, would fit her perfectly. Even if they bore no resemblance to the meager selection she'd brought herself. And she remembered, against her will, what Petronella had said. That two or three lost wives could be a tragedy, but add another three on top of that and there had to be intention behind it.

That, or Benedetto Franceschi, the least hapless man she had ever met, was just…profoundly unlucky.

A notion that made her laugh a little as she found her way out of the dressing room, following her nose. Coffee, if she wasn't mistaken. And she could feel excitement and anticipation bubbling inside of her, as if she was fizzy from the inside out, because she couldn't wait to see him again. His dark, forbidding face that she knew so much better now. That she'd kissed, touched. That she'd felt on every inch of her skin.

Between her legs, she felt the deep pulse of that hunger she would have said should surely have been sated by everything they'd done the night before.

But it seemed her husband left her bottomless.

Her husband, she repeated to herself. Giddily, she could admit.

She pushed the door open to one of the pretty little salons, expecting to see Benedetto there, waiting for her in all his formidable state. But instead, the dour housekeeper waited there with a blank expression on her dolorous face.

Or an *almost* blank expression. Because if Angelina wasn't mistaken, there was a glitter in Signora Malandra's too-dark eyes. It looked a little too much like triumph.

Angelina didn't like the trickle of uneasiness that slipped down her back.

"Good morning," Angelina said, sounding as frosty as her own mother. She pulled the long, flowing sweater she'd found more tightly around her, because it might be the height of summer out there, but old castles were cold. All that stone and bloody history, no doubt.

"I trust you slept well," the older woman said, lifting an accusing eyebrow in a manner Angelina was all too familiar with. "If…deeply."

This woman could not possibly be attempting to shame her master's brand-new wife because she'd slept half the morning away. After her *wedding night*. Surely not.

"Have you seen my husband?" Angelina asked instead of any number of other things she might have said. Because if Margrete had taught her anything, it was that a chilly composure was always the right answer. It made others wonder. And that was far better than showing them how she actually felt.

Signora Malandra indicated the small table near a set of French doors that stood closed, no doubt to control the sea air. And then waited there, gazing back at her, until Angelina realized the woman had no intention of answering her until she obeyed.

Luckily, Angelina had spent her entire life under the thumb of overly controlling women. What was one surly housekeeper next to her mother and sisters? So she only smiled, attempted to look meek and biddable, and went to take her seat. As ordered.

Her act of rebellion was to crack open one of the doors, and then she smiled as the breeze swept inside, fresh and bright.

"Coffee?" the older woman asked. It sounded like an accusation.

Angelina channeled her mother and smiled wider, if more icily. "Thank you for asking. The truth is, I don't care for much in the way of breakfast. I like my coffee strong and very dark, and sometimes with a bit of cream. But only sometimes. I don't like anything to interfere with my walk."

"And where will we be walking?" the housekeeper asked as she poured Angelina a cup of coffee. "Perhaps we have forgotten that this is an island. The castle covers the whole of it, save a few rocks."

It took everything Angelina had not to respond to that. Not to point out that *we* were not invited.

The other woman sniffed as if she'd spoken aloud. "Though I suppose if you are feeling enterprising, you could walk the causeway. It's quite a pretty walk, though I'm not sure I would attempt it until I became more conversant with the tides."

"What a wonderful idea," Angelina said with a sweetness she did not feel. And when she took a sip of the coffee, it was suitably bitter. Which matched her mood.

"I was born and raised in this castle," Signora Malandra said, and again, Angelina could see something she didn't quite like in the older woman's gaze. "It sounds like foolishness, to warn every person who visits here about the inevitability of the tide when the ocean is all around us. But I warn you, mistress." And there was an inflection on that word that made Angelina's stomach tighten. "This is not a sea to turn your back on."

Angelina felt chilled straight through, and it had nothing to do with the breeze coming in from the water. She was glad she'd thought to wrap the sweater around her when all she wore beneath was a light, summer-weight dress that she'd chosen because the color—a bright pop of yellow—made her happy.

She did not feel quite so happy now.

And she did not appreciate having dour old women try to scare her, either.

"My husband?" she asked again, as Signora Malandra looked as if she was headed for the door.

"Your husband is gone," the old woman said coolly. And again, with that hint of triumph in her gaze. "Did you not get what he left you?"

"What he left me?" Angelina repeated, not comprehending. How could Benedetto be *gone?* Did she mean…into town, wherever that was? She tried to conceal her shock. "Has he gone out for the day?"

And this time, there was no mistaking the look on the other woman's face. It was far worse than *triumphant*. It was pitying.

"Not for the day, mistress. Two months, I would say. At the very least."

And by the time Angelina had processed that, Signora Malandra was gone.

This time, when she found her way back into the bedchamber, it seemed ominous again. Altered, somehow. Almost obscene.

Someone had made up the bed in Angelina's absence, and that felt as sickening as the rest, as if some unseen evil was swirling around her, even now—

A sound that could have been a sob came out of her then, and she hated herself for it.

She remembered his face, out there on the balcony last night. That had been real. She was sure of it. Angelina had to believe that what she felt was real, not the rest of this. Not the stories that people had told, when the one he'd told her made more sense. Not because she wanted to believe him, though she did.

But because real life was complicated. It had layers and

tragedies. It was never as simple as *a bad man*. It was never black and white, no matter how people wanted it to be.

There was nothing in the room, not even bedside tables, and she thought the housekeeper must have been playing with her.

Even as she breathed a little easier, however, she realized with a start that the mantel over the fire didn't look the way it should. She drifted closer to the fireplace, her heart in her throat, because there was a bit of paper there with an object weighting it down.

She could have sworn it hadn't been there when she woke up. Then again, her attention had been on that happiness within her that now felt curdled, and the watching, waiting sea.

Her whole body felt heavy, as if her feet were encased in concrete as she moved across the floor. But then, at the last moment—almost as if she feared that someone would come up behind her and shove her into the enormous hearth if she wasn't careful—she reached out and swiped the paper and its paperweight up. Then moved away from the fireplace.

The object was a key. Big and ornate and attached to a long chain.

She stared at it, the weight of it feeling malevolent, somehow. Only when she jerked her gaze from it did she look at the thick sheaf of paper with a few bold lines scrawled across it.

This is the key to the door you must not open.

Benedetto had written that. Because of course, this was his handwriting. She had no doubt. It looked like him—dark and black and unreasonably self-assured.

You must wear the key around your neck, but never use it. Can I trust you, little one?

And for a long time after that, weeks that turned to fortnights and more, Angelina careened between disbelief and fury.

On the days that she was certain it was no more than a test, and one she could handily win, she achieved a kind of serenity. She woke in the morning, entertained herself by sparring with the always unpleasant housekeeper, and then tended to her walk. When the weather was fine, and the tide agreeable, she did in fact walk the causeway. Out there on that tiny strip of not quite land, she felt the way she did when she was playing the piano. As if she was simultaneously the most important life in the universe, and nothing at all—a speck in the vastness. The sea surged around her, birds cried overhead, and in the distance, Italy waited. Wholly unaware of the loneliness of a brand-new bride on a notorious island where a killer was said to live. When the man she'd married had been a dark and stirring lover instead.

Her husband did not call. He did not send her email. She might have thought she'd dreamed him altogether, but she could track his movements online. She could see that he was at meetings. The odd charity ball. She could almost convince herself that he was sending her coded messages through these photographs that appeared in the society pages of various international cities.

Silly girl, she sometimes chided herself. *He is sending you nothing. You don't know this man at all.*

But that was the trouble. She felt as if she did.

She didn't need him to tell her any more of his story.

She knew—she just *knew*—that her heart was right about him, no matter what the world said.

Those were the good days.

On the bad days, she brooded. She walked the lonely halls of the hushed castle, learning her way around a building that time had made haphazard. Stone piled upon stone, this wing doubling back over that. She walked the galleries as if she was having conversations with the art. Particularly the hall of Franceschis past. All those dark, mysterious eyes. All those grim, forbidding mouths.

How many of them had locked their women away? Leaving them behind as they marched off to this crusade or that very important business negotiation, or whatever it was men did across time to convince themselves their lives were greater than what they left behind.

On those days, the portraits she found online of the stranger she'd married felt like an assault. As if he was taunting her from London, Paris, Milan.

And all the while, she played.

Her tower was an escape. The safest place in the castle. She played and she played, and sometimes, she would stagger to the chaise, exhausted, so she could sleep a bit, then start to play all over again.

And if she didn't know better, if food didn't appear at regular intervals, hot tea and hard rolls, or sometimes cakes and coffee, she might have imagined that she was all alone in this lonely place. Like some kind of enchanted princess in a half-forgotten fairy tale.

She played and she played.

And the weeks inched by.

One month. Another.

"Sweet God," said Petronella, when Angelina was finally stir crazy enough to call her parents' home. "I convinced myself he'd killed you already and was merely hiding the evidence."

"Don't be melodramatic," Angelina replied primly, because that was easier. And so familiar, it actually felt good. "He's done nothing of the kind."

Or not in the way that Petronella meant it, anyway. They put her on speaker, and she regaled her mother and sisters with tales of the castle. She'd tagged along on enough of Signora Malandra's tours by then that she could have given them herself, and so spared no flourish or aside as she shared the details of the notorious Castello Nero with her family.

Because she knew they would think wealth meant happiness.

Because to them, it did.

"Everywhere I look there's another fortune or two," she assured her mother. "It's really spectacular."

"I should hope so," Margrete said, in her chilliest voice. "That was the bargain we made, was it not?"

And when she hung up, Angelina was shocked to find herself...sentimental. Nostalgic, even, for those pointless nights huddled together in the drawing room of the dilapidated old *château*, waiting to be sniped at and about. Night after night after night.

Who could have imagined she would miss that?

She would have sworn she could never possibly feel that way. But then again, she thought as she moved from one well-stocked library to the next—because the castle boasted three separate, proper libraries that would take a lifetime or two to explore—she was more emotional these days than she'd ever been in her life.

She'd woken up the other morning crying, though she couldn't have said why. She slept in that absurd bed every night, almost as if it was an act of defiance. But she couldn't say her dreams were pleasant. They were dark and red, and she woke with strange sensations in her body, especially in her belly.

Angelina was glad she couldn't remember the one that had rendered her tearful. Though the truth was, everything seemed to make her cry lately. Even her own music.

That night, she followed her usual routine. She played until her fingers hurt, then she staggered down the stairs from her tower to find a cold dinner waiting for her. She ate curled up on a chilly chair out on the balcony while the sea and wind engaged in a dramatic sort of dance in front of her. There was a storm in the air, she could sense it. Smell it, even.

When she could take the slap of the wind no longer, she moved inside. She was barefoot, her hair a mess, and frozen straight through when she left the master suite and walked down that hallway. The key he'd left her hung around her neck as ordered, the chain cool against her skin and the key itself heavy and warm between her breasts.

And she stood there, on the other side of that door, and stared at it.

Some nights she touched it. Other nights she pounded on it with her fists. Once she'd even gone so far as to stick the key into the lock, though she hadn't turned it.

Not yet.

"I am not Pandora," she muttered to herself.

As always, her voice sounded too loud, too strange in the empty hallway.

She had no idea how long she stood there, only that the world grew darker and darker on the other side of the windows, and she'd neglected to put on any lights.

When lightning flashed outside, it lit everything up. It seemed to sizzle inside of her like a dare.

A challenge.

It had been two months and three days. It was nearly September. And she was beginning to think that she had already gone crazy. That she was a madwoman locked away in a castle, which was an upgrade from the proverbial attic, but it ended up the same.

Alone and unhinged. Matted hair and too much emotion. And an almost insatiable need to do the things she knew she shouldn't.

There was another flash of lightning, and then a low, ominous rumble of thunder following it.

She heard a harsh, rhythmic kind of noise, and realized with some shock that she was panting. As if she'd been running.

And then, when another roll of thunder seemed to shake that wall of windows behind her, she found herself sobbing.

Angelina sank to her knees, there in that solitary hall.

She had waited and waited, but it was nights like this that were killing her. Was this how he'd rid himself of all those wives?

And as soon as she had that thought, she had to ask herself—what kind of death was worse?

This had to be a test. But how long could she do it? She'd had a month of play, and then one impossibly beautiful night with a man everyone insisted was evil incarnate. Her heart had rejected that definition of him.

Could she set that against these months of neglect? She was slowly turning into one of the antiques that cluttered this place. Soon she would be nothing more than a story the dour old woman told, shuffling groups of tourists from room to room.

"I have been a prisoner my whole life," she sobbed, into her hands.

Her piano made her feel free, but she wasn't.

At the end of the day, she was just a girl in a tower, playing and playing, in the hopes that someone might hear her.

All Benedetto had done was trap her. Her family had never wished to listen to her play, but they'd heard her all the same. Now the only thing that heard her was the sea, relentless and uncaring. Waiting.

She lifted her head, shoving the mass of her hair back. Her heart was kicking at her, harder and harder.

She already knew what her mother would tell her. What her sisters would advise.

You've got it made, Petronella would say with a sniff. *You're left to your own devices in a glorious castle to call your own. What's to complain about?*

Angelina understood that she would fail this test. That she already had, and all of this had been so much pretending otherwise. The key suspended between her breasts seemed to pulse, in time with that hunger that she still couldn't do anything to cure.

Before she knew what she meant to do, the key was in her hand. She stared at it, as another flash of lightning lit up the hall, and she could have sworn that she saw the key flash too. As if everything was lightning and portent, dread and desire.

The ring Benedetto had put on her other hand seemed

heavy, suddenly. And all she could think about was six dead women. And a bedchamber made bloodred with dark rubies.

And was she really to blame if she couldn't stay here any longer without looking behind the one door that was always kept closed?

What if he was in there? Hurt?

What if something far more horrible was in there?

Like all the women who had disappeared, never to be heard from again.

Even as she thought it, something in her denied it. Her heart would not accept him as a villain.

But either way, she found herself on her feet.

And then she was at the door, one palm flat against the metal. She blew out a breath that was more like a sob. She thrust the key into the lock, the way she'd done one time before, amazed how easily it went in. Smooth and simple and *right*.

She held her breath. Then she threw the dead bolt.

Alarms didn't sound. The castle didn't crumble to ash all around her.

Emboldened, Angelina blew out the breath she was holding. She took another one, deeper than before, and pushed the heavy door open. She expected it to creak ominously, as if she was in a horror film.

But it opened soundlessly on a stair, very much like the one she climbed every day to her own tower.

Thunder rumbled outside, the storm coming closer. She couldn't see a thing, so she inched inside, then reached out her hand into the darkness, sliding it along the stone, her whole body prickling with a kind of premonition. Or fear. Panic that she would thrust her hand into something terrible—

But she found a light switch where she expected to, in the same place it was in her stairwell. She flicked it on and then began to climb.

Each step felt like a marathon. So she went faster and faster, climbing high, until she reached another door at the top. And her heart was beating too hard for her to stop now. There was too much thunder outside and in her, too.

She threw open the second door and stepped inside, reaching and finding another light and switching it on.

And then she blinked. Once, then again, unable to believe her eyes. Angelina dropped her hand to her side, drifted in a few more steps, and looked around as if she expected something to change...

But nothing changed.

It was an empty room with windows over the sea, just like the tower room she spent her days in. There were stone walls, a bare floor, and a high ceiling where a light fixture hung, illuminating the fact that there was nothing here.

Benedetto had demanded she stay out of an empty room.

That sparked something in her, half a laugh, half a sob.

Angelina thought she heard a noise and she jumped, expecting *something*... But that was the trouble. She didn't know what she wanted. And the room was empty. No monsters. No dead wives. No words scrawled on a paper, or carved into the stone. Just...nothing.

The same nothing these last two months had been.

That made something in her begin to throb, painfully.

She was disgusted with herself. She didn't know if

she wanted to go play her piano until she felt either settled or too wound up to breathe, or if she should crawl beneath that heavy coverlet again to dream her unsettling dreams.

But when she turned around to go, she stopped dead.

Because Benedetto stood in the doorway to the empty chamber, the expression on his face a far more terrible thunder than the storm outside.

CHAPTER ELEVEN

BENEDETTO HAD STAYED away for six weeks. It was easy enough to do, touring his various business concerns. Such a tour would normally have claimed all of his attention, but this time he had found himself distracted. Unable to focus on what was in front of him because he was far more concerned with what he'd left behind.

That hadn't happened in as long as he could remember.

He wasn't sure it had ever happened. But that was Angelina. She was singular even when she wasn't with him.

And since his return to this castle he'd forgotten how to love the way he had as a child, he had become a ghost.

The irony wasn't lost on him. That he should be the one to haunt these old halls, staying in the servants' quarters and wandering in the shadows, both part of the castle and apart from it... Perhaps it was a preview of what awaited him.

Because the other option was that it was a memory of his time here when he was young and had seen the *castello* as his personal playground, magical and inviting in every respect, and that was worse, somehow.

But Angelina had cracked, as he'd known she would. He'd hoped her singularity would extend to this and she might be the one to resist temptation, but she didn't. None of them managed it. Sooner or later, they ended up right here in this empty room above the sea, staring at him as if they truly expected him to come in wielding an ax.

He had come to enjoy, on some level, that they believed all the stories they heard about him and married him anyway. The triumph of his wealth over their fear.

It wasn't as if any of them had touched him the way Angelina had. None of them had seen him, listened to him, or made love to him. None of them had played him music or treated him as if he was a man instead of a monster.

They had married his money. And they all came into this empty room, sooner or later, despite his request they stay away, expecting to come face-to-face with the monster they believed he was. The monster they *knew* he was.

Benedetto had long since stopped minding the way they looked at him when they saw him in the door, as if they could *see* the machete he did not carry with him.

This time, it hurt.

This time, it was a body blow.

"What are you doing here?" Angelina demanded. Her face was pale, her beautiful blond hair whipping around her with the force of her reaction. One hand was at her throat, and he could see the panic in her eyes.

If he was a better man, the fact that *her* fear pierced his soul would drop him, surely. And he would not stand here, wondering why it was that heightened emotion made her even more beautiful.

Or why it reminded him of the look on her face when she'd shuddered all around him, again and again.

Or why nothing about her was like the others—and he *hated* that they were here in this room anyway. Playing out this same old scene. This curse of his he had chosen when he'd never imagined he would want to see the end of it, much less meet someone who'd made it—and him—feel broken from the start.

"Why should I not be here?" he asked, aware as he spoke that he was…not quite as in control of himself as he might wish. Not as in control as he usually was for this scene. "Perhaps you have forgotten that I'm the master of this castle."

"Now that you mention it, you do look vaguely familiar," she threw at him, any hint of fear on her face gone as if it had never been. Instead, she looked fierce. "You almost resemble a man I married, who abandoned me after one night."

"I did not abandon you." He spread his hands open before him. "For here I am, Angelina. Returned to you. And what do I discover but betrayal?"

"You ordered me to stay out of an empty room," she said, as if she couldn't believe it. The hand at her throat dropped to her side, and she took a step toward him, her blue eyes as stormy as the sea and sky outside. "Why would you do that? Do you know what I thought…?"

"But this is a room of terror, clearly," he taunted her, his voice dark, and it was less an act than it usually was. "Look closely, little one. Surely you can hear the screams of the women I've murdered. Surely if you squint, you can see their bodies, splayed out like some horrific art installation."

He watched her emotions move over her face, too

quickly to read. And wished—not for the first time—that it was different.

Lord help him, but he had wished that she would be different.

"That is what you came for, is it not?" he demanded, his words an accusation.

"Are you trying to tell me that is not exactly what you wish me to think?" She waved one hand, the ring he'd put on her finger gleaming like the only blood in this room. "Is that what makes you happy?"

"I gave up on happiness a long time ago," Benedetto growled. "Now I content myself with living down to people's worst nightmares? Why shouldn't I? Everyone needs a villain, do they not?"

Angelina moved toward him, staggering slightly, her bare feet against the cold stone. "I do not want a villain, Benedetto. I want a husband."

"If that were true, you'd be asleep even now, tucked up in the marital bed. It would not have occurred to you to disobey me."

"What you are describing is a dog, not a wife," she snapped at him. "I never promised you obedience."

"Surely that was understood," he shot back. "When I bought you."

And again, he knew that he was far less in control of himself than he ought to have been. He had played this scene out before, after all. He usually preferred an iciness. A cool aloofness that wasn't an act, because it was his usual, normal state.

Nothing about Angelina had been normal or usual. Nothing about this was ordinary.

Even now he wanted to bundle her up into his arms and carry her off. And never, ever put her down again.

"Are you going to tell me what all of this is about?" she asked after a moment, when he'd found himself entirely too entranced by the way her jagged breaths made her body move.

He could see her cheeks were tearstained. She was the one who had disobeyed, the way they all disobeyed, and yet he felt as if *he* had betrayed *her*.

For moment he couldn't understand why.

And then it hit him.

For the first time since he'd met her, Angelina was looking at him as if he really might be a monster, after all.

Of all the things he'd lost, of all the indignities the choices he'd willingly made long ago required that he endure, it was this he thought might take him to his knees.

"Or are these just the kinds of games you like to play?" Angelina asked when he only stared at her. She shook her head, swallowing hard, as if she was holding words back. Or a sob. Or, if that hectic look in her eyes was any guide, a scream. "I am so deeply sick and tired of being nothing more to anyone but a game piece to be moved around a board that is never of my choosing. Is this how you do it, Benedetto? Do you set up every woman you marry in the same way? Do you plot out the terms of your own betrayal, give them the key, and then congratulate yourself on having weeded out yet another deceitful bride? When all along it is you who creates an unwinnable situation?"

He eyed her, amazed that he felt stung by the accusation when he knew it was perfectly true—and more, deliberate. Yet no matter the sting, he was entranced by the magnificence of her temper that reminded him of nothing so much as the way she played that piano. In his weeks here as the resident ghost of his own lost childhood, he'd found himself listening to her play more than he should. He'd found himself sitting behind the stairs, losing himself on the notes she coaxed from the keys.

As if she'd still been playing for him.

Focus, he ordered himself.

"Am I the only one you made sure would fail?" Angelina demanded. "Or is this how you do it? And what do you gain from this? Do you toss us out a tower window, one by one?"

Benedetto laughed, though nothing was funny. "Would that suit your sense of martyrdom, wife?"

She stiffened. "I am no martyr."

"Are you not? Tell me, how else would you describe a young woman who was presented to a known murderer and allowed him a taste of her on that very first night? Do you also write to mass murderers in prison, offering your love and support? There are many who do. I'm sure the attendant psychological problems are in no way a factor."

She looked at him for what felt like a very long time, a kind of resolve on her face. "I didn't believe you were a murderer. I still don't."

And something in him rocked a bit at that. "Because you had made such an in-depth study of my character over the course of that one dinner?" He didn't like the emotion on her face then. He didn't like *emotion.* He growled. "Perhaps, as we are standing here together, stripped down to honesty in this empty room, we can finally admit that what you truly wanted was to escape. And all the better if you could do it while hammered to the family cross."

"Surely a martyr is what you wanted," she replied, displaying that strength he'd heard in her music time and time again. And quietly. "Or why would you go to such trouble to present yourself as a savior, willing to haul a family like mine out of financial ruin—but only for a price."

"I know exactly why it is I do what I do," Benedetto growled with a soft menace. "A better question is why you imagined you could marry a man like me, surrender yourself to my dark demands, and have things end differently for you than the rest. Do you truly imagine yourself that special, Angelina?"

"I don't know," she said, and there was something in her gaze then. A kind of knowing on her lovely face that clawed at him like the storm outside, thunder and flashes of light. "But there were times you looked at me and it seemed clear that you thought so, Benedetto."

She could not have pierced him more deeply had she pulled out a knife and plunged it into his heart. Then twisted it.

Benedetto actually laughed, because he hadn't seen it coming. And he should have. Of course he should have.

Because there was nothing meek about his Angelina. His angel. She was all flaming swords and descents from on high in a blaze of glory, and if he hadn't understood that when he had first seen her—well. When she'd played for him that first night, it had all been clear.

Then he'd tasted all that flame himself.

And there was no coming back from that.

She had introduced music into his life. Now it would live in him, deep in his bones no matter where in the world he went, and he had no idea how he was going to survive without it.

Or without her.

Because these last two months had been torture. If they had been a preview of what awaited him, he might as well chain himself up in his own dungeon and allow himself to go truly mad at last.

It almost sounded like a holiday to him.

"Are you going to kill me?" she asked, and despite the question, she stood tall. She didn't try to hide from him. After a beat he realized there was no fear on her face. "Is that the truth of you, after all?"

And this was the life he had chosen. He had made a promise to his grandfather years ago, and time after time he had kept it.

He had considered it a penance. He had taken a kind of pride in being so reviled and whispered about on the one hand, yet courted and feted all the same because no matter what else he was, he was a man of a great and historic fortune.

Benedetto had considered it a game. For what did he care what names he was called? Why should it matter to him what others said? He had yet to meet anyone who wouldn't risk themselves in his supposedly murderous presence if it meant they would get paid for their trouble.

He had cynically imagined he understood everything there was to know about the world. He had been certain he had nothing left to learn—that nothing could surprise him.

He understood, now it was too late, that the point of it all had been a woman like Angelina.

It was possible his grandfather had expected someone like her to come along sooner, so that Benedetto would learn his lesson. It had never been a game or a curse. It had been about love all along.

Love.

That word.

Franceschis do not love, his mother had told him with one of her bitter trills of laughter. *They destroy.*

Love yourself, his father had said as if in agreement, his tone mocking in response to his wife. He'd cast a narrow sort of look at his only son and heir. *No one else will. Not because Franceschis destroy, or any such superstition. But because the only thing anyone will ever see is your fortune.*

He loves me, Carlota had told him on the day of their wedding. *He knows me. And so he also knows that my duty to you must come first.*

She was joy and she was love, his grandfather had said stiffly on the morning of his grandmother's funeral, staring out at the sea. *And none of each can possibly remain without her.*

I love you, Benedetto, his grandmother had told him long, long ago, when she'd found him hiding in one of the *castello*'s secret passageways. *I will always love you.*

But always had not lasted long.

As far as he had ever been able to tell, love had died along with her, just as his grandfather had said.

Something he'd been perfectly happy with all these years.

Until now.

When it was too late.

Because he knew how this scene between them was about to go. He played the monster and his wives believed it, and he'd been satisfied with that system since the start. There was only ever one way this could go.

He had always liked it. Before.

He raked his hair back from his face, and wished that he could do something about the way his heart kicked at him. Or better yet, about the fact he had a heart in the first place, despite everything.

Surely if he could rid himself of the thing the way he thought he had a lifetime ago, all of this would be easier.

"I am not going to kill you," he told her, his voice severe as he tried to draw the cloak of his usual remoteness around him. But he couldn't quite get there. "Nonetheless, you have a choice of deaths before you. You can consider this chamber a passageway, of sorts. A bridge between the life you knew until today, and one in which you can be anyone you choose. Assuming you meet the criteria, that is."

She swayed slightly on her feet. "The criteria?"

And he had done this so many times. It should have come as easily to him as breath.

But his chest was too tight. That damned heart of his was too big. "The criteria for escape is simple, Angelina. If you meet it, we will create a new identity for you. You can go anywhere you wish in the world under this new name. You will not have to worry about supporting yourself, because I will take care of your financial arrangements in perpetuity."

"Wait…" Angelina shook her head slightly. "Does that mean…?"

He nodded. "My third wife runs a scuba diving business on an island you would never have heard of, off the coast of Venezuela. My fourth wife lives a nomadic lifestyle, currently traveling about mainland Europe in a converted van. It looks modest from the outside but is, I am assured, the very height of technology within.

My fifth wife prefers the frenetic pace of Hong Kong, where she runs a spa. And Veronica, my most famous wife, never able to have a moment to herself in all her days, has settled down on a farm in a temperate valley on the west coast of America. Where she tends to grapes on the vine, raises goats, and makes her own cheese." His smile was a grim and terrible thing. He could taste it. "You can have any life you wish, Angelina. At my expense. All you need to do is disappear forever."

"But if they're not… If you didn't…" She pulled in a visible breath with a ragged sound. "Are you married to all these women at the same time?"

He actually laughed at that. "That is not usually the first question. No, I'm not a bigamist, though I commend you for adding yet another sin to my collection. Murderer and bigamist, imagine! I'm almost sorry to tell you that my marriages have all been quietly and privately annulled. Save the first."

Angelina shifted, hugging herself she stared back at him. "I don't understand. Why would you set yourself up to be some sort of…one-man smuggling operation for women in search of better lives? When you know that the whole world thinks the worst of you?"

"Who better?" Benedetto shrugged. "I don't care in the slightest what the world thinks of me. And you've spent two months acquainting yourself with this castle. It is the tip of the iceberg of the kind of money I have. I could marry a hundred women, support them all, and never feel a pinch in my own pocket."

"So it's altruism then?" She looked dubious, and if he wasn't mistaken, something like…affronted. "If that was true, why not give all that money to charity?

Shouldn't there be a way to do it that doesn't brand you the monster beneath every bed in Europe?"

"What would be the fun in that?"

This was the part where normally, the women he'd married—despite their cynicism or inability to trust a word he said because they feared him so deeply, yet not quite deeply enough to refuse to marry him—began to waver. Hope began to creep in. He would watch them imagine, as they stood there before him, that he might be telling them the truth. And if he was, if he could really give them what he was offering, did that mean that they could really, truly be free?

Of him—and of everything else that had brought them here?

But Angelina was staring at him as if what he was telling her was a far worse betrayal than games with his fearsome housekeeper and a key to a locked tower door.

"What do I have to do to qualify for this extraordinary death?" she asked.

He wanted to go to her. He wanted his hands on her. But the point of this, all this, was that Benedetto wasn't supposed to want such things.

He never had before.

"I already told you that the primary purpose of my existence is to produce an heir," he told her stiffly. "It was why I married Carlota and why we planned to consummate a union that was never passionate."

"I remember the story. But that hardly sounds like reason enough to inflict your unhappy childhood on another baby."

"My childhood wasn't unhappy." He heard the outrage in his voice and tried to rein it in. "My grandmother—" But he stopped himself. Because Angelina already knew too much about him. He had already given her too much. Benedetto gritted his teeth and pushed on. "Ordinarily, this is when I offer my wives the opportunity to produce the Franceschi heir themselves."

"Surely they signed up for that when they said, 'I do'?"

He ignored that, and the flash of temper in her blue gaze. "Should you choose that route, life here will continue as is. At the end of a year, if no heir is forthcoming, the same offer for a new life will be made to you. If you're pregnant, however, the expectation would be that you remain until the child is five. At which point, a final offer will be made. If you choose to go, you can do so, with one stipulation. That being, obviously, that you cannot take the child with you. If you choose to stay, we will have contracts drawn up to indicate that you may remain as much a stranger to the marriage as you wish."

He cleared his throat, because this was all standard. This was the labyrinthine game he and his grandfather had crafted and it had served him well for years. But Angelina was staring at him as if he'd turned into an apparition before her very eyes. When this was usually when that sort of gaze faded and a new one took its place. The sweet, bright gleam of *what if.*

"Of course, in your case, everything is different," he said, forcing himself to keep going. "I always leave after the wedding. Usually while they are locked in the bathroom, pretending not to be terrified that I might claim a wedding night. Then I wait to see how long it takes each wife to open the door to this tower. Once she does, we have this discussion."

Again, the way she looked at him was...different.

He cleared his throat. "But your choices might be more limited, regrettably, because you could already be pregnant. I'll confess this has never happened before."

Her lips parted then, and she made a sound that he couldn't quite define. "Are you telling me…? Are you…? Did you not sleep with all your wives on your wedding night? On all your wedding nights?"

"Of course not." He belted that out without thinking. "Nor do I touch them beforehand. I may be considered a monster far and wide, Angelina, but I do *try* not to act like one."

She let out a laugh, a harsh sound against the storm that battered at the windows outside. "Except with me."

Benedetto ran a hand over his face, finding he was only more unsettled as this conversation wore on. Instead of less, as was customary—because he always knew what his wives would choose. He always knew none of them had married *him*. They'd married his money and hoped for the best, and this was him giving it to them.

"The truth is that you were different from the start," he told Angelina, grudgingly. "I had no trouble whatsoever keeping my hands to myself with the rest. It was all so much more…civilized."

He found himself closing the distance between them, when he shouldn't. And he expected her to flinch, but she didn't. She stood her ground, even tilting up her chin, as if she wanted him to do exactly this. As if she wanted him to make it all worse.

Benedetto slid his hand along her cheek, finding it hot and soft, and that didn't solve a single one of his problems. "But you played for me, Angelina. And you wrecked me. And I have been reeling ever since."

Her mouth moved into something far too stark to be a smile. Far too sad to be hers. "That would sound more romantic if you weren't threatening to kill me, one way or another."

"No," he gritted out. "As it happens, you are the only wife I have slept with on a wedding night."

Her eyes seemed remarkably blue then. "What about your second wife? Your mistress? Surely she—"

"She was paralytically drunk after our reception," he said, not sure if that darkness in him was fury, anticipation, or something else he'd never felt before. Something as overwhelming and electric as the storm outside. "And I was little better. I am afraid, Angelina, that you are unique."

"I feel so special," she whispered in that same rough tone, but she didn't jerk her cheek away.

Even so, Benedetto dropped his hand. And for a moment, they stood there, gazing at each other with all these secrets and lies exposed and laid out between them.

He could feel the walls all around him, claiming him anew. For good this time.

When she left him, as he knew she would because they always did, perhaps he would give up the fight altogether. In another year he could be nothing more than another statue, right here in this room. Another stop along the tour.

There was a part of him that longed for the oblivion of stone.

There was a part of him that always would.

"Why?" she asked, her voice a quiet scrape of roughness that reminded him, forcefully, that there was no part of him that was stone. That there never had been, especially where she was concerned. "Why would anyone go to all this trouble?"

"I will answer any and all questions you might have," he told her, sounding more formal than he intended. Perhaps that was his last refuge. The closest he could get to becoming a statue after all. "But first you must choose."

"As you pointed out, I might already be pregnant," she replied, her arms crossed and even the wildness of her long blond hair a kind of resistance, silver and bright against the bare walls.

Why did he want nothing more than to lose himself in her—forever? How had he let this happen?

"It is true. You might be. I used nothing to prevent it."

"Neither did I. There seemed little need when my life expectancy was all of three months."

And she stared at him, the rebuke like a slap.

He felt it more like a kick to the gut.

"What if I'm pregnant and still choose to disappear tonight?" she asked after a moment, sounding unnervingly calm. "What then? Will you surrender your own child? Or will you force me to stay here despite the choice I make?"

He shook his head, everything in him going cold. "I told you, you are unique. This has never happened before. That doesn't mean that the possibility is unforeseen. Your choice will hold, no matter your condition."

"You would give up your own child," she murmured. Her eyes widened. "But I thought I was the martyr here."

Benedetto realized his hands were in fists. He didn't know which was worse, that he would have to live without her, which he should have figured out how to handle already, or that it was distinctly possible that she would go off into whatever new life she wished and raise his child without him.

But the rules to this game had been always been perfectly clear.

He and his grandfather had laid them out together.

Half in penance, half for protection. He had already lost two wives. Why not more?

Benedetto had never imagined his heart would be involved. He'd been certain he'd buried that along with his grandmother.

"You must choose," he gritted out, little as he wanted to.

And for moment, he thought maybe they were dead, after all. Two ghosts running around and around in this terrible castle, cut off from the rest of the world. That the two of them had done this a thousand times before.

Because that was the way she looked at him. As if she'd despaired of him in precisely this way too many times to count already.

He could have sworn he heard her playing then, though there was no piano in sight. Still, the blood in his veins turned to symphonies instead, and he was lit up and lost.

For the first time since he'd started this terrible journey, he honestly didn't know if he could complete it. Or even if he could continue.

And all the while, his seventh wife—and first love, for all the good it would do him in this long, involved exercise in futility—gazed back at him, an expression on her face he'd never seen before.

It made everything in him tighten, like hands around his throat.

"What if I choose a third option instead?" she asked. Quietly. So very quietly.

Outside, the sea raged and the sky cracked open, again and again. But all he could focus on was Angelina. And those unearthly blue eyes that he was sure could see straight through him and worse, always had.

"There is no third option," he gritted out.

"But of course there is," she said.

And she smiled the way she had when he'd been deep inside her, on that night that shouldn't have happened. The night he couldn't forget.

He heard a great roaring thing and knew, somehow, that it was happening inside him.

"I could stay here," Angelina said with that same quiet strength. "I could have your babies and truly be your wife. No games. No locked towers or forbidden keys. Just you, Benedetto. And me. And whatever children we make between us."

He couldn't speak. The world was a storm, and he was a part of it, and only Angelina stood apart from it all. A beacon in all the dark.

"We don't have to play games. We don't have to do…whatever this is." Angelina stood there and *shined* at him. He'd never seen that shade of blue before. His heart had never felt so full. "We can do what we want instead."

No one, in the whole of Benedetto's life, had ever looked at him the way she did. As if he was neither her savior nor her hero nor even her worst nightmare. He could have handled any of those. All of them.

But Angelina looked at him as if, should he only allow it, he could be a man.

He didn't know how he stayed on his feet when all

he wanted was to collapse to his knees. To beg her to stop. Or to never stop. Or to *think* about what she was doing here.

To him.

"Angelina," he managed to grit out. "You don't know what you're asking."

"But I do." And this time, when her lips curved, it looked like hope. "Benedetto, you asked me to marry you, and I said yes. Now I'm asking you the same thing."

"Angelina…"

"Will you marry me? And better yet—" and her smile widened, and it was all too bright and too much and his chest was cracking open "—will you *stay* married to me? I'm thinking we can start with a long, healthy lifetime and move on from there."

CHAPTER TWELVE

"YOU MUST BE MAD," Benedetto said, his voice strangled.

Angelina couldn't say she wasn't. Maybe the next step was searching out convicted killers and making them her pen pals, as he'd suggested. But she rather thought the only killer who interested her was this one, who'd only ever been convicted in the court of public opinion. And who hadn't killed anyone.

"There is no third option," he said, his voice like gravel. But there was an arrested look on his face that made her heart lurch a bit inside her chest. "I made certain promises long ago. Whether you carry my child now or not is immaterial."

She'd been talking about babies as if she was talking about someone else, but the possibility that it had already happened, that it was happening *even now,* settled on her, then. She slid a hand over her belly in a kind of wonder. Could it be?

This whole night so far had been like one of her favorite pieces of music. A beautiful journey—a tour of highs and lows, valleys and mountains, storms and sunlight—and all of it bringing her here. Right here.

To this man who was not a monster. No matter how badly he wanted to be.

Her heart had known all along.

"I could do it your way," she said softly. "I could sign up for the heir apparent program. I could keep signing up. We could make it cold-blooded and chilly, if you like. Is that what you want?" There was something so heartbreaking about that, but she knew she would accept it, if it was what he had to offer. She knew she would accept anything if it meant she could have him, even the smallest part of him—but she saw something like anguish on his hard face, then. "Or is it what you think you deserve?"

And for a moment the anguish she could see in him seemed as loud and filled with fury as the storm outside. It was hard to tell which was which—but her heart knew this man. Her heart had recognized him from the start.

It recognized him now.

"It's all right if you can't answer me, Benedetto," she said. She went to him then, stepping close and putting her hands on his chest, where he was as hot to the touch as she recalled. Hotter. She tipped her head back, searching that beautiful, forbidding face of his. "If you can't bring yourself to answer, you don't have to. But tell me how we got here. Tell me why you do all this."

He made a broken sound, this dark, terrible man who was neither of those things.

She didn't understand why she knew it, only that she did. Her heart had known it all along. That was why, though she'd feared for her loneliness and sanity here, she had never truly believed she was in actual, physical danger.

He wasn't any more a butcher than she was. And once that truth had taken hold of her in this empty chamber, all the others swirling around her seemed to solidify. Then fall in behind it like dominoes.

She didn't want to leave him. She didn't want to learn how to scuba dive or to live in a caravan. She didn't want to run a spa in a far-off city, or collect grapes and goats.

She wanted him.

Angelina wanted to look up from her piano to find him studying her, as if she was a piece of witchcraft all her own and only he knew the words to her spell.

Because only he did.

God help her, but she wanted all those things she'd never dared dream about before. Not for the youngest daughter in a family headed for ruin. The one least likely to be noticed and first to be sold off. She wanted *everything*.

"Benedetto," she said again, because it started here. It started with the two of them and this sick game he clearly played not because he wanted to play it, but because he believed he had no other choice. "Who did this to you?"

Then she watched in astonishment as this big, strong man—this boogeyman feared across the planet, a villain so extreme grown men trembled before him—fell to his knees before her.

"I did this to me," he gritted out. "I did all of this. I am my own curse."

Angelina didn't think. She sank down with him, holding his hands as he knelt there, while all around the tower, the storm outside raged and raged.

The storm in him seemed far more intense.

"Why?" she breathed. "Tell me."

"It was after Sylvia was swept overboard," Benedetto said in a low voice, and the words sounded rough and unused. She didn't need him to tell her that he'd never told this story before. She knew. "You must understand, there was nothing about my relationship with her that anyone would describe as healthy. I should never have married her. As much for her sake as mine."

He stared straight ahead, but Angelina knew he didn't see her. There were too many ghosts in the way.

But she was fighting for a lifetime. She didn't care if they knelt on the hard stone all night.

She held his hands tighter as he continued.

"Sylvia and I brought out the worst in each other. That was always true, but it was all much sicker after Carlota died. All we did was drink too much, fight too hard, and become less and less able to make up the difference. Then came the storm."

His voice was ravaged. His dark eyes blind. His hands clenched around hers so hard that it might have hurt, had she not been so deeply invested in this moment. In whatever he was about to tell her.

"It took her," Benedetto grated out. "And then I knew what kind of man I was. Because as much as I grieved her, there was a relief in it, too. As if the hand of God reached down and saved me twice, if in horrible ways. Once from a union with a woman I could never make truly happy, because she loved another, and then from a woman who made me as miserable as I made her. The rest of my life, I will have to look in a mirror and know that I'm the sort of man who thought such things when two women died. That is who I am."

"You sound like a human being," Angelina retorted, fiercely. "If we were all judged on the darkest thoughts that have ever crossed our minds, none of us would ever be able to show our faces in public."

Benedetto shook his head. "My grandfather was less forgiving than you are, Angelina. He called me here, to this castle. He made me stand before him and explain how it was that I was so immoral. So devoid of empathy. Little better than my own father, by his reckoning, given that when my grandmother died he was never the same. He never really recovered." His dark, tortured eyes met hers. "There is nothing he could have said to wound me more deeply."

"Was your father so bad then?" She studied his face. "My own is no great example."

He made a hollow sound. "Your father is greedy. He thinks only of himself. But at least he thinks of *someone*. I don't know how to explain the kind of empty, vicious creature my father was. Only that my grandfather suggesting he and I were the same felt like a death sentence."

"Did you point out that he could always have stepped in himself, then?" Angelina asked, somewhat tartly. "Done a little more parenting than the odd hour on a Sunday? After all, who raised your father in the first place?"

And for moment, Benedetto focused on her instead of the past. She could see it in the way his eyes changed, lightening as he focused on her. In the way that hard mouth of his almost curved in one corner.

"What have I done to earn such ferocity?" he asked, and he sounded almost...humbled.

"You saved me from a selfish man who would have sold me one way or another, if not to you," she said, holding his hands tight. "You gave me a castle. A beautiful piano. And if I'm not very much mistaken, a child, too. What haven't you given me, Benedetto?"

He let out another noise, then reached over, smoothing a hand down over her belly, though it was still flat.

She thought of the oddly heightened emotions that had seemed to grip her this last month or so. The strange sensations low in her belly she'd assumed were due to anxiety. She'd felt strange and out of sorts for weeks, and had blamed it on her situation.

But knelt down the hard stone floor of this tower with Benedetto before her, his shoulders wider than the world, she counted back.

And she knew.

Just like that, she knew.

All this time she'd considered herself alone, she hadn't been. Benedetto had been here in the shadows and more, she'd been carrying a part of the both of them deep inside her.

Her heart thumped in her chest, so severely it made her shiver.

"My grandfather reminded me that I have a distant cousin who lives a perfectly unobjectionable life in Brussels. Why should he not leave all this wealth and power to this cousin rather than to me if I found it all so troublesome that I had not only married the most unsuitable woman imaginable, but failed to protect her?" Benedetto shook his head. "He told me that if I wanted to take my rightful place in history, I must subject myself to a test. A test, he made sure to tell me, he did not imagine there was any possibility I would win given my past behavior."

"Did he want you to win?"

He took a moment with that. "All this time I've assumed he wanted to teach me a lesson about loneliness. But I suspect now it was supposed to be a lesson about love."

Benedetto gathered her hands in his again, tugging her closer, and all of this felt like far more important ceremony than the one that had taken place in her father's house. There were no witnesses here but the sky and the sea. The storm. No family members littered about with agendas of their own.

It was only the two of them and the last of the secrets between them.

"My grandfather tasked me with finding women like you," Benedetto said. "Precisely the sort my father had preyed upon, in his time. Women with careless families. Women who might want to run. Women who deserved better than a man with a list of dead wives behind them. I would marry them, but I would not make them easy about my reputation. I would bring them here. Then I would leave them after the wedding night and let them sit in this castle with all its history and Signora Malandra, who is always only too happy to play her role."

"She's a little too good at her role."

"She, too, always thought I ought to have been a better man," Benedetto said. He shook his head. "When they found their way to this tower I was to offer them a way out. One that kept them safe, gave them whatever they wanted, and made me seem darker and more villainous to the outside world. And he made me vow that I would continue to do this forever, until one of these women gave me a son. And even then, I was to allow her to leave me. Or stay, but live a fully supported, separate life. 'You had two chances and you blew them both,' he told me. 'You don't get any more.'"

"How many chances did he get?" Angelina demanded, her voice as hot as that flash of lightning in her eyes.

"But that was the problem," Benedetto said in the same way he'd told her, on their wedding night, that he missed the man who had created this prison for him.

"My grandfather was a hard man. I do not think he was particularly kind. But he loved my grandmother to distraction and never quite recovered from her loss. She was the best of us. He told me that he was glad she had died before she could see all the ways in which I failed to live up to what she dreamed for me, because after my father had proved so disappointing, they had had such hopes that I would be better."

Angelina frowned. "I'm not sure how you were responsible for Carlota's choices on the one hand—in the face of her own family's pressure, presumably—and an act of nature on the other."

"It was not that I was personally responsible for what happened to them," Benedetto said quietly. "It was that I was so arrogant about both of them. Boorish and self-centered. It never occurred to me to inquire into Carlota's emotional state. And everything Sylvia and I did together was irresponsible. Would a decent man ever have let her out of his sight, knowing the state she was in?"

"A question one could ask of your grandfather," Angelina said.

"But you see, he didn't force me into this. He suggested I bore responsibility and suggested I test myself. I was the one who had spent the happy parts of my childhood playing out involved fantasies in these walls. Ogres and kings. Spells and enchantments. I thought I was already cursed after what had happened to Carlota and Sylvia. Why not prove it? Because the truth is, I never got over the loss of my grandmother either, and she was the one who had always encouraged the games I played. In some twisted way, it seemed like a tribute." Benedetto reached over and touched her face again, smoothing her hair back with one big hand. "And if my grandfather had not agreed, because without her we were both incapable of loving anything—too much like my father—could I have found my way to you?"

She let go the breath she hadn't realized she'd been holding.

"I don't care how you got here," Angelina told him, like another vow. "Just as long as you stay here now you've come."

Outside, lightning flashed and the storm rumbled. The sea fought back.

But inside this tower, empty of everything but the feelings they felt for one another, Angelina felt something bright and big swell up inside her.

It felt like a sob. It felt overwhelming, like grief.

She had the strangest feeling that it was something else altogether.

Something like joy.

"I don't want to leave you," she told him. "I don't want to play these games that serve no one. I have always wanted to be more than a bartering chip for my own father, and you are far more than a monster, Benedetto. What would happen if you and I made our own rules?"

"Angelina…" His voice was a low whisper that she knew, without a shred of doubt, came from the deepest, truest parts of him. "Angelina, you should know. I had read all about the Charteris sisters before I ever came to your father's house. And I assumed that I would pick the one who seemed best suited for me, on paper."

"If you are a wise man," she replied dryly, "you will never tell me which one you mean."

And just like that, both of them were smiling.

As if the sun had come up outside when the rain still fell.

"I walked into that dining room and saw an angel," he told her, wonder in his eyes. In the hands that touched her face. "And I knew better, because I knew that no matter who I chose, it would end up here. Here in the locked tower where all my bodies are buried, one way or another. And still, I looked at you and saw the kind of light I have never believed could exist. Not for me."

"Benedetto…" she whispered, the joy and the hope so thick it choked her.

"I had no intention of touching you, but I couldn't help myself. How could you be anything but an angel, when you could make a piano sing like that? You have entranced me and ruined me, and I have spent two months trying to come to terms with the fact you will leave me like all the rest. I can't."

"You don't have to come to terms with that."

"Maybe this is crazy," he continued, wonder and intensity in every line of his body. "Maybe I'm a fool to imagine that anything that starts in Castello Nero could end well. But I look at you, Angelina, and you make me imagine that anything is possible. Even love, if we do it together."

And for a moment, she forgot to breathe.

Then she did, and the breath was a sob, and there were tears on her face that tasted like the waiting, brooding sea.

Angelina thought, *This is what happiness can be, if you let it.*

If for once she believed in the future before her, not tired old stories of a past she'd never liked all that much to begin with.

If she believed in her heart and her hands, the man before her, and the baby she knew they'd already made.

"Our children will fill these halls with laughter," she promised him. "And you and I will make love in that bed, where there is nothing but the sea and the sky. It will no more be a chamber of blood, but of life. Love. The two of us, and the good we do. I promise you, Benedetto."

"The sky and the sea are the least of the things I will give you, little one," he vowed in return.

And the stone was cold and hard beneath her, but he was warm. Hot to the touch, and the way he looked at her made her feel as if angels really did sing inside her, after all.

She wrapped herself around him, high up in that tower that she understood, now, wasn't an empty room at all. It was his heart. These stones had only ever held his heart.

Now she would do the honors.

Because she was the seventh wife of the Butcher of Castello Nero. The first one to love him, the only one to survive intact, and soon enough the mother of his children besides.

There was no storm greater than the way she planned to love this man.

Deeper and longer than the castle itself could stand—and it had lasted centuries already.

And she started here, on the floor of this tower, where he settled her on top of him and gazed up at her as if she was the sun.

And then, together, moment by moment and year by year, they both learned how to shine.

Bright enough to scare away the darkest shadows.

Even the ones they made themselves.

Forever.

CHAPTER THIRTEEN

THE SEVENTH WIFE of the terrifying Butcher of Castello Nero confounded the whole world by living.

She lived, and well, by all accounts. She appeared in public on Benedetto's arm and gave every appearance of actually enjoying her husband's company. As months passed, it became apparent that she was expecting his child, and that, too, sent shock waves across the planet.

The tabloids hardly knew what to do with themselves.

And as the years passed without the faintest hint of blood or butchery, Benedetto found himself becoming something he'd never imagined he could. Boring.

Beautifully, magnificently boring to the outside world, at last.

Their first child, a little boy they called Amadeo to celebrate some of the music that had bound them to each other, thrived. When he was four, he was joined by a little brother. Two years later, a sister followed. And a year after that, another little girl joined the loud, chaotic clan in the castle on its tidal island.

A place only Angelina had seemed to love the way he always had, deny it though he might.

And Benedetto's children were not forced to secrete

themselves in hidden places, kept out of sight from tourist groups, or permitted only a weekly hour with him. Nor were they sent off to boarding school on their fifth birthdays. His children raced up and down the long hallways, exactly as Angelina had said they would. The stone walls themselves seemed lighter with the force of all that laughter and the inevitable meltdowns, and the family wing was soon anything but lonely. There was an endless parade between the nursery at one end, the master suite on the other, and all the rooms in between.

Ten years to the day that Benedetto had brought his last, best wife home, he stood at that wall of windows that looked out over the sea, the family wing behind him. He knew that even now, the staff was setting up something romantic for the two of them in that empty tower room that they kept that way deliberately.

Because it reminded them who they were.

And because it was out of reach of even their most enterprising child, because Angelina still wore the key he'd left her around her neck.

They would put the children to sleep, reading them stories and hearing their prayers, and then they would walk down this very same hall the way they always did. Hand in hand. The bloodred ruby on her hand no match for the fire inside him.

The fire he would share with her up there where they had pledged themselves to each other. The fire that only grew over time.

Benedetto was not the villain he'd played. He was not the boogeyman, as so many would no doubt believe until he died no matter what he did.

But any good in him, he knew with every scrap of conviction inside him, came from his angel. His wife and lover, who he had loved since the very first moment he'd laid eyes on her. The mother of his perfect, beautiful, never remotely disappointing children. The woman who had reminded him of the child he'd been—the child who had believed in all the things he'd had to relearn.

And the best piano player he had ever had the privilege of hearing.

He could hear her playing now, the notes soaring down from the tower that was still hers. These days, there was often art taped to the walls, and the children lay on the rug before the grand piano so they could be near her. So they could feel as if they were flying, too, as their mother played and played, songs of hope, songs of love. Songs of loss and recovery.

And always, always, songs of joy.

These were the spells she cast, he thought. These were her enchantments.

The sun began to sink toward the horizon. Pinks and reds took over the sky. And still she played, and he could picture her so perfectly, bent over the keys with her eyes half closed. Her hands like magic, coaxing so much beauty out into the world.

He could hardly wait to have them on him again, where he liked them best.

Benedetto had so many things to tell her, the way he always did after time apart. Whether it was five minutes or five weeks. How much he loved her, for one thing. How humbled he still was, a decade on, that she had seen the good in him when it had been hidden from everyone. Even himself.

Especially himself.

She had a heart as big as the sea, his lovely wife. She maintained a relationship with her family, and he rather thought her quiet example made her sisters strive to be better than they might otherwise have been. Her mother, too, in those few and far between moments Margrete Charteris thawed a little. And if her father could never really be saved, it hardly mattered. Because Anthony Charteris had as a son-in-law a rich and besotted billionaire more than willing to spend his money on his father-in-law if it pleased his wife.

After all, there was always more money.

Benedetto would spend it all if it made her happy.

He heard the music stop and found himself smiling. He decided he would wait until they were alone to tell her that he had decided to share her piano playing with the world. Whether she wanted to perform or not, he could certainly share her music. He thought the world deserved to know that not only had Angelina soothed the savage beast with her playing, she was one of the best in the world. Accordingly, he'd bought her a record company.

But that would come.

First there was tonight.

He heard her feet on the stone and then she was there beside him, her eyes still the bluest he'd ever seen. Particularly when they were sparkling with music and love and light, and all of it for him.

"Happy anniversary, little one," he murmured, kissing her. He felt that same rush of longing and lust, desire and need, tempered now with these long, sweet years. "I have loved you each and every day. I love you now. And I only plan to love you more."

"I'm delighted to hear that," she replied, in that dry way he adored. "I love you too. And it turns out I have a rather bigger gift for you than planned."

Benedetto turned to look at her in some surprise, and Angelina smiled.

She took his hand in hers—her thumbs moving over the calluses there that it had taken her years to understand he got from performing the acts of physical labor he preferred to a gym membership—and moved it to her belly.

And he had done this so many times before. It was the same surge of love and wonder, sweetness and hope. Disbelief that she could make him this happy. Determination to do it better than his parents had, no matter what it took.

He was already better, he liked to think. If his grandmother could see him now, he was sure he would make her smile. And maybe even his grandfather, too.

"Again?" he asked, grinning wide enough to crack his own jaw.

"We really should do something about it," she said, her eyes shining. "It's almost unseemly. But... I just don't want to."

He pulled her to him, marveling as ever at how perfectly and easily she fit in his arms. "Angelina, my angel, if you wish to have enough children to fill this entire castle, we will make it so."

She laughed, her mouth against his. "Let's not get *that* carried away."

And he kissed her, because the future was certain.

That wasn't to say he knew what would happen, because no man could. Storms came. Sometimes they took more than was bearable. Sometimes they left monsters in their wake.

But he was not alone anymore.

He had Angelina, and together, they made their own

light. And Benedetto knew that no matter how dark it became, they would find a way to light it. And with that light, they would find their way through.

They would always find their way through.

And all the while they would stay here, in this ancient place where they'd found each other. When the tide was low, they would welcome in the world. There would be laughter in the halls, and deliciously creepy stories about disappearances both centuries old and more recent.

But soon enough the tide would come in, and the castle would be theirs again.

Like their heart made stone and cared for throughout time, they would love this place. They would love each other and their children. They would choose light over dark, hope over heartache, and they would do what no other Franceschi ever had across the ages.

They would make Castello Nero a home.

Their home.

And he kissed her again, long and deep, because that was how forever happened when it was made of love— one life-altering kiss at a time.

* * * * *

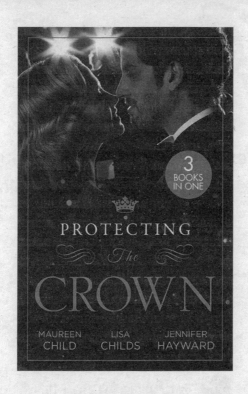

LET'S TALK

Romance

For exclusive extracts, competitions and special offers, find us online:

f MillsandBoon

t @MillsandBoon

○ @MillsandBoonUK

♪ @MillsandBoonUK

Get in touch on 01413 063 232

MILLS & BOON

THE HEART OF ROMANCE

A ROMANCE FOR EVERY READER

MODERN

Prepare to be swept off your feet by sophisticated, sexy and seductive heroes, in some of the world's most glamourous and romantic locations, where power and passion collide.

HISTORICAL

Escape with historical heroes from time gone by. Whether your passion is for wicked Regency Rakes, muscled Vikings or rugged Highlanders, awaken the romance of the past.

MEDICAL

Set your pulse racing with dedicated, delectable doctors in the high-pressure world of medicine, where emotions run high and passion, comfort and love are the best medicine.

True Love

Celebrate true love with tender stories of heartfelt romance, from the rush of falling in love to the joy a new baby can bring, and a focus on the emotional heart of a relationship.

Desire

Indulge in secrets and scandal, intense drama and sizzling hot action with heroes who have it all: wealth, status, good looks…everything but the right woman.

HEROES

The excitement of a gripping thriller, with intense romance at its heart. Resourceful, true-to-life women and strong, fearless men face danger and desire - a killer combination!

To see which titles are coming soon, please visit

millsandboon.co.uk/nextmonth

GET YOUR ROMANCE FIX!

Get the latest romance news,
exclusive author interviews, story
extracts and much more!